T0146494

TRUST NO ONE

Cassidy DiRocco knows the dark side intimately—as a crime reporter in New York City, she sees it every day. But since she discovered that she's a night blood, her power and potential has led the dark right to her doorway. With her brother missing and no one remembering he exists, she makes a deal with Dominic Lysander, the fascinating Master Vampire of New York, to find him.

Dominic needs the help of Bex, another master vampire, to keep peace in the city, so he sends Cassidy to a remote, woodsy town upstate to convince her—assuming she survives long enough. A series of vicious "animal attacks" after dark tells Cassidy there's more to Bex and her coven than anyone's saying. That goes double for fellow night blood Ian Walker, the tall, blond animal tracker who's supposed to be her ally. Walker may be hot-blooded and hard-bodied, but he's hiding something too. If Cassidy wants the truth, she'll have to squeeze it out herself… every last drop.

SWEET LAST DROP
A Night Blood Novel

Books by Melody Johnson

The City Beneath
Sweet Last Drop

Published by Kensington Publishing Corporation

Sweet Last Drop

Night Blood Series

Melody Johnson

LYRICAL PRESS
Kensington Publishing Corp.
www.kensingtonbooks.com

Lyrical Press books are published by
Kensington Publishing Corp. 119 West 40th Street New York, NY 10018

All Kensington titles, imprints, and distributed lines are available at special
quantity discounts for bulk purchases for sales promotion, premiums, fund-
raising, and educational or institutional use.

Special book excerpts or customized printings can also be created to fit
specific needs. For details, write or phone the office of the Kensington
Special Sales Manager:
Kensington Publishing Corp.
119 West 40th Street
New York, NY 10018
Attn. Special Sales Department. Phone: 1-800-221-2647.

Kensington and the K logo Reg. U.S. Pat. & TM Off.
LYRICAL PRESS Reg. U.S. Pat. & TM Off.
Lyrical Press and the L logo are trademarks of Kensington Publishing Corp.

First Electronic Edition: April 2016
eISBN-13: 978-1-60183-423-2
eISBN-10: 1-60183-423-3

First Print Edition: April 2016
ISBN-13: 978-1-60183-424-9
ISBN-10: 1-60183-424-1

Printed in the United States of America

Acknowledgements

To my parents, Nancy and Leonard Johnson, for supporting my excitement to move down south, even though you probably thought quitting my day job for year-round summer and unlimited beach access was poor decision-making. As usual—in my writing, career, and life in general—you always have my back, whether I'm five minutes or five states away. I was brave enough to fly because you gave me the wings.

To Derek Bradley, for making a new home with me in sunshine and sand. Thank you for scouting the apartment, demanding different movers, hulking the furniture three flights, hanging the picture gallery, and taking care of business on the daily. You are an unwavering anchor, and this journey is immeasurably more exciting because I'm taking it with you.

To Carl Drake, for being my go-to IT guy. Without you, I'd still be stuck in the stone ages. Thank you for always pointing me in the right direction, recommending the best software, fixing my code every time I hit a wall, and trying to solve the domain redirect mystery. I finally have a website that looks great and actually works, and I don't know which is more awesome.

To Margaret Johnston, for being my first ever Beta reader! Your feedback and insights were invaluable. I can't truly express how grateful I am for the time and effort you dedicated to reading and revising this manuscript, not once but twice! Thank you so much for your help and friendship.

And last, but never least, to my friends, family, and followers who bought Book One, The City Beneath. Thank you for your support. Your words of enthusiasm, encouragement, and praise keep my creative flame burning bright. I'm so glad you enjoyed the first installment enough to continue reading the series. Taking you on this adventure means more than you'll ever know.

Vampires Bite in the Big Apple- notes from draft 4
Cassidy DiRocco, Reporter

Nightmares are supposed to stay in dreams, but for the past three weeks, absolutely nothing, not even my dreams, are as they're supposed to be. Reality is the nightmare. When murderers, rapists, thieves, and gangs were my choice topics to report, I was sickened and unendurably angry by what people were capable of doing to other people. Now, I'm just sickened by what I'm capable of, and I can't sleep at all.

After sunset I see vampires lurking in every shadow, pressing against every doorway, committing every murder. Reality is further from anything I could have imagined, and I feel helpless against the enormity of Dominic's reach. What's the point of breaking my lease when Dominic will just demand entrance into my new apartment? Who can I confide in about my life after dark without risking their memory, or worse, their life? The one question that haunts me most is ironically one that I struggled to answer long before stumbling upon Dominic's existence. It haunted me after my parents died and I fought Percocet addiction—how long will I search for the answers before buckling under the unbearable truth that my efforts were futile from the start?

My brother disappeared three weeks ago. In another three months, will the agony of Nathan's absence still drive my efforts or drive me insane? When do I draw the line between hope and insanity—in another three years? Unfortunately for me and everyone's peace of mind, I don't think there are lines for love. Love is already insane, so the only answer is to drive toward the truth....

Chapter 1

The bus ride from The Big Apple to Erin, New York gradually descended from the metropolitan area to suburbs, from suburbs to woodsy small towns, and then to nothing but fields and sheds and, of course, cows. I'd never seen so many cows in my life. Considering I'd never actually seen a cow in person, I suppose that wasn't much of a statement, but it certainly seemed like Erin had an over-abundance of them. Their mooing reminded me of Dominic's night blood-and-hamburger metaphor when he'd described how my blood tasted. "You are a rare dish," he'd said, and I'd been terrified by his attraction.

I was still terrified of Dominic, attraction or not, but terror could only hold so much immediacy for so long, especially when the object of my terror was being relatively civil. Despite his consuming responsibilities as Master Vampire of New York City, Dominic had found time to visit me on numerous occasions at the hospital while I recovered from our battle against the rebel vampires. He visited me at home once I'd been released from the hospital. He visited me in the office when I returned to work and outside the office at every starlit opportunity. When he came calling, he was always fully fed, completely gorgeous, and the ultimate gentleman.

I knew better than to believe the illusion.

In his infinite patience, I think Dominic was biding his time, and I suspected it had everything to do with this very road trip to Erin, New York, Ian Walker's hometown and the resting place of Erin's abundantly powerful coven Master, Bex. Dominic's Leveling was approaching in two short weeks, and he'd need all the power and allies at his back as possible to survive the one night he'd be as weak and vulnerable to death as any human.

Dominic, however, wasn't the only man in my life with ulterior motives, although Ian Walker had been decidedly less patient for this visit.

"I can't wait to see you, darlin'," Walker had said at least once per conversation during the daily phone calls we'd enjoyed for the past three weeks. "I miss you."

Walker's voice had deepened salaciously, reminding me of that one night in my office. He'd lifted me onto my desk, and his strong hands had touched me in places I'd never thought I could feel again. I would have found his persistence coming from someone else nauseating, but between all the *darlin'*'s and *ma'am*s, we shared an indelible bond that went beyond incorrigible flirtation.

Walker and I were two of the rare humans who had night blood, a hereditary gene necessary to complete the transformation into a vampire, but just because I had the potential to become a vampire didn't mean I wanted to become one. That was a main point of contention between Dominic and me, albeit one of our more vehement disagreements. Walker, on the other hand, understood and shared my opinion on the matter. He was the only person who could relate to the danger of living with the knowledge that vampires existed.

Despite everything we had in common, I remained skeptical of both Walker and my feelings for him. We'd only physically known each other for one week. How well could I legitimately come to know a person in such a short time? But when I looked back at the week we'd shared and survived, I swallowed my doubts and forced myself to say the words because they were true.

"I miss you too."

And now, after three weeks of nothing but phone time with Walker, I had finally arrived in Erin, New York for what should have been a vacation from all those demons back in the city. Less than twenty-four hours into our reunion, however, and Walker and I weren't any closer to putting the moves on each other. He'd barely had time to give me a proper tour of the town before we were once again staring at a body.

Her name was Lydia Bowser, and she was last seen by her grandmother, leaving the farm for a walk before dinner. According to her grandmother and Walker's detailed notes, she took a walk before dinner every night. She'd loved the last moments of daylight when "the sun had already dipped below the horizon but its rays still lit the sky with a dim, burning glow."

I'd raised my eyebrows at the description, both from its nostalgia and its telling timeframe. Foul play after dark meant only one thing.

Although I'd left the city on vampire business in addition to my business with Walker, I'd especially looked forward to leaving behind a recent stretch of murders. Detective Greta Wahl and Officer Harroway— my personal friends and two of NYPD's finest—were recovering evidence and leads at a snail's pace; considering their slow, nearly backwards progress on that particular investigation, I'd still be able to report their findings when I returned to the city next week. I was due for a reprieve from the usual "doom and gloom," as my boss often referred to my articles, but gazing down at Lydia Bowser, I realized that doom and gloom had, once again, found me.

"The police already called it quits for today. You should have told them the media was coming. It's not as if I can interview the victim." I crossed my arms and glared at Walker. Grief and fear didn't look good on me, but I'd wear sarcasm any day of the week.

Walker looked up from a marker he was inspecting. He might not possess Dominic's mind control abilities, but when his eyes met mine, I had to physically restrain myself from stepping toward him. A smirk tugged at his lips. "Knowing that the media was coming would have spooked them for sure. You can interview the coroner. He'll arrive in a few minutes to officially pronounce time of death and take her body to the morgue."

"I don't want to interview the coroner," I said stubbornly. "I want to interview a witness."

"I doubt an animal attack is what your boss had in mind when he approved your story on city versus rural New York crime fluctuations. You don't need interviews from this case."

I snorted. "Carter will love whatever I give him, although after my last article, an animal attack might be pushing the envelope."

Walker raised his eyebrows. "Animal attacks in New York City certainly warrant headlines, but up here in Erin, NY, darlin', they're the rule, not the exception."

"You're telling me this is truly an animal attack from an actual animal? Not a vampire attack made to look like an animal attack?"

Walker nodded.

"How can you know for sure? How do you differentiate between what's real from the reality that Bex fabricates?"

"Bex would never leave a kill out for discovery." Walker's voice was clipped and uncharacteristically formal. "She's very careful about selecting and disposing of her prey."

"Neither would Dominic, but with the Leveling approaching—"

"Bex's Leveling isn't approaching," Walker interrupted. "Unlike Dominic, she's unfortunately in full, indisputable command of her coven. They don't make mistakes, not like this." Walker gestured to the surrounding woods and the pieces of Lydia Bowser that had been left out for discovery.

I bit my tongue to stop myself from defending Dominic. He was indisputably in command of his coven too, but a faction of rebels was frustrated with his conservative rule. He knew they no longer wanted to hide their existence from humans, but he'd never suspected that Jillian Allister, his second in command, would lead the uprising. In some ways, the blow of Jillian's betrayal had been more devastating to him than his physical injuries. We'd barely survived, but despite her betrayal, Dominic had regained control of his coven.

Considering Walker's unilateral distain for vampires, defending Dominic would only derail our conversation, so instead I said, "I've no doubt that Bex has control of her coven, but mistakes happen. We shouldn't rule anything out."

Walker crossed his arms. "I'll need to measure the bite radius and inspect the tracks to confirm the species and the number of potential predators, but I've no doubt that an animal attacked and killed Lydia, not a vampire."

I held Walker's gaze for a suspended moment, but despite my alligator exterior, even I melted under his velvety brown eyes. I sighed and let some of the anger seep away. "So no interviews."

Walker nodded. "If you insist on discounting the coroner, no interviews."

"Then why bring me here? It's nothing I haven't seen from your lovely tour of the town this afternoon."

"Although it's not homicide, it's still a case I'll be working on while you're in town. I thought you'd want in."

I smiled. "I always want in."

Walker's smirk widened. "So stop wasting our time arguing and get your fill before Berry arrives to transport Lydia to the morgue."

"Berry?"

"Bernard Bershaw, our coroner."

Walker's voice had started off teasing, but by the time he referred to Lydia, his tone had wavered. Here in his hometown, with a population shy of two thousand, Walker probably knew just about everyone. Living in a city of millions, the chances of knowing the victims are slim, but I could empathize. In all my years covering murders and interviewing loved ones, the only victim I'd ever known personally was Jolene McCall, and the memory of her death would haunt me for the rest of my life.

I kept my gaze carefully focused on Walker to distract myself from what little was left of Lydia. "I'm sorry for your loss. I'm assuming you knew her?"

Walker nodded, staring directly at her body. "Her father was the police chief here for years. He just recently retired. We worked on several cases together, and he always carried wallets of his girls. Lydia was his youngest."

Walker wasn't giving me background for the case. His words were more about grief than investigation, but something about his story struck a chord inside me, and God help me, I was hard-wired to pluck at it, grief or not.

From experience, I knew that people didn't respond well to personal questions at a crime scene. They took offense, no matter the intention, because it made them feel suspect. So I made my voice as soft and innocent as I could before asking my question, which, considering my five foot two, one hundred ten-pound frame, could usually sound quite sweet despite my actual disposition. "Did Lydia have a boyfriend?"

Walker's gaze snapped up to meet mine. My tone hadn't fooled him. "What are you getting at?"

I shrugged and kept my gaze honed on his. "It's just a question."

"And I want to know why you're asking it."

"Ex-police chief's youngest daughter takes a stroll at dusk, why? Because she loves the last burning rays of sunlight?" I kept my face neutral and let Walker make the connection himself.

Walker's face flushed. "This was an animal attack."

"It certainly looks like it." I conceded. "But what things are and what they look like aren't always the same."

Walker shook his head, but his mouth clamped shut.

"It's just a question, Walker."

"A question that didn't need asking," Walker insisted. "In this town, we don't look under rocks that best lay put to rest. Maybe Lydia had a boyfriend and maybe she didn't. It's best to let the family grieve in peace without questions and rumors unearthing pain over an animal attack."

"You don't know whether or not she had a boyfriend," I pushed.

He sighed. "I don't know. Her father never mentioned her having one."

"Does she have a best friend? Or is she particularly close to one of her sisters?"

"You're not letting this go, are you? You're gonna poke at wounds and make them fester over what is clearly an animal attack."

"You brought me here knowing my propensity for questions. I'm just doing my job."

Walker crossed his arms. "And what's that?"

"To face the facts and find the truth."

"This was an animal attack," Walker repeated, but he sounded exhausted.

"Yes, and I'm sure she sincerely loved taking walks at dusk," I said, trying to pump sincerity into my voice. "But I'm also sure that's not the whole truth. She told someone the real reason for taking nightly sunset strolls, and that's the person I need to interview."

The crunch of gravel groaned from around the bend in the road. Walker shifted his gaze and waved to the approaching van behind me.

"You can't just knock on strangers' doors and start asking questions like you do in the city. They don't know you here. They'll clam up."

I stared at him for a long moment. "But they know you. Since it's a case you'll be working on, maybe you can help me interview witnesses while I'm in town."

Walker shook his head slowly, but when he met my gaze, a wide smile crept over his features. "You're relentless, DiRocco."

"Only with things that matter," I said.

A car door slammed, and Walker stepped forward to greet the person behind me. As Walker passed he leaned down, and the heady spice of his cologne made me want to lean in.

"I'll see what I can do," he whispered.

                          * * * *

Walker greeted Berry with a back-pounding, handshake-hug. When he stepped back to introduce me, I shook Berry's hand, looked up to meet his gaze, and kept looking up. Berry was a ruddy, solid man whose family life and career choice had replaced what had probably been a promising future in professional basketball. Most people towered over me, but Berry was exceptionally tall, made only taller-looking by his string bean-like appendages. By his slight hunch, I'd wager he was just as aware of his height as I was of mine. He was kind and quiet as he handled Lydia's remains, but despite Walker's claim that animal attacks were a common occurrence upstate, Berry had obviously not grown accustomed to witnessing such carnage.

Lydia had been lovely, with wide doll eyes and wavy, light brown hair. Her face and upper chest were relatively intact; I could still see past the few lacerations across her cheeks and shoulders to the person she'd been before the attack. The rest of her, however, hadn't fared as well.

From her upper chest down, Lydia's remains were scattered in ragged parts, detached organs, and indecipherable pieces. Long shreds of tissue still connected her left arm to her shoulder, but Berry found the marker for her right arm further into the woods. Her abdomen had been raked by claws, spilling her intestines. They stretched in a long, tangled pile next to the unnatural angle of her left leg. The jagged break of her shin tore through the skin just under her knee. Nothing remained of her right leg except shreds of muscle and tendon. If a scrap of skin had survived, I couldn't see it beneath all the blood.

The sight made Jillian stir inside my mind. I could feel her struggle on the opposite end of the mental twine connecting us; she hadn't fed in weeks, not since I'd entranced her to save Dominic from her betrayal. She and her partner, Kaden, were supposed to have been executed for their crimes against the coven, for their crimes against me, but despite Dominic's assurances that their sentences had been carried out, I could still feel her.

One last, frayed thread still connected our minds, and she wouldn't let go.

The sweltering burns over Jillian's body singed mine, as if we were imprisoned inside an oven, roasting in its confinement. I could feel her rage, as searing as the surrounding heat, as she envisioned and reveled in the thought of Dominic's slow and gruesome death.

Examining Lydia's remains was disturbing on many levels, with or without Jillian stirring my thoughts, but worse than the brutality of Lydia's injuries was my reaction to them. Gazing at her blood made my throat convulse in a dry, scratchy swallow. My skin itched from the inside, like I'd resisted a hit and needed a fix, except instead of narcotics, I'd found a gruesome crime scene. God help me, there shouldn't have been anything here to resist.

I glanced at Walker and Berry to see if they'd noticed my distraction. With Lydia center stage, no one was looking at me.

Berry placed two fingers on her neck, but it was a perfunctory measure. Lydia didn't have a pulse. We could see through the right side of her neck and the shredded tissue of her esophagus to the glistening stacks of her spinal column. Her blood was not pumping. Berry glanced at his watch briefly and stood.

"Time of death, 2000 hours."

Walker let a moment pass before he spoke. "How would you like to start?"

Berry cleared his throat. "I have a container as well as the body bag. Let's get as much of her as possible on the gurney and go from there."

Although some of Lydia was still whole and recognizable, not much of her parts were still attached by sturdy tissue. Walker and Berry lifted her upper body, left arm, torso, and left leg into the body bag in one smooth motion, but mid-move, half of her palm and three fingers fell to the ground. Walker picked up the fallen appendage and placed it gently in the container with her other severed body parts, but watching a piece of her physically detach from the whole was somehow worse. Berry couldn't stomach it. He left for a five-minute break, which Walker and I both encouraged him to take, but honestly, I just wanted to finish as quickly as possible and get the hell out of the woods.

If Berry had been a cop, his squeamishness would have been poked and prodded at by his fellow officers until they had either razzed it out of him or he found a new occupation—I'd witnessed Harroway's interaction with some of his new partners and experienced it several times myself from covering cases with him and Greta. Luckily for Berry, he wasn't a police officer, and Walker and I would give him all the time and support he needed. Unfortunately for Walker's animal attack theory, people don't lose their cookies over scenes they witness regularly. Animal attacks might be more common here than in the city, but something was obviously different about Lydia's attack, something which—despite Walker's misgivings—I intended to find out.

Forty-five minutes later, Lydia was safely transported into the back of Berry's van. Berry turned to shut the back doors, and I could see the dread in his expression at the thought of having to reopen them at the morgue. Walker was scanning the ground for anything we may have missed, so before I lost the opportunity for a one-on-one with Berry, I sidled up to the van and slammed one of the doors shut for him.

"Thank you, ma'am. I'm much obliged," Berry said in the same slow, warm drawl as Walker. He slammed the other door shut, so it latched into mine.

"You're welcome. Walker's a good friend, and I'm happy to help."

Berry adjusted his John Deere baseball hat. "I heard the two of you survived a dangerous case in the city. Something about a gang war?"

It had actually been Jillian leading the vampire uprising, but until I figured out how to reveal the existence of vampires without subjecting everyone to their mercy, I just nodded. "Something like that."

"I heard he was glad to have you around then, so we are certainly glad to have you here now."

"Thank you." I took a deep breath. "Would you mind if I asked you a few questions?"

Berry smiled. The movement creased and cracked every plane of his weathered face. "I can't say that Walker didn't warn me."

I raised my eyebrows. "Did he?"

"Yes, ma'am, he did."

"Whatever you say can be off the record, if you'd prefer."

Berry's smile widened. I hadn't thought that his face could further wrinkle, but it did. I couldn't help but smile back. "Ask your questions, Miss DiRocco," he encouraged.

"Just 'DiRocco' is fine."

He nodded.

"How long have you been a coroner?"

"Goin' on twelve years now. My daddy was the coroner and his daddy was the coroner before him. I grew up in the business and wouldn't have it any other way. People in this town often fill in their parents' shoes, and I wasn't much of an exception, I suppose. And proud of it."

I nodded. "It sounds like you enjoy your work."

"In general, yes. There's a lot of great folks in town, and helpin' their loved ones pass, helpin' them grieve, has been more than a business. It's my life's work."

I shared his smile and then deliberately made my face somber, knowing that he wouldn't appreciate my next line of questions. "In all your twelve years of experience, how many animal attack victims do you suppose you've had to pronounce dead?"

Berry's smile wilted. "Little more than a dozen, likely."

"Just over one per year then?"

"I'd have to check our records to be certain, but I'd say that sounds about right."

"Do animal attack victims usually sustain such severe injuries, or would you consider Lydia's injuries exceptionally severe?"

Berry crossed his arms. "Now, Miss DiRocco—"

"DiRocco is just fine."

He shook his head. "If Walker thinks Lydia was attacked by an animal, than she was attacked by an animal."

I opened my mouth, but Berry held up his hand.

"To you that may sound presuming, but to me, it's a testament to Walker's abilities and fine work ethic. I know without a doubt that Walker will research the tracks, determine the animal, and find it. If he determines the tracks are not animal, he'll tell us that, too."

I nodded. "I understand. I feel the same assurance about Walker's work ethic from my brief time working our case in the city, and you've been working together for years."

Berry nodded with me.

"I'm not asking you to question Walker's professional opinion. I'm asking you to give me yours. In your twelve years of experience as coroner of Erin, New York, do Lydia's injuries resemble the dozen or so other animal attack victims you've pronounced dead and their injuries?"

Berry sighed. "No, they don't."

"What's different about Lydia?"

"Her injuries are far more severe. Typically, an animal feels threatened, is protecting her young, or has rabies. In any of those circumstances, the victim may sustain a life-threatening injury, such as blow to the head. Once the victim is unconscious, the threat is neutralized, and the animal goes on its way. Signs of a struggle are sometimes visible and can be substantial, like cuts, bruises, and bites. But Lydia—" Berry's voice caught. He shook his head.

I touched his shoulder softly. "I know."

He cleared his throat. "She was torn apart."

"I'm sorry. I—" I opened my mouth to find a delicate way to ask my next question, but Berry met my gaze. His eyes were red and shone from his welling tears. I reminded myself that these weren't my people. My acquaintance with Walker might encourage their friendliness initially, but if I made grown, weathered men cry after every interview, no one would want to talk to me, about the investigation or otherwise. My next question wasn't an end-all anyway, so I swallowed it. "I'm very sorry. It's especially hard when they're so young."

Berry nodded.

Walker returned empty-handed from scanning the scene. I bid Berry a final thank you for his time, and Berry pounded Walker's back in that same rough handshake-hug they'd greeted one another. One look at Berry's watery, flushed expression, however, was enough for Walker. He narrowed his eyes on me over Berry's shoulder. I blinked back, exuding unperturbed innocence the best I could considering the circumstances, but the moment we were tucked in the privacy of his Chevy pickup, Walker exploded.

"What the fuck was that?"

I matched his glare with an admonishing look of my own. "You said I could interview the coroner, did you not?"

Walker opened his mouth.

"When you brought me here you knew full well I'd ask questions," I said before he could answer. "Apparently, you even warned people. I'm good at what I do because people connect with me. I become a person to talk to, a person to confide in, but if you warn people that I'm a reporter, it only makes me one thing: a reporter. And people don't open up to reporters."

"I warned them for good reason! Berry was crying, for heaven's sake!"

"My questions didn't make him cry, Walker."

"I saw him! He—"

"But it wasn't my questions."

He ran his hand roughly over his face. "I know."

I put my hand on his shoulder. "I'm sorry."

Walker raised an eyebrow.

I smiled. "Not about my questions. I'm sorry about Lydia."

He nodded. "Me too."

Walker started the ignition and followed Berry's van through the narrow gravel road out of the woods. Outstretched branches slapped the windshield and scraped against the side doors as we dipped and popped in and out of man-sized potholes. I winced in sympathy for his tires. The road could hardly be considered a road, even for Erin, and I remembered from Walker's brief tour of the town this morning that it led somewhere specific.

"What's at the end of this drive?"

Walker's jaw tightened.

"If we drove deeper into the woods would we—"

"You can't let it go, can you?"

I blinked. "I'm just making conversation."

Berry pulled out onto the paved road, and his arm lifted from the window frame in a backhanded wave. Walker waved back, turning right out of the woods.

He sighed. "The trail leads to Gretel's Tavern. It's not technically a road. It's his driveway."

"His?"

"Buck McFerson."

I opened my mouth to push my luck with another question, but a shadow moved on the edge of the tree line up ahead.

We still had a few hours of daylight. The sun's rays streamed across the expanse of the road and dappled in glowing spots over the median and into the woods, but on the inner edge of the woods, where the tree line darkened from its leafy canopy and sunlight couldn't quite reach a shadow within the shadows, two glowing orbs blinked through the leaves.

"Walker, there's—"

"Don't start," he snapped. "I'd like to escape from work sometime during the day, and preferably with you, but if you can't separate church from state, then—"

I squeezed my nails into his bicep. "There's a vampire up ahead."

Chapter 2

Walker's muscle flexed under my hand. He stared ahead for a moment, and I knew the moment he caught sight of its reflective eyes. Walker's hand tightened in a trembling vise around the steering wheel. "We can't catch a fucking break."

"The sun hasn't set. How is it out?"

"She keeps to the shadows." Walker took his foot off the gas and sighed. "Daylight doesn't impede her or her abilities anymore as long as she avoids direct sunlight."

I glared at Walker's speedometer. "Why are we slowing down? Do you know her?"

"Of course I know her." His grip on the steering wheel creaked. "There's an old train overpass up ahead."

"Walker, I don't think stopping is the best—"

"Bex can't withstand direct sunlight without bursting into flames, but she'll make short work of us if we cross into the shadows under the overpass."

Bex. I glanced at her again and the road up ahead, and sure enough, the overpass cast its shadow across both lanes, effectively road-blocking our drive.

"So speed up! What could she possibly accomplish in the few seconds we're under the overpass?"

His jaw clenched. "This truck is fairly new. I don't want her denting its grill again."

I blinked. "She's done this before?"

"If we don't stop on our own, she'll make us stop."

I shook my head, both aggravated and impressed. As per my usual experience in dealing with vampires, Bex left us with very few choices, all of which ended in her favor. "She chose this position to deliberately block us, knowing you would stop."

"Or hoping I wouldn't." Walker flipped up the center console. "Take your pick."

I peered into the console's depths and shook my head in appreciation of its contents. "You're certainly prepared," I said, hefting a familiar item in my palm. It looked like a pen, but when I clicked the top mechanism, a wooden stake sprang from its tip.

"Always."

"This one's new," I commented, picking up a men's Invicta skeleton wristwatch. It seemed like a simple watch, but nothing in Walker's arsenal of weapons was ever what it seemed.

He grinned. "One of my newest, actually. The hands detach from the watch on a pressurized spring and fire from the twelve like little spears." He pointed to the tip of one of the watch hands. "The arrowhead design of the watch hands anchor the shot in place, or at least, I'm hoping it will. Once shot, the spear should be impossible to remove without creating more damage."

"Let me guess… silver?"

"It's effective. Why deviate from what works?"

"Very true." I placed the watch back into its holder in the console. "I think I'll just stick with my silver nitrate," I said, reaching into my jacket to pull out the spray I always carried with me, but my fingers slipped through a hole in my right pocket. "Shit."

Walker raised his eyebrows.

"I had spray with me this morning." I abandoned my pocket and tightened my hand around the pen-stake. "Maybe I should hang on to this after all."

"You do that. And take more silver nitrate as well. More never hurt."

"Thanks." I snatched a can of the silver spray from the console and shut its lid. I preferred the silver nitrate over the stake because if a vampire turned the spray against me, it wouldn't harm me. I couldn't say the same about a wooden stake. One stab through the heart would kill me as effectively as it would kill them.

I actually had more than Walker's weapons as protection against vampires, including new silver earrings I'd bought to match the silver necklace Dominic had given me, but I couldn't tell Walker about the necklace. A vial of Dominic's blood hung from the chain in a hollow, glass pendant. I'd shied away from wearing it when Dominic had first bestowed the gift—in general, I made a habit of avoiding jewelry containing bodily fluids—but his blood could heal injuries when applied topically. Anything that could do that was more precious than silver nitrate and stakes combined. Inevitably, no matter the caliber of weapons we carried, I'd need to heal in some capacity after interacting with vampires.

I swallowed nervously as the Chevy rolled to a halt a few feet shy of the shadows. "Just because she'll burn, doesn't mean she won't cross into the sunlight anyway. Dominic once deliberately melted his hand on silver just to prove a point. They don't think of pain and injuries like we do because they heal so quickly."

"I know," Walker said. He opened his truck door. "But she won't."

"I don't want to bet my life on it."

"It's not a bet. It's guaranteed. Bex is very careful not to remind me of her true nature. She doesn't threaten me with her fangs or claws like Dominic. She never allows herself to burn or growl in front of me. I've seen her drink blood from a wine glass, for God's sake, as if that's more civilized than drinking it from the vein. After all her time and efforts to seduce me, I doubt she'll stop now."

I snorted. "I'm doubting," I said, but despite my reservations, I gripped the door's handle and stepped out of the truck to face Walker's Master.

Bex was fully disguised in human-illusion, as I referred to it. Dominic had a similar look right after he fed, like the blood swelled his muscles, shined his hair, and smoothed his skin to healthy perfection, so he looked deceptively human without any of our human flaws. Bex was no exception. Her body, though feminine, was lean and sculpted. She wore dark skinny jeans, brown cowboy boots, and a fitted tee as if she were just another hometown heartbreaker. Her bronze locks swayed in gentle waves past her shoulders, and her glowing complexion looked smooth and tempting. Despite the act, as valiant an effort as it was, Bex couldn't hide the telltale luminescence of her reflective, yellow-green irises that bled to white toward the pupil.

Bex may have looked flawless now, but I knew from experience with other vampires what she'd look like when she didn't drink blood. I'd been stabbed by their gargoyle-like claws and bitten by their razor-sharp fangs. Although Dominic enjoyed flaunting the sculpted perfection of his well-fed body, he also enjoyed taunting me with the monstrous version of himself. To see how long I'd last before flinching. To test how close he could draw near before I stepped back. I called his bluff most days, but one day I suspected, like the wild animal he imitated, his instinct would be to strike.

Bex smiled, carefully close-lipped. "Ian. It's lovely runnin' into y'all," she said, her voice a dainty drawl, more belle and less redneck than the rest of Erin's locals. I wondered if her dialect was an act to lower our guard or if she was truelly southern.

Walker crossed his arms. "Can't say the feeling's mutual."

I stepped around the Chevy and grimaced as pain stabbed through my hip. I'd sat on a bus for most of the day, but I knew by the click and grind of bone on bone that the little time I'd spent on my feet had been too much. Five years had passed since the stakeout I'd taken a bullet for Officer Harroway. The injury had been worth the story I'd scooped, and of course, it'd been worth saving Harroway, but I'd live with chronic arthritis for the rest of my life.

I gritted my teeth against the pain and tried not to limp the ten feet it took to reach Walker. We stood in the shining warmth of sunlight, and like a divider between us, Bex remained confined to the overpass's shadow.

Bex cocked her head. "Won't you introduce me to your friend?"

"She's of no concern to—"

"DiRocco," I said, and Walker groaned.

Bex's eyes flicked to study my face and something, not quite recognition, but something akin to familiarity, sharpened her gaze.

"Cassidy DiRocco, night blood to Dominic Lysander, Master of New York City," I specified. I nodded in greeting instead of offering my hand. She wouldn't extend hers into the sunlight and I sure as hell wouldn't extend mine into the shadows. "Great to finally meet you."

Bex didn't say anything for a moment. I braced myself for her attack, considering the threat she posed to Dominic, but she just stared at me, stock-still. If I didn't know better, I'd say she was shocked. After living a few hundred human lifetimes, I'd imagine that shock was rare. I'd been an iron-clad cynic at only thirty years old; then I'd met Dominic and discovered the existence of vampires. Now, shock was normal.

"Likewise," she said, suddenly animated again. She smiled wider, still close-lipped but lovely nonetheless. Her amiability didn't seem forced, but I'd bet that without that strip of sunlight between us, I'd already be dead, or maimed and writhing at the least. "Your reputation precedes you."

I smiled, but *my* expression certainly felt forced. "All good things, I hope."

Walker leaned in threateningly. "Let it go, Bex."

"You were Walker's partner while he was in the city, is that right?" Bex asked, her glowing, unearthly eyes trained on me.

"Unofficially, yes, I suppose you could call us partners. I covered his back, and he covered mine on numerous occasions."

Bex nodded. "I'd like to extend my gratitude. The rule of New York City's coven is collapsing, and bless your heart, I'm grateful that my night blood had someone to rely on in my stead."

"Your night blood?" Walker asked. His voice was low and growled from somewhere deep and ugly inside of him.

I winced from Bex's opinion of the city. "I'm not sure 'collapsing' is an accurate assessment of Dominic's rule."

"I am."

"You're wrong," I stated, and the depth of my feelings surprised me. It almost felt like loyalty. "Once Dominic survives the Leveling, the coven will once again be under his full reign."

Walker looked at me like I'd sprouted a wholly unwelcome second head.

Bex raised her delicate, carefully sculpted eyebrows. "*If* he survives."

"When," I corrected.

"You sound so certain of Lysander's abilities."

"And my own," I said, nodding. I had my issues with Dominic, but he'd saved my human life when he could have easily taken advantage of my injuries and unconsciousness to have his way and transform me into a vampire. But knowing my preference to remain human, he hadn't. For that, despite my misgivings, he'd earned a sliver of my trust. "We'll weather the storm."

"We," Bex murmured. "Your attitude is refreshing."

I laughed. I couldn't help my reaction. It bubbled up from my gut in a swift burst.

Bex narrowed her eyes.

I raised a hand. "I'm sorry. It's just that not many people qualify my attitude as 'refreshing.' I'm usually a little too outspoken for most people's tastes."

Bex smiled, and this time, she let her fangs slip from between her lips. "I like the taste of you just fine."

"That's enough," Walker snapped. His face was boiling red, and it took me a moment to realize that he was embarrassed, like Bex had exposed something private. "Why did you stop us?"

Her fangs were longer than any other vampire's fangs I'd ever seen while still in human form, even longer than Dominic's. Like a snake's retractable bite, her fangs must slip into sockets in her lower gums. Otherwise, they couldn't fit in her mouth.

"To say hello, of course. It'd be rude to cross paths with y'all and not acknowledge one another," Bex said, her fangs tucked neatly away, once again the dime-a-dozen country sweetheart.

"Hello. So we're done here then," Walker said. He ushered me back toward the truck. "Have a good evening."

"But now that we're all acquainted, it'd be rude not to extend an invitation. You protected Ian with your life, and I would be remiss not to extend my gratitude to such a loyal partner. Are you free tomorrow evening for dinner?"

Walker snorted. "When was the last time you extended an invitation to Ronnie?"

Bex's eyes shifted like two lasers to target Walker. "Bring her as well."

Walker snapped his mouth shut. The muscles in his jaw flexed convulsively, and I wondered if he was chewing on his tongue.

I cleared my throat. "Tomorrow evening works for me."

"No it doesn't," Walker growled.

I glared at him. "Then you don't have to come."

Walker stared at me, his eyes wide and searching, like he was desperate to find something he'd lost.

I turned to face Bex again, and she was much closer, less than two feet away. The setting sun had begun to cast a longer shadow in the five minutes while we talked, and Bex had inched along its growing path toward us. This close, even wearing her human façade, she couldn't pass as anything but the creature she truelly was. Her skin was too flawless, her features too sculpted, and her eyes, those glowing yellow-green swirling orbs, too animal. Looking into her eyes, I knew that her brain didn't feel like ours. She had goals and desires, but when her motivations boiled down to their core, I suspected that she and Dominic and all the rest of the vampires, although capable of love or the memories of love from their human existence, now acted primarily on instinct.

Bex lifted her hand up to my face, and I realized that the overpass angled toward me. I was centimeters shy of its shadow. She ran her fingertips down the line of sunlight between us, mere inches away, and I froze. A thin, rotting stream of twirling steam hissed from the pad of her pointer finger. I stared at that finger as it boiled, the skin beginning to bubble and ooze scant millimeters from touching my hair.

I held my ground, determined not to flinch. Her thumbnail elongated into a claw, but her face remained beautiful. Dominic's transformations were often a result of his emotions and maybe instinct, so when his fingernails elongated, his nose flattened, ears pointed, and brow furrowed. But Bex wasn't losing control of her other features. She had deliberately only transformed her thumbnail.

She sliced her claw-like nail across the lock of my hair. It clipped in half and fluttered to the ground.

I stepped back into full sunlight and out of reach. Bex let my remaining lock of hair slide from between her scabbed fingers. Her hand dropped to her side.

Walker's gaze flicked back and forth between Bex and me, and I didn't appreciate the calculation in his expression.

"Until tomorrow," Bex murmured.

I blinked, and she was suddenly, inconceivably gone. Her reflective, otherworldly eyes had illuminated the shadows like twin halos, rendering the darkness a little deeper in her absence.

I reached up and wearily tugged on the shortened lock of hair. Her swift departure reminded me of Dominic. Despite my growing experience with vampires, his abilities still awed me. It didn't matter that he displayed inhuman physical and mental feats at least once a night. I doubted I'd ever consider his exceptional abilities anything but exceptional.

"Get in the truck."

Walker pounded the gravel in three long strides to his driver's side door. He didn't seem awed by Bex's abilities in the least, but I knew better than most the comfort and clarity of being downright pissed. I bit my tongue and got in the truck.

Walker kicked the ignition, and I held my breath as we drove under the overpass and into the shadows. The cab dimmed for a heart-rending moment. The roar and hiccups of Walker's truck and the squeaking grind of its wheels crunching over the pavement was the only noise between us. Walker didn't offer any assurances about our safety now that Bex was gone, and I wondered if, despite knowing Bex longer than I knew Dominic, or perhaps because of his better acquaintance, he didn't trust her not to double back and attack us.

Light beamed through the windshield as we crossed over, and in the next moment, we were once again basked in the sun's protection.

I released a shuddering breath.

"What does Dominic have on you?"

I turned to face Walker. "Excuse me?"

He wrung the steering wheel in a punishing grip. "He can't control your mind like the rest of us, so the only way I can even *fathom* that you would consent to that circus I just witnessed a moment ago must be blackmail." Walker turned to meet my gaze. "Tell me I'm wrong."

"You're wrong," I said flatly. "Dominic doesn't have anything on me."

He sighed. "I can't help if you don't let me in. Whatever it is, Cass, I'll take care of it."

A laugh burst out from the same deep, dark corner I'd stowed my agony over Nathan, so the laugh sounded sarcastic and hysterical and not funny in the least. "Oh, you'll just—" I snapped my fingers"—take care of it."

Walker locked his earnest, velvet brown eyes on mine; the strength and confidence in his gaze made me believe that he could take care of it, or at least, that he believed he could.

"He might have healed the injuries you sustained in his coven, but make no mistake, healing you was for his benefit, not yours." Walker said tightly. "He wants you. He'll use you, and when he's done, he'll discard you. Dominic Lysander can't be trusted. None of them can," he said, his expression fierce. "If you need help, place your trust in me, Cass."

An infinitesimal blossom of hope ripened inside my chest. The feeling was just a pin-prick of light, but it was more warmth than I'd felt inside myself in weeks. I had to look away before I started believing him.

"You weren't there when I needed you last time," I said softly.

Walker reared back, shocked. "The hell I wasn't."

I nodded, feeling deflated. "We infiltrated Dominic's coven to kill the rebel vampires, but you wanted to kill them all. We were outnumbered and losing daylight, and when I asked you to fall back, you forged ahead with your plan without me."

Walker closed one eye on a wince and massaged his temple. "You're twisting what really happened. When I realized we were outnumbered, I told you to leave while I finished the mission. I was protecting you."

"You never should have finished the mission! You should have left with me because that's what partners do, they stick together, but you were too hell-bent on killing vampires—all the vampires, not just the rebels we had agreed to kill—to recognize a suicide mission when it's slapping you in the face. Or in your case, when it's driving its talons into your stomach."

Walker was quiet for a long moment. I didn't expect him to agree with me. His savagery concerning vampires was an established note of contention between us, but I expected him to say something. He remained silent and continued massaging his forehead.

"Are you ok?" I asked.

"You're right."

I raised my eyebrows.

"I left you alone and without backup because I was greedy to finish the mission and kill the vampires. We should have stuck together because, like you said, that's what partners do. I'm sorry."

My mouth fell open at his honesty. He was such a reasonable and intelligent man in every way except in his single-minded vendetta against vampires; still, I was shocked that he'd admit fault.

Walker stopped massaging his temple and took hold of my hand. His thumb stroked over the inside of my wrist. Shivers shot up my arm to my shoulder. "Can you forgive me, darlin'?"

I pursed my lips against the dual heat and chill his touch ignited. "I've already forgiven you."

Walker narrowed his eyes. "But you don't trust me."

I shook my head. "I accept your apology, but it's one thing to say you're sorry. Even if you mean it, which I believe you do, it's something else entirely to show me."

"Give me the chance to prove myself."

I released a long sigh. The crushing weight of Dominic's situation in New York City and his approaching Leveling was my constant shadow, no matter the distance. "You can prove it to me by joining me for dinner with Bex. I need you to play nice and have my back."

"Play nice," Walker said quietly, nearly inaudible.

I nodded.

"With Bex."

"Dominic needs this alliance. We—"

"I don't care what Dominic needs! We are not visiting Bex's coven for dinner tomorrow night."

"Well I certainly am, with or without you."

"Helping Dominic isn't the answer," Walker ground out. "Whatever he's using as leverage over you, tell me. Let me help you."

"I need you to be my partner and accompany me to dinner. That's the help I need," I pled, the argument familiar and bitter for its familiarity. "Please."

Walker winced and covered his eyes with his hands.

I glanced at the road as we listed slightly. "Are you sure you're ok?"

"Let Dominic mend his own alliances, and if he can't, what do I care if they tear each other apart? Just two less vampires in the world for me to kill."

"Right," I said, realizing that I'd be having dinner with Bex tomorrow night on my own.

"Besides, Ronnie can't go into that hell hole. She'd fall apart."

I put my palms up. "You got her involved. Not me."

A shaft of the setting sun beamed between the forest leaves and through our windshield. We swerved as Walker winced away from the light.

"Maybe you should pull over and let me drive."

Walker glared at me from under his hand as he massaged his temples. "Why would I do that?"

"I'd imagine it's difficult to drive when you're fighting a migraine."

Walker turned his gaze back to the road, but he didn't pull over. He drove us all the way to his house, his eyes barely open and his hands wringing the steering wheel in pain, but we pulled into his driveway in one piece. If tonight was any indication, country life wasn't much different than city life: investigating murders, dodging vampire attacks, and surviving stubborn men. Except I could do all three in boots instead of heels.

* * * *

Walker's house was exactly what I had anticipated a house in the deep woods would look like, but even after seeing it a second time, I couldn't believe Walker actually lived there. The house was essentially a log cabin, a beautiful, three-story log cabin with a wrap-around porch, wood-burning fireplace, and stone chimney. A porch swing was built into the house on the east side of the porch, and on the north side, a hammock was stretched between two awning posts. Gabled dormers jutted from the roof, letting light and space into the attic. The gravel driveway was outlined in heavy stonework; it extended into a wide lot at the side of the house.

When we'd dropped off my luggage earlier this afternoon, the driveway had been empty. Now, two pickup trucks in addition to Walker's Chevy, his Harley, and a Charger were already parked in the lot as we pulled in. I climbed out of the truck gingerly—my hip protesting the movement—and stared, in awe of the sheer magnitude of Walker's home.

"Expecting company?" I breathed.

Walker smiled. "Come on. Let's go inside and get an icy-hot patch on your hip."

"I'm not—"

He held up a hand. "Don't. You were better at hiding it in the city."

The arthritis has worsened since the last time you were in the city, I thought. Instead of speaking my mind, I said. "An icy-hot patch isn't going to cure anything."

"It won't hurt anything either."

I stared at Walker, his face chiding and my hip pounding, and I gave up on pretenses. I used to go through almost an entire day without the arthritis and scar tissue from my old injury affecting my daily life. Today was obviously not one of those days, so I swallowed my stubbornness.

"Well, in that case, an icy patch would be great."

Walker stepped around the hood of his truck and onto the wooden wrap-around porch. A very thin, auburn-haired woman met us at the entrance and opened the screen door for us. She wore an oversized, green sweater, boot cut jeans, and fuzzy green socks. Exactly how thin she'd become was mostly hidden under the layers of baggy clothes, and when she smiled at our approach, her hazel eyes crinkled with genuine warmth. Her smile was wide and bright and had the uncanny ability to transform her delicate features from frail to precious.

Walker smiled back, and his expression was equally warm. Her pale skin and sharp features reminded me of fine china, something of high value but easily broken. I wondered if Walker had noticed the hollows under her collarbone and the frail, protruding bones of her wrist. Walker didn't normally miss much, but if the answering gleam in his eyes was any indication, he was distracted, maybe by more than just her eyes and blossoming smile.

The corner of my heart I had let soften toward Walker over the past few weeks ached.

Shoving my feelings for Walker and those dangerous hopes aside, I gritted my teeth against the pain and climbed the porch's front steps.

Walker bounded up the steps beside me. "DiRocco, I'd like you to meet my partner and very good childhood friend, Ronnie Carmichael. Ronnie, this is Cassidy DiRocco."

Ronnie's smile slipped slightly. She looked almost cautious as she held out her hand.

I took it and forced my own smile. Her hand was rough and her knuckles pink, scaly, and cracking, like she worked regularly with plaster. She covered the back of my palm with her other hand in a handshake sandwich.

"It's great to finally meet you," Ronnie said, and her soft voice sounded genuine. "Ian has told me so much about you. I feel like I know you already."

Walker had divulged absolutely nothing about Ronnie, so I couldn't respond in kind. I simply nodded. "All good things, I hope."

Ronnie's smile brightened. "Any friend who helps Ian on one of his missions is a friend of mine. I'm so glad he found a night blood in the city. I hate to think of him surviving the night alone." She sighed. "Not that being alone ever stopped him."

I smiled, and this time mine was genuine, too. "I was just as fortunate that he found me. He had my back, too. Multiple times."

"I'm sure he did. Some of the other night bloods, like Logan and Theresa, lived in solitude, too, but I think they appreciate having backup now."

"The other night bloods?" I cocked my head, forcing my expression to remain bland. "I thought you and Walker were the only night bloods in the area."

Ronnie nodded. "We were. For years we were the only night bloods we knew existed, but since Walker found Theresa, Jeremy, Logan and his sons, and now you, we're becoming quite a little family."

I glanced askance at all the vehicles in the driveway. "Do Theresa, Jeremy, and Logan live nearby?"

"We can continue this conversation inside." Walker placed his hand firmly at my lower back, ushering me inside.

I turned to protest, thinking he was just trying to derail my question, but when I looked back, I recognized the urgency in Walker's tone. The sun had set and full darkness surrounded the house.

Ronnie extended her hand towards me. "Here, let me give you the tour. You'll be staying in the room across the hall from Walker. Jeremy lives next to—"

"It's been a long day for both of us, Ronnie," Walker interrupted, but his tone was so baby sweet that she nodded sympathetically, like she hadn't been interrupted. I felt nauseated. "I think Cassidy would rather freshen up before meeting anyone. Once she's settled, I'm sure she'd love a tour."

Ronnie looked at me as if to validate Walker's statement, but the truth was that I couldn't care less about a tour, whether it occurred now, after I'd taken a shower, or never. Walker's house was much bigger than I'd expected. Ronnie lived much closer to Walker than I imagined, and my anticipation for this visit couldn't have been more misplaced. I shifted my gaze between Ronnie and Walker, and although they both expected me to respond in some intelligible fashion, I couldn't get past the fact that I was standing in what was essentially a coven of night bloods.

* * * *

"How many night bloods are living in this house?"

I'd followed Walker to the bathroom in tense silence, watched him rummage for the icy-hot patches, and I'd stood stoically while he alternately eyed the patch and my skin. I held my shirt to expose my waist while he eased the band of my pants down slightly to gain better access to my hip. The rough heat of his fingertip grazed along the puckered star of my scar, and goose bumps shivered across my back. A deep, radiating heat stoked through my gut at his touch. My breath caught, and I couldn't hold my tongue any longer.

"Ten night bloods?" I guessed. At Walker's telling silence, I upped the ante and my volume with it. "Fifteen?"

"Not everyone lives here. It's more of a home base, not a home, per se."

"My God, more than twenty?"

Walker sighed. I could hear the frustration expel with his breath, but I refused to let this go.

"The last time we spoke about night bloods, you assured me that we were rare, that the only night blood you'd ever spoken to before me was your partner from home, Ronnie." I lifted my arms and gestured around the bathroom. "Well here we are, home, and Ronnie isn't the only night blood you've been talking to. She's not even the only night blood you live with!"

Walker put up his hands in surrender. "I thought you'd be excited to meet more night bloods besides myself and Ronnie."

I shook my head. "Why did you lie to me?"

"I never lied to you. The last time we spoke about night bloods, Ronnie was the only one living here. She was the only night blood besides yourself that I'd ever spoken to. That was the truth at the time."

I narrowed my eyes. "That was only three weeks ago."

"Yes, ma'am," Walker said, and he had the nerve to look baffled.

"Don't *ma'am* me. After over thirty years of knowing only one night blood, you find twenty in the past three weeks?"

Walker crossed his arms. "I make friends fast. Look at us."

I balled my fists to keep from strangling him. "How are you meeting so many night bloods in such a short timeframe?"

"There's safety in numbers. We get picked off so easily on our own, one night blood at a time, but together, we finally stand a chance against them, against the fate we were born to."

I shook my head, equally awed and horrified. "You're building your own coven of night bloods, an army to fight against the vampires."

Walker didn't say anything, but he didn't have to. I could see the fire deep in his eyes and the effort it took for him not to smile at the thought of fighting and killing vampires.

"Not everyone wants to fight them," I whispered. "I'd prefer to avoid confrontation."

"Dinner with Bex is avoiding confrontation?"

I glared at him. "The vampires are faster, stronger, more lethal, and harder to kill than us. Fighting them is suicide."

"I can't just stand by meekly and let them have me," Walker snapped.

"I'm not saying you should. Protecting yourself is one thing, but seeking trouble is another thing entirely."

Walker sighed. "How is living together under one roof seeking trouble? We're simply protecting ourselves. Safety in numbers, like I said."

"Together or apart, we're no match for them if they decide to attack. Living together just makes it easier for them. The sheep are herded together under one roof now, gathered for slaughter."

"Like shooting fish in a barrel, you're saying," Walker murmured. "You think I've cornered us."

His quiet, unsure tone made me hesitate. He wanted to do the right thing. He thought he'd been doing the right thing. I rubbed my upper arms, lost in thought and mixed, irresolute feelings. "I don't know. Who am I to arrive here one minute and judge you the next?" I bit my lip. "But standing in this house, knowing that over a dozen night bloods are here with me, feels a little like standing in the center of a bullseye."

"It's safe here, Cassidy. I've taken measures to ensure everyone's protection against Bex and her coven."

Walker spread the icy-hot patch over my skin, pressing its frigid length along the curve of my hip. I jerked from the shock of it, but Walker held me immobile against him, his hands steady on my hip as he applied the patch.

I breathed in a sharp hiss between my clenched teeth. "I'm sure you have taken precautionary measures, but—"

"No buts. I have, and I think you'll enjoy meeting the other night bloods. Until now, I've been the only night blood you've spoken to. Maybe sharing your experience with them will help put things in perspective. Help you better see my perspective."

I pursed my lips and tried to harden my resolve, but my will was no match against his velvet brown eyes. "I'll keep an open mind," I relented.

Walker smiled, and I recognized the intention and heat in that slow grin.

I sidestepped around his advance toward the bathroom door, but he blocked my exit.

"Excuse me."

He stepped closer. "I have something else I'd like to discuss, if you don't mind."

"I mind. I'm already late for a phone call."

"Then you can continue to be late for a few more minutes."

I crossed my arms and stared him down, but Walker's grin only widened.

"We haven't had much time alone since you arrived, and with a full house, I doubt we'll have as much alone time as you might have anticipated."

I raised my eyebrows. "So you're taking advantage of the little alone time we have now, in the bathroom?"

He laughed. "Not exactly. I just wanted to make my intentions clear, if they weren't already."

I held my breath for a moment against what I was about to say, but I'd never been one to mince words. "Honestly, they're not."

"They were clear enough that you came to visit."

"That was before I realized that you and Ronnie were living together," I said pointedly.

Walker blinked. "Ronnie?"

I nodded. I'd seen their looks. I'd seen his smile. He could discount their relationship if he wanted, but he'd be lying to me. Worse, he'd be lying to himself.

He leveled his eyes on me. "There's nothing romantic between Ronnie and me. She's my family."

"If that's true, why didn't you tell me that you live together? You've known that I was visiting for weeks. In all that time, you could have warned me."

"It never occurred to me to 'warn you' because there's nothing to warn against. There's nothing there."

I rolled my eyes. "You didn't tell me because whether or not there's nothing or something there, you know how it looks. I'd bet some of the people living in this house think you're a couple. How long did you live together, just the two of you, before you started building your night blood coven?"

Walker pursed his lips, his grin wiped clean. After anticipating this visit for weeks and finally closing the physical distance between us, the inches separating us now felt wider than the miles we'd been apart.

"I guess you have everything figured out," Walker said. He turned away from me, and I let him leave the bathroom without another word.

Chapter 3

I wasn't good at keeping in touch with people, which made distance impossible, even with people I loved unconditionally, like my parents and Nathan. I had the uncanny ability to not see or speak to friends and family for months, and when we finally did visit one another, pick up right where we'd left off. Other people, so I'm told by frustrated friends and family, normal people, need regular phone calls to replace the physical void that distance creates.

Walker was the second person with whom I'd ever achieved a functional long-distance relationship. The emotional closeness we'd developed while we were physically apart still stunned me.

My little brother was the first.

When I moved to California for those four years of undergrad at Berkeley, my parents had fits about my lack of communication. I didn't call. I didn't write. I didn't email. I texted Nathan, which likely only made my silence toward them even more infuriating, but since they wouldn't upgrade to texting, which was all the communication I honestly had time for during the week, I didn't talk to them until I traveled home for Christmas.

On weekends, when I finally had ten or fifteen minutes to breathe between classes, essays, interviews, and a social life, I called the one person I wasn't angry with, who hadn't nagged me all week to call because I knew he could hold a conversation without further nagging. I called Nathan.

I talked to him about the freedom of college life, about staying out late without worrying about curfew, having sleepovers without asking for permission, and eating dessert for dinner. I didn't mention drinking or guys. I just wanted to give him something to cling to in the prison of rules with our parents at home. He talked to me about his budding career as a track star, how he'd medaled at districts and earned a spot in states, how the high school had an assembly for the spring athletes, and he was only one of four students that were presented with plaques directly from Principal Doyle. He didn't mention grades or his restricted social life. He just wanted to give me enough to miss him and my former life, so I'd return home after undergrad.

He knew I'd planned to stay on the west coast after graduation, and my plans were only solidified after meeting and falling in love with Adam. As fate would have it, however, it was my parents who dragged me back to New York City even after being the driving force that had pushed me across the country.

When they died, I moved back home for Nathan.

Although I'd intended to return to California and Adam, it was no surprise that I hadn't been able to make the long distance work, and by the time Adam came to New York to drag me back home with him, I'd buried myself in my career to forget the grief and pain of lost time and memories.

I would have given anything for the opportunity to call my parents just one last time, to tell them everything I'd been too busy and selfish to bother communicating while at school. Now I'd give anything for the opportunity to call Nathan, to hear his voice and make him laugh. To listen to the creak of his floorboards to know if he was lying.

I'd never thought to relive the nightmare of losing my loved ones, but now Nathan was beyond my reach, too.

Of all the people I'd give anything to speak to again, I'd give anything *not* to speak to Dominic, but he was the one impatiently waiting on my call. This time, I'd better make long distance work even if it killed me, because if I didn't, he just might.

I twisted the knob and shut the bathroom door quietly after Walker left. If Walker was right about anything, it was that the bathroom was the best place to achieve a modicum of privacy in a houseful of strangers. The toilet lid chilled my thighs through my thin dress pants as I lowered myself carefully. I tried to enjoy the relief of weight off my hip and let the icy hot patch perform its magic, but if I was honest with myself, sitting didn't particularly feel any better than standing.

The phone only rang once before Dominic's deep, gravelly voice answered. "You're late."

I winced. "No, 'hello'? No, 'How are you'? You might want to work on your phone etiquette."

"Is it not etiquette to call promptly when one schedules a phone meeting?"

Even over the phone, my hair stood on end at his tone. The agreement had been two calls a night, one directly after sunset and the second before sunrise. According to Dominic, this schedule would assure him of my safety in his absence, but as most things according to Dominic, it was never quite that simple. I suspected his calls were also a tactic to keep me focused on the true purpose of my visit. Dominic couldn't bully me in person without risking war with Bex's coven, so bullying me over the phone was his next best option. The fact that he was able to obtain a phone and a service provider when he technically didn't exist to the human population was beyond me, but so were so many things Dominic was capable of that I didn't further question the anomaly.

This was going to be a long conversation if he was already referring to me in the third person. "It's been a long, stressful, busy day, and I got caught up. I'm sorry that I called later than you demand—er, requested, but I'm here, calling you now." *And regretting it*, I thought. I shifted my weight on the toilet seat, and the blazing grind of my hip encompassed my body like a vice.

"Are you well?"

I clenched my teeth against the pain and spoke when I thought I could enunciate clearly and without cursing. "I'm fine."

Dominic was so silent on his end that I couldn't even hear him breathing. Assuming he was choosing to breathe.

"Hello? Can you hear me?"

"Did Bex herself harm you or one of her coven?" Dominic asked casually, but I could hear the dangerous undercurrent in his voice.

"Someone woke up on the wrong side of the coffin this morning," I teased. Vampires slept in beds, not coffins, but apparently, he didn't find my jab at vampire lore as funny as I did.

"You have yet to answer my question, Cassidy," Dominic pressed. "Are you well?"

I doubted that he could exert his mind tricks over the phone and without eye contact, but I swore that even without the in-person influence, his voice had a weighty pull as he spoke my name. "I'm as well as I ever am."

"Elaborate."

"Bex didn't hurt me and neither did any of her coven." Slicing a lock of my hair hadn't hurt, so that was true enough. "Like I said, it was just a long day."

Dominic was silent. Normally, I could hold my silence just fine, but with the threat of him blaming Bex or Walker looming between us, I gave in.

"A long day on my feet. My hip quit on me hours ago."

Dominic was silent a moment longer, but his voice lost its edge when he spoke. "Your pain must be quite severe for you to admit its presence."

I pursed my lips. "I don't know if I'd categorize it as 'severe,' but yes, it's worse than usual." I sighed heavily. "Worse than ever, actually. It's beginning to affect my daily activities, more than I can ignore for much longer." I laughed to lighten the mood. "Too bad you can't just lick my hip and heal me, huh?"

"You think I wouldn't if I could?" Dominic said, his voice low and thick.

I didn't know what to say, stunned by the emotion in his words. "I, well—"

"They have surgery now for your condition," he interrupted. "It can reduce the bone spurs and scar tissue associated with advanced early arthritis after an injury. I'm told that it can delay further symptoms and temporarily relieve pain, especially in young, otherwise healthy patients."

I gaped for a moment before I could gather my wits enough to respond. I'd never thought of Dominic considering human medicine or of me in that way. "What do you know about my condition?"

"Although painful, your condition is no longer an injury. But there are other options to consider. You don't have to live with the pain."

"Bex approached me today," I said, switching gears. Scary, when vampires become the choice topic of conversation.

Dominic let it go. "As I suspected she would. She enjoys exerting her control. How was her approach?"

I frowned. "How do you mean?"

"Did she threaten you? Did she issue any demands for me through you? I wasn't sure how receptive she would be to your presence."

"Bex was friendly compared to the reception I received from your coven," I said. "No broken bones or bloodshed."

Dominic snorted.

"She invited me to dinner tomorrow night."

Silence.

"Hello? Domin—"

"She what?" he asked sharply.

"Um," I delayed, trying to fathom how my statement could have angered him. "She invited me to dinner?"

"Pack and return home now," he ordered.

"What? Home to the city?"

"Yes."

I blinked. "What are you talking about? I just got here."

"I don't trust that she has invited you willingly into her coven for a friendly dinner. She shouldn't trust you. She shouldn't want you to know where her coven is located or how to infiltrate it. You are to pack your belongings and come home immediately."

"We had a deal," I said, livid. "I'd liaise between you and Bex if you'd search for my brother. If this is your way of snaking out, then—"

"You have completed your favor to me, and I will continue to search for Nathan for you. I'm simply relieving you of further debt. Come home."

I hesitated. "You'll still search for my brother?"

"Of course." Dominic sounded offended. "Like you just stated, we had a deal. You have fulfilled yours, and I intend to fulfill mine."

"I haven't fulfilled anything! Your strength is deteriorating daily. You need Bex's alliance to survive the Leveling. You said so yourself."

Dominic sighed over the phone, and I knew he knew I was right. "We have a couple weeks. We'll find another way."

"A couple weeks is nothing. No, we'll see this through." I said firmly. "I'm already here, and I'm not leaving until it's done."

"DiRocco!" Walker's voice called from the other room. "Come here. You'll want to hear this."

I muffled the phone in my hand. "What is it?" I shouted back to Walker.

"The police scanner."

I could just barely discern Ronnie's breathy whisper. "You should wait until sunrise."

Walker's voice was smooth and soothing, a tone he'd never wasted on me. "Listen to the police scanner and keep me updated. I'll call if I need you."

"You never call unless it's from the hospital. Lydia's attack is different, and you know it. Visit the scene in the morning. Please."

"DiRocco!" he called.

"I'll be there in a second. Just finishing up here." To Dominic I said, "I need to go."

"That's our Ian Walker's voice I hear in the background," Dominic said calmly.

It didn't matter that Dominic was over three hundred miles away, nor that we were only talking over the phone; the dead chill in his tone still spiked fear through my gut. My heart leapt into my throat, and I imagined that even across such a distance, he could still hear its accelerated pace.

"He doesn't know you're speaking to me," he commented.

I took a calming breath, but my heart still slammed. "I try not to make waves."

"You're a reporter. It's your job to make waves, and I dare say, you're very good at it." Dominic paused, and I envisioned him staring at me, cocking his head in that unsettling, bird-like movement of his, as if he could ferret the truth from seeing into my brain.

I shivered.

"Does he know the true motivation of your visit? Does he know about your brother's disappearance?" He paused again, and I suspected that like everything Dominic did, he paused deliberately – to make me sweat. "Does he know of our deal?"

"It's not as if I could invite him to dinner with Bex and her coven like a double date." I lied, fear making me angry. Of course Walker didn't know. He'd die if he knew I'd made a deal with Dominic. Even I couldn't deny it was akin to making a deal with the devil.

"I approve of Ian Walker as your backup, but you still need to take precautions against him. Although he is skilled and will probably protect you, he will have no qualms about risking your safety for the chance to kill a vampire, especially Bex," Dominic said, his tone stern and less terrifying, but I could understand terror from Dominic. This advising, almost parental tone coming from his gravelly, rumbling voice was confusing.

"I know what Walker is capable of," I said flatly, the memory of Jolene McCall's buckshot-blasted face still raw in my mind. Strange and random things reminded me of her, like jaunty baker's hats and fondant. It's the details that refuse to disappear even after the pain is buried far and deep, undetectably, inside. I hadn't eaten a cupcake in three weeks.

"You *think* you know what Walker is capable of, but he has hunted Bex for nearly a decade. His hunger to kill her will surely outweigh any other interest. When it comes to your *primary* goal as my liaison," Dominic enunciated, as if I could forget, "you will be on your own."

I would be more on my own than he realized since Walker had refused Bex's dinner invitation. I touched the vial of his blood that hung from a chain under my shirt, rubbing the smooth glass with the pad of my thumb. "More than a decade?" I asked, deciding to keep the focus on Walker.

"He hasn't spoken of his fair Juliet?" Condescension masked the sharp edge in his voice.

"DiRocco! Now or never! I'm leaving in five!" Walker shouted.

I sighed. "I've got to go," I said to Dominic.

"Ask Ian about Julia-Marie Frost, and maybe then you'll understand the minefield between him and Bex."

"Maybe you should worry less about Walker's loyalty and more about your own," I said hotly. His words reminded me of how little I really knew about Walker and his past, and having Dominic throw that ignorance in my face made my temper boil over. "It's been weeks since Nathan disappeared, and you have nothing to show for your efforts. Assuming you've put forth any effort to find him."

"If you're late to call me going forward, I will assume the worst and come for you," Dominic said, ignoring me. "This is your only warning."

"You wouldn't dare," I whispered. "What about the truce? Bex would consider your presence an act of war, or so you've claimed. Isn't that why I'm here in your stead?"

"The war that will ensue should you force my presence will be on your shoulders," Dominic hissed. "I expect you to call five minutes before dawn, so I know that you have survived the night without injury."

"What about Nathan? You remember him—five foot eight, nose ring, my hair, my eyes? It's been weeks, and you aren't any closer to finding him than when you started."

"We made a deal, and if you uphold your end of the bargain, I promise you, I will uphold mine," Dominic purred. "Have a good night, Cassidy DiRocco. I'll look forward to your next call."

"You have no trouble finding me wherever I am," I said, exasperated. "I don't see why it should be so difficult for you—"

The phone went dead.

"—to find Nathan."

I shoved the phone in my right jacket pocket, but remembering the hole, I switched it over to the left with Walker's borrowed silver nitrate spray. I bit my lip as Dominic burdened my thoughts. He wouldn't risk breaking the truce with Bex. He'd sent me here deliberately to avoid initiating a war with her, but his words made me wonder. I knew how fast he could move. I knew how fast he could fly. Was the 300-mile distance a false sense of security? If he decided to come for me, could he really?

"I meant five seconds, not five years, DiRocco!"

I opened the bathroom door and caught the barrel-end of his bellow. "Coming, Walker," I called back. I left the bathroom and walked into the kitchen.

Ronnie looked up at my approach. Her mascara was smeared across her cheeks to her temples from wiping at tears. I raised my eyebrows and glanced at Walker.

His expression was set like molded plaster.

"You still have the silver nitrate spray?" he asked.

I patted my pocket. "Armed and dangerous."

"Then let's go."

"Go where?" I asked.

Ronnie sniffed. I glanced at her and then back at Walker.

"What's going on?"

Walker glanced at Ronnie, and then he met my eyes, his expression unreadable. "There's been another animal attack, under the old train overpass on Elm Street."

I raised my eyebrows. "Under the old train overpass?"

Walker nodded tightly.

"Where we just stopped to speak to Bex?"

"Yes," he bit out.

Ronnie's gaze sharpened on Walker. "When did you speak to Bex? The sun just set after you came home."

"We've got to go," Walker said, ignoring Ronnie.

I nodded slowly, still trying to puzzle together why Ronnie was near hysterical. "Do you know the victim personally?"

"Victim*s*," Walker said, emphasizing the plural. "John Dunbar and his wife, Priscilla. Sounds like their car was found abandoned on the side of the road, their bodies yards away. And torn apart."

"Torn apart? Is there any connection between the Dunbars and Lydia?"

Walker shook his head. "I need to research Lydia's wounds and examine the Dunbars before we assume anything. If the Dunbars have the same injuries, maybe the same animal who attacked Lydia this evening attacked the Dunbars tonight."

"And maybe they're both vampire attacks."

Walker leveled his gaze on me. "We won't know 'til we examine the Dunbars. You ready?"

I shook my head. "If country vampires are anything like city vampires, my vote's with Ronnie. We should wait until sunrise. There's nothing we can do now that we can't do in daylight."

"Berry, Keith, and Riley are expecting me," Walker said, exasperated. "I'm tracking the animal on this case, remember?"

"I don't care about Berry, Keith, and Riley," Ronnie whispered, still sniffing. "I care about you."

"Berry, Keith, and Riley?" I asked.

"You just met Berry, the coroner. Sheriff Keith Pitston and his deputy, Officer Riley Montgomery, will be at the scene and expecting me," Walker explained. To Ronnie he said gently, "Bex won't kill me. You know as well as I do that I'm less at risk than anyone else out after dark."

"No, she'll turn you, and then you'll be as good as dead anyway. Isn't that what you always say, Ian? That you'd be dead to us?"

"I'll be fine. I'll have DiRocco with me," Walker assured her. "I've seen her entrance a vampire as easily and completely as they entrance us. She's better equipped to protect us than all of my weaponry combined."

I shook my finger at him. "Don't put this on me. I came here with specific goals in mind, and none of them involved protecting your coven of night bloods. I'm here to find the facts, not to save lives, and the facts can wait until sunrise."

"Will they?" Walker stepped closer and tipped his voice in a deep, taunting whisper. "If you don't come with me tonight to interview witnesses and report tonight's murders, you know damn well someone else will. You'll be out-scooped."

Rage swept like a backdraft through my veins, and I opened my mouth to blast him with its heat. Before I could articulate my anger, he turned his back on me, opened the front door, and left the house.

Since discovering the existence of vampires and my own identity as a night blood, I'd struggled to balance my career and survival, but as Walker had just so accurately stated, I couldn't interview witnesses and out-scoop my competition while hiding in my apartment. This crime fluctuation feature, in addition to being an excuse to visit Walker, allowed me to trick my boss, Carter Bellisimo, into thinking I was still in the game as a competitive crime reporter. In reality, I was swiftly becoming a hermit obsessed with the sunrise/sunset calendar.

I watched Walker's back as he strode across the yard, confident and empowered and purposeful, and I ached inside. This was what my experience with vampires had done to me. They'd stripped my ability to live according to my own terms. They'd confined my life according to their schedule, and they'd compromised my abilities as a reporter.

My rage switched targets, and I stepped out of the house into the night.

"You're going with him?" Ronnie asked, shocked.

I looked back at her. "Did he leave me much choice?"

Ronnie pursed her lips. "Don't let his demands become your only choices. His goals and intentions are very important, but that doesn't make yours any less important. I have to remind myself of that every day."

I considered her words carefully before I spoke. "You didn't know that Bex could survive in daylight, did you?"

Ronnie shook her head. "I don't get out much."

"She just needs to stay confined to the shadows," I said, "but otherwise, she doesn't need to wait for sunset to leave her coven."

"So in the hours between sunrise and sunset, we're still not entirely safe."

I opened my mouth, but Ronnie had already turned her back and walked into the house, leaving me on the porch between the two of them, my head safely inside with her and my heart torn somewhere between Walker's pickup truck and common sense.

* * * *

John Dunbar and his wife, Priscilla, had been sixty-three years old, high school sweethearts, and enjoying dinner with their daughter, Alba. She was attending cake decorating classes at the local bakery, Hot Buns, and her parents had been so impressed by her new fondant skills, they'd stayed later than usual to have a slice of her newest creation—strawberry-vanilla marble cake with chocolate icing and a flip flop-shaped fondant topping. The Dunbars left Alba's apartment shortly after sunset without taking their extra slice, so she packed the slice in a Tupperware container and drove after them.

Alba only made it five minutes down Elm Street before finding their upturned car on the side of the road. Their bodies had been thrown so far from the car that Alba hadn't found them until Officer Riley Montgomery and Sheriff Keith Pitston arrived at the scene, which was actually very fortunate considering their injuries. Officer Montgomery removed Alba from eyeshot of her parents' remains—what little there was left—and brought her to his car to recover. I kept her company while more officers flooded the scene, examined the bodies, and gathered evidence.

Berry had arrived in his van a few minutes ago. Although they wouldn't move the bodies for several hours, after all evidence had been collected and photography had been captured, he was deep in conversation with Sheriff Pitston. If the Sheriff's deepening crease between his brows were any indication, I'd need to snatch another interview from Berry. For the moment, until the activity at the scene settled, I contented myself with interviewing Alba.

I leaned on the frame of Officer Montgomery's cruiser as Alba huddled in the passenger seat. I tried to keep my interview light and unobtrusive, but I didn't need to ask Alba questions to encourage her story. She couldn't stop talking about her parents. I listened and wrote some brief notes, but throughout the entire conversation, I couldn't help but think, *dear God, not another baker.*

John and Priscilla were the golden couple, according to their daughter, and their love was why she was still single. They'd taught her to never settle because once she found the right love, she'd have the rest of her life to enjoy it. She'd never settled, so she was alone. Now, being an only child, she was completely on her own.

Alba clammed up after that. She covered her mouth with her hand and just shook her head in shock. I didn't have the words to comfort her—I knew how deep and sharp grief could stab—so I just sat with her in silence until Officer Montgomery returned. He was in his late twenties, like Alba, and from the looks he was shooting her, Alba wasn't as alone as she felt.

"Is this woman bothering you, Alba?" he asked

Alba shook her head, but she hugged herself a little tighter and started rocking back and forth from her perch on the passenger seat.

Officer Montgomery turned to me. "If you don't mind, ma'am, I think you've done enough here. Please be so kind as to leave the scene and Miss Dunbar to me."

"Have I done something wrong, Officer?" I asked congenially. I reminded myself that this was not my turf and reined in my temper.

His face flushed. "If you can't see what's wrong here, there's nothing I can do for you, ma'am. You can teach manners, but you can't teach morals."

I raised my eyebrows. "I'm not sure what you're referring to. I've been keeping Alba company. Seems to me like she needed it."

As I'd hoped, Alba's name sparked her awareness. She glanced up and smiled wanly. "Hi, Riley."

"Is this woman bothering you?" Officer Montgomery asked again, pointing at me.

"No, not at all," Alba said, shocked. "She's been wonderful company. I've never met a better listener. I just can't believe that—" Alba covered her mouth, and her throat made horrible squealing noises as she tried and failed not to cry.

He placed his hand on her shoulder and squeezed. "I'm sure Ms. DiRocco is the best listener," Officer Montgomery said, glaring at me. "We're just finishing up at the scene. I'll stay with Alba, if you don't mind."

"I don't mind at all," I said, ignoring the implication that I should leave.

"I'm not askin' your permission," Officer Montgomery said, his twang sharpening. "I'm tellin' you, ma'am. You've outstayed your welcome."

His tone penetrated through Alba fog. She frowned. "*You're* being rude, Riley. Why should Cassidy leave? She's Walker's friend, and she's been wonderful company."

"She's a reporter, Al." Officer Montgomery said, as if he were unveiling the man behind the curtain.

Alba nodded. "I know."

Officer Montgomery frowned. "What do you mean, you know?"

"She told me. She works for *The Sun Accord* in New York City. Walker brought her here to write a story on crime comparison between country and city life, and she asked if she could sit with me. And that's what she's done, just sit with me."

Officer Montgomery looked back and forth between us, and whatever he saw, he obviously didn't like. His face flushed a dark crimson in mottled patches across his cheeks. He stepped in close and tipped his voice to a whisper, but in stepping closer to me, he was closer to Alba as well. "I know your type."

I raised my eyebrows. "My type? I'm not sure you know me well enough to know—"

"I don't need to know you to know where you're from. You city hot shots think you're better than us. You'd do anything for a story. You're taking advantage of a woman's grief, but I ain't gonna let that happen."

Anger, like hissing steam, flashed through me and heated my face. I opened my mouth to to say something I'd regret when a glint behind Officer Montgomery caught my eye. I hesitated. A glowing orb blinked a few yards into the woods, like a mirror reflecting the moonlight. I knew that glint almost better than I knew my own reflection.

I glanced around to see if anyone else had noticed the vampire watching us from the woods, and another movement caught my gaze. Walker was shaking his head at me. He had joined the conversation between Sheriff Pitston and Berry, but my argument with Officer Montgomery hadn't been as private as I would have hoped. A few other officers were staring at us, most of their expressions disapproving and aggravated. Walker, however, looked furious.

He was shaking his head at my argument with Officer Montgomery. He hadn't seen the vampire. No one had.

"You've worn out your welcome, Ms. DiRocco," Officer Montgomery said. "I'm telling, not asking, you to leave Miss Dunbar alone."

Alba's mouth dropped open. "Riley! That's completely uncalled for!"

"It's all right, Miss Dunbar." I patted her knee and then held out my hand for Officer Montgomery to help me stand. "He's right. I've worn out my welcome."

Montgomery hesitated a moment before taking my hand and helping me to my feet. He didn't trust my easy acquiescence, but he wanted me gone badly enough to accept it without question.

"Before I leave, would you mind giving me a statement?"

Officer Montgomery's face pinched. "You'll have to speak with Sheriff Pitston about statements."

I nodded. "I certainly will. Thank you for your help."

He returned my nod but eyed me carefully as I walked away. I could feel the heat of his gaze as I walked toward Walker's truck. Had he been Greta or Officer Harroway or nearly any city cop, I would have cajoled my way into squeezing more information about the case, but I didn't have the clout or notoriety here that I had in the city. In fact, if Officer Montgomery's treatment was any indication, I was starting from the very bottom of the totem pole, lower even than when I'd started in the city simply because I was from the city. But if I could write a book about anything, I could fill page after page about how to claw my way back from the bottom.

Walker had rejoined his conversation with Sheriff Pitston and Berry. I waited until Officer Montgomery turned back to Alba. He knelt in front of her, giving her his undivided sympathy and affection. While everyone else was distracted by other conversations, I ducked behind Walker's truck and into the shadowed overpass toward the police tape. I squinted into the darkness beyond the police parameter, scanned the surrounding trees, and waited.

After a minute, my gaze caught the glint again. My eyes were drawn to it, and I could feel the deep, wrenching pull of its mind connecting with mine. Its strength couldn't compete with anything I'd experienced with Jillian or Dominic, but nevertheless, it rooted deep inside me, shaping my will. It wanted me to step toward it. I could feel the force of its desire stimulating the synapses in my brain to move my legs, one foot in front of the other, to walk toward it.

The force of its command was light and coaxing. I could resist if I wanted, but if I resisted now, I wouldn't have the advantage of surprising it with the depth of my own strength. From experience, that slight advantage could make the difference between bleeding and surviving.

Vampires were willing to sacrifice anything, even their own anonymity, to get what they wanted, and at the moment, with dozens of police officers and emergency personnel to choose from, this vampire wanted me. As prejudiced as Officer Montgomery and the rest of Sheriff Pitston's team might be, they didn't know the dark like I did. I could talk a good talk to Walker about being here to report the facts, not to save lives, but when faced with the reflective double glint of a vampire's eyes staring at me, staring into me, I was glad that mine was the life on the line. I didn't want anyone else getting caught in the kill zone between me and the vampires.

I took one halting step and then another into the woods, away from the illusion of protection that the police provided, and toward the vampire.

* * * *

A heavier, denser darkness lived in the woods compared to the train overpass. Its thickness was like trying to see underwater; just when I thought I'd approached what looked like a boulder or tree branch, I'd reach out to catch my bearings and touch nothing but shadows. The reflective glint was only a dozen yards away now. I stumbled uncertainly, and my heart leapt to pound on my eardrums.

The musk of damp dirt, leaves, and pine thickened the air, and for a moment, I inevitably thought of Dominic. As frightened as I was of his power, influence, strength, and intentions, I realized that his presence in the city had also given me a measure of security. Not one vampire had attacked me in three weeks, and I knew it wasn't because of my own muscle. Dominic's loyal protection—albeit motivated by his own selfish desires to control me—ensured that I survived the night. Now that I was facing the creatures that bump in the night alone, I appreciated his ability to bump back. I could feel the void of his protection like a tightrope walker performing without her net.

The glint, which had flashed a few yards to my left, streaked mere feet in front of my face. I stumbled, but before I could fall, my back bumped flush against something tall and bone cold. Arms wrapped around my body, but they were distinctly not human. Its knobby joints protruded under its rough, gray skin, like bat claws. One hand bound around my waist, clamping my back to its front. The other gripped my neck, tipping my head sideways with the unbelievable strength in its fingers. I could feel the cutting pressure of its talons rake against my stomach as it held me, but unfathomably, I also felt its reserve. The talons didn't slice my skin. Its grip hadn't torn my muscles or broken my ribs. I was still unharmed and whole.

I was playing the human, a performance that had saved me on previous occasions. I knew I needed to act unaware of anything but the smooth, calming limbo the creature was trying to flood through my mind, but I couldn't help the deep tremble that shook my chest and vibrated through my body like a swift, deadly undertow.

Lips—if you could call the thin skin stretched over its massive fangs lips—kissed the skin beneath my ear. "Be calm, little one." He spoke and the growling timbre of his voice belied the meaning behind his words.

The swift boil of my anger at being called "little one" helped douse some of my trembling. I deliberately slowed my breathing, so he would think I was under his influence.

He rubbed his cheek against my cheek. "Hmm," he murmured on an inhale. I felt a tremble course through his body. His talons tightened just short of breaking the skin as he composed himself. "Lovely."

The slick slide of his tongue flicked out in a hot swipe over my neck. I almost lost my nerve. I clenched my teeth to stop myself from jerking away when his mouth clamped over my carotid in a punishing, penetrating lock. Fangs pierced through my skin, and my knees gave out as he sucked a long, fiery gulp of blood.

Pleasant, soothing pleasure kneaded my body in pulses. Unlike Dominic's bite, which could blow my mind in orgasm, and Kaden's bite, which tore through flesh like a rabid dog gnawing its bone, this bite massaged around my body like a cloud. It wasn't overwhelming or violent, like the other bites I'd experienced. It soothed my aches and worries. I floated in oblivious bliss, and perhaps this bite was more dangerous for its gentility because despite having kept my will, I didn't want to pull away.

The vampire released the pressure on my neck, healed the wound with a quick, efficient lick, and stepped back from me after only one swallow. I slumped to the ground. From my prone position, I could finally see the vampire behind me. He hadn't fed yet besides the one swallow of my own blood, but that one swallow hadn't been enough to transform him back from his gargoyle-like form. His ears stood at attention. His nose was flat and flared, and although his canine teeth were fanged, every tooth in his mouth came to a sharpened point.

Like all the other vampires I'd seen in this form, his body was slim, nearly skeletal, and his legs, which I had to focus on not seeing, were jointed backwards. Vampires were difficult to differentiate in this form, but I noticed a slight difference in his. This vampire, unlike Dominic and any other vampire I'd known, had webbed fingers.

The vampire stared down at me, incredulous.

"You're a night blood."

I blew out a long breath. "What gave me away?" I asked sardonically. The jig was up the moment he'd tasted my blood.

He cocked his head, and after a suspended moment, he shot me a smile. The smile would have been reassuring if not for the rows of needle-sharp teeth.

"Humor," he said. "It's been a while."

I tensed to move from my prone position. The vampire disappeared and was suddenly beside me, scooping me from the ground and carrying me in his arms deeper into the woods. He dodged between trees and flashed over logs and catapulted over what looked like a small river dividing the forest, moving at that nearly invisible speed that they could all move. The few times Dominic had carried me as he moved at that speed, I tried to focus on something central, like the freckle above his collarbone, to keep my bearings, but focusing on this vampire was more sickening than the world warping in a dizzying blur around us. Focusing on him meant staring at the rough grayness of his chest, the five-inch talons curved under my knees, and the glowing amber of his reflective, nocturnal eyes.

His focus shifted at my perusal, and our eyes met.

I stiffened in his arms. "Shouldn't you watch where you're going?"

"Does my gaze make you uncomfortable?" he asked, and he deliberately smiled wide enough to showcase every pointed inch of his teeth.

Of all the vampires to attack and abduct me, I'd found the comedian this time. I shouldn't complain. Last time, I'd found the serial killer.

"It's not you, it's me," I said, and the vampire snorted. "If we crash into a tree at this speed, you'd survive just fine, but I'd be dead." I gave him a long look. "The police would have another murder to investigate, and the last thing your coven needs with a serial vampire on the loose is more attention."

The vampire sobered. "We don't know who's responsible for the murders, serial vampire or not. Bex will be busy tonight finding out, but despite the murders, I think she'll make time for you."

I blinked. "You're bringing me to Bex?"

"You know Bex?"

I nodded.

"That's impossible," he dismissed. "I know every night blood here."

"I'm not from here."

A slow smirk widened his lips. "That I believe."

The wind whipped my hair around us, smacking him in the face. A deep rattle vibrated through his chest as he breathed in my scent. I watched his fangs elongate and his lips thin like a dog with its hackles raised.

He looked away, ignoring me to focus resolutely on the path in front of us.

I gaped. "You haven't fed yet, but you're resisting me."

He didn't meet my eyes this time when he spoke. "You're not intended for me. You could be just what my Master needs to find herself again. I can't take that from her."

"How could I possibly do that?"

"She hasn't found a willing night blood in years, not since Walker refused her." The vampire spat Walker's name like it was something vile.

"She must accept what can't be hers and be content with finding someone else, anyone else, before it tears us apart."

I opened my mouth to correct him, to let him know that I wasn't what Bex needed. I already had a Master, and I wasn't willing. But it dawned on me that the only thing preventing him from feeding from me was his intention to bring me to Bex.

"What's your name?" I asked instead.

"You may call me Rene."

I raised my eyebrows. "Just Rene?" I needed to know his first and last name to have a hope of entrancing him.

"Knowing a vampire's full name is earned, not given."

Damn it. "Oh. Why is that?"

He smirked. "Asking to know my full name is tantamount to a man asking to see your breasts on a first date. I don't know you well enough to reveal all of myself, and it's rude to ask."

Rene described it like a social nicety, but I suspected the real reason he wouldn't give me his last name was survival. Knowing and saying a vampire's full name increased my hold on its mind when I entranced it. Most night bloods couldn't entrance vampires, but Rene didn't know that I wasn't like most night bloods.

"Sorry," I muttered. "Far be it for me to be rude while I'm being abducted."

Rene laughed. "Valid point. My name is Rene Roland. What's yours?"

"DiRocco," I murmured, deliberately only giving him my last name and determined not to feel guilty for my deception. I was food to him, nothing but meat and blood with a sence of dry humor that he apparently appreciated, but this piece of meat was not being eaten. Not tonight. "Most people call me DiRocco."

"It's lovely to meet you, DiRocco. My apologies that our paths couldn't cross under more favorable circumstances."

I couldn't imagine a favorable circumstance in which we could have met, but I kept my lips sealed and simply nodded, not trusting my smart mouth to remain polite.

We stopped in front of an overgrown cave imbedded on a hillside. Vines spread over the embankment and grew along the edges of the cave's mouth, blurring exactly where the ground ended and the cave began. Rene set me on my feet, but between the thick, impenetrable darkness of the deep woods and my fear of the coming confrontation with Bex, I could already feel the confines of the cave's walls closing in around me. I leaned fractionally over its edge, peeking into the abyss. Even as my eyes adjusted, they couldn't penetrate through to the cave's bottom. Assuming the cave had a bottom.

Rene pulled me back. "We're waiting here. Many of our newest coven members still haven't fed."

"Is this the entrance to your coven?" I asked, surprised.

Rene nodded. "I don't want the first human they lay eyes on after waking from their day rest to be a night blood. They wouldn't be able to resist drinking from you, and once they started, they might not stop. Your blood is like—"

"Like cinnamon and spice and everything nice," I said, drolly. "Or so I'm told."

He smirked. "Yes, it is."

"I appreciate your concern, but if you didn't want me in harm's way, why bring me to a coven full of unfed vampires?"

"It's not you I'm worried about. You would survive, but they wouldn't."

I frowned. "*I* would survive, and *they* wouldn't?"

"Bex would never tolerate another vampire in her coven draining a night blood."

I stared at Rene, incredulous. "Bex would kill a vampire for attacking me?"

"Of course. Night bloods are potential vampires, and the only vampire who can transform a night blood is Bex. An attack against a night blood is considered an attack against Bex herself."

I nodded. His logic made a strange sort of sense, more sense than how Dominic ruled his coven, and I wondered at the difference. Maybe Bex was more powerful and therefore better able to control her vampires. Maybe Dominic only seemed less powerful because his Leveling was approaching in two weeks. Or maybe Dominic was not as effective a Master—all possibilities worth considering, but I knew better than to utter them aloud, especially the last. Even 300 miles away, I wouldn't be surprised if Dominic overheard me. I'd regret it, but I wouldn't be surprised.

"What have you brought home, Rene? I thought I taught you better than to play with your food?"

Bex materialized in front of us. It must have been a trick of the darkness and her own speed and stealth because actually materializing from nothing was impossible, even for a vampire. Then again, so much lately that should be impossible was real; I couldn't really question what may or may not be possible. I only questioned what occurred: I was alone with Rene one moment, and the next, Bex was in front of us, her reflective, yellow-green irises refracting the moonlight.

I tried to breathe normally, knowing their senses could detect every minute internal change in my body, but I couldn't help it. My body started to tremble.

"Master." Rene bowed his head. "I present a new night blood in our territory. She calls herself DiRocco."

I took a calming breath, but the tremble in my chest worsened. The vial of Dominic's blood was a hot weight around my neck. I caught myself reaching to touch it and forced my hand to remain at my side.

"DiRocco, I present—"

I waved my hand at Rene dismissively, annoyed at his formality while Bex was frying a laser through my chest with her unwavering, alien eyes. "Yes, I know, you present Bex, the Master Vampire of Erin, New York, from Chemung to Wayne County and everywhere in between."

Bex grinned. "Walker taught you well."

"Walker doesn't speak of you in that way."

Rene looked between the two of us, weary regret heavy in his expression. "You've already met?"

Bex lost the grin. "Why would Lysander concern himself with my expanding territory?"

"Dominic makes everything his concern."

"That I most certainly believe. What I'm not quite certain I believe is why you were brought here." Bex shifted her gaze from me to Rene with a flick of her golden-green eyes, and I almost felt bad for Rene. Almost.

Rene cocked his head, not looking particularly worried about being on the business end of that look. "She's a new night blood in our territory. I wasn't aware of her presence, and I definitely didn't know that you were previously acquainted. Upon discovery, why wouldn't I bring her to you?" Rene narrowed his eyes, and despite his obvious loyalty, returned Bex's laser look with heat of his own.

Bex lifted her chin defensively. "She might be new to us, but she's not new to our territory. She's Lysander's night blood, and by bringing her to me you risk—"

"When has territory ever stopped you from claiming what's yours?" Rene interrupted. His chest vibrated in a low, rattling growl, and his lips thinned across his sharpened teeth. "DiRocco is in your territory, and anything in your territory is rightfully yours to take. Lysander knew that when he allowed her to leave his territory. You shouldn't need me to explain this to you."

I pursed my lips and wondered if what Rene was saying was accurate. He seemed to be a font of vampire etiquette, and if Bex's expression was any indication, Dominic had thrown me to the wolves, almost literally. Except wolves might have been preferable.

"She doesn't want me as her night blood," I interjected, hoping to turn the heat under someone else. Walker was certainly a subject of contention between them, so I'd play on that. "Or at least, she doesn't want me enough to risk war with Dominic. The only night blood she'd risk anything for is Walker."

"By pursuing Walker, she risks everything," Rene growled.

"Enough," Bex growled back.

"Other night bloods exist beyond Walker." Rene continued. "They might not be the night bloods you want, but they're the night bloods your coven needs. Your love of Walker has blinded you from the destination we've worked so hard to reach, and if you continue leading us astray, someone will come along to right our path."

Bex's chest rattled. "Is that a threat, Rene?"

"Never, Master. I serve only you, but as your loyal servant, I fear for the stability of our coven."

"I've lived many lives with many covens, and I've transformed many night bloods. In all that time, I've gained something that I didn't possess in my former life as a night blood, nor after I was transformed, for many, many years: patience. Walker is my night blood, and when he's ready, I'll be there. Looking back years from now at the time it took for him to accept his destiny, you'll see that the extra time we waited was a mere blink in our existence. Y'all haven't realized this because you've only lived one human life, but when you've lived five, ten, one hundred human lifetimes, you'll understand this inevitability."

"I understand, Master," Rene growled through clenched teeth, his tone anything but understanding. "But in the meantime, while you're exercising patience with Walker, other night bloods are ripe for the transformation."

"Night bloods must be chosen carefully. If they're unwilling—"

"Walker is unwilling!" Rene snapped.

"DiRocco isn't worth the trouble that changing her would stir with Lysander," Bex finally admitted, and as the words tumbled from her lips, she realized her mistake.

"You fear Lysander and his growing power, despite his approaching Leveling," Rene accused.

Bex lifted her chin higher, refusing to bend. "I fear nothing."

"Then if you don't want the night blood, and you don't fear Lysander's wrath, may I drink from her?" Rene asked darkly.

I looked back and forth between Bex and Rene in the sudden, quelling silence. The exchange had escalated so rapidly that I wasn't sure how their attention had once again shifted to me, but I held my breath as I became the focus of both their honed, targeted gazes.

Bex froze for a moment, her expression like chiseled stone. She'd trapped herself between pride and fear, and my heart sank. In her place, I knew which I'd choose. Quickly, nearly imperceptibly, she nodded.

I didn't wait to see if Rene would make good on his request. I didn't care if he just wanted a taste or if he was only proving a point, he wasn't drinking a single drop from me.

"Rene Roland," I said, and like butter, my mind melted around his, seeping into the cracks and crevices of his thoughts.

I felt shock and fear sting his heart like bees.

"Rene?" Bex asked sharply.

"Stand in front of me, Rene Roland, and shield me from Bex with your body," I commanded.

Rene flew in front of me, shielding me from Bex. He didn't even attempt to reflect my command.

Bex gaped at me. "It's true."

I would have smiled at her expression if I hadn't been so terrified. Bex's astonishment was my only upper hand. Before she could recover, I hooked my fingers around the vial of Dominic's blood, snapped the necklace from my neck, and whipped the silver chain around Rene's throat in a makeshift garrote. The moment the silver touched Rene's skin, a noxious steam hissed from his burning flesh.

Rene tensed, but because of my command to shield me from Bex with his own body, he couldn't move.

"You are full of surprises, little night blood," Rene whispered.

"I'm sorry."

Rene bared his teeth in a semblance of a smile. "Never apologize for surviving."

Bex recovered from her shock and released a growling roar. It blasted through us. I felt the compelling urge to bend to her power. Rene trembled to cede to her, but he remained firmly planted in front of me, as per my command. No matter her control over Rene as a member of her coven, I wasn't hers to control. My grip on his mind was deeply rooted where Bex couldn't reach, and until I chose to release him, my grip was unbreakable.

I could taste the strength of my bond in the flavors of Rene's kaleidoscope of emotions. His rage burned through my stomach. His fear spiked through my heart. And a swell of grudging respect filled him painfully, like a Thanksgiving feast. He thought I could be the wedge between Bex and her destructive pursuit of Walker. He hoped I could be his coven's salvation.

He'd have to get in line.

Bex stepped closer.

"Don't." I tightened the necklace around Rene's throat. His skin gave easier than I would have expected; like a hot spoon through ice cream, I could have scooped the silver straight through to his spine. He hissed, but the sound was gargling and wet. I eased my grip before I decapitated him by mistake.

"You will release Rene," Bex growled.

"You will step back," I said. I tugged on the necklace for emphasis and it imbedded a little deeper into Rene's charred flesh.

Rene trembled. "Master, please."

Bex didn't take another step closer, but she didn't move back either. "You can't cross into my territory and threaten my vampires without retribution. I thought Lysander wanted to prevent war, not start it."

"I'm not here to threaten you or your vampires. I'm protecting myself!" I could feel my hands trembling on the cold stillness of Rene's neck. *If I were really Dominic's night blood in heart and not name alone,* I thought, *what would I do?* I took a long, deep breath and spoke again. "Dominic is the only vampire who may drink from me. You are his ally, but he is my Master. My *only* Master."

Something flashed in Bex's eyes, a bright, burning mix of longing and frustration and jealousy that I knew all too well. I'd looked at other couples that way after my breakup with Adam and felt that impossible, bitter longing for the love they had while simultaneously condemning their love to fail because mine had failed. In that moment, I knew that Dominic had been right about Bex.

She wanted from Walker what she thought Dominic had achieved with me. She wanted a willing and loyal night blood. My relationship with Dominic was mostly illusion—I certainly wasn't willing and I was only loyal enough to uphold my end of our deal for Nathan's sake—but I'd delivered the impression Dominic had wanted, and Bex believed it.

Bex crossed her arms. "What do you want?"

"I want your word that my status as Dominic's night blood will be respected. That means no drinking," I said, and I directed that last part to Rene by tightening the necklace around his neck.

Rene stiffened. "Got it."

"I'm here on Dominic's behalf to mend bridges," I continued, meeting Bex's gaze. "I'm here to express Dominic's sincere regret that Walker suffered in his care, and as a show of good faith, he sent me. As Walker returned to you whole and otherwise not permanently damaged from Dominic's coven, Dominic is expecting the same courtesy for me."

Bex pursed her lips. "I'm listening."

"I accept your dinner invitation for tomorrow night, but only if you ensure my safety. If you're at all interested in rebuilding a truce with Dominic, you should keep in mind that I report directly to him."

"Excuse me?"

"The report of my visit thus far won't speak well of your hospitality."

Bex narrowed her eyes. "Is that a threat?"

"I'm only reminding you of the reality of our situation and my position, so you can make a choice. If you allow vampires, like our comedian here," I said, indicating Rene, "to drink from me, Dominic's attempt to mend fences will stop before it's even really begun."

"I don't need your advice to rule my coven, bless your heart. I've survived my enemies, and my vampires have flourished under my rule for longer than you've been alive. You think you can cross into my territory and threaten my vampires? You think that you can threaten me?" Bex growled. "You don't want me as your enemy."

"No, I don't. You have a choice to make, a choice that will affect you and your coven as well as mine, and I'm here to make sure you choose correctly."

Bex's nostrils pointed, the first slip I'd ever witnessed in her control. "You don't know shit about choices, little girl."

"You think on it. I'll see you tomorrow night for dinner."

Bex snarled and stepped forward.

"Pick me up and fly me back to the crime scene," I whispered to Rene. "You will leave me there, fly back here, and not return for me. Now!"

Rene didn't hesitate. We flew through the air faster than my eyes could track the surrounding woods, so fast that the trees and foliage and blanketing darkness blurred on either side of us. His arms cradled my body. His embrace was strong and secure and without even a twitch to indicate the inner struggle he was surely battling. I remembered my struggles to fight Dominic's mind games. I'd screamed and fought against him on the inside while physically following his every command on the outside, but I'd never followed them blindly. My struggle was apparent in the nuance of my responses and my trembling hesitation as I battled for control of my body.

Rene wasn't strong enough to display his struggle, but I could feel it. On the threads of my mind that plucked at his, I could hear him screaming.

My feet abruptly touched the ground. The blur of the surrounding forest shifted into focus, and I lost my purchase on the forest floor before I even knew I'd found it. The world tipped sideways. I fell hard on my side, and pain flared through my hip. Gritting through it, I turned to block Rene's attack.

But as per my direct command, he was already gone.

Chapter 4

"Had you stayed in the police cruiser with Alba, this wouldn't have happened," Walker chided. His tone was deliberately calm and measured, but I could tell by the clench of his jaw that he wanted to shout.

"Officer Montgomery shooed me away from Alba because I'm a big, bad reporter from the big, bad city," I said. I was trying to be reassuring, but I couldn't keep the sarcasm from my voice, even for Walker.

"You're not that easily shooed," Walker grumbled. "On a scale from one to ten, how badly does your hip—"

"A pain rating? Seriously?" I shook my head. "*I'm fine*. What happened with the Dunbars? What did Berry and Sheriff Pitston say about the case?"

"Had you stayed with Alba, you could have interviewed them yourself."

"Had I stayed with Alba, someone else would have been abducted."

Walker crossed his arms stubbornly. "Exactly. Someone else might have been abducted, but not you."

I pinched the bridge of my nose and prayed for more patience. I was sorely running low, and although I struggled with the existence of a graceful, omniscient deity, it would take a miracle to get through this conversation without losing my temper. Walker and I had argued over who was to blame for my abduction from the moment he caught me limping back from the woods, while he helped me to his truck, and as he drove us back to his house. From the stubborn clench of his jaw, the argument wasn't ending anytime soon.

Despite his temper, Walker insisted on replacing the icy-hot patches on my hip when we reached his house, and since I couldn't step without wincing, I wasn't in much of a position to resist when he led me back to the bathroom.

Without much room to maneuver, he had me sit on the toilet seat to reapply the icy-hot. I tried to find a position that I could sit comfortably without shards of my hip digging into nerve endings. I had the feeling that my efforts to convince Walker and sit comfortably were a lost cause, but until he included me on the details of this case, I wasn't letting it go.

I took a deep, calming breath. "We're lucky I was the one adbucted. Had it been anyone else, they wouldn't have stood a chance."

"They would have been fine. Bex's vampires don't kill their prey. As a powerful Master, she controls her vampires," Walker said. I narrowed my eyes, not liking the subtle dig at Dominic, but Walker continued before I could comment. "They would have fed, clouded the person's mind, and returned him generally unscathed."

"I was returned generally unscathed, but Bex obviously doesn't have the iron control over her vampires that you're giving her credit for, *bless her heart*. Lydia and the Dunbars were completely scathed."

Walker snorted. "Bex has been Master of her coven since before we were born—"

"So I've been told," I muttered.

"—and in all my experience dealing with her—over thirty years of learning about them, nearly becoming one of them, and eventually *hating* them—none of her vampires have ever left evidence of their victims. Our experience in the city with Kaden was the first time I'd ever witnessed such a public display of vampire kills. That's rare, not the norm." Walker scrubbed his palm over his face. "These murders are *not* vampire attacks."

I snorted. "Both victims were attacked at night," I ticked off one finger. "The Dunbars were attacked in the exact location that Bex stopped your truck earlier this evening," I ticked off a second finger. "And you said so yourself that if we didn't stop the truck voluntarily, Bex would stop it for you," I ticked off a third finger and stared at Walker, my point solidified. "Something obviously stopped the Dunbars' car for them, and that something screams vampire to me."

"They seem like vampire attacks to you because of your experience with Kaden in the city, and if we were in the city, I'd be inclined to agree with you. But we ain't in the city, *darlin'*, and I'm telling you that Lydia and the Dunbars were not attacked by vampires."

I sighed heavily. "Fine, I'll play along. What else could it be?"

Walker opened his mouth and then hesitated. "Off the record?"

I rolled my eyes. "You do realize that you brought me here under the pretense of writing a newspaper article?"

Walker stared at me with those velvet brown eyes, and I could feel my frustration and anger slip away into the depths of his gaze.

I shook my head at my own weakness. "I have to write *something* worth publishing while I'm here, and it's not as if I can write about vampires," I snapped. Weakness made me angry. "And now you of all people are going to prevent me from writing an article I can actually publish?"

"Sheriff Pitston needs to play this case close to his chest." Walker leaned in and tipped his voice low. "You know how copycats are. They might copy the crime, but if they don't know the details, the police can separate the copycats from the real murderer."

I nodded, curiosity humming through my veins at Walker's tone. "I can keep this under the radar until you give me the go-ahead."

He pursed his lips and nodded. "The hearts are missing."

I raised my eyebrows. "The hearts are what?"

"The hearts of all three victims are gone from their chest cavities, completely severed from the aorta and connective tissue. Berry returned to the scene after Lydia's autopsy, but no evidence of her heart can be found in the surrounding area." Walker said bluntly.

I tried not to gape. After everything I'd seen and survived, even before stumbling upon the existence of vampires, I should have taken the news in stride, but the human mind is a curious thing. Despite the violence I'd witnessed for years at crime scenes and stakeouts, and most recently, the horrors I'd endured at the hands of vampires like Kaden and Jillian and even Dominic, Walker's news took me aback.

I gaped.

"My thoughts exactly." Walker's expression was grim.

I touched my chest over my own heart, still not quite accepting the facts. My fingertips brushed against Dominic's vial of blood, once again securely looped around my neck and dangling low beneath my shirt. Dominic would be pleased that his gift had come in handy, although not in the manner he had intended. Even this far from the city, a piece of him was still with me, protecting me. Keeping my blood in my own body. Keeping my heart in its chest.

I shook my head. "The hearts of all the victims are gone," I repeated, coming to terms with this new development and everything it implied.

Walker nodded. "Berry thought Lydia was so torn apart that we simply missed an organ along with some of her smaller parts, like we—" Walker cleared his throat. "—like we almost did her hand. But both John and Patricia are missing their hearts, too. Once could be chance. Twice could be a coincidence, but three times—"

"Three times is a pattern." I rubbed my hands down my cheeks. "I don't suppose vampires typically include human hearts in their diet?"

"No, not typically."

"So who does? An animal, like you originally thought?" I asked. "Do hearts even offer specific nutritional value that other muscles don't?"

Walker let out a sudden bark-like laugh. It sounded bitter and not his own. "No, I can't say I know of any animal that would eat the heart specifically for its nutritional value. Sheriff Pitston is thinking more along the lines of a killer's trophy."

I blinked. "A trophy?"

"These are murders, DiRocco. Sheriff Pitston is contacting the FBI. If he's right about the hearts, we might be dealing with a serial killer."

I frowned. "You can't think a human is responsible for these killings."

He shrugged. "It would explain the missing hearts."

"How could a human inflict the damage that was done to Lydia's body? How could a person stop a moving vehicle to attack the Dunbars? That doesn't make sense, Walker."

"Have you forgotten how creative humans can be? Lydia's injuries could be achieved with a blunt object, like a sledge hammer or an axe, and the Dunbars could have been stopped by someone pretending to hitchhike." Walker shrugged. "It could have been a human."

I shook my head. "But what's the connection between Lydia and the Dunbars? Nothing, except for the missing hearts and that they were attacked after sunset."

"If these are serial murders, there doesn't necessarily need to be a connection. Their first kill is often personal, but after that, it's not nessisary for serial killers to actually know their victims. They kill for the sake of killing."

"I still think the murderer could be a vampire."

Walker made a face. "A serial killer vampire?"

"I wouldn't be surprised. You wouldn't consider Kaden a serial killer?"

"All vampires kill humans. They're all serial killers."

"No, most vampires hunt to eat. You said yourself that Bex's vampires don't kill humans."

Walker shook his pointer finger at me. "I said that Bex's vampires don't leave their kills out for discovery. There's a difference."

I sighed, still trying to make my point. "They consider us their food. We don't consider people who eat hamburgers serial killers, do we?"

Walker smirked. "A vegan might."

I waved away his comment. "But if the intent of the vampire is to kill simply for the sake of killing, *then* we can consider it a serial killer. In this case, we need to find the one who collects hearts."

"Maybe," Walker admitted, "but I've got twenty that says it's human."

"I'm not taking that bet. I'd prefer it be human. At least then I could write an article about it." I dug the heel of my palms into my eyes, smearing what little eyeliner wasn't already smeared. The familiar suffocation of helplessness and doomed fate that always accompanied thoughts of vampires swelled over me, and my throat constricted. Being one of the few who knew about the enormity of their influence and power was drowning. "If the FBI get involved, and it's a vampire, what are we going to do?"

I heard the deep groan of Walker's sigh. "The same thing we always do: deny we know anything, and when the time comes, kill the vampire responsible."

I looked up and gave him a questioning stare. "We're going to deny we know anything to the FBI?"

"Yes." He groaned again. "I don't know. What else can we do?" His frustration was deeply rooted, from the darkest, unexpressed core of his being. I could empathize. Giving in would be like giving up, but until then, the burden of our secret was in itself a slow death. Sometimes I didn't know which was worse: living in ignorance of vampires and therefore dying their victim or the constant struggle to survive.

Someone knocked on the door.

"Come in," Walker called out.

The door opened slowly. Ronnie peeked her head inside and inexplicably, the bathroom was suddenly too small. Walker's broad shoulders occupied the majority of the space. The heat of his hip was flush against my shoulder—a heat I hadn't even noticed until that very moment—and I felt that heat travel to my face, embarrassed as if she'd caught us indecent.

"Sounded like someone could use a pick-me-up," she said. She opened the door wider and stood in the doorway between Walker and me, a plate of chocolate chip cookies in her hands. I cringed inwardly. At least they weren't cupcakes.

Walker had the grace to smile. "Just what the doctor ordered, darlin'. Thank you."

"Of course." She smiled back at Walker and then offered me the plate.

"Thanks." I grabbed a cookie and bit into a clump of chocolate chips. They were gooey and sweet, and despite my bleak mood and sour disposition, I heard myself release an audible *yum* as I chewed.

Ronnie smiled. "How about I leave these here with you," she said, placing the dozen cookies in front of Walker, "so I can finally give Cassidy the tour I promised her."

Walker nodded, his mouth already too full of cookie and chocolate to properly enunciate.

"That'd be great," I said, anything to escape the confines of that bathroom and Ronnie's overly innocent looks. I stood haltingly, my hip giving me its usual grief, and snatched another cookie from the pile before Walker hoovered the plate clean.

* * * *

At first glance, the house seemed like any other house—albeit stunningly beautiful, well kept, and white glove tested—but unlike any other house, the history was fascinating. I'd known Walker was handy and knowledgeable, but I'd never imagined the extent of his skills. And seeing them here in the house on full display was breathtaking.

Walker had tiled the backsplash above the kitchen counter himself. He had sanded, stained, and polished the hardwood flooring that spanned the entire downstairs, and the stonework in front of the fireplace had also been hand-laid by Walker himself. According to Ronnie, as she continued her tour and the running list of hand crafted features, Walker's father had built the house in 1982 for his wife, and when they passed, Walker had taken over the renovations and maintenance himself with the same custom, earthy flare of his father. The entire house was very log cabin-esque, with wood beam structures, exposed brick, and doilies on every flat surface, but I suspected the doilies were Ronnie's touch.

The only feature of the house not in theme was the basement, or as Ronnie referred to it, the "safe room." The basement was a silver box in the ground as protection against Bex and her coven; Walker had stocked it with enough supplies, food, and weapons to keep a small army hidden and alive for weeks, and a small army was exactly what I feared Walker had in mind.

I reminded myself that I was on assignment—undercover as Dominic's willing night blood and under orders as Carter's lead crime reporter—and I'd return to the city in a week. I tried to harden my heart and convince myself that Walker's problems didn't have to be my problems. I could choose to leave Erin and Walker in my rear view, but I couldn't deny that the thought of leaving him behind, hardened heart or not, made a deep, hollow part of my chest ache.

Although the house's history was certainly interesting, it wasn't Walker's handiness that struck my report's tuning fork.

"Did you ever meet Walker's parents?" I asked, wondering how recently they'd died.

Ronnie glanced behind her, where Walker was now sharing the crumbs of his cookies with a tall, unnaturally lanky teenager with red hair. The boy had clearly just endured a growth spurt. He was all arms and legs and no coordination, and was just now filled with cookies. Ronnie smiled. She turned back to me.

"I grew up with Ian. Our parents were the kind of neighbors who borrowed sugar to finish a batch of brownies and walked in unannounced to share a six-pack for a game. Ian's like the brother I never had," Ronnie said, and although her face smiled, her voice had wavered. She recited by rote what Walker likely told everyone, that they were like brother and sister, but I'd bet my own brother that wasn't how Ronnie felt.

I nodded, pretending I hadn't heard the waver in her voice. "It must be nice still having your parents so close."

Ronnie's smile twisted painfully. Her hands shook on the granite kitchen countertop she was leaning against, and she crossed her arms to hide their trembling.

"I'm sorry, was it something I—"

"No, not at all," Ronnie said hastily. "It's been years. Ian could talk about it without batting an eye, but I still—" She took a deep breath, and her voice was steady afterward. "—it hurts like they died yesterday."

"I'm sorry, I didn't realize—"

"No, really, it's fine."

I leaned in close. "I don't think Walker could talk about it any better than you. I think he just chooses not to talk about it at all."

Ronnie wiped away the tears that had spilled over her cheeks. "That's probably very true."

"How long ago was it?"

"I was five the day of the fire, so Mr. and Mrs. Walker died eighteen years ago. They found my mother the day after. She was buried under the collapsed porch awning. My dad lasted a little longer. He suffered in the hospital for weeks afterward, lost both his right arm and leg from infection, and the pain—" She pressed her fist against her lips and cleared her throat. "—he trembled constantly from the pain of the burns. Ian brought me to the hospital just the one time to say goodbye, but I'll never forget. That one time had been—" Ronnie shook her head. "—I know why Ian thought I should see him. If it had been his father, he'd have stayed by his side the entire time, tried to ease his passing, and said a proper goodbye, but in nearly every way that a person can be different from another person, I am not Ian Walker."

"That and you were five," I said, reliving the depth of my own grief from losing my parents. "Both of your parents died in a fire?" I asked. I fought to keep my voice even so she'd continue her story, but all I could see from the description of her father's suffering was my own mother, trembling and dying from her burns.

"In the same fire," Ronnie said. "We were having a movie night or watching the Giants. I don't remember exactly what was on the TV, but we were in the living room and eating popcorn."

Ronnie waffled her hand in the air as if it didn't matter what they were watching, but I knew better. I couldn't remember the last conversation I'd had with my mother, whether it was in person or over the phone, and the inability to recall our last words still haunted me even after all this time.

"No one's entered the house in years," Ronnie continued. "It's not structurally sound. I've lived here with Ian ever since."

"Where's the house? You said you were neighbors, but there aren't any houses nearby."

"The woods are too thick to see neighbors, but they're there," she assured me. "My house was less than a quarter mile through the woods, due south. The path between our houses is overgrown now, but years ago we visited each other every day, and there was a distinct path we used to walk."

"You and Walker were lucky to have escaped the fire," I commented.

"Yeah." Her face darkened. "We were lucky."

"If you were five, Walker must have been around eleven or twelve?"

"Thirteen."

"Still, that's pretty young to escape the fire on his own. You were *very* lucky," I pushed.

"Well, as it turns out, we were never actually on our own." Ronnie's voice was clipped. She pushed away from the kitchen counter and led me to the staircase. "Care to see the second floor?" She turned away and walked up the stairs before I could reply.

I followed behind at my own excruciating pace, and for once, I took my time, wondering about the statistics behind house fire mortalities, and more pointedly, the statistics behind house fire mortalities for the parents of night blood children. My own parents had died in a fire, and during

Dominic's human lifetime, several lifetimes ago, his father had been maimed in a house fire. Although Dominic claimed the kiln explosion had been an accident, I was very good at sniffing out fact from fiction—my job required that skill as essentially as it required long days, longer nights, and the competitive drive to expose the truth—and the fact that all of our parents had been killed or nearly killed by fire did not smell accidental. It smelled like arson.

I doubted Dominic had been involved directly in my own parents' deaths—my existence as a night blood had been quite the surprise to both of us—but he wasn't the only vampire in the area. From personal experience, his vampires were known to act on their own desires.

Perhaps Bex had acted on hers.

It wasn't until I reached the second floor landing that Ronnie turned the tables on me.

"Ian tells me that you're here on business."

I nodded, trying to breathe past the throbbing in my hip enough to respond. "Yes, I'm writing an article."

Ronnie led me toward the first room, an open parlor that overlooked the living room and kitchen below in a balcony-style sitting area. Decorated with an overstuffed recliner, a three-cushion sofa, end tables, coffee table, and no TV, the room was a classic family room.

"This is beautiful," I commented. "I love how it overlooks the first floor."

"What breaking news is occurring in little old Erin that you'd leave the city for us?" She asked, ignoring my compliment.

I smiled warily. "Breaking news is admittedly the great love of my life, but we've had a falling out recently. I needed a vacation, and honestly, the chance to report something real."

"Breaking news isn't 'real' news?"

"It used to be my favorite kind of news. The rush, the immediacy, the race: it's a sport, and I was my team's star player." I sighed. "Or I liked to think so. But since I discovered the truth about Dominic and Bex and, and—" I hedged, hesitating to say it.

"Vampires," Ronnie said helpfully, her smile understanding. "Since you found out that you're a night blood."

I nodded. "And since I realized that vampires are the cause of many, if not most, of the violent crimes in the city, I've felt disenchanted about my job. Maybe when Dominic gains better control of his coven after the Leveling, I can go back to reporting news like I used to, but until then—" I shrugged. "Here I am."

"It'll never go back to the way it was. Once you find out about them and who you are, everything else in life becomes nothing but background." Ronnie wrung her hands. "Did Ian invite you to stay with us, or did you need somewhere to stay while on assignment?"

I leaned against the arm of the nearest couch to alleviate some of the pressure on my hip and crossed my arms. "I could have chosen any county for on-site research on my article, if that's what you're implying. I chose Erin because Walker encouraged me to visit."

She worried her bottom lip with her teeth, nodding.

I shook my head. "If you've got something to say, you may as well say it. Everything is just background anyway, right?"

"That's my point." Ronnie said. She crossed her arms too, but it seemed to me like she was holding herself together. "You could have chosen any county upstate, but you chose Erin, New York because of Ian. Whether you came here to learn more about being a night blood or to learn more about Ian, I don't know and it's really not my business, but I know Ian a little better than you do. Whether he's invested in you as a night blood or a reporter, or whether he's actually invested in you, it doesn't matter compared to his investment in the great love of *his* life: vampire hunting. He's got a personal vendetta against Bex and a deep rooted hate for all vampires, and rightfully so, but you will never hold a bigger place in his heart than the one that Bex already carved out."

It took me a moment to respond. Of all the things to come out of Ronnie's mouth, I hadn't expected a warning against Walker for my sake.

"I suspected as much," I said quietly.

Ronnie frowned. "So you're not here for Ian?"

"I didn't say that. I'm here for multiple reasons. It's complicated."

"Anything involving vampires always is." Ronnie turned away from the parlor and walked down the hall. "How would you like to meet some of the other night bloods living here?" she asked, her voice forcibly chipper.

I raised my eyebrows. "Aren't most people asleep at this hour? It's past midnight."

"Most of us live a nocturnal lifestyle. Who can sleep knowing the vampires are awake and potentially outside your window?"

"Well then, lead the way."

Everyone was friendly and welcoming as we knocked door to door. Walker's residents greeted me with varying degrees of excitement to have another "night blood sister," as Theresa gushed. Ronnie introduced Theresa as the first to move into the house after herself. Logan and his sons— Keagan, Douglas, William, and Colin—recently moved into the room across the hall from Theresa and were still unpacking. Ronnie explained that I'd only just discovered my "heritage" three weeks ago. Logan's youngest, Colin, had promptly commented, "It's fucked up, right?" only to be smacked lovingly in the head by his barrel-chested father.

"You'll have to excuse my son," Logan said, his eyes rolled heavenward. "Nothing, not even the vampires, could curb that kid's tongue."

Colin stuck the said appendage out at his father, only to be snatched around the neck in a headlock by William—or maybe he'd introduced that son as Douglas—and they both disappeared back into the room. I shook my head at the chaos.

Theresa, watching from her doorway across the hall, laughed. Despite her youthful appearance, she laughed like a cackling witch.

"Those boys will be the death of you, Logan!" she shouted between cackles.

"Care to babysit?"

Theresa raised her hands in mock surrender, backed into her room, and slammed the door. I could still hear her grating cackles through the wall.

Logan had black hair and was a mountain of a man, built of pure muscle and spit, but all four of his sons were gangly redheads. I wondered about their mother, presumably the mass contributor to the boys' genes, but it seemed like everyone in the house had at least one missing loved one and a past filled with blood and sadness. Everyone was here because they'd survived their siblings and spouses. They'd survived their parents.

Ronnie knocked on the last door on the second floor, but no one answered.

"Jeremy?" She knocked again. "It's Ronnie. We have a guest staying with us if you'd like to make her acquaintance."

She waited a moment, but her knock was only answered by silence.

"He's our newest tenant," Ronnie whispered to me. "He doesn't socialize much, but that's how Keagan was, Logan's oldest son. Eventually, he came around. Jeremy is about Keagan's age, maybe a little younger. He'll come around, too."

"I can hear you talking about me," Jeremy said through the door.

"If you'd open the door and talk to her yourself, I wouldn't have to," Ronnie said.

Silence.

Ronnie met my eyes and shrugged. "You'll have plenty of time to get aquainted. Your guest room is right here, across the hall from Jeremy's. I know you dropped your luggage off in a rush earlier today, but please, make yourself at home."

I smiled. "Thanks, Ronnie. I appreciate that."

We turned away to walk back down the hall when I heard the lock unlatch. The door opened, and my breath caught.

Jeremy was my height, made a little shorter as he leaned bare-chested against the doorframe. He crossed his arms and pinned Ronnie and me with a hot stare, daring us to comment on the four rows of stitches across his abdomen. They were tiny, neat stitches, and the cuts looked clean, albeit fresh. From his mop of shaggy brown hair to his ripped skinny jeans, he looked about sixteen with a sixty-pound chip on his shoulder. But who was I to judge? I was thirty with a three-hundred-pound chip on mine; I'd just gained the maturity to hide it better.

"Jeremy," Ronnie said, her voice squeaky with false cheer. "Thank you for opening your door."

Jeremy raised his eyebrows.

Ronnie ignored his wound and continued her introductions. "Jeremy McFerson, I'd like you to meet Cassidy DiRocco. Cassidy is a reporter for *The Sun Accord* in New York City and a good friend of Ian." She turned to me. "Jeremy just moved in last week."

My stomach turned at the sight of Jeremy's wounds, but I followed Ronnie's lead and held out my hand.

He didn't uncross his arms. "You're from the city?"

"That's right."

"What made you leave for this Godforsaken place?"

I grinned. "A combination of work, Walker's insistence, and my own curiosity. And for the record, the city's no better," I lied. I wiggled my fingers, trying one more time for the handshake. "You can call me DiRocco. Everybody does."

Jeremy looked me up and down, his cornflower blue eyes sharp and quick. He nodded to Ronnie. "She didn't."

I met his eyes with my own hard gaze. He wasn't the only one in this hallway who could be difficult. "Jeremy McFerson. Any relation to Buck McFerson?"

He looked away. I could see the muscles of his jaw shift as he clenched his teeth, and I let my hand drop to my side.

Ronnie whispered, as if Jeremy wasn't just in front of us and couldn't hear. "Buck's his uncle."

Ah, I thought. *Lydia.*

His head snapped up. "Shut up."

She raised one eyebrow. "Excuse me?"

"My business is none of her business," Jeremy hissed.

"I plan to make it my business," I said. "Those are some pretty deep scratches you've got there."

Jeremy glared at Ronnie a moment longer before turning his glare on me. "Yeah."

"If they're as new as they look, you should keep gauze over them for a few days."

"What do you know about it?"

"I know a lot," I said calmly. "Like I know that those cuts from their spacing are fingernail scratches."

He laughed. "You can't get cuts like this from fingernails."

"No, not from human fingernails."

Jeremy stopped laughing and just stared at me.

"Did you visit your uncle last night?"

He scoffed. "I don't know what you're talking about."

"Did you know Lydia Bowser?"

"I don't want to talk about it."

I leaned in close. "Did you see her before or after she was torn apart?"

"I said I don't want to talk about it!" Jeremy shoved passed me and into the hall. My hip blazed with a sharp, cutting pain and gave out. I ended up on my ass on the floor.

"Jeremy McFerson!" Ronnie shouted. "When your uncle hears abo—"

"Shut up!"

He pounded down the hall and would have continued down the steps except that six feet of broad muscle blocked his way.

"What the hell is going on up here?" Walker asked, his voice low.

He looked over Jeremy's shoulder to me on the floor, and his eyes widened. He shoved Jeremy back against the wall and opened his mouth to blast him, but whatever words had boiled to the surface turned to steam when he caught sight of the stitches across Jeremy's abdomen.

"It's my fault," I cut in. Ronnie offered me a hand up, but I waved her away, using the wall for support. "I pushed him too far."

"What did this?" Walker asked Jeremy.

"It wasn't a vampire," Jeremy said quietly. His surly attitude toward Ronnie and me evaporated in Walker's presence.

"Next time he acts up," I whispered to Ronnie, "maybe you should threaten him with Walker, not his uncle."

Ronnie snorted.

"What *was* it?" Walker repeated.

Jeremy shrugged.

"You're under my roof, and I'll be damned if I don't know what's going on under it. I can't ensure our safety, the safety of everyone living here, if I'm blind. Knowing is s—"

"Knowing is surviving," he interrupted. "I know."

Walker raised his eyebrows.

Jeremy opened his mouth. He closed it, cleared his throat, and tried to start again, but his face twisted. He flushed a bright red and cleared his throat again, louder than before, and this time, I could hear the wetness in his throat. He was struggling not to cry.

"How about we move this conversation out of the hall and take a seat in the family room?" Ronnie offered.

Jeremy nodded, jumping on the opportunity to compose himself.

I grunted, still trying to leverage off the floor.

Ronnie gave up on watching me struggle, gripped my arms above the elbows, and yanked me to my feet. She had some muscle hidden somewhere under her skin and bones. The next thing I knew, I was back on my feet, and she was steadying me as I swayed over the gnawing ache of my hip.

"Thanks," I said grudgingly.

"You're more stubborn than Ian." Ronnie said, shaking her head. "That's something I never thought I'd say."

Walker glanced between the two of us, his eyes narrowed. I smiled back, acting deliberately obtuse. Walker shook his head and turned around, leading Jeremy by a firm grip on his shoulder to the family room. When I turned to look at Ronnie, I realized that she had been forcing a strained smile at Walker, too.

* * * *

"I met Lydia at Gretel's Tavern last night, like we do every night before dinner."

Jeremy, Ronnie, Walker, and I were all seated in the family room. Jeremy and Ronnie took the couch, and Walker and I scooted two of the overstuffed chairs from the other side of the room, so we all faced each other.

"How long have you been meeting her at Gretel's?" Walker asked.

Jeremy wrung his hands. He wouldn't meet Walker's gaze as he spoke.

"Two months. Her dad hates me, always has, but after I was suspended from school for that damn pen, he forbade that we continue dating. We've been meeting at Gretel's ever since."

She didn't have a boyfriend, huh? I thought, looking at Walker.

My thoughts must have been pretty loud; he frowned at me before responding to Jeremy.

"What happened this time when you met that was different from the other times?"

Jeremy shrugged. "Nothing. We made out. Ragged about her old man and Mrs. Secor for clicking that damn pen."

"Why is a pen the feature in this story?" I asked.

Walker sighed. "He brought one of *my* pens to school."

"Ah," I murmured. The wooden stake that sprang from its tip would certainly be a surprise to an unsuspecting teacher. "Poor Mrs. Secor."

"Poor me! I don't get out of practice until six," Jeremy snapped, sounding defensive. "It's dark by then."

Walker put up a hand. "I know. No one's saying that you don't need a weapon to protect yourself. You just needed to implement a better method of concealing it or find a different weapon. Which we did."

Jeremy closed his mouth and stared down at his hands again. He nodded.

"Which is why you need to tell me what's going on, so we can figure out the tough stuff together." Walker said, but he glanced at me when he said the last.

Jeremy just shook his head, holding his silence.

I pursed my lips. "Did Lydia get angry when you complained about her father?" I asked.

Jeremy finally looked up, frowning. "No. She complains about her old man all the time."

"But he's her dad. I bet she didn't like *you* 'ragging' about him."

"It wasn't like that."

"Then how was it?"

"It was like any other night." Jeremy said, and then his jaw dropped. "You think that I, what happened to Lydia, you think that was my fault?" Jeremy asked, his eyes frantic.

Walker shook his head. "You tell me what happened, Jeremy."

"I don't know what happened!" Jeremy burst. "One second we were kissing and talking and she was laughing and kissing me back and then—" He ran both hands through his hair to the back of his neck. "—then something crashed into us. The only light behind Gretel's is what little shines through the bathroom windows, so I couldn't see shit, but whatever it was, the thing was on top of Lydia. And she—" he took a deep breath, but when he continued, his voice cracked. "—she was screaming. It didn't hypnotize her like the vampires usually do. It didn't strike at the neck or her carotid, and it didn't just suck her blood. It looked like it was actually *eating* her."

Jeremy stopped speaking. He looked away and after a moment, when I thought he would continue, tears spilled down his cheeks. He wiped them away with a jerk of his arm.

Ronnie squeezed his knee.

"This is bullshit!" he exploded. "What the fuck was that thing?"

Walker shook his head. "That's what I'm trying to find out."

"I tried to get it off her," Jeremy said, still wiping away tears. "But it swiped its hand out, it just fucking backhanded me, and I slammed into a tree. I couldn't move for a minute, and Lydia, God, she screamed the whole time. It was a while until she finally stopped screaming. And this," Jeremy looked down at the slashes on his stomach, "this was from its backhand. It wasn't even attacking me, and its claws nearly spilled my guts."

"What did you tell the doctor who stitched you up?" I asked.

Jeremy narrowed his eyes on me. "What's it to you?"

I looked at Walker. "His blood is at that crime scene, and when the labs come back with his blood alongside Lydia's, her father's going to demand answers." I looked back at Jeremy. "What do you think he'll do when the sheriff tells him that his daughter was with you in the woods that night?"

Jeremy blanched.

"What you said at the hospital matters. The police will look into that."

He shook his head. "I didn't go to the hospital."

Walker made a scrambled noise in his throat. "You went to Theresa, didn't you?"

Jeremy shrugged.

I pointed my thumb down the hallway. "This Theresa?"

Ronnie nodded. "She's a surgeon."

"Was. She's retired." Walker swiped his hand down his face. "That was a good move, but you should have come to me, too."

"I wanted to, but—" Jeremy shook his head.

Walker pressed forward this time. "But what?"

Jeremy pounded his fist into his thigh. "Lydia kept screaming! And I just laid there while she screamed and that thing *ate* her and she died. I just laid there, Walker. Is that what you would have done?"

Jeremy's shouts rang through the entire house, making the resulting silence heavy between us.

"Sometimes," I whispered, "simply surviving is all you can do."

Ronnie nodded.

"Amen to that," Walker said, "but now we need to clean up the mess."

Jeremy frowned. "What do you mean?"

"DiRocco's got a good point," Walker said, nodding to me. "What the hell are we going to do about your blood at the scene?"

Jeremy's eye widened. "You don't think Bex will take care of it?"

"Bex alters evidence and memories to keep the existence of vampires a secret. If this wasn't a vampire attack—"

Jeremy shook his head. "I don't know what it was."

Walker shrugged. "Then I don't know what she'll do."

My phone vibrated against my side, Maroon 5's *Maps* jamming from inside the inner pocket of my jacket. I glanced out the window at the matte, black night sky. The moon was still bright and high, but the stars were dull, nearly invisible in the dim early morning. Dominic's threat to visit if I didn't call before sunrise was like the burning jolt of a cattle prod. I jumped to my feet and regretted the instant electric pain that tore through my hip.

Walker, Ronnie, and Jeremy stared at me.

"I'm sorry. I've got to answer this."

Walker opened his mouth. By the set of his eyebrows, he looked about to argue the interruption.

"Of course," Ronnie said graciously. "Nothing too serious, I hope."

Jeremy squinted at Ronnie like she was an idiot. "What could be more serious than my blood at the scene of a murder investigation?"

"Don't be dramatic," Walker said coolly. "At the moment, it's still an animal attack."

"The FBI doesn't get called in for animal attacks," I murmured.

Walker glared at me. "If we play it right, they'll just consider him a victim."

"FBI?" Jeremy asked. "I *am* just a victim!"

My phone stopped ringing, but the resulting silence only heightened my urgency. "I'll be back in a minute."

I turned on my heel into the hallway and eased down the steps. My hip protested painfully, but I needed privacy for a conversation with Dominic. Walls were thin, and I didn't want anyone, especially Walker, knowing that I confided regularly with the enemy.

The only enclosed room on the first floor that I had at my disposal was once again, unfortunately, the bathroom.

* * * *

Adam Levine's clear, prepubescent singing voice pierced the air just as I shut the bathroom door behind me. I locked it this time.

I fished my phone from my pocket, and sure enough, the bat I'd uploaded in lieu of Dominic's picture flashed and vibrated in rhythm with Maroon 5. The time flashed at me, too, and my panic eased slightly. He was calling me fifteen minutes before sunrise. I hadn't missed my scheduled phone meeting again; he was calling me early.

I sighed with relief and slid my thumb over the screen to answer. "I still had another fifteen minutes," I said. Feeling anxious and uncertain always made me angry, so I added, "What happened to your hard-won, everlasting patience?"

My question was met with silence.

"Hello?"

"I thought you'd be interested to discover a curious development in Detective Greta's investigation. Such a conversation would likely exceed five minutes, but perhaps I was mistaken."

I smiled. Dominic's tone was more formal than ever, but I heard an unmistakable hitch and tremor in his voice. He was amused. He knew how much I wanted information on Greta's murder investigation. I'd want to know enough to happily endure an extra ten minutes on the phone with him.

Dominic sighed dramatically. "I can leave you to your business with Walker if you prefer."

"No, that's not necessary," I said hastily. "I appreciate the call."

"Ah," Dominic said, and this time, I could actually hear the light puffs of his laugh. "That's what I thought."

"It figures, though," I muttered, "that there would be a break in the case as soon as I leave the city."

Dominic snorted lightly. Even his snort sounded formal. "I thought you would be happy on behalf of your dear friend's good fortune and the good fortune of the city without thinking of your own personal agenda. I'm sorry you cannot capitalize on her success."

I pursed my lips. "I *am* happy for Greta, but still, I—"

"Nevertheless," Dominic interrupted in a sudden, theatrical tone. "You may rest assured that no such break has occurred in her investigation."

"But you said—"

"I said there was a curious development. You jumped to the inaccurate conclusion that Greta solved something. The police department is no closer to discovering who is responsible for the murders than I am."

I rubbed my eyes. "This could have easily been a five-minute conversation if I was having it with someone else. Anyone else."

"I'm glad to hear you've retained your sense of humor despite being in Walker's constant presence."

I eased myself onto the toilet seat's lid, resigning myself to his lengthy, circular logic.

"Are you all right?" Dominic asked, his tone suddenly serious.

"Yes, of course." I said absently, thinking about the case. "If there wasn't a break in the investigation, what is the 'curious development?'"

My question was once again met with silence. I resisted the urge to say 'hello' again. I knew he was there, but it took more willpower than I'd like to admit to wait him out.

My patience didn't go unrewarded.

"You are not all right. I heard your intake of breath and your heartbeat accelerate a second ago," he said finally. "You released an audible wince."

I made a rude noise in the back of my throat. "Can you please stop using your vampire senses on me and hold a normal conversation?"

"I don't need vampire senses to hear you wince. You are in pain. Did Bex—"

"I'm always in pain," I snapped. "It's just a part of my life now, and it always will be."

Dominic paused a moment. Silences during our conversations were always dead silences because unlike everyone else, Dominic didn't always bother to breathe. Breathing was more for my benefit than his, but more often than not, he preferred to forgo my peace of mind in favor of reality. I'd been sickened by Dominic's true nature, but now, having met Bex and her attempts to humanize her appearance for Walker, I was finding new appreciation for Dominic's honesty.

"You will not always be in pain," Dominic said in a low voice.

"Yes, I will." The phone trembled against my ear, and I realized how hard I was squeezing it. "Even if I get the surgery you mentioned earlier today, it's only a temporary solution. I'd have to endure physical therapy again, and after struggling through recovery, I'd be in the same boat five or ten years from now when the scar tissue and bone spurs build back up. I don't even need to bear weight anymore for the pain to spike. I can barely walk." I felt the hot spring of tears fill my eyes as I voiced the festering, expanding fear, the greatest fear of my life, even since discovering the existence of vampires. "In another few years, I'll need a wheelchair to be mobile."

"No you won't," Dominic said in that same low, steady tone. "Vampires do not bear the pain of their human afflictions. You'll keep the scar, as I have," he said, referencing the jagged, raised scar across his lip and chin, "but your body will transmit pain differently as a vampire. Your nerve endings will no longer register the pain of your arthritis."

"I will never be a vampire, so that doesn't apply to me," I said automatically.

Dominic sighed, audibly taking a breath over the phone. "In your limited understanding, you perceive many disadvantages to the transformation, but there are numerous advantages as well, some as simple as the cure to your physical ailments."

"I've been in pain since you met me. You have connected with my mind on several occasions. You've felt what I feel on a daily basis."

"I can feel what you feel right now if I concentrate hard enough."

I let that comment slide as it was disturbing on multiple levels. "Then why, in all this time, is the topic of my chronic arthritis being discussed? Why now?"

"I only bring it up now because of the hopelessness I hear in your voice," Dominic admitted. "I would not want you to lose hope in your human life and do something drastic to ease the pain before I turn you."

"Listen to the words coming out of my mouth," I gritted from between clenched teeth. He was so bull-headedly infuriating. "You are not turning me. Ever."

"But there are more advantages to the transformation than you could ever imagine, some that I couldn't even describe to you sufficiently enough for you to comprehend. Some things you simply must experience," he said, ignoring my frustration. "I've already divulged too much."

"Why have you divulged too much?" I asked, baffled and curious despite my anger.

"Because I want you to embrace the transformation in loyalty, knowing that you will be a serving, faithful member of my coven. If you embrace the transformation solely for selfish motivations, you could destroy my coven, and I will not allow that to happen, not ever again."

"Ah," I said, "You don't want me to be another Jillian."

"Precisely."

"So don't turn me," I said breezily. "Problem solved."

"Like I said, there is more to being a vampire than you could ever imagine without experiencing it. One day, you'll understand."

"No I won't," I said stubbornly. I wasn't the only one here who was bull-headed. I glanced at the phone's screen to check the time. "We now have five minutes, and you have yet to divulge anything about Greta or her investigation. The last I heard, our unsub was working toward body number fifteen, and Greta's team didn't have one suspect."

"Unsub?"

"Unidentified subject. It's a term the FBI used when they joined her investigation last week." I pinched the bridge of my nose to stave off a coming headache. "Tell me his kills haven't escellated. Tell me we have a real lead on this guy."

"On the contrary," Dominic said, "no one was killed last night."

I waited for more, but my waiting was met with more silence.

"That's it?" I asked, nearly squeaking with disbelief. "That's your big news?!"

"I don't want to jinx it, but considering that sunrise is mere minutes away, I think I can safely say that no one has been killed tonight, either."

I massaged my temples. "Nothing. You got me excited for literally nothing." Then the light dawned. "You think the murders are vampire-related."

"I said no such thing," Dominic said, his tone scolding.

"You didn't have to. You said, 'considering that sunrise is minutes away,' implying that the murderer is bound by the sun, in turn, implying a vampire." I said.

"Nice try, but no," Dominic said coolly, his tone less amused. "If the murderer was a vampire, I would know."

"Not to pick at fresh scabs, but Jillian was a vampire, and you didn't know about her rebellion. I think it's entirely possible that a vampire is committing mass murders and you might not know."

Dominic let out a choking noise. When he finally spoke, he growled. "That wound has not scabbed yet, and since Jillian, I have tightened my control of the coven—"

"You're losing more of your powers every day as the Leveling approaches."

"—and you would appreciate that tenuous control if you had ever seen me in command of my full powers. Not all of my vampires want to usurp my rule. In fact, most want me to survive the Leveling."

"But the few who don't might be committing mass murder."

He growled louder. "You are missing the point of my news entirely."

"Fine," I conceded. "What is your point?"

"My point," he snapped. "Is that the murderer has killed one person every night for the last two weeks."

"I'm still waiting on your point."

"One person every night. It's a pattern. Your FBI refers to it as an M.O. Why now, all of a sudden and for no apparent reason, has he not struck two nights in a row? Why would his M.O. change?"

I sighed. "A serial killer satisfies his or her urges through killing. There's usually a cooling period until the urges return, and then he kills again. Our guy's cooling period is relatively short, and he kills the next night." I frowned. "If anything, his cooling period would diminish over time, not lengthen. He should be killing more people per night, not less, and he certainly wouldn't stop entirely."

"Well, Greta's serial killer has stopped entirely for two nights in a row, and neither Greta nor the FBI seem to know why."

"Wonderful." I sighed. "At least you're right about one thing."

Dominic snorted. "I'm right about everything."

"I'm not missing out on breaking news. I can only hope when the FBI arrive, they'll be more helpful here than they've been in the city."

Dominic didn't speak for a long moment. "Why would the FBI follow you from the city to Erin, New York?"

"Because instead of bringing the weather with me, I brought the crime. We have two murder scenes and three victims in the span of two days, and the Sheriff here didn't wait for a third scene before calling in the feds."

"In the span of two days or two nights?" Dominic asked. "The same nights that our murderer didn't strike here?"

I opened my mouth and closed it, shocked into silence. "It can't be the same murderer," I whispered.

"Little Erin, New York experienced the two murders that we were supposed to experience here in the city. It's entirely possible."

"I was just joking about the crime following me." My heart pounded through my sternum, its beat frantic. "Why would he come here to Erin, of all places?"

"What do you know about the case?" Dominic asked. Of all my interaction with him, I'd never heard his voice sound so calm and yet so utterly serious.

"Not much, actually. Greta was very tight-lipped about it. But—" I hesitated. One lead linked the murders here in Erin, and now that I thought about it, if the murderer had indeed followed me, it may have been the very reason why Greta was so tight-lipped.

"But…" Dominic encouraged.

When I first met Dominic, I thought he was a sociopath capable of murders—degrading, unimaginable murders like the cases we were investigating—and I wouldn't have thought twice about blaming him for them. I thought he was a monster with no regard for other people's pain, suffering, life, or loss. Now, I knew Dominic cared about many things, myself included. He was still a monster and manipulative, cold, calculating and for a man to be powerful—physically, mentally, in every way possible for a man to be powerful—but I also knew that Dominic was not responsible for these murders. He was certainly capable of them, there was no doubt, but leaving kills out for public display and eating their hearts wouldn't have served his purposes or brought him closer to achieving any of his goals.

"But…" I said, slowly. Knowing he wasn't responsible for the murders, I knew I could trust him, but confiding in him would break my confidence with Walker. I sighed. "Walker wasn't as tight-lipped about the case here."

"Of course he wasn't," Dominic said, and a tinge of jealousy crept into his tone.

"He could have easily kept the information to himself," I said defensively. "The police here in Erin aren't as forthcoming as Greta and Harroway."

"I wouldn't expect them to be. You've never saved their lives like you have Greta and Harroway. They don't owe you any favors."

"Greta and Harroway don't owe me anything."

"But I have no doubt—" Dominic continued as if I hadn't interrupted, "—that Walker will share all of his information with you, whether he owes you anything or not."

"Which is good of him, considering we need to know all the information we can get," I argued.

"Yes, it is good of him. I never said otherwise, however—"

"Your tone said otherwise."

"*However*," Dominic pressed, "I wouldn't get too paranoid about the case until we have proof that the crime literally followed you. All we have thus far is speculation, and it's a bit far-fetched."

"Vampires exist," I said grouchily. "Nothing is far-fetched."

Dominic sighed. "What information did our Ian Walker confide in you?"

I sighed, equally frustrated. "The hearts are missing."

Silence.

"Hello!" I snapped. "I can't infer what you're thinking by your expression because I can't see you. When you're on the phone with someone, you actually have to speak to them to carry a conversation!"

"How exactly are the hearts missing?"

I blinked. "In how many ways can a heart be missing?"

"In shredded, bitten pieces. In pieces, but whole. Entirely, but nearby. Entirely missing. From under the sternum. Through the ribs. From over—"

"I get your point," I said hastily, before he could finish his recitation. "Entirely missing. The first victim was so torn apart, I doubt the medical examiner could determine the means of removal. I'm not sure about the other two victims, but from what I've gathered, their bodies were found in the same state as the first victim. In pieces."

"I thought they were found in the State of New York."

I opened my mouth and after a moment of stunned silence, I closed it, resigning myself to not having a response.

"Too soon?" he asked.

"A few weeks ago, you never would have made that joke," I said quietly.

I could hear Dominic's breathing in the silence this time. "A few weeks ago," he said softly, "I didn't know you."

The line went dead.

Chapter 5

When I was in high school, my parents had strict rules against piercings and tattoos, so in rebellion, I had my belly button pierced on my fifteenth birthday. Mandy Hopkins and I were in newspaper club together, and her brother, Morgan, was practicing to become a tattoo artist. He had gnarly-looking tattoos of random animals, skulls, and bands intermixed with blobs of indeterminate shape and color covering his entire body—his first attempts at artistry. There was definitely a learning curve to tattooing.

Morgan pierced me in their parents' guest bedroom. He had me lay on a padded table that I suspected his mother used for massage therapy, he wore surgical gloves, and he sterilized the needle and ring. He was quietly professional and well-mannered, and his shyness, combined with the loudness of his tattoos, drew me to him. I remember being both embarrassed and excited to reveal my stomach for the piercing, but as his little sister's friend and a customer, he was very efficient. He pierced my belly, charged me five dollars, and reminded me that I was still too young to legally consent to the piercing. He didn't know it because he didn't know me, but he didn't have to worry. Even as just a member of high school newspaper club, I knew to protect my sources.

Morgan was one of the piercers at I.P.P. (Inked Pierced & Proud) by the time Nathan wanted a nose ring. He was fourteen at the time, and frankly, I was surprised that he hadn't come to me earlier. I took Nathan to see Morgan, and being eighteen, I pretended to be Nathan's legal guardian. Morgan knew I was lying, but he also knew that I could keep a secret. He pierced Nathan's nose, charged him fifty dollars, and I complimented Morgan on how well his career was progressing.

He smiled, and by the way his eyes lingered, I suspected that he didn't see me as his little sister's friend anymore. But I was leaving for Berkeley in the fall. I wasn't interested in keeping permanent ties in New York City because once I left, I wasn't ever coming back.

I returned his smile anyway.

When our parents saw Nathan's face, his nose ring like a glittering F.U. on display, they threw a fit. Nathan promptly threw me under the bus, asking them to explain the difference between his nose ring and my belly ring when he knew damn well they hadn't known about my belly ring. He accused them of being unfair and sexist and closed-minded, but in the end, when they demanded he tell them who had pierced him, a minor without parental consent, his mouth was a steel trap. He'd known when to keep a secret when it mattered.

Later that week, when he'd finally groveled enough for me to speak to him again, I thanked him for not ratting on Morgan like he'd ratted on me. I'd never forget his response. He shook his head and said, "I didn't rat on you. I threw them a bone." He gave me a look. "You're welcome."

That was a skill Dominic had also mastered, but even after twelve years, I was still learning—how to give a little to throw someone off the scent of something more important. To me, everything seemed important and everyone needed protecting. Although I could appreciate the benefits of prioritizing, lately, my biggest priority was just surviving.

* * * *

The house was quiet as I left, making the creaks and yawning cracks of the floorboards under my hiking boots seem deafening in the silence. All the other good little night bloods were asleep in their beds, but I couldn't sleep. Despite having been thoroughly mentally and physically drained, memories of Nathan kept me awake. After three hours of tossing and turning on the twin bed in my guest room, I'd finally given up on the pretense of sleep and decided to explore the area. If I couldn't do what I wanted, which was rest, I may as well do what I'm good at: snooping into business best left alone.

I'd decided to find Ronnie's abandoned childhood home.

According to Ronnie, the search wouldn't be difficult: due south through the woods. From habit, I'd packed my silver spray along with my recorder and phone. We still had a few hours until sunset, but I'd never regretted being over prepared. Thanks to the balmy May weather, I forwent my jeans in favor of fitted cargo shorts and the hiking boots Walker had insisted I pack for the trip. I owned multiple pairs of flats, boots, heels, sandals, sneakers, and slides, but little did he know, his request had actually required me to buy hiking boots.

Navigating the woods was far easier than I expected, and not because Ronnie's house was due south. It wasn't. To give Ronnie a little credit, the house was in a southerly direction, and I probably wouldn't have missed it following her instructions. The house was unmistakable, even hidden in the thick of the woods, because the path between it and Walker's house wasn't as overgrown as Ronnie had claimed. I followed the winding trail for a quarter mile and it led me right to the house.

The roof crested behind the rise as I hiked. Once I reached the top and could see the house in its entirety, I took a moment to catch my wind and enjoy the view. The structures of the house that had survived the fire were lovely, from the wide, wrap-around porch to the gabled roof dormers. Ronnie's house was smaller than Walker's, but what it lacked in square footage it made up in charm; she had lived in a veritable gingerbread cottage. The stone chimney was still standing, and even after all this time and weed overgrowth, the matching stone landscaping for flowerbeds and garden walkways were intact. One walkway in particular led to a tree swing. Woodchips were laid under the swing, and I imaged Ronnie as a little girl, her parents pushing her on the swing, her legs pumping strong and high. I felt my throat tighten from my own loss.

Like Two-Face, with his handsome left profile and grotesque right, the quaint beauty of the house was tainted by the devastation of the fire. The roof had collapsed into the front porch awning, so the awning lay smashed under its weight. The half-exposed second floor siding and walls were nothing but charred skeleton beams on one side. On the other, they'd collapsed, reduced to rubble.

I didn't visit my parents' apartment after the fire. Everything during that time had been a whirlwind of grief and preparation for the viewing and funeral, and after those formalities, going through the motions of normal life—returning to work when I wanted to curl inside myself, eating when I felt nauseated, and speaking when I wanted to alternately scream and cry and punch someone—consumed my energy. Their apartment had been repaired over time, and another couple lived there now. The light had been off the few times I'd passed their building, but a new name was labeled on the outside intercom. With the rubble cleared and new tenants occupying the space, the only remnants of my parents were memories, pictures, and a few pieces of jewelry. The firemen had recovered Mom's crucifix and Dad's cufflinks, but other than those few items, everything had been lost.

The thought of those damn cufflinks threatened to overwhelm my composure. I felt my throat contract around the burn of tears.

No one had cleared the rubble here for Ronnie and no new tenants were likely to take root anytime soon. I wondered which was worse: watching as new life filled my parents' apartment even as my heart remained a hollow shell or living with the physical reminder of her parents' deaths for a lifetime.

Taking deep breaths to regain my composure, I continued toward Ronnie's house, forging onward, as usual, despite the pains in my hip and in my heart.

I shuffled down the rise toward the house carefully, avoiding the prickly vines and thick undergrowth with high, methodical steps. My joints ached. Tripping down the rise would hurt my hip much worse, so I clenched my teeth and bore the pain until I reached the embankment at the bottom.

Hesitant to actually enter the house in its state of disrepair, I circled around it. I'd walked over the cobbled driveway to the collapsed roof when I noticed something rusty smeared along the base of the awning. I stepped over some of the rubble for a closer look and froze. The rusty smear was blood. That particular smear was old, browned, and crusty, but I could also smell the metallic sweetness of fresh blood nearby, and inexplicably, the smell made me irrationally and undeniably thirsty.

When had I gained the ability to smell blood? I thought, followed by an even more disturbing question. *Why did I want to drink it?*

I searched for the source of the smell and sure enough, fresh blood was splashed along the base of the house near the garage. Turning away from the sight, I eyed the house speculatively. It had withstood the elements for over ten years; it would hold for another ten minutes. A combination of curiosity and nostalgic kinship with the burned house finally got the better of common sense, and I decided to peek inside.

I had to climb over fallen planks, step on crushed rubble, and cross the line of fresh blood to enter the house, and it took more willpower than I'd like to admit to pass the blood without stopping. I didn't want to analyze why I wanted it or what I wanted to do with it. I could feel the answer to that second question scrape the back of my dry throat, so I walked on, fastidiously ignoring the blood as I stepped into what had once been a very homey living room. Doilies, now soot-stained and charred, decorated some of the wood end tables. Picture frames that had once propped on those doilies or had hung from the walls were smashed on the ground, their glass like the glitter of snowflakes across the floor. They crackled and popped under my boots as I stepped.

The smell of blood dissipated as I reached the middle of the room, but as I crossed to the other side of the house, the air sweetened again. My stomach cramped. Goose bumps broke out over my arms, and I felt the craving claw from inside my skin. Saliva swelled in my mouth. I swallowed, and an image of myself licking the blood from the ground flooded my mind.

I jerked back, disgusted and sickened by my own thoughts, and tripped over the protruding leg of a broken coffee table. I hit the floor on my knees but caught myself on a couch cushion before my hands hit the ground, too. A billowing cloud of soot and dust burst into the air. I waved my hand, trying and failing to clear the soot from my face. Even holding my breath, the dust floated up my nose and down my throat. I coughed, and gasping in more soot-dusted air, I coughed harder. I leveraged myself slowly, painfully, to my feet, alternately coughing and waving my hand against the dust.

I limped to the other side of the room and crossed back over the rubble for some fresh air. My first lungful, free of dust and soot, was laced with a tempting, salty sweetness. Identical to the side I'd entered, blood was splashed across the house's concrete foundation on this side as well. I hunkered down—the movement more cumbersome now that I'd further stressed my hip, and pressed my fingers into the dirt. The ground was sticky and moist, and when I turned my fingers over, my prints were stamped red with blood.

I swallowed, staring at my bloodstained fingers for a long, excruciating moment. My hand began to shake as I resisted.

"They were arguing the night of the fire."

I whirled around at that deep twang, my heart stuttering and my arm elbow-deep in my shoulder bag, clutching the silver spray.

"Walker," I gasped. I'd recognized his voice, but the suddenness of his arrival was still a shock. My face flushed, like he'd caught my hand in the cookie jar. I quickly wiped the blood off my fingers on some rubble as I stood, but when I faced him, Walker wasn't looking at me. He was looking at the house.

"Ronnie remembers it like a slumber party with movies and popcorn. Maybe someone had given her food as a distraction, but that's not how I remember that night at all."

I crossed my arms against a sudden chill. "How do you remember it?"

"Mr. and Mrs. Carmichael were terrified. They'd packed bags, loaded the car, and were leaving at first light. My parents were begging them to stay. They'd built their home as a fortress against the vampires, and where

else do you take shelter during a war? You take shelter in your fortress."
Walker shook his head, disgusted. "But the Carmichaels wanted to run.
They offered to take me with them, and my parents—" he paused to clear
his throat, "—my parents hesitated. They considered for a moment the
benefit of letting the Carmichaels take me."

I frowned. "Why did the Carmichaels want to leave? And what would
make your parents consider giving you up to them?"

Walker linked his hands behind his neck, his muscles tense. They
shifted under his shirt as he mulled over my questions, the answers to
which he'd likely been mulling for a lifetime. "I don't know. But they
never had the opportunity to leave, with or without me. As our parents
argued, the fire ignited. By the time they realized what was happening, it
was too late. The house was already engulfed in flames."

"But not for you and Ronnie."

Walker looked up sharply. "Excuse me?"

"It was too late for your parents, but you and Ronnie escaped."

Walker pursed his lips. "Bex saved us."

He'd spoken the words so softly, I wasn't sure I'd heard him
correctly. "Bex?"

He nodded. "Ronnie and I were screaming, trapped by the flames and
coughing. I remember the scorching heat around us, like the house was an
oven and we were being baked alive. The air scorched our lungs, and our
screams turned more and more hoarse until we struggled to breathe. Bex
was suddenly there, out of nowhere, and she pulled us out."

"Did you know who she was back then?"

"I knew *what* she was, if that's what you mean," Walker said bitterly.
"But at the time, despite everything my parents had taught me, she was
my hero. She was the first vampire I'd ever actually met, and she'd saved
my life." Walker shook his head at the memories. When he met my gaze
again, his lips grinned but his eyes were shadows. "I was such an idiot."

"You were thirteen," I chastised softly. "There's a difference."

Walker snorted. "Ronnie really does talk too much."

I nodded. "Don't be too hard on her. It's me after all, and as you know,
I always get my scoop." I winked, trying to lighten the oppressive mood.

Walker laughed. "Nevertheless, I should start tailing her house tours.
God only knows what else she's saying about me."

"Only good things, I assure you. Since she gave me a tour of your
house, it's only fair turnaround that you to give me a tour of hers," I
suggested playfully.

Walker shook his head. "You're incorrigible."

I raised my eyebrows. "Does that mean I get a tour?" Anything to escape the sickly sweet smell of blood. My heart hadn't stopped racing since I'd touched the blood, and I could feel that once familiar, now returning itch crawl beneath my skin in a tide of goose bumps and nausea.

Walker sighed; it sounded pain-filled, but he smiled. "Yes, darlin', you get a tour." He stepped over the rubble, into the house, and spread his arms wide. "This once spacious room was the living room. My family would visit every Saturday to watch Syracuse games." He walked a few steps toward the broken wall. "We grilled out on the stone porch during the summer. Ronnie's dad could make a mean burger."

I smiled. "That stone porch outside is called a patio."

"No interruptions mid-tour," Walker said, shaking his pointer finger at me. "Save your questions for the end."

I zipped my lips with my fingers.

"And this lovely view—" Walker waved his hand through the air, Vanna White style, indicating the collapsed banister and rubble, which allowed for an unhampered view of the woods. "—was a short hallway to the upstairs." He pointed upstairs, and we both looked up through empty air to the half-collapsed roof. "But I can't show you that part of the house today, ma'am, as it's currently under renovations."

I tried to laugh but couldn't hide the sadness in my voice despite our mutual attempt to lighten the mood. "It's lovely."

"Sorry, I'm not much of a tour guide." He grinned down at me, his smile tinged with the same sadness in my voice, but with the sun glowing like a halo behind the sparking highlights in his curls and his velvety brown eyes crinkling at the corners, I couldn't help but feel the warmth of his presence blanket over me.

I smiled back. "I must confess, my request for a tour had an ulterior motive."

Walker gasped in mock horror. "You don't say."

"Come on, *darlin',* I have something to show *you.*" I grabbed him by the hand and showed him the smeared blood on either side of the house, both old and fresh. "What do you make of that?"

Walker narrowed his eyes. "It doesn't look like accidental blood spatter. Someone or something put that there deliberately, I'd say."

I nodded. "You're right, it doesn't look accidental, but why would someone smear blood around the perimeter of the house?"

"We'll have to take samples to the lab," Walker said, shaking his head.

"Ronnie told me that this house was abandoned. That she hasn't returned here in years."

"She hasn't."

"Well, someone has, and if not Ronnie, then who?"

Walker sighed. "That's something I intend to find out."

A cloud shifted position in the sky, and the full light of the sun brightened the house. With the broken rafters and half-collapsed ceiling, its rays uninhibitedly poured over the living room, through what was once a doorway, onto the patio, and onto its concrete foundation. The blood around the perimeter of the living room was fresh and pungent, and as it warmed from the sun's spotlight, it perfumed the entire house with its metallic sweetness. The sharp contrast of the bright red smear against the rough, gray concrete foundation was brilliant, ripe, and succulent.

A thready laugh tugged at my mind, and I could feel Jillian surface. She was still suffering an unending, excruciating death, but underneath her pain, I could sense a small kernel of sadistic pleasure.

You want to drink that blood, she thought, still laughing at me despite her pain.

My heart slingshot into overdrive. *I do not want to drink that blood,* I told myself firmly, even as my throat became parched. The feeling was more than want. I desired the blood. The sensory image of those tacky, salty-sweet smears against my tongue made my breath hitch.

I'd been losing pieces of myself and finding new ones recently, pieces of strength and fortitude and determination that I'd always thought I'd had, but when tested against the immediate danger of nearly dying and the lasting danger of my acquaintance with Dominic, those pieces of myself had a whole new meaning. I could add unnatural hunger and desire to that list now, too.

"Is something wrong?"

I looked up, and Walker was a hairsbreadth away from my face. My heart pounding and my breath heaving, I couldn't think past the crawling need beneath my skin. The warmth of Walker's velvet brown eyes, the brilliance of his springy blond curls, and the plump ripeness of his lower lip weren't enough to pull me back from the deep. He wasn't nearly enough, but he was all I had.

"You're bleeding."

I looked down at myself to where his gaze had dropped, and he was right. Both my knees were cut, trickling blood down my legs and soaking into my socks. A few drops had spattered onto the floor. I glanced passed him, following their telltale path. The glass scattered next to the coffee table sported two little pools of blood, one from each knee.

"I tripped and fell on my knees," I said lamely. "The glass must have cut me."

Walker turned to follow my gaze, and when he turned back, his eyes had sharpened. "You should be more careful."

I cleared my throat, but my voice still rasped like scraping gravel. "I don't suppose you have a first aid kit stashed here."

"I haven't visited this house in years, let alone stored supplies," he said, shaking his head. "I'm becoming your own personal paramedic, DiRocco, always bandaging you up. Let's get back to my house where we can dress that wound properly. God only knows what bacteria is growing on that glass after all these years."

"Thanks for that lovely image," I grumbled. "I thought paramedics were supposed to be reassuring."

"You suffer an injury worse than scraped knees, I'll be reassuring."

"What could be worse than scraped knees?"

"Hmm," Walker murmured, and I recognized the heat in his eyes as he scanned me head to toe.

"Nothing comes to mind?"

Walker grazed his fingers along the waistband of my shorts. "A stomach injury would be worse."

My breath caught. Like the burst of a backdraft, I hadn't expected the mood to ignite between us, but my craving for blood morphed into a different craving as Walker's fingers trailed along my hip to my back.

He slipped his other hand under my hair to cup the back of my neck. "Your neck, maybe."

I opened my mouth, but Walker's hand slid from my neck to cup the side of my cheek. He rubbed his thumb along my bottom lip.

"Your lips, definitely."

Walker leaned closer, his lips nearly touching mine.

"Walker?" I whispered.

"This is the first time we've had a moment alone."

That wasn't entirely true. We'd been alone in the bathroom while he applied the icy-hot patch, and we'd been alone in his truck on our way home from both crime scenes, but admittedly, this was the first time we were alone since I'd arrived that we weren't arguing.

"And I've been thinking about this moment since our last kiss on the desk in your office."

His fingers were rubbing maddening circles at the small of my back. I opened my mouth.

"You can tell me that you're here to write your story on crime rates, but I'll be damned if you're not here for this, too," Walker interrupted before I could speak. "Tell me you're here for me. Let me forget about Bex and the fire and the night bloods under my care for just a moment, and let me be here in this moment with only you."

The scent of warmed blood still permeated the house. I could still hear Jillian's manic laughter, and I could still feel that deep ache in the pit of my stomach, half nausea and half anticipation. I wanted the blood, but I was familiar with resisting addiction. It wasn't a matter of what I wanted. I could want to swallow handfuls of Percs all day, and I could want to drop to my knees and lap the blood from the concrete with my tongue, but I chose to resist.

I closed my eyes and let Walker kiss me because addiction was a matter of choice.

His lips pressed against mine. This close to his skin, I could smell the spice of his aftershave and the mint of his breath, and I breathed in the scent of Walker as long and deep as I could to expel every other scent, every other desire except for this man in this moment. I rocked my mouth against his, our tongues dipping and shifting against the other, moving in unison yet daring for more with the same breath. Walker groaned. His grip on my neck tightened. His other hand moved under my shirt, so the rough calluses of his palm scrapped down my spine as he pulled me into the warmth and security of his arms.

Dominic was so incomprehensively strong that the few times he'd touched me—especially during the day, when he touched my delicate, very breakable skin with his gargoyle-like claws—he was exceedingly careful with my body. His advances, although fervent, were reserved. Walker had no such reservations. My lips felt raw as his teeth ground against mine. My back felt scraped from the strength of his fingers pulling me closer, and what had begun as a whisper of heat from his gentle caress at my lips exploded into a battle over each other's body parts.

I scraped my fingernails down his back. He cupped my ass through my shorts. I pressed my palms along the ridges of his sculpted abs. He dug his fingers beneath the underwire of my bra, and suddenly, I felt suffocated. The minty taste of his tongue mingled with the wet metallic scent of blood, and his arms, so strong around me, were a cage. He rolled my nipple between his thumb and forefinger, and I bit his lip.

He jerked back, fingertips touching his bottom lip. When he pulled his hand away, I saw that I'd drawn blood.

I winced. "Sorry. I just felt—" *trapped,* I thought. His deep, velvet eyes, so patient and understanding, made me want to scream. "I guess I just got carried away."

"That's quite all right, darlin'. You're not the only one who got a little carried away. We're in Ronnie's old house, and I hadn't meant to, well, rather, I hadn't expected us to—" He took a deep, unsteady breath.

"You hadn't expected the fireworks?" I asked helpfully.

He smiled. "Exactly. Sun will be setting soon, and this place is too full of memories to make new ones here. It's just—" His voice trailed off, but I couldn't help him find the words this time. Finally, he muttered, "It's been a long time."

I laughed. "It's only been three weeks."

"That's long enough, but I wasn't referring to us kissing."

"Oh," I said, at a loss for words.

"Come on, let's get back to my house and clean your knees. I suppose your legs are important body parts, too." He winked.

"Sure, you say that *now* that I've cut you off from the other parts." I pushed his shoulder, teasing, but amid the torrent of claustrophobic panic and the addict-like itch beneath my skin, I was unaccountably disappointed.

I followed his lead from the house. Once outside and walking into the woods, away from the blood, I breathed in the fresh afternoon air. Some of the itching need dissipated as the smell of blood faded incrementally into the smells of moist moss and pine, and eventually, the sickly sweet smell along with the itching need faded entirely. We walked single file along the path toward his house in silence, only the crunch of twigs and stones beneath our boots.

Even wearing a t-shirt, Walker's back muscles bunched and coiled noticeably through the fabric. My lips still burned, thinking of how we'd collided—his hand at my back, pressing me closer; his minty breath, breathing into me; the heat of his skin on my skin, sparking my heat.

Even with the taste of Walker's desire still seared on my tongue and the goose bumps from his touch still tingling over my body, we were walking back to the house and away from privacy because of sunset. Ronnie was right; once you know the truth about the creatures who hunt in the night, everything else in life—no matter how tempting—becomes nothing but background.

* * * *

The view from my window in the guest bedroom was due west and showcased the sun's descent. I hadn't witnessed a sunset like that in years.

The sky was stained orange and purple and the wispy edges of each cloud glowed blood-red, like backlit fire. I had a half hour until full dark, but the day was so much darker at this time than I was accustomed to in the city. As the sun set here, a blanket of complete, utter blackness threatened, and within the half hour, when the sun fully dipped below the horizon, I wouldn't be able to see five feet outside my bedroom window. As it was, with the sun still lingering above the tree line, the woods surrounding the house was shrouded in opaque shadows. Bex could be in those shadows now, watching me prepare for our dinner. She would be able to see me in the light of my room, but I wouldn't be able to see her.

In preparation for dinner with Bex, I wore Dominic's necklace, snapped matching silver earrings through my ears, and slipped a silver ring on each finger. The rings looked excessive, but we were dining with vampires tonight; no amount of preparation was excessive if it prevented me from becoming the meal.

Finally, I changed into dark skinny jeans, a black tank, and a black leather jacket. I'd learned my lesson with dresses and skirts and fabrics that could be easily ripped, clawed, and bitten through. Dresses and skirts left my femoral artery exposed, and short sleeves gave easy access to my brachial artery. The leather jacket had a high collar, which was admittedly pretty badass, but more importantly, it blocked a direct attack to my carotid. When the vampires decided to bite—whether in violence, warning, or temptation, they always do—it took longer for their fangs to tear through jeans and leather, and that extra moment was my only chance to bite back.

I refreshed my eyeliner, laced up my hiking boots, and packed every pocket for war. I had backup weapons for my backups, and tonight, I had the uneasy feeling I'd need them all.

Dressed and armed for dinner, I needed to do one last thing in preparation for tonight. Dominic wasn't going to like it, but without a viable alternative, I was going to do it anyway.

The sky still had about fifteen minutes of light remaining. Dominic wouldn't answer his phone until full night had fallen, and knowing that, I was going to call him early. Dinner with Bex was at sundown, and I still needed to convince Walker to join me. Dominic either got his call now or never, and I wasn't crazy enough to choose never.

I pressed "Call" under his name in my contacts, and as I suspected, his phone shot directly to voicemail. At the beep I said, "Dominic. It's Cassidy. My day went well. I hope your day rest went well, too." I winced at my own awkwardness and rubbed my forehead. "I've got dinner tonight with Bex, so she'll know what a willing and loyal night blood you've turned me into. Wish me luck!" I continued, but I couldn't help the sarcasm from creeping into my tone. I cleared my throat. "I'm looking forward to hearing the progress you're making on your end of our bargain." I bit my lip, thinking about Nathan. I had to focus. "If you find him, or find news about him, text me. I'll be busy with Bex, but I'll still want to know."

I rolled my eyes at myself; as if Dominic could text. The man had needed instructions on dialing a number. "Texting is when you type a short message to me. You press the icon with the talk bubble. It's a different icon than the "Call" button. After you type your message and click send, I'll get a notification on my phone. It's easier than calling for quick communication, and Bex won't realize you're in touch with me. Unless she sees my phone light up or can sense electronic waves. Either way, it's more subtle than calling." I pounded my palm into my forehead. *Stop talking. Stop talking.* "I'll call you in the morning before sunrise. Bye."

I pressed "End" and shook my head at my phone. I was going to pay for that. I stuffed my phone in my pocket and decided to worry about Dominic at sunrise. By that time, I'd be back in the guest bedroom, safe and sound, and with any luck, Dominic would have news concerning Nathan. To get to that point, however, I needed to survive dinner with Bex.

I walked downstairs, not unaware that with my leather and fully loaded, I looked a little reminiscent of Trinity from *The Matrix*. Most of the house's occupants were downstairs when I walked into the kitchen. Ronnie was mixing a bowl of batter. Jeremy was sitting on one of the barstools at the breakfast counter next to Logan's oldest son, Keagan, presumably waiting for whatever Ronnie was mixing. Theresa, Logan, and his younger sons, Colin, William, and Douglas, sat around the wooden kitchen table. Walker stood next to Logan, and the two of them were lecturing the boys, but only Colin was really listening. The other two had that glazed look of boys who'd heard the speech before and hadn't heard a word of it the first time, either.

My boots pounded into the floor with an audible clunk as I stepped from carpet to hardwood, and everyone looked up. I waved hello as I walked in, but they kept staring. Keagan's lips quirked into a wide smile. Logan blinked at me several times. Walker instantly glowered, and Ronnie, if I wasn't mistaken by the whisk in her hand hovering above her pancake batter, Ronnie started shaking.

"Good evening," I said to the room in general. I leaned over Jeremy at the breakfast counter. "Did I smear my eyeliner or something?"

He raised his eyebrows. "Or something."

"Right." I faced Walker. "Can I talk to you for a second?"

"In a minute. I'm in the middle of—"

Logan shook his head. "No, go ahead. I've got it here," he said to Walker, but he never took his eyes off me. I'd have been offended, but his eyes were anything but salacious. In fact, he looked a little angry.

"Thank you, Logan," I said, feeling self-conscious. "It really is urgent."

The muscle in Walker's jaw ticked. I knew he wasn't happy with the interruption, but I only had another ten minutes before sunset.

Walker led me to the living room, and we sat adjacent to each other on the couch.

I leaned in and whispered, "What's with everybody?"

Walker glanced around the room where everyone was now surreptitiously whispering and glancing at us, obviously eavesdropping.

He met my eyes. "You tell me, Lara Croft."

I blinked. "Excuse me?"

"You come down here, eyes lined with fresh war paint, skintight armor, and brass knuckles ready to swing, and wonder why everyone is staring." Walker shook his head.

I looked down at the rings on my fingers. "They're silver, not brass. You think I overdid my eyeliner?"

"You know what I'm saying. This house is a refuge. Night bloods come here to feel safe, but you're compromising that, dressed for battle. What's going on?"

"What's going on?" I repeated, my temper spiking. I tipped my voice low since we were still center stage, squelching the urge to scream. "Maybe it slipped your mind, but tonight is my dinner date with Bex."

"No, tonight is the night that you're skipping your dinner date with Bex," Walker said.

"No, I'm not, and neither are you. She's expecting us."

"No, she's not," he said, wagging his finger at me. "I remember having this conversation with Bex, and I distinctly remember refusing her invitation. I also remember having this conversation with you, and I distinctly remember my reply. We cannot trust Bex. Even if she only invited the two of us, I'd have said no. But we're not the only night bloods that she wants at her dinner table tonight." Walker dipped his voice low. It broke slightly as he referred to Ronnie. "And I'm not putting her at risk."

I glanced at Ronnie where she spooned the bowl of pancake batter onto the griddle, the only person in the kitchen not staring at us. She deliberately blocked out the drama unfolding around her, about her, to focus solely on her pancakes. By the smell of them, they were banana nut. My stomach growled.

"I know," I whispered, ignoring my stomach. Some things, although admittedly not many, were more important than pancakes. "But I'm only asking for *you* to come with me."

"You don't think Bex will punish us for not bringing her? You don't think she'll punish her for not coming?" Walker snorted. "It's better if we don't come at all."

"You said so yourself; this house is the safest place for a night blood. She'll be protected from Bex and her punishments here while we're at dinner. We only have to worry about Bex retaliating against *us*."

Walker's jaw tightened in that stubborn flex that was becoming frustratingly familiar. "We're not going," he said, and his voice was definitive.

"But I—"

He placed both hands on my shoulders. "Listen to me. We are not going."

"*You're* not going," I hissed, to hell with being center stage. I shrugged off his hands. "But that doesn't mean that *I'm* not going."

"Oh, yes it does."

"Oh, no it does not," I snapped right back. "You can choose not to come. You can choose to protect Ronnie here at home where she'll be safe while I face Bex alone. Whatever. But I *am* going," I enunciated.

Walker crossed his arms. "You think I can't stop you?"

"Seriously?" I shook my head. "Everyone needs a partner. I need someone at my back. I'm going no matter what, but I'd rather not go alone."

"If you're going no matter what, then why are we even having this conversation?" he asked bitterly. "Just go."

We stared at each other, two bulls trying to bluff the other. Having dinner with Bex in her coven was stupid enough, but having dinner with Bex in her coven alone was not only stupid, it was suicidal. I needed Walker there with me, but more than that, I needed to uphold my end of the bargain with Dominic if I expected Dominic to uphold his. Normally, I wasn't stupid or suicidal, but I'd do anything to get my brother back, including having dinner with Bex, and God help me, I was having dinner with her alone.

"Fine." I stood. "I'll be back before sunrise."

Walker watched me from his perch on the couch as I stormed from the living room, crossed the kitchen, and slammed the front door behind me. I made it off the porch and down the driveway before I even realized that I didn't have transportation to Bex's coven.

I stood in the middle of Walker's driveway in the pitch darkness, looked back at the screen door, and took a deep breath. He wasn't chasing after me. I could stare at that door all night, but it wouldn't change a damn thing. I was dining with Bex alone, assuming I even made it to the coven without being torn to shreds by a wild animal, or worse, by the serial killer collecting hearts.

Sunset was minutes away, and whatever had attacked Lydia, Patricia, and John—vampire or otherwise—was still out there. The winding country road stretched for miles, and taxis didn't exist this far from civilization. I rolled my eyes at the inconvenience of country living and started walking. If Bex was anything like Dominic, she'd come find me when I didn't arrive in time for dinner, and with any luck, she'd find me before I became the victim at our next crime scene.

I only wished I had Walker—hell, I wished I had anyone—at my back when she did.

* * * *

Ten minutes later, the dim dusk evening doused into full darkness. Without streetlights, porch lights, or light of any sort, I stumbled along the road, tripping over roots when I strayed too far from the curb. The sky, with its stars and half moon, was more illuminated than the unlit road. The sight of such a swirling mass of starlight was stunning. Strangely, it reminded me of the city and a moment I'd experienced with Dominic only a short three weeks ago. After everything I'd experienced and learned since then—everything I'd learned about life and myself—three weeks felt like a lifetime.

In that moment with Dominic, I'd thought I was dying. I'd been attacked by Kaden and the other rebels, and Dominic had saved me. He'd torn the vampires from my body, literally, as they drank from me and flown me to a rooftop, away from danger. I'd laid in his arms, too weak and scared to do more than stare at the impossibility of having been *flown* anywhere, let alone a rooftop. As I'd stared out at the expanse of the city lights below, I couldn't help but feel the awe of insignificance in the presence of its enormity.

I felt the same awe now as I gazed at the mass of stars overhead, and strangely enough, I felt the same fear. Instead of being afraid of Dominic, I feared the unknown. The buzz of cicadas filled the silence. The hiss and chirps and rustles of God only knew what echoed from the woods, and the hard shuffle of my boots kicking gravel only sounded louder as I quickened my pace.

I was on the verge of admitting idiocy and making an about-face when a single headlight beamed from behind. The winding road was suddenly in full spotlight, the woods on either side casting lined shadows across the road from overlaying branches, and the deep roar of an engine came upon me. Maybe it was half habit from hailing taxis, and half desperation, but I put up my arm for a ride.

As the roar slowed to a rumbling purr, I realized two things: one, my hail had worked and the vehicle was stopping, and two, the vehicle was a motorcycle. My heart dropped. The rider coasted next to me, and I shielded my eyes against the brightness of its beams.

"When you need a pick-up in the country, you don't hail a ride like you would a cab, darlin'. You stick your thumb out. It's called hitchhiking."

Even after my eyes adjusted, I couldn't discern the man's features through the shield of his helmet, but I didn't need to see him to know that voice or recognize the chrome and matte black Harley-Davidson beneath him. Walker had invited me for a ride once before, but in the city, where cabs are readily available, I'd been able to politely decline without causing a fuss. I looked out into the darkness of the woods, then back at the motorcycle warily. A cab wasn't going to zoom around that bend to save me from the darkness. All I had was Walker and his damn Harley-Davidson. I wondered if I would have been better off on my own.

"What happened to your truck?" I asked.

Walker took off his helmet and rested it on his knee. "Hello to you, too."

I crossed my arms and raised my eyebrows.

"Not impressed?"

"Not particularly. Your truck offers more protection should dinner with Bex—" I considered my words. "—stray off menu."

Walker laughed. "Should dinner with Bex stray off menu, we'll need speed and maneuverability." He patted the seat behind him. "She's exactly what we need. Trust me."

"We?" I asked. My heart bounced a little flip flop in my chest at the thought. "Finally come to your senses? Are you joining me for dinner with Bex?"

Walker sighed. "I never lost my senses, but I'm wondering about yours, out here in the woods after sunset with a murderer on the loose." He shook his head. "No sense there, far as I can see."

"I doubt you can see very far at all in this darkness."

"I've said it before, and I'll say it again," Walker said, laughing. "Don't quit your day job."

I shrugged. "Joking aside, I'm not going back to your house. I'm—"

Walker waved my words away with his hand. "You're going to meet Bex for dinner. I know. And apparently, I'm going with you."

"Apparently?"

"After you left, it got pretty hostile at the house. I've never considered the night bloods a democracy—it's my house, after all—but there's no arguing with a unanimous vote. You need backup."

"I know I do. Although, I'd prefer a willing partner, not one that needed votes."

"I'm willing, darlin'. If I was only endangering myself, you know that I'd be your backup anywhere."

I frowned. "But you said the vote was unanimous."

He nodded. "It was."

I raised my eyebrows. "Even from Ronnie?"

"Especially Ronnie," Walker admitted. "She called me a hypocrite."

I frowned. "Why would she say that?"

"She's my partner, but when my feelings changed toward Bex, when I finally saw her for the monster she really is, Ronnie wouldn't be my backup. She abandoned me when I needed her most, and I was forced to confront Bex alone."

I reached out and touched his shoulder. I couldn't not touch him when he looked like that, like the memories were splitting him in two. "I'm sorry."

He shook his head. "It's all right. I understand now that she was afraid, and still is, actually, and what I was asking of her was beyond what she was capable of giving. But like you said, everyone needs a partner. Everyone needs someone at their back, but when I needed Ronnie most, she wasn't there for me. No one was. I had to face Bex alone, and I'll be damned, *apparently*, if I do the same to you."

I laughed at his tone. "Despite the fact that you were forced here by Ronnie's guilt trip, I appreciate the backup."

"Good." He reached behind him and produced something from a zippered pouch. "Hop on."

I realized after a long second that the object he was extending to me was a helmet. "I don't think so."

"It's a rule. I don't let anyone ride without a helmet."

"That's very responsible of you, but I'm not riding. I have rules, too, and one of them is having the metal body of a car and airbags surrounding me while cruising over thirty miles an hour."

"Don't worry, darlin', we'll cruise well over thirty."

I glared at him. Although he probably couldn't see my expression through the darkness, he could undoubtedly feel the heat of it because he laughed.

"This motorcycle should be the least of your worries. We're in full darkness in the middle of the woods. Besides the murderer and vampires, we've got bear, wolves, and coyotes in these parts. It's a forty-minute drive to Bex's coven. You want to walk there yourself?" He offered me the helmet a second time. "Take it and hop on. I'm not telling you again."

I snatched the helmet out of his hand just as I felt my phone vibrate. More to stall than actual curiosity, I checked my phone before strapping on the helmet but couldn't contain my laughter at the message waiting for me.

Walker raised his eyebrows.

"Trying to boss me around all the way from New York City." I rolled my eyes.

"Carter?"

I nodded, hating to lie, but I knew that he wouldn't receive the truth well if I told him that Dominic had just texted me. I pursed my lips, trying not to smile at his message:

I might be four hundred and seventy seven years old, but I know how to text. Good luck.

"I haven't had the opportunity to help you research crime rates like I promised," Walker admitted sheepishly, and it took a moment before I realized that he was referring to Carter and the article I was supposed to be writing for his paper. "As soon as you got here, we got slammed with homicide after homicide."

I sighed regretfully. "I know, but we'll make time eventually. It's only my second night here. How better to get a grip on crime rates than to experience it firsthand?"

Walker snorted. "We've had enough experience. I'm personally looking forward to the research."

I eyed the helmet in my hands dubiously as Walker spoke. I hadn't known the gravity of agreeing to be a motorcyclist's passenger the last time I'd put on a helmet.

"You don't need to examine the thing. It's in full working order, I assure you."

"Yeah, I'm sure." I smoothed my hand over its hard, fiberglass surface. Adam had been scrupulous about auto maintenance for all his vehicles, but for his motorcycle and my equipment in particular, he had been meticulous. No amount of preparation and precaution, however, can prevent a driver from spilling scalding coffee in his lap and running a red light. That's why they're called accidents.

"Once you put it on, we can get going. The sooner we get to the coven, the sooner we can put this disastrous dinner date behind us."

"We don't know that dinner will be disastrous."

"Anything involving Bex is a disaster waiting to happen."

I nodded, but I wasn't really listening. I was still seeing the round, inset headlights of a Dodge Challenger barreling toward us. My scream was fast and vibrated strangely inside my helmet, but Adam's reflexes were faster. He throttled forward and swerved out of reach. The Challenger narrowly missed our back tire by the tips of my split ends and slammed into the car behind us. I watched it unfold—the shriek of brakes, the stink of burnt rubber, and the grind of metal on metal—and as the passenger, I'd only been able to hang on tight for the ride.

Being a passenger on a motorcycle meant literally entrusting the driver with your life. You could try to say the same for any motor vehicle, but on a motorcycle, there was nothing between your body and 4,000 pounds of metal except luck and reflexes. Adam was an excellent driver. He'd unequivocally saved our lives that day, but I never wanted to be that completely helpless to save myself ever again.

"I'm a great driver, DiRocco," Walker drawled, as if he could hear my thoughts. "I've had vampires flying on my tail and trees to navigate and passengers to protect, but I've never crashed. I've had close calls, not gonna lie, but my wheels have always stayed on the ground."

I breathed a deep, indecisive sigh. "I'm sure you're an excellent driver, but I've had close calls before with excellent drivers. I promised myself, never again."

Walker leaned forward. "You trust me at your back against Bex?"

I nodded. "Of course."

"You trust me to protect you and bring you back from dinner in one piece?"

"I trust that we'll protect each other, and together, we'll do our damnedest to survive."

Walker nodded. "So trust me now. Put on the helmet, hop on the bike, and let's go."

The one had nothing to do with the other, and Walker knew that. Just because I trusted an environmental science expert and animal tracker with a lifetime of night blood experience as my partner against the vampires did not mean I trusted him on that bike. The cicadas continued buzzing and the crickets continued chirping in a pulsing chorus while Walker waited on my move.

In the end it came down to a simple decision despite my indecisiveness. It didn't matter that Walker was an excellent driver nor that I trusted him with my life. It didn't matter that his vendetta to kill vampires was more important to him than saving lives, and the promises I'd made to myself concerning motor vehicle safety didn't matter, either. What mattered was that we were in the middle of the woods, miles from the coven after sunset, and we were late for dinner with a Master vampire.

I strapped on the helmet and swung my leg over the bike.

Walker laughed, but I heard it through the helmet's headset rather than from him. "Just put your arms around my waist and relax. You're gonna love this."

"I doubt that," I said, just to be obstinate. I knew I'd love it: the speed, the adrenaline, leaning into the turns and accelerating into the stretches. The purr of the bike between my legs. Hugging the ridges of Walker's back. There was no doubt I would love it. I'd always loved it, even with Adam, but loving something and recognizing whether or not it was good for you were two completely different things. I consciously chose not to ride on a bike ever again, just like I'd chosen not to ingest Percs ever again, because I chose to live instead. The joys that motorcycles and Percs offered weren't worth the risk to my life.

I wrapped my arms around Walker's waist. He revved the ignition, and my stomach bottomed out as we jetted forward.

Chapter 6

"He's lost his damn mind," I grumbled to myself.

Walker and I were standing outside the entrance to Bex's coven. We'd ridden the back roads of the woods for about twenty minutes. The experience of riding was just as thrilling as I'd remembered, but thanks to my hip, the experience was also quite painful. We'd cut off road onto a dirt path for five minutes before dismounting and walking another fifteen or twenty minutes through thick foliage. My hip couldn't endure such intense physical activity anymore. Sparks of grinding pain shot through my leg, and I fought not to noticeably limp.

And now that we'd finally reached the coven entrance, after riding for twenty minutes and stumbling through the dark for another twenty, Walker started pulling ropes, anchors, and harnesses from his pack.

I stared alternately at the cave's entrance and its vertical drop to the equipment that Walker was knotting and looping and preparing for us, and I knew, without a doubt, that he'd lost his mind.

I grumbled as much beneath my breath, and he looked up. "What was that?"

"You think I'm climbing down there?" My question ended on a squeak, and I pointed down at the cave. "You've lost your mind," I repeated. I stared down into the cave's fathomless depth and shook my head.

"No," He said, and his voice was calm and steady, the way you talk slowly to a child on the verge of a meltdown. "I think you're rappelling down there."

I nodded. "Yep. You've lost your mind."

"It's easy. The ropes and pulleys distribute your weight, so there's essentially no work involved on your end. You just lower yourself down with the ropes and steady yourself against the cave walls with your feet. When the wall expands away from you, just relax and lower yourself to the bottom." He spread his hands as if to encompass all the equipment in front of him and everything he'd just said. "Easy."

"The wall's going to expand? So I'll be dangling hundreds of feet above the vampire coven in midair." I shook my head. "Are you serious?"

He stared at me, not seeing a problem.

"You're going to make me say it, aren't you," I grumbled, annoyed at him for not seeing my limitations but mostly annoyed at myself for having them.

"I don't understand why you're balking. You've faced worse odds against Dominic and Kaden and Jillian, and you faced them head on. I get that it's a deep, dark cave, and that the cave is filled with vampires. It's scary, I get that, but—"

"I'm not scared—" I said automatically and then shook my head. "Well, I'm actually terrified, but that's not the point. I was just as terrified when facing Dominic and Kaden and Jillian, and I faced them anyway."

Walker put his hands on his hips. "Then what's the problem?"

"I can't physically do it." I said it fast, like ripping the bandage off a wound, but the sting from the rip still hurt like hell.

"Sure you can. Just lean back on the harness, and let the ropes and pulleys do the work for you."

"Just lean back?" I asked.

"Yep."

"The harness goes around my waist, and you want me to lean back on my hips?"

Walker opened his mouth, about to agree, when he finally understood my point. "Your hip," he murmured.

I nodded.

"I know it pains you. I've noticed you limp sometimes, but—"

"It hurts all the time," I admitted. I looked down into the cave, and it killed me to admit it to myself, let alone to Walker, but I was not going to be able to rappel down. "It hurts whether I move or stay still. It hurts whether or not I'm weight-bearing. It hurts constantly and relentlessly. I can still grit my teeth and bear through it enough to walk and work and maybe even run when I'm being chased, but this—" I looked at the equipment and shook my head. "—I've always believed whole heartedly that I could do anything I set my mind to achieve, but Walker, this is impossible."

"Nothing's impossible. I'll add more harnesses to distribute the weight off your hip."

"Walker, you're not listening. I can't—"

"It's the only way down, so if you still want to move forward with this insane dinner date, than step in." Walker offered me the harness, holding the straps wide for my feet.

"It's not the only way down," a sultry voice whispered from the other side of the cave.

Walker looked up at the voice and curled his lip.

Bex was balancing on the small ledge of the cave opposite us. She was smiling, still wearing skinny jeans and the beautifully detailed, leather cowboy boots from last night, but her top was sexy and strappy and showed a lot of skin. I'd wager that top was not for *my* benefit. Her wavy bronze hair was curled into ringlets, and each ringlet gleamed ethereally in the moonlight.

Since I was the only one of us who planned to fake cordiality, I smiled back. "Good evening, Bex. How was your day rest?"

She waited a moment, still staring at Walker to gain his greeting, but when it became evident she'd be waiting a while longer, she flicked her gaze to me. "Good evening to y'all as well. My day rest went very well, thank you for asking. How was your day?"

"No one died, so I can't complain."

Bex blinked at me for a long, silent moment, her face bland, and then she laughed. Her face transformed like the spread of butterfly wings, one moment set still, motionless, and carefully sculpted to keep its true nature hidden, and then the next, it fluttered free and wide, flashing its genuine, exquisite, unmatched beauty. Her ringlets bounced with each tremor of her laughter and the sound, light and joyous, lit the air.

I glanced at Walker, but his eyes never left Bex's face. His expression looked pained.

Her laughter settled on a sigh. "Rene was right," she said, shaking her head. "You've quite a sense of humor."

"Thanks," I said blandly. I poked my thumb in Bex's direction. "Did you catch that, Walker? The vampires appreciate my sarcasm."

Walker grunted. "That's not a compliment." He wiggled the harness impatiently. "It's go time."

I shook my head at Walker, exasperated. "What part of 'I can't' don't you understand?"

"The 'can't' part," Walker gritted from between his clenched teeth.

"There's no reason for Cassidy to suffer unnecessarily. Rene is on his way, and then we can bring y'all down to dinner. Both of you."

"The hell you can," Walker bit out.

"What he means is—" I amended, thinking fast, "—we wouldn't want to inconvenience you. I'm sure we can manage on our own. Somehow." I looked at Walker. "Without rappelling."

"This is the only entrance," Walker whispered to me, although Bex, being Bex, could certainly hear him. "We either rappel down, or we don't go down at all."

"It's not an inconvenience in the least," Bex assured, ignoring Walker. "It would be my pleasure to assist you. Isn't that right, Rene?"

Rene shot up from the depths of the cave on cue. His leather coat flapped around his knees with an audible whipping noise as he whirled past us and flew overhead. He descended slowly to land on the ledge next to Bex, and his landing—complete with flapping coat and whirling, chin-length, golden hair—was dramatic and flashy. He locked eyes with me, his grin cocky and daring, and I realized that just as Bex's skimpy top was for Walker, Rene's showmanship was for me. But what exactly he was daring of me, I could only guess.

His features were very delicate and femininely handsome, no longer the gargoyle-like creature he'd been when we'd first met, which only meant one thing: he'd fed since waking from his day rest.

"Yes, it will certainly be my pleasure to assist you, DiRocco," Rene purred smoothly.

The wound on his neck from my necklace garrote wasn't quite healed. Feeding had obviously helped—the wound wasn't bleeding or fresh—but when he spoke, his Adam's apple moved beneath the split skin, widening and closing the wound as he spoke like a second mouth.

I hesitated, simultaneously horrified by the sight of his wound and proud for successfully defending myself, but a nagging, cautious part of me wondered how Rene would retaliate.

The direction of my thoughts must have shown on my face because Rene said, "I meant it when I told you to never apologize for surviving. I don't hold a grudge against you for my injuries."

I nodded, trying to think of an appropriate response. My knee-jerk reaction was   to flip him off, but that was the old me. The new me was a liaison for Dominic.

"Thank you," I said. "I appreciate your level-headedness, Rene. I hope that after tonight, I won't feel the threat of survival. Our Masters are neighbors, after all. There's no reason we can't be—" I tried to think fast and ignore Walker as he gaped at me. "—neighborly."

Walker leaned in to whisper-shout in my ear. "I can think of several reasons!"

Rene extended a hand across the cave, ignoring Walker. "You will trust me to escort you to dinner?"

I stared at his extended hand, at the thin, nearly translucent webbing between his fingers, and swallowed.

Walker shook the harness with a hard *clank* and held it out for me to step in. "We can escort ourselves, thank you."

I tried locking eyes with Walker, but he was glaring at Bex. I touched his hand holding the harness. He glanced at me, but his expression didn't soften.

I sighed. "Listen, Walker, I can't rappel down. It's impossible."

"Yes, you can. You just—"

"You're not listening. I physically cannot do what you're asking of me." I sandwiched one of his hands between both of mine. "I know my strengths and my limits. How many times have I ever told you I wasn't capable of doing something?"

Walker opened his mouth and hesitated.

"How many times have you told me that I should rest, that I was pushing myself too hard, that I needed to recognize when to back down, so I could heal?"

Walker let loose a deep sigh. "Too many times."

"You know how stubborn I am. You know I would grit my teeth and forge ahead if I could, but I'm telling you now that I can't. My hip has worsened since we last saw each other, and I cannot rappel down this cave."

Walker nodded, finally accepting what I was saying as truth. "But it's the only entrance into the coven."

"I know." I turned away from Walker and locked eyes with Rene. "It would be an honor if you could escort me to dinner."

Rene smiled, his fangs long, sharp, and prominent in his mouth. He extended his hand again, his gaze darting to his outstretched palm and then back at me expectantly.

I breathed in a deep, long-suffering sigh. This was going to be a long night.

I took Rene's hand, weaving my fingers between his webbed ones.

"No, Cassidy!" Walker shouted. "Don't—"

Rene yanked me forward, and I fell into the cave.

* * * *

My heart clutched in that sick, suspended panic just before my feet left contact with the ground, and I thought I could still save myself. Walker's hand was outstretched, and I felt the ghost of his fingertips at my back. I twisted and stretched my hand to his, the insurmountable distance between our fingertips the space between two heartbeats.

And then I was falling.

I was midair, the cave's mouth suddenly overhead with the black shadows of Walker and Bex looking down at me. I thought I would have screamed. I think most rational people, when faced with their imminent and certain deaths, would scream. The circle and safety of the cave's mouth was shrinking away from me, the cavern floor with its jagged stalagmites was rushing toward me, and I was going to die in the next breath, but my thoughts weren't cohesive enough to scream. My thoughts were a snapped wire. Its frayed, mismatched ends couldn't circuit the reality of smashing one-hundred and twenty miles per hour into the earth, so through the gut-wrenching panic, instead of screaming, I held my breath.

Something cold and strong wrapped around my body. It couldn't have been death, since I was still falling, but then I saw his face. In a sense, death *was* wrapped around me. Rene slowed my descent, his arms holding me safe and secure against his body, so by the time we hit bottom, we landed as gently as if he had carried me a step between rooms.

He smiled down at me, and I could see his valiant efforts at trying not to laugh. I gasped for air, starved for oxygen and stability. Somewhere inside myself I was angry with him, but for the life of me I couldn't feel anything but the excruciating need to breathe.

Rene lost his own personal battle and laughed. "You should have seen your face. Priceless."

I pinned him with my best glare. "People can die from shock, you know."

"Some people might, but not you."

I laughed, incredulous. "Believe me, I can die just as easily as all the rest."

"Cassidy-dy-dy-dy!" My name echoed in a deep bellow from above.

I looked up. Walker's shadow hovered over the cave's mouth.

"I'm OK! Rene caught me!" I yelled back.

"I'm coming down!"

"Be careful!"

The rappelling rope fell from above a second later, and as soon as it hit the ground next to us, Walker was midair, cruising down its line into the cave.

I shook my head. "I guess Bex won't have the pleasure of escorting Walker to dinner, although I must admit, from experience, my escort leaves something to be desired."

Rene laughed, but it wasn't genuine this time. He sounded bitter. "Walker will never allow Bex to escort him to dinner. Having you here as an example of how life could be with a willing night blood, maybe Bex will reconsider her choice." Rene looked up to watch Walker as he rappelled. He shook his head. "We can only hope."

Bex growled. It echoed in strange, dissonant vibrations from above as she watched Walker from outside the cave.

"You can hope all you want, but I wouldn't place any bets."

Rene laughed, and he sounded like himself again. "I've heard quite a lot about you, but rumors failed to mention your delightful personality."

I frowned. My personality had never been described as delightful. "Heard from who?"

"You know, just here and there."

No, I didn't know. I'd only been in contact with Dominic and members of his coven. I hadn't expected rumors about me to spread to other covens. "All lies, I'm sure."

"That's what I had assumed when I heard how you could connect and control our minds, like we do humans, but that was true. What else is true about you, Cassidy DiRocco? I heard you helped the Master of New York City regain control of his coven when he didn't have the power to stand against them alone, and with you as his added strength, he survived a coup to overthrow his rule. I heard you gave him your blood to help him survive."

When were rumors ever that accurate? I thought. To my own ears they sounded like lies, the events were so fantastic, but those last few moments beneath the city, fighting against Jillian and Kaden, witnessing Dominic's heartbreak at their betrayal, and struggling to survive were etched permanently into my memory.

I'd never forget the vibrating rumble of the coven descending on us. Dominic was unconscious, hemorrhaging after losing his battle against Jillian. I had slit my own wrist and fed Dominic my blood to revive him. Dominic wouldn't have survived without me, but I'd never have survived against his coven without him.

To Rene, I shrugged. "You can't always trust what you hear."

"That's what I thought, too." Rene leaned forward. A golden blond lock fell over his face. "Until you controlled my mind."

Once I'd caught my breath, Rene set me on my feet, and I followed him deep into the cave, away from humanity and civilization, away from the safety of sunlight with only my status as Dominic's night blood as protection. The cavern air was damp. I could taste its stale moisture from the stagnant water pooled at the cave's bottom. Rows of stalagmites jutted from the water, some my height and others gigantic, towering over my head and nearly kissing the few stalactites hanging from above. As he led me through the cavern, I couldn't help but compare this coven entrance to the only other coven I'd ever had the misfortune of entering. Dominic and his vampires lived in the bowels beneath New York City, within a labyrinth of abandoned subway tunnels and sewer drains. His coven's entrance was dank and dark and underground as well.

Although Bex and Dominic couldn't enjoy the sunlight, I'd imagine that living underground in stale air and seclusion, was a type of prison all its own. If I were a vampire, despite all their enhanced senses, strength, and capabilities, I'd still want fresh air and moonlight if I couldn't have sunlight, and I knew from experience—from Jillian's betrayal and the other rebels in Dominic's coven—that I wasn't the only one who shared that opinion.

Rene stopped in front of an Old World, brass and oak door. He turned the knob, and the door opened with an ear-splitting, scraping creak that echoed in shaming reverberations throughout the cavern.

Rene winced. "It's the moisture. The wood expands, and it's hell to open."

"You could install a new door," I said. I held back a giggle at the thought of Rene, with his long blond hair and black leathers, with a tool belt.

"Bex loves this door, among other things." Rene sighed. "This way, please."

Rene stepped inside, and I gaped. The coven wasn't built from a natural cave. We were walking through a restored mining shaft. Dark, glossed hardwood had been laid as its floor, but the vertical beams and struts of the original mining shaft were sanded, stained, and finished. The beams lined the walls in four-foot intervals and every other beam sported an antique kerosene lamp. The flame in each lamp flickered hypnotically, creating a beating, romantic pulse. I walked forward through the entryway, out of the cavern, and into the hall, feeling like I was stepping back in time.

The air was less damp in the hall. Rene closed the door behind us, and we walked through the mining shaft in semi silence. Our shoes clipped on the hardwood. The sound echoed, seemingly in pulse with the flickering light. I had questions, so many damn questions that my body felt stretched thin from their unspoken potential, but the flames flickering sedately against the wood beams pulled my thoughts inward. I swallowed my questions and simply absorbed the experience. This mining shaft was built long before my birth, was used for mining before the vampires had claimed it as their home, and would exist as their coven long after my death. Moments like this, when the world is narrowed and timeless and infinite compared to the blip of our existence, the only right answer to the many questions is silence.

We reached the end of the hall, and Rene opened that door with significantly less ruckus than the first. It swung out gracefully and soundlessly to reveal the dining hall. I caught myself gaping again in open-mouthed awe and made a conscious decision to close my mouth. The hall was stunning. More dark glossy floors and vertical wooden beams accented the space to match the mining shaft, but the kerosene lamps were replaced by crystal candelabra. Their light sparkled over the walls, glittered across the floors, winked down the dark tapestries, and shimmered along the banquet table, brightening the entire hall in subtle iridescent hues.

Rene strode directly to the banquet table. He pulled out one of the middle seats—a high-backed, cushioned number lined with brass tacks—and gestured for me to sit.

I eyed the table speculatively. It was already set with four place settings.

I walked to Rene at a more sedate pace compared to his purposeful clip—my hip was grinding against my last nerve—and sat graciously in the chair he offered.

"Thank you," I murmured.

Walker joined us a minute later, led by Bex, seemingly no worse for wear from having rappelled into the cavern. He sidestepped Bex, scraped his chair out from the table, and sat next to me without waiting for her gesture. Bex ignored Walker's mood, smiling as if we were all old friends finally gathered together to dine. Her cowboy boots, jeans, and strappy top were strangely modern and misplaced here in the world she'd created within the mining shaft. Dominic had created a whole city beneath New York City, complete with tunnels and passageways and a labyrinth of corridors and rooms. Bex, on the other hand, hadn't just created a city. She'd created a passage in time, a world apart from the outside in which her coven could not only inhabit but also thrive.

Yet Bex herself was dressed like a twenty-year-old cowgirl ready for a night out and looking for a good time.

Rene removed his leather coat and stood next to the table wearing dark jeans and a button down. He tugged at the collar of his shirt, looking uncomfortable with the top buttons against his throat. As Bex approached, he scooted the chair across from Walker out from the table. Bex sat, and Rene tucked her in place. She nodded, Rene left the room, and the timeless, candlelit silence turned suffocating.

Bex met Walker's gaze and smiled. "Thank you for joining me for dinner. Both of you," she said, looking between the two of us. "I know y'all are swamped with a murder investigation, and I appreciate that you've taken the time to keep our dinner date."

I nodded. "Of course."

"As if we had a choice," Walker murmured.

I jammed the heel of my boot into his shin under the table. He kicked me back with his other foot.

"There are always choices," Bex said, her expression and tone still pleasant despite the edge to her words.

Rene returned with two plates of salad for Walker and me. He filled our glasses with white wine and Bex's glass as well as his own with a dark crimson, more viscous liquid from a separate decanter. The smell of her drink burned the back of my throat, and Jillian stirred inside me.

I glanced sideways at Walker.

He picked up his fork and glanced sideways at me, just as hesitant.

"Please," Rene gestured. "Enjoy."

I swallowed preemptively, speared a cucumber and spinach leaf in my fork, and took a bite of salad.

The dressing was sweet and tangy and complimented the crumble of blue cheese over the greens. I swallowed, relief like the warm spread of wine through my limbs, and I forked up another bite. I don't know what I expected. Despite being invited to dinner, I somehow hadn't anticipated being fed. As Walker had once warned me, poison wasn't their style, but as far as I was aware, neither was hosting dinner parties.

"The dressing is quite good," I commented truthfully.

Walker grunted, having taken his first bite.

Bex nodded. "So Cassidy, what brings you to Erin, New York? Surely Ian isn't the only reason for such an unexpected visit."

I raised my eyebrows, reminding myself that I was here for Dominic. As his night blood, what would be considered an appropriate response? I took my time chewing and swallowing another bite of salad before answering.

"Surely my visit isn't unexpected, considering that Dominic is my Master."

Walker kicked my shin with the back of his heel. I grimaced and kicked him back this time, but he toyed with his salad, seemingly unfazed by my retaliation.

The corner of Bex's lip twitched as she fought not to grin. She took a sip from her glass before speaking. "Yes, I expected Lysander to respond in some way after Ian was harmed in his care."

Walker frowned. "In his care? I'm not—"

"Dominic sends his deepest apologies," I interrupted. I gritted my teeth against Walker's heel as it slammed into the same bruised spot over my shin again. "He never intended Walker any harm. As you know, Dominic's Leveling approaches, and Walker's injuries were an unfortunate result of the rising civil war in the coven. I was injured that night, too, but Dominic restored order and healed us as best he could."

Bex swirled the liquid under her nose. The crystal from the chandelier winked in the sparkle of the glass and illuminated the liquid a brighter red. "A civil war in which two night bloods are injured doesn't speak well of the control Lysander is maintaining within his coven."

I narrowed my eyes. "He maintained control of the coven just fine. As I said, they *attempted* an uprising, but Dominic restored order."

"I heard differently," Rene said. He'd settled in the chair next to Bex after serving the salad, but he hadn't yet touched the liquid in his own glass. "I heard that Lysander didn't restore order to his coven. I heard that you did."

I braced my shin for Walker's strike, but he didn't kick me this time. He just stared at me, his face like granite.

I took another bite of salad, mulling over my answer before speaking. "I did my part, but my actions are an extension of Dominic's power. Despite what you may or may not have heard, Dominic *will* maintain control of his coven during the Leveling. I'll make sure of it."

Walker choked on his salad.

I patted his back. "Are you OK?"

He glared at me and moved away from my hand.

I sighed. This was going to be a long dinner.

"I accept Lysander's apology on Walker's behalf," Bex said. She set her glass aside on the table and stared into my eyes, her gaze unwavering. "You just recently discovered your existence as a night blood, is that right?"

I nodded. "Until about a month ago, I didn't even know that vampires existed, let alone that I had the potential to transform into one."

Bex rapped her finger on the table. "Lysander must be quite persuasive to have inspired such loyalty so quickly."

"He can be persuasive when he wants to be, but he learned from the beginning that I can be just as persuasive." I smiled, and I'm sure that my smile looked as cocky as it felt. I was very proud of my abilities to entrance vampires. "My loyalty is based firmly on mutual respect, not coercion, if that's what you're implying."

Bex blinked, and I got the distinct impression that not many things took her by surprise. But I did. "I wasn't implying anything. My apologies."

"Yes, you were," Walker said snottily. He finished his salad and threw his fork on the plate with a clatter. "All you know is coercion."

"I have *never* coerced you into any decision. You might delude yourself into thinking coercion explains the demons that you have lurking inside you, but let me assure you, those demons are all your own," Bex growled.

The intuitive creature that he was, Rene chose that moment to stand, gather our finished salad plates, and escape back into the kitchen.

"You're the demon," Walker snapped.

Bex shook her head sadly. "When will you forgive me for Julia-Marie's death? It was an accident."

"It was no accident!" Walker exploded. "You killed her!"

"I did no such thing," Bex said patiently. "She wasn't strong enough to complete the transformation. I knew better than to try, but when you insisted, I couldn't deny you. I can't deny you anything."

I got the distinct impression that this was an age-old fight, so I took Rene's cue, bit my tongue, and let it play out without my input.

"I grieve for her, too," Bex said softly.

"Bullshit! You killed my parents to worm your way into my life, and you killed Julia to worm your way into my heart. You're a monster and a murderer. You don't know how to grieve," Walker hissed, his voice the nastiest and rawest I'd ever heard.

I held my breath for Bex's reaction.

She stared at him a long moment, took a longer sip from her wine glass, and finally, she leaned forward, her beautiful green and yellow-tinged eyes pleading. "I don't know what I can do to show you that I never intended for any of those things to happen. I'm not to blame for the fire that killed your parents. I don't know why Julia-Marie's blood couldn't sustain the transformation. I'm not responsible for the things you've always accused me of, and I don't know what on earth I can do to show you that I care. Tell me what to do to rewind the damage, and I'll do it."

Walker crossed his arms and leaned back in his chair. "You want to rewind back to when I agreed to be your night blood?"

Bex nodded. "Of course that's what I want. It's what I've always wanted."

"I agreed to be your night blood to save Julia. My decision had absolutely nothing to do with you and everything to do with saving her. But you failed. I'll never agree to be yours again," Walker said coldly.

Bex leaned away from the table. I waited for her to explode, transform into a gargoyle, and tear Walker's throat out—a woman enraged—but she didn't. She picked up her napkin, patted her lips with its corner, and stood.

"I'd better check on Rene to see what's holding up your dinner," she said.

She turned her back on the dining hall, leaving Walker and me drowning in the wake of her tense, angry silence.

"You've never mentioned Julia before," I said softly.

"I don't like talking about her. She uproots memories I'd rather leave buried."

I understood better than anyone the benefits of putting the past to rest, but I had to know. The reporter in me wouldn't let it go, and if I was honest with myself, the woman in me wouldn't, either. "Julia was the reason you agreed to become a vampire?"

Walker rubbed his palms along the grooves of the table. He stretched his fingers wide over the expanse of wood, studying its texture as he spoke. "Yes. Julia-Marie Frost was my high school sweetheart. She was the love of my life, and of all the luck, she was a night blood. She understood my lifestyle. She understood me. She was the only other person I'd ever met, beside Ronnie, who could share my entire world: no lies, no betrayals, no judging." He swallowed, but I could still hear the thickness in his voice when he added, "She was my entire world."

"That sounds wonderful," I said softly, but I ached for him. I knew this story didn't have a happy ending.

He released the table and rubbed the corner of his temple. "She was diagnosed with leukemia shortly after our engagement party. I was devastated, but Julia—being Julia—accepted the news graciously as God's plan." A muscle in Walker's jaw ticked as he spoke about God. I bit my tongue and let him continue. I had the feeling that if I commented now, he wouldn't finish the story. "I waited as long as I could, but eventually, I couldn't live with her suffering any longer. I brought her to Bex to transform her onto a vampire. Bex refused, claiming that Julia-Marie was too weak to complete the transformation, but I insisted. I told Bex that if she transformed Julia, I would willingly allow her to transform me, too."

Walker stopped speaking, and by the strain in his jaw and temple, I didn't think he could finish even if he wanted to.

"But when Bex drained her, Julia died," I surmised, finishing the story for him.

He nodded.

"I'm so sorry, Walker."

"It was a long time ago, nearly ten years now." He laughed harshly. "Although sometimes, it still feels like yesterday."

"Leukemia," I said thoughtfully. "Isn't that cancer of the bone marrow and blood?"

Walker nodded. "Yes, it is."

"Maybe Bex wasn't lying. Blood is crucial to the transformation, and if Julia had cancer of the blood...." I shrugged, at a loss for words. "Bex warned you that Julia wouldn't survive the transformation."

"Bex was always jealous of Julia and me," Walker snapped. "Bex wanted me for herself, so when she saw her opportunity to kill Julia and get her out of the picture, she took it. She's a vampire, Cassidy. Just like all the rest, she's a monster."

Bex didn't need an opportunity to kill Julia to get her out of the picture, I thought. *Julia was already dying.* I opened my mouth to say as much, but Walker's expression stopped me cold. The pain of Julia-Marie's death was still fresh. The wound hadn't healed over time, it had festered, and poking at it would only cause more pain. I pursed my lips and kept my thoughts to myself.

Bex and Rene returned from the kitchen before I could think of an appropriate response to Walker's pain and deep, seething anger. They were holding dishes of—I squinted, my brain refusing the register what I was seeing—baked macaroni and cheese and toasted chicken club melts on pretzel rolls.

I stared at the food in front of me, stunned. "I haven't had baked mac and cheese in forever."

"It's my favorite dish," Walker said, his voice devoid of emotion.

"I know. That's why I had it made," Bex said, her voice equally hollow.

"Thank you," I said, genuinely surprised. It smelled like heaven. "It looks delicious."

"We might not eat solid food anymore, but if we hope to attract the many night bloods in town recently, we'll need to feed them. Food is, after all, the route to everyone's heart," Rene quipped.

Walker glared at him. "Keep your eyes off my night bloods."

"I doubt it's my *eyes* you're worried about," Rene said, smiling wide to show off his fangs. "Can't look anywhere these days without spotting a night blood. With this kind of spread," he motioned to the mac and cheese, "it's you who must worry about them keeping their eyes off me."

I rolled my eyes. Without a doubt, Rene was the worst comedian of us all. Walker was still glaring, so I leaned in and whispered. "He's joking."

Walker looked down at me and raised an eyebrow.

"I didn't say he should quit his day job."

Rene laughed. "Too late. I quit my day job years ago. Ninety-eight years ago, to be exact."

I burst out laughing, realizing my mistake, and when I glanced at Walker, the edges of his pursed lips were trembling. He didn't want to laugh. Monsters didn't make jokes, and people who hunted monsters didn't think they were funny. He hid his amusement behind a cough and scooped up some macaroni.

Dinner continued with Rene's humor lightening the air, and without further discussion on the topics of Julia-Marie, night blood loyalty, or vampire transformations, I was actually able to enjoy the fresh baked macaroni and grilled sandwiches.

"Are you sure y'all won't stay for dessert?" Bex asked when Rene had cleared our dinner plates. She blinked several times, and her beautiful green and yellow eyes ringed by those doe lashes were hard to resist. Physically, they were lovely, but mentally, I could feel the pull of her will shaping my tongue: *I'd actually love dessert.*

The evening had progressed so well I might have accepted the offer, but if she was resorting to mental compulsion to force us to stay, I wasn't sticking around to find out why.

Walker spoke before I could swallow the rest of my wine. "Actually, I'd love—"

I kicked his shin.

"Ouch! What the—"

I swallowed and pasted on a smile. "We would love to stay for dessert—"

Bex smiled and half rose from her chair.

"—but unfortunately, with a murderer on the loose, we'd better leave sooner rather than later. At the rate and viciousness of these recent attacks, the murderer will more than likely strike again tonight."

Bex settled back in her seat, an expression of carefully crafted understanding on her face. "Of course. It's too bad y'all can't stay just a *bit* longer."

Walker shook his head, frowning as if he wasn't exactly sure what he'd been thinking a moment ago.

I knew exactly what he'd been thinking: Bex's thoughts, just like I had. The only difference was, when I heard her thoughts in my mind, I could differentiate them from my own.

I folded my napkin from my lap and set it on the table. "Thank you for dinner. The food, as well as the company," I grinned at Rene, "was lovely."

"Y'all are very welcome," Bex said, nodding graciously.

I pushed my chair back from the table.

"Before you go, however, I do have one item of business I'd like to discuss."

I raised my eyebrows in question, but my gut sank. *Get out, get out, get out,* it screamed. A small, hopeful fraction of my heart hoped it was overreacting, but the few times I hadn't listened to my gut, I'd regretted it.

"Business?" Walker asked.

Bex nodded. Her expression looked contrite, but the gleam in her eyes said otherwise. "I believe I invited three of you to dinner, but here you are, just the two of you." Bex looked between us, her expression still carefully crafted, but the crease between her eyebrows and the little frown tugging at her lips was all an act. She was relishing this moment.

Walker stiffened next to me.

"Where's Veronica?" Bex asked, and her voice was nothing but sweet curiosity.

I glanced at Walker from beneath my lashes.

"She had a long day and didn't feel well," Walker said succinctly.

Bex wiped her mouth with the corner of her napkin and placed it on the table in front of her. "It would have been nice to hear that from Veronica herself. Honestly, it feels as if she purposefully rebuked my invitation."

"She sends her sincerest apologies," Walker said, but his voice sounded anything but sincere. Coming from his lips, even with his charming country twang, the words were flat and fraud.

"And yet, you didn't bother to apologize on her behalf until I broached the subject." Bex clucked her tongue in a succession of tsk-tsks that somehow shot from her mouth and whipped through the air like slaps. I physically felt their sting from across the table.

"You're lucky we even—"

"We're sorry that we forgot to mention how poorly Ronnie felt earlier in the evening." I interrupted. I wasn't sure where Walker was leading with that intro, but it hadn't started well. I doubted it was going to end any better. "It wasn't our intention to offend you. When we tell her about that mac and cheese, she'll doubly regret not being able to attend tonight." I stood.

Walker followed my lead. He pushed back from his chair and stood as well.

"Ian Walker. Cassidy DiRocco," Bex commanded.

She looked at both of us as she said our names in turn. I knew that tone. Dominic used that tone on me when we'd first met, and I used it every time I was about to entrance a vampire. I envisioned a mirror between the two of us, a giant mirror with a fortified, silver gilt frame surrounding my entire mind. Nothing, not her words or her will, was getting through my mental barriers.

"Sit down," Bex commanded. "Now."

Walker sat instantly.

I felt the pound and rumble of her command hit my mental barriers like thunder. They shook from the power behind her words, but they didn't break. Her command reflected off the mirror and hit her. She was already sitting, so Walker couldn't tell that her command had reflected. He only saw that I didn't sit, and by the swift swivel of his head and the blazing look in his eyes, he was astounded by that alone. But I could tell. Bex's eyes widened in fear and anger, which I expected, but they also widened with something I'd hesitate to define. I wanted to name it "recognition," but that didn't make any sense.

Rene whistled. "Your Master must simultaneously worship and rue the day he met you."

"Is this a game?" I asked darkly, ignoring Rene. "Dinner went so well. I was looking forward to relaying a favorable report to Dominic. But not anymore. What business is it of yours to force us to stay?"

Bex pursed her lips tightly, but she nodded. "Understood. Please, sit. My business is not with you."

I hesitated. I didn't like the way she'd worded that last sentence. It didn't bode well for whomever she did have business with, but at least she hadn't commanded me to sit this time.

I sat.

Bex locked eyes with Walker. "When was the last time Veronica left your house?"

Walker frowned. "It's not safe outside the house after sunset. I wouldn't want her—"

"I'm not talking about after dark," Bex dismissed. "In general, when was the last time she stepped foot outside your house?"

I glanced at Walker, my eyebrows raised.

Walker crossed his arms. "I don't know what you're talking about."

"Let me enlighten you. Veronica hasn't left your house after dark since y'alls parents died, but she hasn't stepped one foot outside your house *at all* in the past five years."

Walker opened his mouth, but whatever he'd been about to say, he thought better of it. I could almost see him thinking, backtracking through their shared history, and from his weathered expression, he concluded that Bex was right.

"Your point?" Walker asked tightly.

"No matter if Veronica felt well or not, she wouldn't have joined me for dinner."

"If Ronnie doesn't want to leave the house, that's her business," Walker said. "I don't make her daily routine my concern."

"It's your concern now." Bex raised her wrist to her mouth and bit into her own vein. I gaped at the violent suddenness of seeing her blood. I'd expected blood tonight, but after an entire meal spent in pleasant, if not tense, conversation, I'd become comfortable. I'd let my guard down just a crack and allowed myself the naïve, selfish hope that I'd actually leave here unscathed.

Stupid. Stupid. Stupid.

"Bex?" Walker's voice was like razor blades. I'd never heard his tone so sharp and devoid of expression.

"Just one lick, and you may leave."

Chapter 7

Walker shook his head, and I knew that stubborn set to his jaw all too well. It meant that he wasn't budging. Even if one little lick guaranteed our safe passage, he wouldn't concede. On some level, I understood. I knew firsthand that even one drop of blood meant tightening whatever bonds he had with Bex a notch tighter, but I also knew that sometimes, conceding meant escaping. And there was certainly something to be said for just getting the hell out of dodge when the going was good. I was at that point now.

Walker, on the other hand, wasn't bending one inch. Never had, and by the steel look in his eyes, he never would. He'd rather break than bend because he believed he'd never break again.

I glanced between the two of them and eased the silver nitrate from my pocket into my palm.

Bex leaned across the table, offering her wrist. Blood flowed freely from the wound and puddled in a path of bright red drops on the smooth wooden table. I could smell its sweet, cinnamon heat from my seat. Dominic always described my blood as having a spiced quality. As inexplicable as it seemed, I could smell blood, too, and the last few days—at Lydia's crime scene and at Ronnie's abandoned house—I'd been overwhelmed by its cloying sweetness.

Bex's blood also smelled sweet, but it contained deeper nuances that singed my nostrils. I imagined that's how my blood smelled to Dominic and the reason why Kaden became obsessed with possessing me. It was the reason why my eyes hadn't left her wrist and my mouth flooded with saliva.

Her blood smelled delicious.

Taking a deep breath, I tried to conceal my reaction, but the spice from Bex's blood was poignant on my tongue. My skin turned clammy as I stared, craving a dose of something unidentifiable.

I shifted in my seat, uncomfortable with Bex and my reaction to her blood. My hip flared in a grinding burst of pain. The more my hip throbbed, the more my stomach cramped with inexplicable craving, and I felt trapped inside a body that had betrayed me.

"Think of it as your toll for coming without Veronica," Bex said. "One lick, just one, and you may leave as planned."

Walker snorted. "I thought you were playing human, trying to show me how alike we really are." He waved his hand over her bleeding wrist. "This isn't how humans say goodbye. A handshake would have sufficed."

"For years now, I've attempted to assimilate to your preconceptions of beauty and humanity. I've been very patient with you, Ian Walker. I've waited for you to come around, to see me as you once did, to see the truth. I've been very, very patient as you killed my vampires and insulted my reign and power. Now I'm thinking my patience was wasted." Bex glanced at me and then back to Walker with a micro flick of her eyes, but I didn't miss it and I doubt Walker did, either. "I know Lysander, and I know how he rules. He can be polished and posh when he wants to be, but that veneer is a façade. He is an animal at heart. He rules by strength and loyalty and public displays of justice. He takes what he wants in the moment without regret. Night bloods usually don't remain night bloods very long in his territory."

I swallowed, wanting to defend myself but not wanting to betray my arrangement with Dominic.

Bex locked eyes with me. "You've seen Lysander in his true form," she asked, but her words didn't rise at the end in question. She already knew the answer.

"Yes. I've seen his true form. I've also seen him polished and posh, as you put it. I've witnessed him hunt and fresh from the kill. I've seen him when he first rises, malnourished and skeleton-like before his first meal, and I've witnessed his transformation into muzzle, talons, pointed ears, flared nostrils and all. I've seen him in every form."

Bex cocked her head to the side. "And you accept him? You accept that you'll become that creature too, after your transformation?"

Bile rose in my throat at the thought of becoming that creature. I composed my expression and replied, "I anticipate it."

"That's enough!" Walker burst. He stood from his seat without Bex having released him. His chair shot backward and hit the wall behind us.

I shook my head. "Walker—"

"We're leaving. Now."

I opened my mouth to argue, my natural reaction, and then realized that leaving was exactly what I wanted. I stood. "OK."

The kitchen, mining shaft, and back hall doors slammed shut in succession. I could hear the bolt of their locks slide into place with an audible finality that didn't bode well for a timely exit. I walked to the door of the mining shaft anyway and tugged on the handle—call me Thomas—but the door was unmovable. It didn't even rattle.

I turned to face Bex. She was staring at Walker and smiling. She held out her wrist to him a second time.

"Fuck you!" Walker spat.

Bex sighed, long and theatrical. "I'm sorry to hear you say that. Just one lick, Ian, that's all I'm asking. But even to save yourself, you're incapable of compromise."

Rene was suddenly behind Walker, restraining his hands behind his back.

"There's no compromising with coercion," Walker spat, struggling against Rene's iron grip. Walker heaved his body forward, trying to dislodge his hands and slip free. Rene didn't budge. He didn't even look strained.

The only blood that had spilled thus far was from Bex herself, but the optimist that I wasn't, I stood still and silent, waiting for the strike.

My grip on the silver spray was slick from my sweaty palm.

"Rene, please escort Walker to my private chambers. I'll be there momentarily."

Rene nodded and began dragging Walker across the dining room. Walker turned into a spitting, cursing Tasmanian devil, but Rene didn't even break a sweat. Despite Walker's struggles, the two of them were nearly at the door.

I stepped forward to follow.

"It was lovely meeting you, Cassidy DiRocco. Lysander is a lucky man indeed with you at his side." She gestured to the mining shaft. "I'll see you out."

I blinked. "You'll see me out?"

Bex smiled. "I told you, my business isn't with you."

"I'm not leaving without Walker."

Her smile widened, and her fangs gleamed in the candlelight. "Then you'll be here a while."

"Cassidy! Go! Get out of here!" Walker bellowed from across the room.

I could leave. I could go back to the safety of his house without having been bitten, bled, attacked, or in any way physically harmed tonight. I could face Ronnie, eye to eye, and say that I'd survived only by leaving Walker behind, and the woman that she was, allowing Walker to face the night alone, I think she'd understand. I think she would leave if she were standing here in my place, except she'd never be in my place because she couldn't leave her own house. I could leave, I probably *should* leave, but I wouldn't. If I left, I wouldn't be able to face myself.

Walker's life and humanity were at risk, and I couldn't leave him to face that alone, even if it meant my own life and humanity. Over the past three weeks, I'd learned that there's a fine line to cross to becoming a monster, and it has nothing to do with transforming into a vampire.

I could still feel a thin mental chord between Rene and me from our connection last night. It linked us, and I stroked that chord experimentally. It vibrated a low, deep bass, and I realized it wasn't nearly as thin as I'd thought. The chord was inconsequential when ignored, silent and therefore unheard, but when I plucked at it, even gently, it expanded in a strong, deep swell of sound that was inescapable.

Rene paused in his struggles with Walker. He looked up at me, his mouth a wide O.

"Rene Roland," I commanded, and the chord struck a loud, demanding note between us. "Release Walker and restrain B—"

A blur of movement knocked the silver spray from my hand, and I was suddenly smashed on my back into the stone floor. Bex's hand squeezed around my throat, cutting short my command. She'd moved like Dominic could move, faster than my brain synapses could fire, and her strength was incredible. I couldn't breathe. I tried to flex my neck to sip a hiss of air between the squeeze of her fingers, but struggling against her was useless. If she truly wanted to kill me, I had no doubt that she could break my neck with a simple twitch of her fingers. She could twist and pull with the inhuman strength in her arms and decapitate my head from my body without straining a muscle.

She watched me impartially for a moment, her luminous yellow-green eyes scanning my face. Walker was free from Rene and threatening Bex. She ignored him, obviously unconcerned by his threats, but she eased the pressure from my throat slightly. I gasped, squeaking a thin stream of air into my starved lungs before she closed her grip on my throat again.

Walker had missed it. He was still shouting and waving one of his weapons in her direction, and he'd missed that she was letting me breath.

She wasn't letting me live for his benefit.

Bex doesn't want to break the alliance, I realized. She was actually reining in her strength, restraining herself to only choking me, but even that was a ruse if she was letting me breathe.

She allowed a few more stolen sips of air into my lungs. When she closed her grip again, cutting off my air supply, I gasped and choked—ineffectual but desperate for more—like sucking ice cream through a straw. She was letting me live, but I wouldn't last long without more than a few sips of air. Black spots and bright starbursts were starting to cloud my vision, and my neck was burning.

At first, I thought the pressure of her vise-like grip was straining my throat, but the burning became intensely focused. A thin whisp of noxious steam sizzled between us, similar to the sizzle of vampires being burned by silver.

My necklace.

The silver chain should have protected me, but instead of pulling away when the necklace burned her hands, she squeezed tighter, embedding the necklace deeper into my throat as it scorched both of us.

I opened my mouth to scream, but I couldn't breathe in, and the scream couldn't escape out. Something like cinnamon and cloves dripped into my open mouth and over my tongue. That persistent, addictive itch beneath my skin flamed to life, and my eyes, like laser targets, focused with inhuman clarity on the source of that stolen drop.

Her blood. The wound on her wrist was still bleeding, and as she twisted to ward off Walker, a warm drop dripped into my open mouth.

Jillian roared inside my head. *SWALLOW!*

Between Bex's hands around my neck choking me, Jillian's voice screaming at me, and my own desperation to breathe, I did the unthinkable. I swallowed Bex's blood.

The itch beneath my skin became claws, as if something alive and unbidden was trying to escape from inside me. Walker did something to her then, I couldn't see what, but Bex turned to fend him off. Her wrist grazed my lips, and the suppressed creature inside me burst free. I sealed my lips around the wound at Bex's wrist, sucked a mouthful of her blood, and swallowed.

Like a soothing balm, the blood soaked under my skin, dampening the flames. I couldn't move for a moment. Jillian sighed across the mental twine between us, and instant relief swept over me in a numbing, limp lethargy. I stared overhead, letting the blood overtake my body, and then like a sudden backdraft, the blazing itch returned. It scorched up my throat like fire, and I realized the craving was neverending. I wanted more blood. I'd always want more blood.

Why can't Walker want me like that?

The thought was in my mind, but it wasn't my own and it wasn't from Jillian. Unlike the other thoughts Bex had projected at me, it wasn't a command either. She was just watching me and thinking a simple thought without intending for me to hear.

But I'd heard.

I could hear all of her—the Master of New York State, Rene's maker, Walker's protector—everything within her heart that composed her being. I could feel the heat of her blood nourishing her muscles. I could hear the snap of synapses, like a network of neurons throughout her nerves, firing over her arms and legs, allowing her that blinding speed and unimaginable strength vampires naturally possessed. I could see her still, physically useless human heart, which was still broken. She had walls that, even with my newfound connection, I couldn't scale, but the connection I did have was more than enough for my purposes.

Get the fuck off me! I thought.

Bex's hands released my neck instantly. She stared down at her palms, pure, dumbfounded shock blanking her expression.

"I heard you inside my head," she whispered. Her voice shook as she met my gaze. "And I listened to your command."

I gasped, struggling to breathe through my bruised throat and coughing instead.

Rene was suddenly beside me, his arm behind my shoulders to help me sit up. "Are you OK?" he asked.

I looked askance at Rene and nodded. Walker was standing next to Bex, inexplicably checking the time on his wristwatch. I narrowed my eyes on him, wondering why Rene was the one helping me up.

"You don't look OK. Breathe in slowly." Rene advised. "I'm sorry that things escalated so quickly. You should have left when you had the chance."

I didn't have the wind to breathe yet, slowly or otherwise. I couldn't stop coughing.

"You don't even know my full name," Bex said, staring alternately at me and her betraying palms. "All you needed was a sip of my blood, and I was yours to command."

"I'm guessing that doesn't happen often," I croaked, finally catching my breath.

Bex's smile was weary. "Not in a very, very long time. I don't suppose that you—"

Walker tapped the face of his watch, and Bex's hands whipped up to cover her face. She doubled over, shrieking a high, piercing wail from behind her hands.

Walker hadn't been checking the time. He'd been aiming.

Rene was gone from my side, and just as quickly, Walker was missing a chunk of flesh from his neck. He screamed and covered the wound with his hand just as another chunk was ripped from his shoulder. Walker backed up wildly, aiming his watch while he backpedaled, but his watch and the flesh under it tore violently from his wrist. Blood spurted from the wound.

I opened my mouth to command Rene to stop.

Walker tripped backward, cracked his head on the corner of the dining room table, and hit the floor hard.

Rene stopped the attack without being commanded. I scrambled across the floor to kneel next to Walker and help him, but something was wrong. He was moving strangely and not getting back to his feet.

I put pressure on the wound at his wrist with my own hand, the deepest of the Rene's bites. "Walker? Can you talk to me?"

Walker vomited. His eyes rolled back, and his body shook violently.

"Oh God." I knelt beside Walker and cupped his head to protect it from hitting the stone floor. "You're OK. You're going to be OK," I said, more for my benefit than his. I didn't know enough about seizures to know if he could hear me or not.

My heart sank as my brain caught up to what I was seeing. Walker was having a seizure.

Bex rushed beside me. I glanced up at her, and despite the urgency of the situation, I stared. Walker had shot Bex in the eye. One of the hands from his wristwatch was imbedded deep in the center of her iris. Blood and a thicker, more viscous liquid dripped over her cheek like tears as she blinked around the protruding watch hand.

Rene was staring at Bex, too. "Master," he whispered, and that one word said it all.

I'd witnessed vampires heal worse wounds—Dominic had expelled an entire spray of silver bullets from his body and stood moments later like the injury had never occurred—but it was her *eye*. I had a very bad feeling that if she attempted to pull the watch hand free, she'd pull her eye out with it. Evidently, Rene was thinking the same thing.

Bex ignored Rene and dropped to her knees next to me.

"What happened?" she demanded.

"He tripped backward and hit his head. Obviously he hit it hard if he's—" I couldn't finish my sentence.

My throat was already swollen from being choked, but now it clogged with tears. I tried to swallow them back, but they flowed down my cheeks in a hot panic.

"You're going to be fine, Walker." I repeated. "Just hang in there."

"It was an accident," Rene added. "He shot you, and I was protecting—"

Bex held up her hand to Rene, and he fell silent.

"He's having a seizure," she said, her voice calm and steady.

I nodded.

"He's had these before, twice recently that I know of, since returning home from the city. The doctors say it's not uncommon for those who suffer from TBI."

I blinked. "TBI?"

"Traumatic brain injury."

"Oh," I whispered, but I couldn't process what she was saying and what was happening. In all the weeks we'd spent getting to know each other, hours of sharing our lives over the phone since we couldn't in person, Walker had never once mentioned having seizures.

"Lysander healed Walker as best he could, but healing some injuries are even beyond our capabilities," Bex said, and a note of condescension in her tone made me wonder if she was thinking of herself as well as Walker. "Brain injuries are as much a mystery to us as they are to humans. We cannot heal the brain with vampire blood or saliva like we can other body parts."

"Walker told you about having a brain injury? He told you about his doctor appointments?" I asked. Nothing about this made any sense.

Bex snorted. "Ian doesn't tell me anything. But he doesn't need to. I know when he wakes in the morning and eats his oatmeal. I know when he leaves at night to hunt and which weapons he carries. I know when he fucking sneezes, so I damn well know when he has a seizure." Bex sighed. "I've just never actually seen him have one. Not that it matters, since I can't heal it."

"There is the little problem of getting past his skull," I said testily.

Bex shrugged. "With or without the skull, it makes no difference. I've witnessed injures in which the brain was exposed, and I attempted to heal the night blood. Both blood and saliva failed."

I imagined Bex healing a brain the way Dominic often licked my wounds to heal them. I gaped, horrified.

"The brain doesn't respond to vampire blood like other human muscles and organs," she explained, oblivious to my expression as she watched Walker. "I pieced the brain together and healed the skull around it, but the person was still severely mentally impaired afterward."

I just stared. Between listening to Bex talk about exposed brains and holding Walker as he seized, I didn't know what to say.

"Getting past the skull, as you stated, would be difficult without incurring serious, permanent deficits, worse than the injury he already has," Bex said, "so I left it alone."

Her tone and her expression as she watched Walker seize sounded as if she regretted that decision. The mental image of her cracking open Walker's skull to lick his brain was more than I could bear.

"He'd be left a vegetable!" I screamed.

"I know." Bex blinked at me, annoyed. "That's why I left it alone."

"You're fucked up." I snapped. "We need to get him to a hospital! Now!"

"No hospital," Walker whispered.

He'd stopped seizing. His eyes fluttered open and closed, but other than that, he hadn't moved.

"Walker? Can you hear me?" I whispered. My hands holding his head were shaking.

"Yeah. How many times did I seize?"

"Just once. Less than a minute," Bex said wearily, as if she'd answered that question before. "Do you feel another coming on?"

"No. Can you help me sit up?"

I stared at the lines of his face, his eyes, his mouth, the wrinkle between his brows, and a million questions ripped through my mind. *How long have you been having seizures? How often? How many? What else did the doctors say? Is that why you've been having headaches? Should you be driving? Are you taking medication?*

But one question, more insignificant than the rest but by far more insistent, nagged at me.

Why didn't you tell me?

I couldn't voice any of those questions now, so instead, I did the one thing I could do. I helped him sit up.

Walker made a noise in the back of his throat. I tensed for a second, thinking he was about to seize again, but I realized he'd noticed the vomit. He shook his head.

"I'm sorry you had to see that," he said. Even through the thready weakness in his voice, I could hear the bite of his anger.

"I'm not sorry. I'm thankful I was here. What if you'd been alone? Or worse, what if you'd been—" *here with only Bex,* I thought. I stopped myself short, realizing that she was still beside me. "—in danger. I'm your backup. This is what I'm here for."

Walker shook his head. "I'm *your* backup."

"It goes both ways, *darlin'.*" I turned to face Bex. "It's been a lovely dinner, but we're leaving. Now."

Bex didn't take her eyes off Walker. "You can't just—"

"Let me fly you to the nearest hospital," Rene interrupted. He stepped forward, his expression pleading. "You need me to fly you from the coven anyway, and it's no problem to land at the hospital. He can't possibly climb back up the cavern in his condition."

Bex's mouth tightened infinitesimally at Rene's interruption, but she nodded.

I sighed. The last thing I wanted was more "help" from Rene, but he was unfortunately right. "Thank you," I gritted from between my clenched teeth. "I'd appreciate that."

"That's not necessary," Walker said, "We'll see ourselves out."

"Of course you will." The disgust in Bex's voice was palpable, and I realized that she'd anticipated his response.

I leaned into Walker, not that Bex or Rene couldn't hear me—they could probably hear me whisper from miles away—but the instinct to whisper made me lean into his ear anyway. "You just had a seizure. You need—"

"I'll tell you what I need. I need to be alert and focused. I need my freedom to work and track the animal responsible for those murders. The hospital is going to take away my license, put me on drugs, and prescribe ongoing treatments that I don't have the time to—"

"You make the time!" I burst. "Maybe you need those drugs! Maybe you shouldn't be driving!"

"I don't feel like me on medication. I can't—"

"So you try different medication until you find one that works!"

Walker shook his head. He used one of the dining room chairs to leverage himself to his feet. "It was only one seizure. I'm fine."

I blinked as I watched him struggle to stand. The picture I was slowly piecing together was one I didn't recognize or understand. "You've had more than one seizure before," I said.

He knew it wasn't a question, and he knew better than to deny it. Instead he said, "And I know that since I only had one, I'm fine."

He let go of the chair and took a step. His legs visibly trembled from the strain of holding his own weight, but he didn't fall. I shook my head, torn between helping him and letting him struggle.

"I know the feeling well," Bex said beneath her breath.

I looked at her sharply, wondering if she could read my mind as easily as I'd been able to read hers.

She turned to Rene and cocked her head toward the entrance. She didn't need to ask twice. Rene was just a blur and in the next instant, Walker was just a cursing blur with him.

"He's not taking him to the hospital," I stated, my voice deadpan. "Is he?"

"That's Ian's decision, and he's chosen to be stubborn, bless his heart. Maybe in the future he'll choose differently—" Bex's voice was strained, and I knew that choosing to go to the hospital wasn't the only choice she was waiting on. "—but in the meantime, he'll be waiting for you outside the coven."

I nodded. "Bless his heart," I muttered. I thought of all the questions I couldn't ask Walker, of all the uncertainty between us compounded by everything he hadn't confided in me—the night bloods living with him, Ronnie living with him, and now, his health—and I felt anger, like a deep, vibrating tectonic plate, shift over my heart.

Rene was suddenly, unaccountably in front of me.

I sneered at him.

Rene's smile widened. "Your turn."

I tipped sideways in his arms, his grip tight around my body, and we were gone. Out of the dining room, through the flickering dim of the mining shaft, and rocketing up the cavern, passed stalagmites and rock structures, away from the world Bex had created with her kerosene lamps and tapestries and timeless beauty, and toward the steep pitch of the present, we soared.

* * * *

Rene dropped both of us unceremoniously outside the coven. I decided to rise above my anger and the million festering questions inside of me and offer Walker a hand to help him stand. There wasn't one question I could ask here that I couldn't ask from the safety and comfort of his living room.

"Let's get the hell out of the woods and go home," I said.

He ignored my hand and met my gaze. "What the hell was that back there?"

I blinked. "Excuse me?"

"That loyal night blood bullshit. You're not Dominic's little day servant. You don't answer to him and his coven. You don't answer to anyone!"

I let my hand drop to my side. "Things changed while you were gone. I've learned to survive on my own, to co-exist with Dominic in peace."

"There is no peace between wolves and lambs." Walker spat. "Only slaughter."

I shot him a quelling look. "Am I the lamb in this analogy? Really?"

"When we were in the city together, you—" Walker shook his head at me. "—but you obviously aren't the same person I met back then."

"Not everything has to be war," I hissed. "Sometimes, in order to survive, you need to compromise."

"Maybe you should have told me about your *compromise* with Dominic before you came to visit," he snapped.

"Maybe you should have told me about having seizures before I came to visit," I snapped back. "Maybe you should have told me that you lived with Ronnie and an entire houseful of night bloods! You haven't been exactly forthcoming either."

"You let me go into that dinner thinking we were on the same side," Walker said in a low voice.

I rolled my eyes. "We are on the same side!"

Walker jabbed his finger toward the cave opening. "From what I just heard down there, you're on *their* side! Compromising with a vampire," Walker shook his head. "It's bullshit, is what it is."

"What does my compromise with Dominic have to do with anything?" I asked. "I'm surviving the best way I know how. If I'm alive and *healthy*, what does it matter?"

"It matters. When push comes to shove and Dominic tries to turn you, will you agree to that, too?"

Hell no, I thought, but I couldn't answer truthfully because Bex might overhear. I settled on a different truth instead. "When we were in the city, you told me that it's my decision to make, not yours and certainly not Dominic's. Was that a lie, too?"

Walker shook his head and looked away.

"When were you planning to tell me about the seizures?"

"I've only been having them for a few weeks. The doctors aren't even sure if—"

"You never would have told me," I said quietly, in shock. "If you hadn't seized right in front of me, you never would have told me. Does Ronnie know? Does anyone know?"

Walker closed his mouth and didn't say a word.

"We're going to the hospital," I insisted.

"No, we're not. When we first met and I rescued you from Dominic's coven, did we go to the hospital like I suggested?"

I shook my head. "That's not the same thing and you know it."

"You told me you were fine, and even though I knew you weren't, I brought you home anyway because I respected your decision."

"I also remember a different time, when I begged you to take me to the hospital, and you didn't. Nothing was more important than your vengeance to kill vampires."

"Not much is," Walker admitted. He struggled to his feet on his own. I caught his arm to steady him, and his fingers brushed against my bruised neck as he groped for balance. I winced back with a hiss.

"Careful," I muttered. "We should take it slow. We still have a long hike back to the Harley."

"Your neck has third degree burns. They could easily become infected out here in the woods," He said, and when he held his fingers up, they were glossed with my blood.

"Let's get the hell out of the woods then," I snapped.

He took hold of my chin and tipped my head for a better look at the burns. "We need to get you to a doctor."

I shook off his grip. "We don't have time for a doctor. The murderer is still out there, and we—" I stopped short, catching the glint of Walker's teeth in the moonlight as he grinned at me. "You're such a brat."

He wiped my blood off on some dry leaves outside the coven and took my hand. "You're right about one thing, darlin'. We need to get the hell out of here."

An hour later, we finally entered his house. Ronnie was shelving newly washed dishes. Logan and his oldest son, Keagan, were continuing their conversation on the couch. Jeremy was eavesdropping on their conversation from a nearby chair and still scowling. My whole world had shifted tonight in the span of three hours, but everything here in this house, everyone we'd left behind, had remained the same.

Maybe we should live more like Ronnie and never leave the damn house.

Walker shut the door quietly behind us, and I wondered at the likelihood of being able to sneak upstairs to my room without anyone noticing our presence. Evidently, Walker didn't want to face anyone, either. He didn't greet Ronnie. He didn't even take off his shoes. I followed suit, and we swallowed our grunts of pain, limping silently across the kitchen, passed Ronnie and Logan and the kids, toward the stairs.

We were almost home free. I'd reached the end of the hall just outside the bathroom, Walker three steps behind, when Ronnie shrieked. "Ian! Oh God!"

The horror, I thought, and I looked back.

Ronnie gaped in dismay. Her hands shot up to cup her cheeks. At her shriek, Logan, Keagan, and Jeremy looked up, too, so every eye was trained on us. I sighed. The glow of the kitchen's overhead light wasn't flattering. A few leaves were stuck in Walker's hair. Blood was crusted on his left cheek, neck, the back of his head, and his wrist from Rene's attack. His expression looked ragged and pinched with pain, and I doubted I looked much better.

Ronnie dropped the bowl she was drying back in the sink and darted around the island. "Are you OK? What happened? Jesus, Ian, your wrist!"

His wrist, I thought, shaking my head. If she only knew. I met Walker's gaze before he turned around, and he must have read the intention in my eyes. He shook his head, but I couldn't stand next to him, knowing what I knew while Ronnie stared at us with her battered heart in her eyes. Walker had a serious health condition, and after a lifetime of living together, she deserved the truth. Walker obviously disagreed.

He turned to face Ronnie, and I did both of us a favor and ducked into the bathroom.

I shut and locked the door behind me, flicked the light on, and gaped. I'd been gaping a lot lately, but sometimes, there's nothing to say or do when reality stares back at you and it's not anything you ever thought could possibly exist.

The reflection staring back at me from the bathroom vanity was a stranger. My hair was a mess of tangles and leaves. My eyeliner had smudged in dark, dripping circles, and blood was crusted over my lips and between my teeth. The thought of swallowing Bex's blood made my stomach simultaneously queasy and ravenous. Jillian didn't voice her thoughts this time, but I could feel her stretch inside of me, luxuriating in the lethargic glow of a full stomach. She was satisfied. For now.

Bex's blood mixed with my own injuries. I touched a solidified glob of her blood on my cheek, and when I pulled away, her blood stretched in a thick rope between my cheek and finger. I gagged and tried scrubbing her blood off my face. A scrape on my cheek burned as I scrubbed. I scrubbed harder, desperate to clean my face and stop the burning, but just as suddenly as the burning had started, it stopped.

The scrape was healed.

I stared at the blood and my healed cheek for a long moment, trying to come to terms with my life, with the many disturbing realities that still seemed like nightmares, but there wasn't enough time in a lifetime to find a resolution. The best I could do, the best I'd been able to do for three long weeks now, was damage control.

I twisted the faucet and cleaned my face.

Fifteen minutes later, I'd plucked the leaves from my hair, used the globs of Bex's blood to heal the burns at my throat, and washed the remainder of the blood, dirt, and grime from my face. I nearly looked like myself again, except for the deep purple bruises around my neck.

I still looked like hell, but at least I was clean. As far as damage control, that was the best I could do.

Thinking of hell reminded me of my own personal devil. I'd blown Dominic off at sunset, leaving him that God-awful, rambling voicemail, and he'd taken it in stride. Maybe he deserved the courtesy of another phone call.

I rolled my eyes, thinking of being courteous to Dominic, the man with fangs and talons and unfathomable strength. The man who had a silver cage and handcuffs in his bedchambers to keep me "safe" from his coven.

The man who, when presented with the opportunity to get exactly what he wanted from me, to turn me into a vampire, had chosen to save me as a human.

Reluctantly, I punched in Dominic's number. The phone only rang once before he answered.

"How was dinner with Bex?"

"Hello to you, too," I said teasingly. "We really need to work on your phone etiquette."

"Hello," Dominic said, and I could hear the patience waning in the snap of his tone. "How was dinner?"

"If you're asking if Bex believes that I'm your loyal night blood, forging alliances on your behalf and anticipating my transformation into a vampire, then dinner went swimmingly. She's jealous of us and is doubly determined to have Walker. Bless her heart," I added, Bex's phrase growing on me.

"I'm sure our Ian Walker is loving the spotlight. Bless *his* heart." Dominic said, and it sounded as if he relished the thought. "Bex is something, isn't she? She's originally Southern, from Georgia I believe."

I snorted. "She's something, all right."

"If Bex handles this right, she'll strengthen her standing in the coven. Walker has run amuck for far too long, killing vampires and refusing her rule, without being curbed."

I snorted. "I got the impression that her coven wants her to choose a different night blood. They're impatient with Walker."

"I'm sure they are. He's killed many of their family and friends. Even if Bex eventually won him over and he agreed to the transformation, he wouldn't have many allies in his new home."

I hesitated, Dominic's logic startling since I'd never thought of the coven's perspective. I doubt I'd made many allies in Dominic's coven, but since I was never agreeing to the transformation, I suppose the point was moot.

"You've done very well, Cassidy," Dominic continued. "I won't forget it. How was dinner otherwise?"

I glanced at my reflection, at the bruises around my neck still darkening as we spoke. I thought of Walker seizing and vomiting on the stone of Bex's dining room floor. I thought of our argument on the way home, and I looked away from the mirror.

"About as good as could be expected, I suppose," I said. "We both made it out alive and with all our limbs accounted for." I couldn't say the same for Bex. I thought of her eye and shuddered.

"You're not telling me something."

I sighed. "I'm not telling you a lot of things, but I did what you wanted me to do. I stabilized your alliance with Bex. You should be grateful."

"I'm very grateful, and I thank you for acting as my loyal night blood. I appreciate your efforts, but—"

"This wasn't a favor," I reminded him. "We had a deal. Do you have any leads on Nathan?"

Dominic made a noise over the phone. It sounded like a sigh and a groan and something more, something like pain. "I've doubled my efforts and scoured the city for his scent. I fear that any trace of him that once existed may no longer."

"You haven't found anything," I accused.

"I *will* find out what happened to your brother, Cassidy. As you so often remind me, we made a deal, and you upheld your end of our bargain. I *will* uphold mine."

I didn't like his phrasing. "I don't want you to find out what *happened* to him. I want you to find *him*," I snapped. "Deal or no deal, you need to find my brother because his disappearance means that a vampire in your coven kidnapped a night blood behind your back."

"Or killed."

I sucked in a sharp breath. "Don't."

The silence was a palpable, throbbing bruise between us. I refused to break it. I feared that if I did, I wouldn't sound rational.

Eventually, Dominic spoke. "I think you should prepare yourself, Cassidy, for the distinct possibility that your brother is dead. He disappeared three weeks ago, and there has been no trace of him since."

"No," I said, but my voice was reduced to the raw whisper of restrained tears. Nathan was my little brother. It didn't matter if he was missing for three weeks or three years, I was still holding on to hope.

"A young vampire may have fed on Nathan," Dominic pressed, "and once begun, it's possible he couldn't stop. The vampire would need to erase Nathan's identity to erase his crime, and that may be why we can't find any trace of your brother. It's possible that the vampire is still loyal to me and only made a mistake."

"A mistake. Killing my brother is a *mistake*?" I shrieked, and I could hear the hysterical squeak in my voice.

"Cassidy—"

"That's not possible," I ground out slowly, trying to get a grip on my anger and fear. "Even if the vampire drained Nathan dry, Nathan can survive large amounts of blood loss and still survive."

"Assuming he's a night blood."

"Of course he's a night blood!" I snapped, my voicing squeaking back into hysterics.

"Calm yourself. You—"

"Rene's a young vampire, and he had the strength to stop feeding. When he realized I was a night blood, he brought me directly to Bex." I said rationally, stamping home my point. "If a vampire was truly loyal, he would have stopped and brought Nathan to you. If Nathan's dead, which he isn't, then it's no *accident.* Maybe you don't have as much control over the rebellion as you'd like to think."

"Rene who?" Dominic asked softly.

"Rene R—" I stopped myself, realizing the blades beneath the silk of Dominic's tone. "He's a young vampire, Bex's prior night blood."

"And he decided to feed from you during dinner? I thought Bex was more civilized than to substitute the guest of honor for the main dish."

I sighed. "He didn't bite me at dinner. We were in the woods, and he didn't know who I was, and—"

"In the woods?" Dominic said, sounding scandalized. "Among the trees and dirt and wilderness?"

"There isn't anything here but wilderness." I thought about that a moment and corrected myself. "And cows." I shook my head, realizing we were off topic. "The point is, have you asked your vampires about Nathan?"

Dominic snorted. "Of course."

"And?"

"Nothing. My vampires are loyal at present, thanks to you."

"All your vampires?" I asked, thinking of the allegedly executed Jillian still alive in my mind.

"Every last one of them. I assure you, my vampires did not deliberately harm your brother, and if an *accident* did befall him, it was not committed in deliberate disloyalty to me."

"Fine," I conceded, not appeased in the least but willing to let it slide for now. At least until I found a lead that proved otherwise. "How's Greta and her case? Any breakthroughs?"

"Greta is well, but her case is not. Two nights in a row now the murderer hasn't struck again."

I tapped my finger against the sink, thinking. "One victim a night for two weeks, and then nothing. The pattern shouldn't have stopped or altered unless the investigation missed something at that last crime scene, something to indicate that his work was complete. What does Greta make of it?"

"The police are considering the possibility that he suffered an accident, perhaps unrelated to his last victim. There's nothing to suggest that his last kill went afoul or was a completion of his work. If anything, his kills were becoming more savage. He wouldn't have stopped of his own volition."

"I didn't ask what the police thought. I asked what Greta thought."

Dominic laughed. "Greta's instincts and will are her greatest assets and will one day be her downfall. She reminds me of someone else I know," he said, still snickering to himself. "I think it's the depth of her loyalty that keeps her from listening to her instincts about you, but that will only last for so long. One day she will discover our secret, and that will be the day her instincts fail her. You know that I won't compromise my coven's secrecy, so if you don't keep Greta leashed, I will."

"Is that a threat?" I hissed.

He paused a moment. "How do you usually put it?" he asked. "I'm just calling it as I see it."

"You're avoiding my question," I snapped. "What does Greta make of the sudden stop in murders? She doesn't think the unsub was involved in an accident, does she?"

"No, she doesn't," Dominic admitted. "She's comparing this case to last month's case and how evidence disappeared. She's remembering how everyone thought the wounds were inflicted by knives, when in reality, they were animal bites. And she's remembering that you were the one who knew the truth."

"Me? What do I have to do with anything? I'm out of town."

"Exactly. It hasn't escaped her notice that the murders stopped the moment you left."

"That's ridiculous," I scoffed. "Once again, we were *joking* that the murders followed me here. I don't have anything to do with this case!"

"I know," Dominic said quietly. "I'm simply telling you what Greta is thinking."

"Right." I nodded, more to myself than to Dominic. The thought that Greta was suspicious of me again made my heart sore. "I've got to go. It's been crazy here, too, and I'm exhausted."

"Cassidy, I—"

"Have a good rest of your night. I'll call you tomorrow." I cut him off and ended the call.

I sat for another few minutes in silence, mulling over everything Dominic and I had discussed and left unsaid. I thought about Jillian's voice in my head. I thought about Bex and her destroyed eye. I thought about Walker's seizures. I both mourned and raged at the thought of losing Nathan. I ached over Greta and her case, and I wondered if my life would ever get back on track. I couldn't pinpoint exactly when everything had derailed, but I feared that the track I'd always known and had planned to continue traveling was too far gone to ever find again.

If I hoped to restore a semblance of a life worth living after this nightmare, I'd have to lay down new tracks of my own.

* * * *

I flushed the toilet for appearances' sake, opened the bathroom door, and nearly walked into the chest of a lanky red-headed boy I recognized as one of Logan's sons.

"Oh, sorry," I said, looking up. "You're Logan's oldest, right? Keagan, is it?"

He nodded. "And you must be the infamous Cassidy DiRocco," he said. His voice was just as deep as his father's.

"I don't know about 'infamous,' but you've found me," I said, holding out my hand.

Keagan took my hand, his shake firm but gentle, and I could tell he'd had practice despite his age. He pointed behind me to the toilet. "You've got to run the water after you pretend to use the bathroom or people won't want to shake hands."

"I'll keep that in mind," I said, cracking a smile. "How much did you hear?"

"Enough to know you weren't actually using the toilet."

I nodded. "Fair enough."

"And," he glanced sideways to the kitchen where Walker was attempting and failing to placate Ronnie before leaning down to whisper, "enough to know you were talking about Lydia."

I narrowed my eyes. "I didn't mention anything about Lydia."

"Maybe not this time, but you've talked about her in the bathroom before."

"You've been eavesdropping on me?"

Keagan shrugged. "Jeremy's not the only one who cared about Lydia. I want to know what really happened."

"You knew Lydia, too?"

"Of course. Everyone knew Lydia. Jeremy's story doesn't check out, does it?"

I pursed my lips as he voiced my own suspicion. I doubted Jeremy was capable of the carnage I'd witnessed, but still, Keagan was right. His story didn't quite check out. "I thought you two were friends."

"We are, but Lydia deserved a lot better. Growing up a night blood is hard business for everyone, but Jeremy doesn't get it. He lived with his uncle as a regular human for too long to really understand."

I frowned. "To understand what?"

"That we can't live like everyone else. We can't stay late at football practice and date pretty girls who can't see vampires. That's how you and people around you end up dead. He didn't grow up on hunts and stakings and fallout shelters. As shelters go, though, this is the best one we've ever lived in." He spread his arms out, indicating Walker's house.

"It certainly is a beautiful home," I commented, but something in the way he'd specifically said, "fallout shelter," as opposed to, "home," stuck with me. "What makes it the best?"

Keagan shook his head. "I have questions of my own."

"What kind of questions?"

He smiled, and I noticed that his left canine endearingly overlapped with its neighboring tooth. "Bathroom questions." He nodded his head at me. "Get back in there."

"Excuse me?"

"Do you want to know about fallout shelters or not?"

I narrowed my eyes. "You mentioned that on purpose, knowing I'd be interested."

Keagan shrugged. "Walker said that you're new at being a night blood, that I should be informative and make you feel at home."

I raised an eyebrow. "This bathroom interrogation is supposed to make me feel at home?"

"I'm being informative. Did you know that you can turn your city apartment into a relatively safe fallout shelter in less than an hour? Not as sealed tight as this house, but better than nothing in a pinch."

I bit the inside of my lip. Walker had never mentioned turning my apartment into a fallout shelter.

"Would a fallout shelter work, even after giving a vampire permission to enter?"

Keagan nodded. "For sure. It wouldn't be the best protection, but like I said, anything's better than nothing. It'd certainly be more effective than in the country. More witnesses to slow them down."

I laughed. "Have you ever lived in the city?"

Keagan shook his head. "My dad's got roots that run pretty deep. We move a lot, but he prefers the country."

"Most city vampires, in my experience, don't care how many witnesses they incur. I've had a vampire attack me in front of an entire police department, take down the officers and surrounding witnesses, and then take a hostage to bargain with me."

"Attack you?" Keagan asked, looking shocked. "To kill you? But you're a night blood."

"It doesn't matter, not in the city. The Master vampire there doesn't have control over his vampires like Bex does here," I said, and I couldn't keep the bitterness from my voice as I admitted the truth to myself.

Keagan shook his head. "That's insane."

I nodded. "More witnesses don't necessarily mean less danger. It just means that the vampires have more people to entrance."

Keagan was still shaking his head in awe.

"So about fallout shelters…" I began.

He pointed into the bathroom.

"I just told you about city vampires. It's your turn to spill," I countered.

"That wasn't one of my questions, but I appreciate the information all the same."

"You want to play hard ball?" I asked, narrowing my eyes.

"I have specific questions, and I'm willing to trade information for answers." He raised his hands innocently. "That's all."

"That's all," I grumbled, but I stepped back reluctantly into the bathroom. Keagan followed, shutting the door behind him. "You're a pretty persuasive kid. You should consider becoming a reporter when you grow up."

He leaned against the sink. "Remember what I said about Jeremy living a normal life? Having a career is part of living a normal life. Night bloods don't get that."

"I have a career," I pointed out.

"Yeah," He said, flashing that snaggle tooth. "And how's that going for you lately?

I narrowed my eyes, his question too on target for comfort. "You get three questions."

"Deal."

"And you tell me about fallout shelters after question two."

He hesitated this time, but then nodded. "That's fair."

I cocked my head and waited.

"How do you know that the person who killed Lydia also killed Mr. and Mrs. Dunbar?"

"There's evidence to suggest they were killed by the same person," I answered vaguely.

Keagan snorted. "Obviously. What kind of evidence?"

I crossed my arms. "That's confidential information in an ongoing investigation. Next question."

"Confidential information that you told Dominic. How would Walker feel about that?"

I shrugged. "It doesn't matter what Walker feels. I can't answer that question, so I guess we're done here."

I stepped to the door and grasped the handle.

"No! I have more questions!"

I turned back to face him. "Then ask them."

He nodded, but a moment past before he gathered his thoughts. "What's the Leveling?"

I raised my eyebrows. "They don't teach you about the Leveling in night blood university?"

He snorted. "I must have skipped that class."

I grinned. "Every seven years, on the anniversary of their making, Master vampires lose their powers to their successor for one night. It's the coven's opportunity to empower a new Master, if they so choose. If the current Master survives the night, his powers are returned to him, and he continues his reign over the coven."

"And if the Master doesn't survive?"

I sighed, this problem all too real. "Then the successor would take reign as Master vampire.

"Is Dominic your Master?"

"I get my question now," I interrupted. "Tell me everything you know about fallout shelters."

Keagan made a rude noise in the back of his throat, but he didn't argue. "Any place can potentially be a fallout shelter, granting that it's essentially an enclosed space with a threshold to cross. The easiest way to prevent a vampire from crossing the threshold is to not invite him, but as you probably already know, vampires can be persuasive."

I nodded. "Exactly. And once invited, you can't take it back."

Keagan frowned. "You can take it back."

I blinked. "What?"

Someone knocked on the door.

Keagan stared at me, eyes wide.

I held a finger up to my lips. "Sorry," I said to the door. "The bathroom's occupied."

"I know," the person whispered. "Let me in."

I stared at the door, shocked.

"It's Jeremy," Keagan said and let him in.

"Don't—" I hissed, but Jeremy was already inside and locking the door behind him.

"When you didn't come out, Ronnie got worried, so I said I'd look for you."

I snorted. "How magnanimous of you."

"I heard what you said."

"Is that so?" I asked dryly.

Jeremy nodded. "Is Bex losing her powers? Is that why she didn't remove my DNA from the scene?"

"Wait your turn." Keagan elbowed Jeremy in the ribs. "I get one more question."

I pinched the bridge of my nose. "Actually, I believe I get information on fallout shelters before either of you get anything." I pointed my finger at Keagan. "Go."

"Fallout shelters?" Jeremy looked at me and then Keagan like we were insane. "What's there to know about an underground safe room? It's made of silver because vampires are allergic to silver and you hide in it."

Keagan rolled his eyes. "There's more to it than that. There's precautions you can take, like having a location that's clear to the east with lots of windows. Soaking blood into the earth helps, too, if you have access to that sort of thing. You need a lot of it."

Jeremy shook his head. "Between a safe room and blood-soaked earth to protect me against the vampires, I'll take the safe room."

"We're protected here because of all the precautions Walker takes, not just the safe room." Keagan hissed at Jeremy before looking sheepishly at me. "Although the underground safe room is the main component."

"But how does that translate to my city apartment?" I asked. "If a vampire has permission to enter, I don't have an underground safe room to hide in. I live five stories off the ground."

Jeremy snorted. "Move to the country."

Keagan rolled his eyes. "Take as many precautions as possible. Pick an apartment with lots of windows that isn't overshadowed by another building. In a pinch, your apartment will be exposed to the first rays of dawn. Don't underestimate the timing of the sun."

I laughed. "You're preaching to the choir. I live by the rise and fall of the sun."

"We all do," Keagan said. "With enough windows, your apartment will soak in the sun's light and warmth all day. The more windows the better. You might think that windows, since they're breakable, would make it easier for them to enter, but if your fallout shelter is working, it won't matter if every window is open, they can't cross the threshold."

I nodded. "All right, what else?"

"Try to find an old apartment, one that's been soaking up the sun for years. If it has real metal door hinges and door knobs, that helps, too. The antiques are made with brass and cast iron. Don't go for porcelain or glass door knobs; they're pretty to look at but they don't do shit against vampires."

"Why brass and cast iron? Not silver?" I asked

"They don't make door knobs in silver, it's too expensive. Although Walker might if you asked nicely."

I stuck my tongue out at him.

He laughed. "There's something about the metals, even if they're not silver, that doesn't sit well with vampires. They're uncomfortable entering a house that's filled with it."

Jeremy scoffed. "That's bullshit. How will that prevent a vampire from entering her apartment?"

"It's not guaranteed to work, but the sunlight combined with antique metals and human blood gives you a chance. Even if he can still physically enter the apartment, your vampire might at least hesitate, and in that moment, revoke your invitation."

My skin prickled in anticipation. I might actually regain a measure of control in my life. "You mentioned soaking the earth with human blood," I said thoughtfully. "How does that help? Wouldn't blood actually attract vampires?"

"Vampires are attracted to our scent because new night bloods mean potentially new vampires. They're attracted to human blood for food, but specifically, they're hunting warm, circulating human blood in a live human. Stagnant human blood is unappetizing, like stale bread, so pouring human blood into the ground, or in your case, smearing it around the perimeter of your apartment, will keep you off their radar."

I blinked, and a sudden rush of understanding swept over me. "So smearing blood around the perimeter of my apartment, across door frames, will help ward off vampires?" I asked, thinking of the blood smears around the entry of Ronnie's old house. Someone was using her house as a fallout shelter.

Keagan nodded. "For sure."

"And Walker knows about all this stuff? About fallout shelters and smearing blood across doorways to keep vampires at bay?"

He nodded. "Of course. He taught me."

"Are you good now?" Jeremy asked impatiently. "Because I heard you say something about Lydia and the Dunbars, and anything to do with Lydia I—"

"No, we're not good." Keagan snapped. "I get one more question, so you can just—"

Someone knocked on the door.

The three of us stared at each other, startled into silence.

Jeremy opened his mouth, and I covered it with my hand.

"Just another minute," I said through the door. "Sorry."

"Take your time, darlin'," drawled an unmistakable twang.

I closed my eyes in embarrassment. *Shit,* I thought. *Now what?*

Jeremy disappeared from under my hand. I opened my eyes only to witness Keagan dragging him into the shower stall. I shook my head at the ridiculousness of it.

Keagan nodded back at me.

I rolled my eyes, but despite my better judgment, I didn't have a better idea. I flushed the toilet.

Keagan pointed at the sink and rubbed his hands together.

I waved him off and washed my hands. Jeremy slowly and silently slid the shower curtain closed, hiding from plain view. I took my time drying my hands, only delaying the inevitable, but hoping Walker would wander back into the kitchen. I could hear the plodding creak of footsteps, but in a home this old and housing so many people, the noise could be anyone.

Taking a deep breath, I twisted my hand around the doorknob and opened the door.

Walker was leaning against the door jam, his arms crossed.

I smiled. "It's all yours."

Walker smiled back. "Funny, I could have sworn I heard someone talking back to you in there."

I snorted. "Speakerphone works better than my regular phone."

"Using speakerphone is pretty inconvenient in your line of work," Walker said. "Conversations tend to be confidential."

I nodded. "That's true."

Walker's hard, locked gaze was unwavering.

He waited what felt like a full minute before breaking eye contact, reaching behind me in a quick lunge, and yanking the shower curtain wide open. I closed my eyes, mortified.

"I know Keagan was in here with you."

I turned sharply at the accusation in his voice and stared at the empty shower, stunned. "Keagan?"

Walker turned back to me with a hot glare. "And Jeremy, too, if I'm not mistaken. I could hear those two bozos through the door, clear as day."

I shrugged. "I told you, I was on speakerphone. And as you can see," I said, spreading my hand out for his perusal, "No one's here except me."

He stared at me for another moment, willing me to break, but I crossed my arms and met his gaze without flinching. Knowing how vulnerable I felt in my city apartment, he could have told me about fallout shelters, but he'd kept that information to himself.

Well, I could keep information to myself, too.

Walker sighed. "I guess I was mistaken," he said. He touched my shoulder, and I could feel the solid warmth of his touch through my leather jacket.

I eyed him skeptically. "Why would Keagan be in the bathroom with me?"

Walker's laugh was self-deprecating, but I kept my anger wrapped around me like a blanket against the chill of my guilt.

"Just something he said to me earlier while you were touring the house with Ronnie."

"Oh?" I asked. "What did he say?"

He rubbed the back of his neck with his hand. "He had some questions about my time in the city, about you, and how you survived when you didn't have other night bloods at your back."

"It certainly hasn't been easy, especially these last few weeks. I can't remember the last time I felt safe," I admitted.

"You can feel safe here." He said, but his smile was a little deflated.

Walker stepped out of the bathroom. As I turned with him, a shard of sunlight pierced through the window next to the shower. Dawn. The longest stretch of safety we ever had in a day was the moment the sun broke the horizon.

I narrowed my eyes on the window. The sunlight dabbled on the bathroom floor as it shone through the lacy white curtain, but the corner of the curtain was caught in the window and fluttered outside.

I smiled silently to myself, thanking God for the fearless spontaneity of teenage boys.

Chapter 8

Of course Walker knows everything I know about fallout shelters. He taught me.

I was lying on my bed in the guest bedroom, staring at the twirling overhead fan. Keagan's words replayed over and over in my mind. Walker had taught Keagan about fallout shelters, but he hadn't taught me. We'd pondered the smeared blood across the doorways of Ronnie's abandoned house, but he'd recognized the blood for what it was all along.

And once again, he hadn't told me.

I'd confided in Walker several times over the last three weeks about how violated I felt in my apartment. I told him how excited I was to see him, to get away from the city and escape the invasion of privacy I felt from Dominic's constant presence. Granted, Dominic hadn't taken advantage of the privilege. He often requested entrance, and lately, he even knocked, but we both knew the truth. His politeness was an act. He'd call it something less conniving, like a concession, but a spade is a spade whether it's a seven or an ace. Dominic had access to my home, and he'd utilize that access if necessary whenever he wanted. He simply hadn't found it necessary to break our tremulous truce, but there would be a day—and I suspected it would be sooner rather than later—when he would break that truce and break into my home. When he did, I wanted the arsenal stockpiled and prepared to fire. I'd thought Walker was the biggest asset to loading my arsenal.

Obviously, I'd thought wrong.

A commotion was brewing downstairs. If I wasn't mistaken, a conversation between Ronnie, Walker, and Logan had turned heated.

Their shouts had woken me after only an hour of restless sleep and had kept me awake for the past fifteen minutes.

A door slammed, and a minute later, Walker's motorcycle rumbled to life. I peeked out the window just in time to catch the tail end of his bumper disappear into the woody trail between his house and Ronnie's.

Curiosity finally got the best of me. I climbed out of bed, changed into a fresh, fitted t-shirt and jeans, masked the bruises on my throat with makeup, and ventured downstairs to do what I did best: snoop into things that were none of my business. Except when I reached the kitchen, the only person still there was Ronnie, and she was sobbing hysterically.

She was doubled over with her elbows on the counter, a hand over her mouth, and tears poured from her eyes like geysers. I'd never seen someone with tears so physically large. They rolled out of her eyes and down her cheeks the size of dimes to splatter onto an expanding puddle on the counter.

I stomped on the last step to make her aware of my presence, but she didn't notice. She continued sobbing, her eyes fixated on the space of countertop in front of her.

"Ronnie?" I ask softly. "Are you OK?"

She let loose a particularly loud sob.

"Ronnie!" I said, a little louder.

Her head jerked up, and she blinked at me in shock, the tears still flowing.

"I heard the commotion a few minutes ago," I said, gently this time. "What's going on? Are you all right?"

She breathed in a shaky breath. "No. I'm not all right." She grabbed the bowl of pancake batter and the whisk next to her and started beating the mixture furiously. "I... they...." She stuttered, her chin quivering, and the twin geysers erupted again in fresh sobs.

I looked around, feeling awkwardly self-conscious by her emotional display, but for the first time since arriving, no one else was in the kitchen or living room. We were alone. "Do you need me to get Walker? I could call—"

"No!" Ronnie shouted.

She reached out as if to stop me, and then realizing her outburst, she covered her mouth again with her hand. But at least she had stopped crying. She turned her back to me, her spine ramrod straight, and poured little blobs of batter onto the steaming griddle.

"I hope you're hungry. You're the only person in this house who hasn't tried my banana nut pancakes, and you can't avoid it this time. You're the only one here to eat them."

I raised my eyebrows at *her* avoidance. "Why don't you want me calling Walker?"

"Ian doesn't like being interrupted during an investigation. Besides, I wouldn't want him seeing me like this."

"I'm sure he'd want to know why you're this upset, investigation or not."

Ronnie looked away. "He knows why I'm upset. It's fine. I'm fine. I just needed to let it out."

I shook my head, wondering why Ronnie had suddenly changed her tune. "No."

She met my eyes. "What?"

"Something horrible happened, and Walker left you here alone to deal with it. That's not fine."

"He had to," she defended. She waved a hand at me, dismissing Walker as she scrutinized the hole-pocked pancakes. "Ian didn't want to leave, but he was needed at the scene."

I narrowed my eyes on her. "What scene? I thought you said he went to work on the investigation?"

Ronnie snapped her mouth shut. "He did," she gritted from between clenched teeth.

"No, you just said he left for a scene. A new crime scene? Another murder?" I let that sink in before I whipped out my cannon. "I saw him ride through the trail to your parents' house."

She wiped the tears from her cheeks and looked away to flip the pancakes. "You're twisting my words."

"I'm not twisting anything. I'm just telling you what I saw."

"It's personal." Ronnie pursed her lips. "Do you take syrup with your pancakes?"

"Will you stop cooking for one second and focus on this conversation?" I snapped. "What does it matter if I take syrup with anything? There's a crime scene at your parents' house."

Ronnie met my gaze. "Do you take syrup with your pancakes or not?"

I stared at her, taken aback by her tone. She was not budging until I made a decision on the syrup.

I sighed. "Yes, I take syrup."

She turned, snatched the syrup from the shelf, and pounded it onto the counter in front of me.

"Why did Walker leave you while you were so upset?" I pushed.

"Ian warned me that you might press me for information. I don't have to answer your questions if I don't want to."

"I'm not asking you questions as a reporter. I'm asking you questions as Walker's friend. I thought you two were close, like brother and sister?"

Her face tightened into a knot. "We are."

"Then why did he leave? Doesn't he care that you were so upset?"

"Ian left because he had to, not because he wanted to," Ronnie snapped.

"What was so urgent that he had to leave before taking the time to comfort you?"

"He didn't know I needed comforting!" she shouted. "I don't let him see how much it kills me when he leaves!"

"What was so important that he left?" I repeated.

"I don't know the details of his investigation. I don't like being involved."

"No, you like to hide behind the safety of these four walls and let everyone else risk their lives for your safety."

Ronnie snapped her eyes to meet mine. "You don't know anything about me."

"I know you haven't left this house after dark since you were a little girl. I know that you let Walker leave every night to fight your battles alone, and that he hasn't had someone to watch his back in years." I waited a moment to let that sink in before I hooked her. "Until me."

"I'm glad he has a friend in you. He needs backup," Ronnie said magnanimously, but her lips trembled while she said it.

"I don't think that's altogether true. You want someone to have his back, so you tolerate me. But you wish that backup could be you."

Ronnie clenched her teeth, staring daggers at me.

I pushed harder. "I think you wish you had the courage to leave this house, to be at his side when he needs you most, but you don't."

Tears pooled in her eyes. I could tell she was fighting to keep them, but eventually she blinked, and those abnormally large drops streamed down her cheeks.

"It's daylight, though. It's safe to leave and be his backup, so why aren't you there beside him, helping him now?"

She crossed her arms, but instead of a power stance, it looked like she was holding herself together.

"He doesn't want your help, does he?" I pushed as hard as I could, pressing all her buttons. I knew that my questions were cruel, but I needed to confirm if there was another murder scene and where. I needed to know why the hell he'd left without me. "He doesn't trust you."

"Fuck you," she whispered. "I could have gone with him if I wanted to!"

"Are you afraid to leave, even during the day?" I scoffed. "You're worse off than I thought, and I didn't think your agoraphobia could be much worse."

"My fears are not unfounded!"

"But they *have* consumed your life, haven't they?"

"He left you out of the investigation, too! He left you behind just like he left me!"

"Where did the murderer attack this time?" I asked softly. "It was close to home, wasn't it? That's why you're so upset."

Ronnie's eyes welled, and like a burst damn, she broke. "It was my home. They were killed in *my* home!"

"Who are 'they'?" I asked, sickened by the thought of more victims. "Who was killed?"

"Ian warned them against leaving the house after dark! Logan sat them down and forbade them from playing in my parents' house. I told them that the woods was off limits," Ronnie said between sobs. "I promised Logan I'd watch them more closely while he was at work."

"Who was killed, Ronnie?" I asked softly. I suspected I already knew the answer, but I needed her to say it. It wasn't real unless she said it.

"Logan's youngest sons," Ronnie whispered. "William and Douglas are dead."

She blinked in a sudden flurry, the smell of burned batter startling her from her grief. "Shit, I'm burning the pancakes!" She scooped them off the griddle and onto a plate, but only the first was burned. The rest were golden brown, fluffy, and perfect.

I looked away from the pancakes and took a deep breath, letting her words settle in a heavy lump at the bottom of my gut. I remembered Walker and Logan lecturing the boys yesterday. They must have been the ones to smear blood across the entrance of her house. They thought they'd made her house into a fallout shelter. They probably thought they'd been safe.

I felt sick. "What about Colin?"

Ronnie sniffed. "What about him?"

"You said William and Douglas were killed, but Colin was playing at your house with William and Douglas, wasn't he?"

Ronnie nodded.

"So where was Colin?"

She shook her head. "I don't know. The police didn't mention him. They'd only identified William and Douglas."

Identified, she said. I swallowed, remembering the other scenes. I didn't want to imagine William and Douglas in the same state as the other victims, but I didn't have to imagine. I was about to find out.

"Where's Keagan?" I asked.

"At school. Logan wanted to identify the bodies, to know for sure that they—" Ronnie's voice trembled. "To know for sure before he pulled Keagan out of school."

"We need to find Colin. He might be our only surviving witness."

"How are we going to find Colin? We don't know where he is."

"We don't, but Keagan might." I strode passed Ronnie toward the front door. "Come on."

"Where are you going?"

"We're going to talk to Keagan, and then we're going to your parents' house."

"We?" Ronnie squeaked.

"Yes, we. I can't pull Keagan from school, but as his babysitter, you can."

"I most certainly cannot!"

"Do you want to help find Colin?"

"Well, yes, but Ian said I should stay here. He said—"

"It's daylight, and I'm going to need backup," I interrupted, thinking, *Screw Walker.* "Do you want to help catch the monster who killed Douglas and William? Do you want to help stop the monster from killing again? It could be you or Keagan or *Ian* next on this psycho's hit list." I leaned forward. "Are you in or out?"

Ronnie met my eyes. "I'm in. But only if you eat these pancakes. You really don't eat enough."

I rolled my eyes. "That's quite a statement considering I've only ever seen you cook in this kitchen. When was the last time *you* ate?"

She blushed.

"We'll eat them together."

"And then we'll pick up Keagan?"

I nodded. "And find Colin."

"All right then." Ronnie handed me a fork, slathered butter on the plate, and drizzled long pools of syrup over the pancakes, and I discovered what all the fuss was about in Ronnie's kitchen every morning.

Her banana nut pancakes were to die for.

* * * *

"What the hell are you doing here?" Walker whispered. He didn't want to draw the attention of the cops at the scene, but by the throbbing vein in his forehead and the clenching tightness of his jaw, I knew that if he could, he would have shouted.

Keagan and Ronnie were waiting in Walker's pick-up around the bend in the road, so Walker could see them, but for the moment, the officers processing the scene hadn't noticed their presence. If I were still in the city, I'd have skirted the perimeter until Greta, Harroway, or someone else from the department recognized me and let me through. But I wasn't in the city. Walker was my only connection, so I had to play nice since Ronnie and I hadn't exactly played by the rules.

Ronnie had pulled Keagan from school, and I'd grilled him about Colin. We'd found the information we needed, but Keagan was too smart not to put the pieces together. We weren't grilling him to find Colin because Colin was missing. We were grilling him to find Colin because he was the only one of his brothers we hadn't found. Ronnie and I had known better than to bring Keagan along, but we couldn't just send him back to school knowing two of his brothers were dead and one was missing.

We were all here to find Colin and help solve this case, but by Walker's expression, he didn't want our help.

"I would have come alone if I could, but I couldn't talk to Keagan without Ronnie, and once I had both of them with me…" I shrugged. "I know the police won't like the spectators, but they won't leave the truck. I told them to sit tight."

Walker's expression turned skeptical. "When was the last time *you* listened when someone told you to sit tight?"

I waved away his concern. "That's me. We're talking about Ronnie. I practically needed the Jaws of Life to extract her from the house. She'll sit tight."

He shook his head. "Besides, this isn't about them. You can't be here, either."

I crossed my arms. "You need me here. I have important information pertinent to this investigation. I'm here to help."

"You're already too involved in this case. You're not a police officer or detective or medical examiner. You're a reporter, and you're not welcome anymore."

"I'm never welcome, but that's never stopped me before. It's never stopped you, either, before now." I narrowed my eyes on him. "You deliberately left the house without me. You deliberately left me out of this scene."

Walker nodded. "You're damn right I did."

"I thought we were partners. Partners don't leave each other in the dark."

"We're partners against the vampires, but in the real world, I'm involved professionally in this case and you're not. Let it go, and get out while you still can." Walker glanced over his shoulder at the scene behind him.

"I'm just as involved in this case as you are. You're the one who got me involved in the first place." I watched him carefully, trying to deduce why he was freezing me out from one scene to the next. "Is this about dinner last night?"

"Logan is going to kill you for talking to Keagan without him and for bringing him here," Walker said, avoiding my question. "And I've said it once but I'll say it again: you're not welcome at this scene. The police will bring you in for questioning if they find you here."

I shook my head. "Why would they go after me?"

"Get back in that pick-up and drive home before you make this scene more of a mess than it already is."

"I'm not going anywhere," I said, standing my ground. "I came here to help you find Colin, and that's exactly what I'm staying here to do."

Walker frowned. "Douglas and William were found at the scene. Not Colin."

"Exactly. So where's Colin?"

He opened his mouth and closed it. He glanced up at where Keagan was sitting in the truck behind me, and when he locked eyes with me again, they were resolute. "Colin wasn't at school."

"Nope."

"Shit." Walker scrubbed his palm down his face. "If he was here with Douglas and William last night, he might have been abducted."

I nodded. "Or he might have escaped and hidden somewhere in the woods. He might still be out there."

Walker placed a hand on my shoulder. "Thank you."

"We need to band in groups and fan out. If we plan to find him before sunset, we need to comb every inch of—"

"We as in the police. Not you. We'll take care of it." He turned me by the shoulder and nudged me away. "You need to get in that truck and drive back to my house. Now."

I dug my heels in the dirt and stared at him. "Excuse me? I just turned the tables on this case. This was my tip, and I'm helping you find him."

"I appreciate the tip, and yes, it significantly helps this case, but that doesn't change the fact that you're not welcome here." He crossed his arms. "Go back to my house and stay there. I'm not telling you again."

I stared at Walker, at his unflinching, unmovable expression, and I felt something inside me turn sour. "The fact that Colin didn't go to school today wasn't the only tip Keagan gave me."

Walker raised his eyebrows. "There's more?"

"Keagan confirmed that his brothers were making Ronnie's old house into their own fallout shelter to play in. They were using human blood to ward off vampires and hiding there at night, like a club house."

I watched his expression, but Walker didn't so much as blink.

"But you already knew that the moment you recognized the blood smear around the perimeter of Ronnie's house," I whispered. "Didn't you?"

It took a moment, but eventually, he nodded.

"Why didn't you tell me? When you saw the blood smear, why did you let me question its existence when you knew exactly why it was there?"

His expression hardened, but otherwise, he didn't say anything.

"Jesus, Walker, you told me that you needed to take samples," I said, laughing at how genuine he'd seemed and how stupid I'd been to trust him so completely. I thought of our moment together afterward, of how thoroughly and passionately he'd kissed me after he'd just as thoroughly lied to me, and I embraced my rage, so much sweeter than the bite of his betrayal.

"Why didn't you tell me about fallout shelters?" I shouted, and I didn't care. "All this time there were steps I could've taken to fortify my apartment, and you kept them to yourself. I could have found a new apartment. I could have warded myself against Dominic's intrusion." I shook my head in wonder at his deception. "I could have felt safe."

"Stop shouting," Walker hissed at me. He turned to see if we were attracting any attention from the surrounding officers, but they were preoccupied with the murder scene. "Feeling safe is an illusion. You're never safe. Ever. But you're safest here. There is no better fallout shelter than the one I built. Anything you'd have attempted in your city apartment would have paled in comparison."

"Ah ha!" I said, pointing my finger at him. "And there's the boiled truth. Once again, you would rather give me the help you think I need rather than the help I want. You deliberately withheld information from me, so I'd need you to feel safe, and that's bullshit."

"Dominic is to blame for you not feeling safe in your apartment, not me," Walker said. "But you can feel safe *here*, far away from Dominic."

The finger I pointed at him trembled, I was so angry. "New York City is my home, and I'm not leaving. I wanted to feel safe in my home, but you deliberately withheld information I could have used to feel safe, so I'd think I needed *you*," I said slowly and succinctly, so he'd understand.

"You could never achieve the fallout shelter I've built by smearing blood around the perimeter of your apartment. My father built that house, and over the years, he modified it, and over my lifetime, I've fortified it. If I told you how to fortify your apartment, you would only achieve a false sense of security. I'm offering you a real one."

I breathed deep and even, and let the clean, fresh air of the woods and the heat of the sunshine soaking my skin bathe me. That was the only way I could stand in front of him and still see him, and not just see a wash of red.

When I did speak, I made my voice quiet and calm, trying to keep the crazy contained. "You should have told me how to protect myself anyway, so when I came here, I could make my own decision whether to return to the city and my own shelter or to stay here, protected by yours. Instead, you tried to make that decision for me."

Walker snorted. "It wasn't much of a decision, so much as common sense."

I did see red then. I shoved him back with every ounce of anger and frustration and strength inside me. "Partners help each other survive! They don't put each other in danger to remind themselves that they're needed."

Walker stumbled back a step. By the clench and unclench of his jaw, however, I could tell that Walker was losing his patience as well. He glanced at the officers behind him and a few were watching us now.

I took a deep breath to pull myself together.

Walker turned to face me. "We'll finish this conversation later. In *private*."

"You've kept everything a secret," I whispered. "From the day I arrived, you've lied about Ronnie living with you, night bloods living with you, the fallout shelter, and about having seizures. How can I trust you? What else aren't you telling me?"

Walker winced and rubbed his forehead rhythmically.

I stepped closer, concerned. "Are you all right?"

He glared at me and his expression was so intense that I stopped mid-step. "I've been a night blood my entire life. I can't possibly teach you everything I've learned in a lifetime in a few days, so I brought you here, not only for me but also for you to interact with other night bloods. To talk to them and learn from their experiences. You're bound to learn things from them that I haven't taught you, but it's not because I've 'deliberately withheld information' from you.

"I let you ask me any questions you wanted, any at all, and in all that time, did you ever ask me how to revoke Dominic's invitation to your house? Did you ever ask me how to better fortify your apartment?"

I opened my mouth and closed it, feeling uncertainty like a deer caught in the headlights, torn between flight and immobility. "No," I said in a small voice, "Dominic said that the invitation couldn't be revoked."

"And that's your problem right there. Listening to a vampire," Walker said coldly. He crossed his arms and stared at me. "Maybe instead of blindly believing Dominic, you should have just *asked* me."

"I asked you about the blood smears around the perimeter of Ronnie's old house, and your response was that you needed to take blood samples," I said sharply. "You didn't tell me the truth when I asked you," I pointed out.

Walker groaned, sounding as exhausted as he looked. "What do you want from me, Cassidy? To tell you I'm sorry? Because I'm not. If I had the chance to do it over, I'd do it all the same. You're safest here with me, not in some half-ass, fortified city apartment. A few blood smears and some silverware isn't enough protection against Dominic and his coven. I've lost a lot of people because of that mistake, people who thought they could survive on their own. Now we've lost William and Douglas." Walker leaned in close. "I'm not about to lose you, too. Not when I can protect you."

I swallowed. "I don't want you to tell me you're sorry. What's done is done. I want you to make it right. Let me help you find Colin."

Walker shook his head, his expression carefully masked.

"Keagan says that Colin left with his other brothers last night, like he does every night," I pushed. "If he was with them when they were attacked, he might have seen the murderer."

His mask slipped for a moment, and I saw something light his face that I hadn't seen in a while. "He might know what really happened."

"Exactly." I smiled. "I'm more than just a pretty face."

He rolled his eyes. "You know I know that."

"Then why did you leave me behind? Why didn't you bring me to this scene like you did the last two scenes?"

"I meant it when I said that you can't be here." He whispered, "They specifically told me not to bring you."

I frowned. "I know Officer Montgomery isn't my biggest fan, but I—"

"This doesn't have anything to do with Riley." Walker glanced at the scene behind him again.

I stood on my toes to see over his shoulder. "Who else could possibly have a grudge against me?"

Walker turned to face me again. "The FBI."

I blinked. "Come again?"

"There's a pattern forming. They left their case in the city to continue it here. It's officially a serial murder investigation, Cassidy."

"What the hell does that have to do with me?"

"Everything," Walker swiped his hand down his face again, stress like a grease he couldn't seem to wipe off. "They know you were lead reporter for your paper on this investigation back in the city."

"Yeah, me and a dozen other lead reporters from a dozen other papers. What does that prove? It's not as if this is the same case."

"It *is* the same case, and so far, you're the only connection between the two."

"Me?" I asked, incredulous.

Walker nodded, his expression grim.

"I didn't follow the murders here," I said, exasperated. "I didn't even know this was the same case! I came here for you and to write my crime fluctuation piece for Carter."

"Of course *I* know that, but I can see how it looks to the FBI. To them, it doesn't look good, Cassidy."

"If the only thing they have on me is circumstantial, they don't have anything."

"Your fingerprints and blood are at this scene."

I blinked. "I was in Ronnie's house yesterday with *you*," I reminded him, "And they can't possibly know that yet. They haven't finished processing the scene, let alone analyzing fingerprints and blood samples at the lab."

"But they'll find it, and when they do, the further away you are from this case the better. You need to create some distance to protect yourself."

"Helping to solve this case can only work in my favor. I'm staying."

Walker shook his head. "They found your silver nitrate spray on Buck McFerson's driveway."

I raised my eyebrows. "*My* silver nitrate spray?"

He smirked a little sheepishly. "They found my spray, the one I gave *you*, and it has your prints all over it. They told me this morning when I got the call about William and Douglas."

I shook my head, feeling like a bobblehead. I was a suspect in a serial murder investigation. Unbelievable. "I'm not running from this. I'm innocent."

"Leaving isn't running. It's smart. It's called survival." Walker's face darkened with frustration. "Do you want us to find Colin?"

"Of course," I said. "That's why I'm here."

"Every moment I spend arguing with you is a moment that I could be tracking Colin."

"Then stop arguing and let me help."

Walker bared his teeth on a grimace. "You are not—"

"Is everything all right over there, Walker?"

Walker turned at the voice. An officer had ducked under the police tape and was striding toward us from the scene. As he came closer, I realized he wasn't an officer. He was an agent.

Walker leaned down to whisper in my ear. "Get out of here, and stay with Ronnie while I'm gone. I might not be home tonight, and she can't protect the house by herself." We locked eyes. "Go."

I peeked over his shoulder at the agent behind him. He reminded me a little of Officer Harroway: block-jawed and stony-faced. He was a burly man's man, but when Officer Harroway opened his mouth, the only thing that man took seriously was how deeply he could crawl under my skin. This agent wore a Kevlar vest, like Walker sometimes wore on a mission, but unlike Walker, "F.B.I." was emblazoned on his chest in white block letters. I didn't want to find out what that man had to say when he opened his mouth any more than I did when Harroway opened his. Despite my misgivings about running while innocent, I listened to Walker, turned on my heel, and left.

Not two minutes later, Ronnie, Keagan, and I drove into a road block. Three police cars and one SUV formed a barrier across the dirt road.

"I guess your conversation with Ian was worse than you thought," Ronnie commented.

"Are they going to interrogate me about my brothers?" Keagan asked. His voice was monotone and had been ever since we'd pulled him from class.

Ronnie shook her head. "They're probably here for me. The scene's at my house, after all."

"No, they're here for me," I admitted.

Ronnie looked askance at me. "You? What do they want with you?"

"The FBI think I'm involved in the murders."

"The FBI?"

"Then why the hell didn't you drive faster?" Keagan asked, his monotone voice somehow still expressing his annoyance.

"Language," Ronnie admonished.

I rolled my eyes. Of all the times to admonish. "Speeding away would only look guilty." I turned to Ronnie. "Drive straight home with Keagan.

If Walker's not home by six o'clock, lock yourself and Keagan in the fallout shelter."

"But you'll be home before sundown, right?"

I turned to Keagan. "Take care of each other and don't be a hero. Be safe. Got it?"

Keagan nodded. "Got it."

Someone pounded on the passenger-side door and all three of us jumped. Ronnie squeaked.

The block-jawed agent who reminded me of Officer Harroway was standing outside Ronnie's passenger side window. She lowered the window and blinked at him.

I leaned forward to see him around Ronnie. "Can we help you, sir?"

The man ignored me. "Veronica Anne Carmichael?"

Ronnie nodded. "Yes?"

"I'm going to need you to come with me."

Ronnie looked at me and then back at the man. "Me?"

"There must be some mistake," I said. "I—"

He locked eyes on me. "Cassidy Lee DiRocco?"

"Yes. But I don't think you need—"

"And Logan Keagan McDunnell?"

Keagan raised his hand. "Present."

"I'm going to need all three of you to come with me."

Ronnie looked at me and raised her eyebrows.

I sighed. It wasn't the first time I was wrong, and by the steely look in the block-jawed agent's eyes, I wasn't taking any bets that it would be the last.

Chapter 9

Officer Riley Montgomery was a methodical man. After sitting across from him for the last four hours in the Erin Police Department's interrogation room—alternately answering a barrage of pointed questions, correcting his allegations about my involvement in the murders, and listening to him ramble about my future incarceration—I learned three undisputable truths: Officer Montgomery was in love with Alba Dunbar and had been likely since birth, he unquestionably believed that I was in some fashion directly involved with the murders, and he was determined to expose me to solve this case. Maybe he thought exposing me would endear him to Alba, and once he solved the case and gave her a sense of retribution for her parents' deaths, she'd ride off with him into the sunset. But he didn't know what prowled the night after sunset. I did, and I was not going to sit through another hour of interrogation, answering the same questions and fending off the same allegations, until dark.

Officer Montgomery was in the middle of a rant, being deliberately raunchy while describing the many uses inmates have for cleaning supplies—brooms and mop handles in particular—when I interrupted him.

"I don't need to listen to this bullshit. Up until this moment I've been accommodating and cooperative for you, your department, and this case. I came here willingly. I've answered your questions to the best of my abilities, and I've provided you with information that will hopefully help you find Colin and further this case. I've always maintained good relationships with the police, but unless you plan to charge me here and now, I'm done."

The door suddenly opened, and the block-jawed FBI agent reminiscent of Officer Harroway walked into the interrogation room. He looked at Officer Montgomery and jerked his head toward the door, dismissing him.

Officer Montgomery flushed a deep red. "She might be done here, but I'm not. I—"

"Cassidy DiRocco is not under arrest, so she can leave whenever she wants. Before she leaves, however, I'd like a quick word with her." He looked at me. "If you don't mind."

I leaned back in my chair and crossed my arms. "I was wondering if you'd make an appearance. Does the FBI always allow local law enforcement to interrogate their suspects?" I asked congenially.

Something flashed in the agent's aquamarine eyes. Humor, I think, but then it passed and his expression never faltered. "Never. You're not a suspect."

"She is the only—"

"Out," the agent said. His didn't shout, but his voice reverberated with power and command, like Dominic's voice could carry physical weight in his words, except Dominic's words were powerful from a blood-bond formed with his coven. The weight in the FBI agent's words were simply from experience and confidence. Whatever the reason behind the power, the agent's words were just as effective as Dominic's. Officer Montgomery closed his mouth and walked out.

I turned my attention to the man now sitting across from me. The FBI agent was handsome, devastatingly handsome with his clean-shaven, chiseled jaw, bright aquamarine eyes, and sharp features. Like Officer Harroway, he had that burliness that reminded me of ham-fisted lumberjacks, and nothing was sexier than a lumberjack in uniform. Harroway always ruined the illusion the moment he opened his mouth and cracked a joke at my expense. From the looks of him, however, this man hadn't cracked a joke in years.

I smiled. "Cassidy DiRocco," I said, and I held out my hand, "But you already knew that."

The agent took my hand in a brief, firm grip and shook. "I'm Harold Rowens, an Agent of the Federal Bureau of Investigation."

Maybe I'd been in the same room without fresh air for too long, or maybe Officer Montgomery had rattled me more than I'd ever admit, but I couldn't help it. What were the chances that the man's name who resembled Officer Harroway was Harold Rowens? Even their names were similar. I giggled.

Rowens cocked his head. "Is something about this situation amusing, Ms. DiRocco?"

I turned my laugh into a cough and sobered. "Not at all. You remind me of a friend I have in the NYPD. Officer Harroway." I shook my head. "In physical appearance and name alone, I assure you," I added in case he was somehow familiar with Harroway. I wouldn't want to insult the man.

"Officer Harroway." Rowens opened one of the files he'd brought with him and rustled through a few papers. "You took a bullet for him while on a stakeout with him and Officer Wahl for the Mars Killington drug trafficking case five years ago."

"You've done your homework. But it's Detective Wahl now."

Rowens nodded. "Yes, I see that. I also see that you quote her in the majority of your articles pertaining to drug trafficking, gang related crime, and murders."

"Those are the nature of her investigations, and considering she's the lead detective of those investigations, you're damn right I quote her," I said.

"No one else quotes her."

I raised my eyebrows. "Is that a question?"

"Your shared history encourages Detective Wahl to give you statements that she doesn't feel inclined to give other reporters, is that right?"

"I don't know, and I can't speak for her. That's something you'll have to discuss with Detective Wahl yourself."

"I have." Rowens put down the papers. "But she declined to answer. Do you want to know what I think, Ms. DiRocco?"

"I've got a feeling you're about to tell me whether I want to know or not."

"I think that your shared history would encourage Detective Wahl to do a lot more than give you exclusive statements for your articles. I think she knows that *you* know more about Lydia Bowser, John and Priscilla Dunbar, William and Douglas McDunnell, and all the other similar murders in the city than you've admitted to knowing."

"I have nothing to do with those murders. I went through each alibi with Officer Montgomery for the better part of three hours. Tell me I didn't stay here for reruns." I stared at him. Hard. "If that's the case, like I said, I'm done here."

"Your alibis check out, and like *I* said, you're not a suspect. But that doesn't mean that you don't have more information about this case than you're letting on."

"I did have information about this case, and hopefully, your team is using that information as we speak to find Colin."

"I'm not denying that you've been helpful and cooperative, but you haven't divulged everything you know. When I find out what you know, it could go one of two ways: I find out now, in which case you continue to help this investigation, or I found out later, in which case you and Detective Greta Wahl will be charged with obstruction of justice."

"That's ridiculous," I spat. "I'm not obstructing anything! You've said so yourself that I've helped further this investigation!"

"I think you're helping to hide what you *really* know. I think Detective Wahl knows that you know something big, but she wouldn't point the finger at you even if every finger was pointed at her. When I take you down, she's going down, too."

"Greta and I are trying to solve this case, just like you. We're on the same side, and the more time you waste on us, the less time you have pursuing real leads."

Rowens leaned back in his chair and crossed his arms. "It's up to you. When will you tell me what you know: now or later?"

Vampires are responsible for these murders, I thought. I didn't know that for sure, but even if I did, he wouldn't believe me. What else could be responsible for ripping out human hearts? "There's nothing to tell. I don't know anything about this case."

"That's impossible."

I rolled my eyes. He hadn't even spotted the tip of the iceberg of what was and wasn't possible. "Why is my ignorance about this case impossible?"

"Because you are the linking factor in every scene here in Erin, and I have no doubt that when we deepen this investigation, you will be the linking factor in every scene in New York City."

I blinked. "What?"

He tossed a manila folder across the table at me. "Your prints on a can of spray at Lydia Bowser's murder." He tossed another manila folder across the table. "Several locks of your hair at the Dunbar murder." He tossed a third folder, and they landed in a fan of damning evidence in front of me. "And your blood at the McDunnell murder."

I shook my head, stunned. They'd processed the evidence faster than I'd expected in a small town. I suppose the FBI had ways of expediting the process. I tapped my pointer finger on the first folder. "This doesn't prove anything except that I was present at these specific places at one time before the murders. Walker and the medical examiner were present at the Bowser scene, too. That doesn't mean that they committed these murders, and it doesn't mean that I did, either."

"No, it doesn't, and I don't think that you did. But I *do* think that you know more than you're admitting. The victims range in age, gender, race, and social standing. Nothing about them or the locations where they were murdered is a common thread tying this case together," Rowens stared at me this time. Hard, like I'd stared at him. "Except you."

"You have nothing on this case, and you're grasping at straws to solve it." I stood. "This conversation is over."

"I'm going to find out how you fit into this puzzle, and when I do, Greta won't be there to cushion the fall. She'll be falling right beside you."

"Threats don't scare me when there's nothing to support them," I said, but my hand was cold and shaking when I grasped the door's handle. "Goodbye, Agent Rowens."

"Just remember, Ms. DiRocco. You still have a chance to come clean if you talk now. Talk later, and you'll have a bed of your own making to keep you warm at night, and as Officer Montgomery so eloquently described, you won't be the only one lying in it."

I slammed the door on my way out.

* * * *

Ronnie, Keagan, and I turned into Walker's driveway just as the sun started its descent. We were cutting it closer than I liked, considering that Bex didn't need the full cover of night to leave her coven, but my final conversation with Agent Rowens had rattled me more in ten minutes than the entire four hours I'd been harassed by Officer Montgomery.

Rowens didn't mince words and the few he'd uttered rung with a resonating certainty. Unless the real murderer or a real lead was found soon, Greta and I would be the scapegoats for this case. Just as Dominic had predicted, her loyalty to me had put her in danger, albiet not the danger I had anticipated.

I would have answered Agent Rowens' questions to protect us if I could, but Dominic and Bex wouldn't allow him or anyone he told to live with the knowledge of their existence. To protect the people I knew and loved, I kept the truth to myself. If I wanted to survive in both worlds—bridged between the humans and vampires—I needed to find evidence of my own to prove my innocence without exposing the vampires. And I needed to find that evidence before the humans found more evidence connecting me to the murders.

I didn't believe in coincidences. The fact that the murders had followed me combined with the fact that each murder scene had my prints or DNA was a pattern I couldn't deny or ignore. Someone was framing me to protect the real murderer, and I only knew one person who might have the power and motivation to pull that off.

Bex was the one who had sliced a lock of my hair where the Dunbars had been killed only a few hours later. She'd tasted my blood and could probably track my scent to Ronnie's abandoned childhood home, where I'd cut my knees. I don't know how she knew about the silver nitrate spray—maybe she had tracked my scent there, too—but I didn't care. If a member of her coven was responsible for these murders, I had no doubt that she'd cover the evidence to keep her coven's existence a secret. Just like Dominic, I'm sure she'd do anything to protect the anonymity of their existence, but make no mistake, she'd regret turning the evidence on me.

During our ride home from the police station, Ronnie had tried and failed to rouse conversation. Keagan and I had been somber and silent. I was brooding over my murderous thoughts concerning the case, and Keagan was likely grieving. Ronnie, unfortunately, could pull conversation from thin air despite the mood.

"I'm sure it was very difficult for you," Ronnie said to Keagan, her voice soft and consoling. It made me sick. "You were brave to talk to the police about your brothers. I know you already know this, but any and all information at this point will help them find Colin."

"I know," Keagan said.

"Did they ask you any questions that didn't involve your brothers?"

Keagan shrugged.

"If you want to talk about it, I—"

"I don't want to talk about it."

"I understand." Ronnie turned to me. "Did they—"

"I don't want to talk about it either," I cut her off.

Ronnie crossed her arm. "I didn't even finish my question. You don't know what I was going to ask."

"I don't care. I've answered enough questions. I'm not in the mood to answer yours, too."

Ronnie stared at me in silence.

Guilt diluted my anger enough for me to regret being rude. Snapping at Ronnie was like kicking a puppy for nipping your hand. It couldn't help that it was just trying to play. "Sorry."

"Do you think they'll come after me?" Ronnie asked in a small voice. "It's my house, after all."

I rolled my eyes. "You haven't left Walker's house after dark in years. Your alibi is solid. You don't have anything to worry about."

Ronnie bit her lip. "Did they—"

"I said I don't want to talk about it."

Ronnie stared at me in silence again, but that time, I let her stew.

By the time I parked in Walker's driveway and killed the engine, Logan was already out of the house and striding toward us. I squeezed the steering wheel nervously. Normally, I'd say he'd need to get in line with all the other people I'd pissed off lately, but by the pace of his stride, he was cutting ahead of the crowd.

He didn't even wait for me to get out of the truck. He yanked the driver's side door open and dragged me from the seat by my waist.

"Dad! Cassidy was just trying to help!" Keagan shouted. I heard his feet hit the gravel as he jumped out of the truck.

"I know," Logan rasped. His voice was thick and wet, and I realized belatedly that he was crying. He buried his face in my shoulder as his own broad shoulders shook, and his grip around my waist tightened. My feet still hadn't touched ground as he held me in his arms, and like my feet, my mind was failing to find its purchase, trying to decide if Logan was trying to squeeze the life from me or hug me.

He was panting something between the silent sobs that racked his big body, and that's when I finally knew he was hugging me. I could just decipher the rough mantra of him repeating over and over again, "Thank you. Thank you. Thank you."

I tried to pull back to see his face, but he only buried his face deeper into the curve of my neck. His tears had soaked my shirt.

Keagan was suddenly next to us. I felt one of Logan's arms leave me to encircle his son, but my perch against Logan's chest didn't slip, even with only one of his arms holding me.

"I'm sorry for pulling Keagan out of school," I wheezed through the pressure around my lungs. "I was trying to help. To confirm if Colin had left with William and Douglas last night. I thought maybe we could still find Colin."

"You thought right," Logan said.

I stiffened in his arm. "They found Colin?"

Logan shook his head. "They found his hat."

My hopes deflated. "I'm so sorry."

"He's still out there. They haven't found his—" Logan couldn't finish his sentence, but I knew what he was about to say.

They haven't found his body.

"He's still out there," I repeated his words back to him, the only words I had, which were both a comfort and a curse. They hadn't found his body, but the sun was setting. Unless they found him soon, he'd still be out there after dark with the vampires and the same murderer that had killed his brothers.

Logan nodded. He set me on my feet. The splintering protest of my hip stabbed down my leg as it bore weight. I gritted my teeth against the pain and concentrated on the plan I'd developed on the drive back from the police station.

"I need to ask you for a favor, Logan."

He raised his eyebrows. "What is it?"

"I need you to take Keagan and Ronnie to Walker's fallout shelter below the house and protect them tonight."

Logan shook his head. "I can't stay there tonight. I need to join the search. I need to help find Colin."

"I'm coming with you," Keagan interjected.

"You're staying here," Logan said, his tone low and pained and brooking no argument.

"I can't stay here tonight, either. I need to help!"

"I can't lose all my sons in one night!" Logan bellowed. "You are to stay here and stay safe until sunrise!"

Keagan snapped his lips shut, the worry and grief etching his face deeper than his years. I glanced at Logan, but I couldn't look at him without seeing the indelible impression of his sons' features in his own face.

I leaned forward and lowered my voice. "You're right that Keagan should stay here, but he needs you to stay here, too."

"Colin needs me, and right now, he's the one in danger. I need *you* to stay here with Keagan and Ronnie." This time he leaned forward, his whisper intense and urgent. "Keagan can't protect himself and Ronnie. They need you. Please."

I looked down at my own petite frame and laughed. "I'd just be another liability, worse than Ronnie."

"I can hear you," Ronnie said from behind Logan, her hands on her hips.

"Don't play dumb." Logan ignored Ronnie, his expression like stone. "I've heard of your abilities. You can control vampires like they can control us. You can entrance their minds."

I crossed my arms. "Walker told you about his time with me in the city."

He nodded. "What you lack physically you make up in mental strength. He asked you to stay here tonight to protect Ronnie and Keagan, and I'm asking you to do the same."

"I can't. I have business to take care of tonight." I pursed my lips, deciding how much to divulge. "You know that vampires can twist evidence, right? Make people forget they were attacked. Make people think they saw only shadows when really they saw vampires."

"Of course. They'd do anything to hide their existence from humans."

"The evidence they're twisting is pointing at me, and I need to fix it before I'm blamed for these murders."

"You're being blamed for these murders?"

"Not yet, but I need to keep it that way."

Logan glanced alternately at the woods and back at me. "I can't sit here and do nothing while Colin's out there. I'll go crazy."

"I can't risk another murder tonight, linking me to this case. I'll be arrested."

"We don't need either of you," Keagan said tightly. "If we stay in the fallout shelter all night, we'll be fine. That's what the basement is designed for, isn't it? The entire house could collapse on top of us, but the fallout shelter would keep us safe."

Logan pursed his lip, his gaze unwavering. "How long will you be?"

"How long will it take to find Colin?" I countered.

He looked taken aback. "As long as it takes."

I nodded. "Exactly."

Logan blew out a long, deep breath and then faced Keagan squarely. "You are to lock yourself in the fallout shelter and not leave until dawn. Agreed?"

Keagan nodded.

I turned to Ronnie. "I'll be back as soon as I can."

"You shouldn't leave after dark alone," she whispered.

I raised my eyebrows. "Are you going to come with me?"

She balled her hands into fists. "You don't know me. You don't understand."

"I know enough to know that you're going to watch me leave, like you've watched Walker leave a hundred times, to face Bex alone." I whispered. "You can't hide inside your entire life, Ronnie. You have to fight for it."

"Like you're letting me fight for mine?" Keagan cut in.

Logan glared hotly at me before answering. "That's different," he told Keagan. "I can't focus on finding Colin if I'm worried about you."

Keagan locked eyes with his father for a long moment. "You're going to find Colin."

"You're damn right I am."

Keagan's face turned to stone, just like his father's. "What if he's already dead, like William and Douglas?"

Logan swallowed. His lips trembled this time when he spoke, but his voice was steady. "I'm going to find him."

Keagan nodded, understanding all too well what his father meant. Dead or alive, Logan planned on finding his son. Tonight would be a long night for Logan and the officers as they combed the woods, searching and praying to find Colin, and an even longer night for Keagan and Ronnie as they bunkered here at the house, waiting and praying for everyone's safe return. I thought of my plans for the night and cringed inwardly.

Tonight would be a long night for everyone.

Chapter 10

I silvered up on jewelry, donned my leather coat despite the mild weather, and took the liberty of borrowing Walker's truck again. Public transportation wasn't an option here in the woods. God, I missed the city. Walker's truck was my only option; without streetlights, the trees, insects, and dense solitude—that horrible, unshakable itch that you were not alone yet completely on your own—were worse than street bums, muggers, and traffic. I wasn't repeating that experience, so until taxis were once again a viable option or until Walker was present to stop me, his truck was mine to borrow.

Navigating the woods was easier this time since full dark hadn't descended. Maybe I could finish my business with Bex and join Ronnie and Keagan in the fallout shelter without Walker being the wiser, but I doubted it. If my plan worked, I'd find the murderer and maybe Colin, too, so Walker would know I'd confronted Bex on my own.

If my plan failed, however, Walker and Logan might be planning a search party for me next.

I parked the truck in the woods where we'd parked Walker's motorcycle last night for dinner with Bex and finished the trek to her coven on foot. Even with the sun's rays penetrating between the trees, the coven's entrance was well hidden. Shadows from the ledge's rocky overhang blended with moss and stone, covering the cave's mouth. Someone unfamiliar with the area would likely pass and allow the cave to exist unnoticed, but I knew where to look. I recognized the chafed bark where Walker had secured the rappel rigging. I remembered the jut of the overhang and the tilted angle of the cave's mouth. The stones that had given way when Rene had yanked me into the cave exposed a patch of dirt in an otherwise stone-lined entrance, so I recognized the coven despite its seclusion.

A green-tinted, reflective light blinked at me from beneath the shadows of the stone overhang. Just one light blinked instead of two, but I didn't need the reminder of her injury to recognize who was lying in wait, staring at me from the far side of the cave's opening.

Bex was the only vampire I knew who could tolerate the shadows of darkness before the sun had fully set.

I stopped in front of her, the cave between us. "Hello, Bex."

"Cassidy." Her voice purred from the darkness, but I could only see the solitary green tint of her reflective eye. Otherwise, her body was completely shrouded in shadow. "I hadn't expected the pleasure of your company so soon after your last visit."

"I hadn't expected to visit so soon, either." I fingered the can of silver nitrate in my pocket, triple checking that the trigger was unlocked and ready to spray. "To be honest, I would've preferred that last night be both my first and last visit to your coven."

"It pains me to hear you say such things," Bex said, the blatant sarcasm in her voice oddly comforting. "We are still allies, are we not?" she asked.

I narrowed my eyes on that one reflective orb in the darkness. I couldn't discern her from the shadows. I couldn't see her expression or read her posture, and her voice revealed nothing. Did she still fear losing Dominic as an ally, or was she searching for a reason to break the truce?

I decided to err on the side of caution. "Dominic desires you as an ally. He sent me here to mend the ties between you. Since you are his ally, you are my ally."

"Ally by default," Bex laughed, and the melodic loveliness of her voice was like the brush of a feather against the inside of my skull. It made my skin tingle and raised goose bumps along my nape. "I like that."

"I'd prefer to think of it as ally by *loyalty*, but to each her own."

I caught a movement in the shadows that might have been her head nodding. "I regret how we left things between us after such a pleasant dinner."

Pleasant dinner, I thought dismally. I'd hate to discover what she considered unpleasant. Although, truth be told, before Walker had refused her blood, before she'd strangled me, and before he'd shot her in the eye, concussed his head, and seized, we all would have left physically well and relatively unscathed.

But that's not how dinner had ended.

"I regret how things ended, too." *And I won't forget,* I thought, but I kept that part to myself. "How's your eye?"

"That wasn't your fault. Walker was only protecting you. I won't hold my injury against y'all, I assure you."

How gracious of you, I thought, but I bit my lip and kept that to myself, too. My sarcasm would only get me into trouble, as usual, and my agenda only involved getting *out* of trouble.

I inclined my head, like Bex had done, but it didn't escape my notice that in addition to being "gracious," she'd avoided answering my question. Removing the silver spear from her eye probably hadn't gone well.

"How is your throat?" she asked. "I see it's still bruised."

I touched my throat instinctively. "I'll live."

"I apologize for attacking you. Let me know if there's anything I may do to right that wrong and prove to you that I'm the loyal ally Lysander expects of me."

I pursed my lips. This was too easy. She was speaking very formally and deliberately, like Dominic, and I wondered if her formality was for my benefit, like her skinny jeans and cowboy boots were for Walker. No one suspected an enemy in friend's clothing, but she didn't know that Dominic wasn't my friend.

"Actually, there is something you can do, and if you help me, I'd consider a clean slate between us," I said. I'd never consider a clean slate—I wasn't Dominic's loyal servant and she wasn't my ally, by default or otherwise—but she didn't need to know that.

"Anything for Lysander's loyal night blood," she said, her voice a low, rattling purr.

She knows, I thought, and then I banished the thought as deeply and behind as many silver fortified walls in my mind as possible. If she was anything like Dominic, and God knew she was likely stronger, she could read my thoughts if she tried. Unless I slipped, unless I thought the very thing I didn't want her to know, there was no way for her to know my deal with Dominic.

I took a deep, fortifying breath and gripped the silver nitrate spray a little tighter. "I need you to choose me over one of your own vampires in a gesture of loyalty."

"And how do you intend for me to do that?"

"Give up the vampire responsible for the murders of Lydia Bowser, Mr. and Mrs. Dunbar, and the McDunnell brothers, and make the humans think that the case is solved."

Bex laughed, but this time, the sound was grating. "How do you expect me to give up one of my own vampires to the humans without exposing our existence?"

"I've witnessed Dominic's skills firsthand when he wants to rearrange a murder, and I know you possess those same skills. You can kill the vampire as you see fit, arrange the scene so he looks human, and convince the officers in charge of this case that they found and killed him while he resisted arrest."

Bex smiled. I could just discern the whites of her teeth against the darkness of her lips. "Very clever. Every time our paths cross, I admire Lysander's taste."

I tensed. Her tone didn't match her complimentary words. "Thank you."

"There's one problem."

I raised my eyebrows. "And that is?"

"As I've told you repeatedly, I don't know who's responsible for the murders."

"Yes, so you've said, repeatedly, but saying something a second and third and fourth time doesn't make it any more believable than the first."

"I give you my word," Bex said solemnly. Her voice was so genuine and pressing, urging me to believe her, that I was stunned by her callous ability to lie.

Dominic certainly had a forked tongue, but when he wanted me to take him at his word, he swore by the sun. The sun was a final and certain death for him, like the passage of time was for me, and that was how we knew the other would keep their word.

I narrowed my eyes on Bex. "Swear to me that you don't know who is committing these murders. Swear by the sun."

"Where did you learn that phrase?" Bex asked. Her voice hitched on a strangely pitched note. If I didn't know better, I'd say she sounded frightened.

"Will you or will you not swear by the sun that you don't know the vampire responsible for the murders?"

Bex's voice tipped low and breathy. "You don't know what you're asking of me."

"I know exactly what I'm asking of you, but you won't swear because you can't. You know who's responsible for the murders, and you're twisting the evidence so the police focus on me and not your vampire," I accused.

"That's ridiculous," Bex scoffed. "If my vampires were responsible for these murders, I'd execute them and create a scene to pacify the humans, just like you've asked. It's how our existence has remained a secret all these years, by eliminating any and all threats to our coven, even if the threat is the coven itself."

"I know. That's what you *should* do, but it's not what you're doing this time."

Bex barked a laugh from the back of her throat. "I've executed members of my own coven to enforce the sanctity of our secret, and I'd do it again if I knew who was responsible for the murders. But I don't."

"Yes, you do," I insisted, "and you're using the murders to get rid of me without breaking your alliance with Dominic."

"As if *you're* more important than the protection of my coven." I caught the flash of Bex's smile again. "Why would I want to get rid of you?"

"Because in our short acquaintance, Walker is more in love with me than he will ever be with you."

Bex growled. The rattling hiss vibrated like an impact tremor; pebbles jumped and danced on the stone overhang. She stepped out of the darkness, and without the impenetrable pitch of the overhang, I could see her expression. It took every ounce of willpower and courage I could muster to hold my ground.

She hadn't bothered transforming into the irresistible country belle that she'd postured for Walker. She hadn't bothered transforming at all. Her ears were long and pointed, and her nose was flattened and flared to tips at each nostril. Her hands were sharp, long, skeletal-like talons. Her legs, which were once lean and perfect in skinny jeans and cowboy boots, were still lean, but the knees bent backward in those bat-like hind legs that made me queasy.

I swallowed. Worse than her transformed ears and nose and talons, even worse than her legs, was her eye. She only had one. The other eye, the one that Walker had speared with the silver watch hand, was just a bloody socket in the otherwise smooth perfection of her face.

She should have been able to heal the eyeball and placed it back in the socket after removing the silver broadhead—with a little blood and saliva, I'd witnessed Dominic heal devastating injuries—but whether she'd been unable or unwilling, she didn't have a left eyeball. The muscles twitched in the socket as her remaining eye shifted over my expression. I tried to keep the revulsion I felt from showing in my face, but I must have failed because Bex smiled.

"You're right," she said. "Ian Walker is incapable of loving me the way he loves you, and if I'd known the murderer, I might have framed you for his crimes to drive a wedge between you." She laughed at the thought.

"I doubt Ian would be interested in conjugal visits, but even that is more likely than him choosing me over you."

"So you admit to framing me?" I asked. She was sticking to her story, pretending that she didn't know who was responsible for the murders. But she knew. She had to know, because if she didn't, who else could possibly have the motivation and capability to frame me?

"I admit that the idea has merit, but even if I did frame you, even with you out of the picture, Ian wouldn't come to me." She laughed, and I winced from the pain lacing her voice. "I've justified his actions in the hopes that he'd come back to me, but everything I've hoped for, everything I convinced myself would be worth the sacrifice, were all lies to deny the truth. And the truth is that no matter what I do or say, Ian will only see me as a monster."

"You're not human." A deep voice suddenly spoke from behind me. "So what else could you be?"

My head whipped around at the interruption, and Walker stepped out from behind the trees and shadows into view beside me.

"How long were you—" I began.

"Long enough to know that your conversation with Officer Montgomery didn't go well if you think someone's framing you," Walker interrupted blandly.

I scoffed. "I could take Officer Montgomery all day. My conversation with Special Agent Rowens, however, not so much." I sighed. "How did you know I was here?"

"Logan told me when he joined the search. You can't do this alone."

"They need your help to find Colin. You can't just—"

"They can search for him with or without me, but you need me here." Walker turned away from me to face Bex. "We're done here. You tell Bex that we're waiting, and we won't wait long. She's familiar with my limited patience."

I stared at Walker, confused.

Bex grinned. The pointed tips of her teeth poked through the bottom of her tight-lipped smile. "Yes, that I am, and y'all are familiar with the infiniteness of mine."

Walker frowned.

I leaned in, as if she couldn't hear me whisper. "That *is* Bex."

It took a few seconds, but I knew the moment he recognized her. He openly gaped.

I stared at Bex and Walker's reaction to her, shaking my head. "You never saw Bex in her true form?"

Walker blinked several times, before turning to face me. "I've seen other vampires in this form."

"But not Bex."

Walker shook his head.

Bex smiled a full, teeth-baring smile, and every tooth was pointed. "Knowing I have a day form and seeing it are two very different things. I've always been of the philosophy that Ian couldn't see past this appearance to the woman beneath, so I only let him see my beauty and strength in the hopes that when he loved those forms, he could come to love every form. Ease him into the frigid water, so he could acclimate, you might say, instead of shocking him with full-body submersion."

Walker's struck-dumb expression had shifted to pure disgust, so I'd say her philosophy was right on target.

"But after speaking with you, Cassidy, I know what my philosophy should have been all along."

I was almost afraid to ask, but I was too curious not to. "And what is that?"

"Submersion." Bex cocked her head thoughtfully. "Dominic has tempered nothing from you. He's shown you his true form, his thirst, strength, power, and lethal nature as surely as I've withheld them from Walker. He didn't ease you into anything. He pushed you head first into the very darkest, bloodiest, ugliest parts of his world, but even after everything you've witnessed from him, you accept him for the creature he is."

"I accept honesty," I said, laughing ruefully. "In that respect, in showing me the true forms of himself, Dominic is brutally honest."

"I thought that shielding Walker from my true form would ease his assimilation into the coven, but he's fought me at every turn."

"I fight you because I don't want to be a vampire. It wouldn't have mattered when you showed me this...this..." Walker gestured at Bex, searching for the words.

"True form?" I supplied.

"Monstrous form. Seeing you like this doesn't change anything. It just confirms what I already know, what I've always known: that despite your beauty and strength, you're a monster inside."

Bex's expression didn't waver. She ignored Walker and met my eyes. "After speaking with you, I've had a change of heart. I don't want Ian to join my coven until he can see past this form, as you can see the man beneath Lysander's form." Bex tapped her forefinger against her chin. "Despite the power struggle in Lysander's coven, he's had great success with you. Maybe speaking with him about you would help me with Ian."

"Stop speaking about me like I'm not here!" Walker burst.

"Do you think Lysander would help me?" Bex asked me.

And there it was. Dominic's plan had succeeded with the spectacular finality of fireworks, New Years confetti, and party blowers. I imagined him patting me on the head, the good little night blood who had mended fences between covens and enticed the opposing coven to seek counsel.

But it didn't feel like a cause for celebration to me. I glanced alternately at Walker and Bex, and it felt like an impending storm about to strike lightning between us.

"You're his ally," I murmured. "I'm sure it would be Lysander's pleasure to help you if he can. I'll let him know you asked."

"Yes, please do relay the message. And thank you, Cassidy, for opening my eyes," she continued in a smooth purr. She pinned her gaze on Walker, and the muscles in the scooped curve of her eye socket shifted and twitched in response. "Or should I say, eye."

I could almost hear the rumble of thunder in her voice.

"You're welcome," I whispered.

"Until then, I will *not* hide my true nature, nor resist my true form. You will see me as I am, so when the time comes, you'll accept me and my coven in our entirety, in this form and every form, and you'll relish the thought of living in this form with me for eternity."

Bex's voice never rose above a low rumble, but the power in her voice shook the earth. I could feel it press against my chest and the vibration of her will hurt my heart.

Walker cringed. He must have felt her power, too.

Abruptly, the pressure against my heart lifted, Bex stepped back into the shadows, and Walker and I were left alone in the woods in a void of utter silence.

I squinted into the darkness. "Bex?" I whispered, but I couldn't see or hear anything to indicate whether she was still present. Walker looked up into the trees and around at the surrounding woods. The sun had nearly set during our conversation, so the trees' shadows were longer and beginning to merge into one blanket of darkness.

My phone vibrated.

Shit, I thought. That was likely Dominic, impatient with how I'd ended our last conversation, but now wasn't the time or the place to talk. My stomach knotted, hoping that Dominic had found a lead on Nathan. I knew he probably hadn't. I knew that he believed Nathan was dead, but knowing didn't loosen the knot. I wondered, not for the first time, how long I could hold on to only hope.

I glanced at Walker. "Is Bex still here?"

He shook his head. "I don't know. We should leave now, while we're ahead."

"We're ahead?" I snorted. "I came here for answers, and I'm not leaving until I get them."

"I don't want a repeat of last night. We leave now, before anyone gets hurt this time."

"I don't want a repeat of last night either, but after my conversation with Montgomery and Rowens, I need answers about those murders, and I need them now. You can go if you want, but I'm staying."

"You're not doing this alone, and we need more weapons if we're going to do this right," Walker hissed, exasperated. "If we leave now, we'll live to fight another day. Isn't that what you told me the last time we had this conversation, when I was the one who wanted to stay?"

"This is different. I—"

"I should have listened to you, but I was angry and vengeful and I didn't know that I was in over my head until it was too late. *I should have listened to you*," Walker insisted. "Please, listen to me now. We'll go back to my house, you'll tell me about your conversation with Rowens, and we'll figure it out together."

I took a deep breath. I could hear the rationality in his plan but that didn't ease the impenetrable knot in my chest. I wanted to find Colin and solve the case now, before anyone else was killed and before I was blamed for it. I'd thought that I could leverage Bex to show her hand. I'd thought that I could put this case to bed tonight. And looming over everything I thought I could do, like approaching thunderheads on the horizon, I thought that Dominic would've found Nathan by now. I'd been wrong about so many things that I didn't know what was right anymore.

I nodded. "OK. Let's figure this out together."

"Don't take another step." A light flashed in my eyes, blinding me. "No one is going anywhere."

* * * *

Walker shielded his eyes with his forearm and squinted through the spotlight. "Riley?" He stepped forward.

"Stop walking and raise your hands above your head!"

By the panic in his voice, I'd guess that Officer Montgomery was aiming his gun at us. I couldn't see anything past the blinding flashlight, but I wasn't leaving anything to chance. I froze in place and raised my hands.

Walker stopped walking, but he didn't raise his hands. "Riley, is this really necessary? What's happening out there? Did you find Colin?"

"We still have parties out searching for Colin. It's gonna be another long night if we don't find anything more than his hat."

Walker frowned. "If the search is still on, why are you—"

"Why am I here in the woods with you instead of helping the search party?" Montgomery finished. He laughed. "I'm here to ask you the same damn thing. I thought maybe you were following your gut, but instead, I find you here with Cassidy DiRocco. I don't think that's a coincidence, do you, Rowens?"

"I don't believe in coincidences," Agent Rowens' deep voice intoned.

I squinted into the flashlight, but my eyes still hadn't adjusted. I could discern a second blob next to the first, whom I assumed was Rowens, but if more officers were out there, I couldn't see them.

"I don't know what it is you *think* you know, but you're mistaken, Riley. Put down the gun, and let's sit down and talk about this man to man." Walker took a step forward.

"Not one step closer, Walker, I'm warning you! And put your hands on your fucking head!"

I balled my hands into fists, trying and failing to stop their trembling. Montgomery reminded me of Walker, barking orders from the business end of his gun, but this time, I was the one on target. Jolene's ruined face sprang to mind, and I shuddered. I didn't want to die, but I especially didn't want to die like that.

"Tone it down, Montgomery." Rowens' deep, steady voice interrupted.

"I told you we'd find them together," Montgomery hissed.

"I know you did, and here they are," Rowens agreed. "Cool it."

"She wasn't the only one present at all the crime scenes. Ian Walker was with her. They're conspirators!"

"No one's conspiring with anyone," I snapped.

"You've known me our entire lives, Riley." Walker inched forward. "You can trust me. Put down the gun."

"Stay where you are!"

"I said, calm down. You're pissing me off, Montgomery," Rowens said, "And if you take one more step closer, Walker, I'll shoot you myself."

"That's not necessary," I said.

"I'll determine what is and isn't necessary," Officer Montgomery continued. "People got hurt last night, and you don't want a repeat, remember?"

"You're taking our conversation out of context and twisting it," Walker said.

"I know what I heard."

My eyes were finally beginning to adjust, and I could see that Montgomery and Rowens were the only officers there. Although Montgomery still had a gun in his hand, it wasn't pointed at us anymore. I let my arms drop to my sides.

"You're wasting your time here on us," I said, trying for reason. "Every second counts in a missing persons case. If you don't find Colin tonight—" I sighed and shook my head. "It might already be too late!"

"You'd better pray we find him tonight or that's on you, too." Montgomery stepped forward.

"Montgomery," Rowens warned.

A soft but distinct growl rattled from behind us, and I remembered that Bex was still hidden in the shadows across the cave. If Montgomery moved too closely or too suddenly—if Bex thought Walker was in mortal danger—Rowens and Montgomery were toast.

Walker stiffened. He'd heard her growl, too. "You don't know what you're poking your nose into, Riley. Back down."

"Are you threatening him?" Rowens asked, his tone low and dangerous, but not as dangerous as Bex behind us. "Montgomery might be hot-headed and jumping to conclusions, but he was right. I'm inclined to believe what he's saying, so you might want to start explaining yourself."

"There's nothing to explain," I said.

Rowens ignored me. "What are you doing out here with Cassidy that's more important than finding Colin? You're lead on this search, Walker, yet you left us."

"Now *I'm* lead on the search?" Walker crossed his arms. "You were singin' a different tune a few hours ago."

"I'm here to lead this investigation, but you know damn well we needed you out there tonight," Rowens said calmly. "You know these woods like the back of your hand. You grew up here. You've tracked game and other missing persons, and you should have fought me for lead on this search. You did, in fact, right up until you left."

"Are you building up to a question or did I miss it somewhere in all that bullshit?"

Rowens cocked his head. "What did Logan say to you before you left?"

"The one has nothing to do with the other."

"What did he say?" Rowens pushed.

Walker threw up his hands. "He asked how the search was going and how close we were to finding his son. Jesus, what else would he say?"

"I don't know. You tell me."

Montgomery was twitchy with the need to act—that man was a loose cannon—but Rowens was unflappable. He looked comfortable with the thought of standing in the dark woods all night if it meant getting answers.

My gut twisted. We didn't have all night.

"Was it the guilt?" Rowens continued when Walker didn't answer. "Was reassuring Logan too much, knowing he'll never find his son's body? After all, no one knows the woods like you."

Walker tightened his hands into fists. "You've crossed the line."

"Looks like Officer Montgomery's not the only one jumping to conclusions," I muttered.

"Maybe," Rowens said, "Then again, Montgomery's conclusions were right, so maybe not."

"Then why did you leave the search?" Montgomery insisted. "What are you—"

Montgomery was knocked down by a shadow the size of a mountain. Flashlights went flying. Their light beams swirled the air in a crazy strobe before hitting the ground and dousing us in complete darkness.

The sun had set.

Montgomery shrieked. Blood sprayed the air like a macabre fountain and splattered across Rowens' Kevlar. Rowens rushed forward, gun first, but Montgomery had already stopped screaming.

The shadow lifted its head to face Rowens. Its muzzle glistened with Montgomery's blood.

Rowens squeezed off two shots. Walker grabbed my shoulders and dragged me down with him as he hit the ground. The shots didn't seem as loud as they should have, not nearly as deafening as Walker's sawed-off shotgun, but my hands snapped over my ears reflexively anyway.

The thing didn't even flinch. Rowens had shot it point blank in the face, and it didn't so much as *flinch*.

It reared over Rowens and knocked him to the ground. Rowens squeezed off an entire clip. The monster clawed at his chest, unfazed by the bullets. It started growling, that low, deep, rattling growl I knew so well from the vampires, but this creature was different. Although its ears were pointed, its hands were like talons, and its legs bent back like the hind legs of a bat, just like the others of its kind, this creature had scales, and from the effect Rowens' bullets weren't having on its body, I'd say those scales were impenetrable.

It continued clawing at Rowens' chest, and like the sweet, fresh inhale of an epiphany, I realized that Rowens wasn't screaming. His Kevlar was protecting him from the creature's talons. I didn't know how long the

Kevlar could hold against its assault, but by the pinched, grim expression on Rowens' face, I wasn't betting on the Kevlar for very long.

Walker reached inside his vest and pulled out a gun. I yanked out my silver nitrate spray from the inner pocket of my leather jacket, but as defense against this creature, the spray seemed woefully inept. Walker shook his head and searched the other side of his vest. He pulled out a curved-tipped bowie knife. I accepted it, squeezing the handle tightly in my sweat-slicked palm.

Rowens slammed a second clip into his gun and squeezed off another round.

The creature reached out with its massive claw and crushed Rowens' gun hand. Rowens did scream then, loud and shrieking, and the creature tore the gun away, and with it, Rowens' right arm.

The arm tore at the shoulder, ligament ripped from ligament, so fast that one moment I mourned for the use of his crushed hand, and the next moment, the bone snapped with a wet, suctioned *pop* and there wasn't even a hand to mourn. The creature tossed his arm to the side to resume clawing at Rowens' chest. I stared at the limp, detached arm a few feet away. The hand was a mangled, bloody mess of twisted fingers and protruding bones.

I swallowed bile.

Staring at Rowens wasn't any better. His shoulder had torn in long strands of skin that dangled from his collar onto the ground like wilted daisy petals. Blood sprayed in a wide crescent and was now squirting from the missing limb in pulses.

I glanced at Montgomery, where he'd fallen and hadn't moved since. His arms were shredded from the monster's claws and his chest was now a gaping wound where his heart used to be. I looked past the carnage and fear and narrowed my eyes on Montgomery's missing heart, *his missing heart*, and I realized with delayed, dawning recognition that this wasn't just any vampire. This was our murderer, and we were its next victims.

I turned back to Rowens. His residual limb was still squirting blood in pulses and the creature, that mountain of a creature, was still on top of him, clawing at his chest.

I leaned into Walker and covered my mouth around his ear as I whispered. "It's going for his heart. This is our guy."

Walker nodded. He aimed the gun, and I braced myself for its fire. Seconds that felt like minutes passed, but Walker didn't shoot.

"Shoot, damn it. What are you waiting for?"

Walker turned his lips to my ear and whispered, "Rowens' bullets didn't penetrate. Shooting will just piss it off. We need to ease back slowly."

I blinked. "What about Rowens?"

Walker's face hardened. He turned his face away from mine to stare at the creature and what was left of Rowens, giving me his profile. The muscle in Walker's jaw ticked.

"If that were me," I whispered, "would you just stand by and watch? Would you 'ease back slowly' as I was ripped apart and that thing ate my heart?"

Walker glared at me. "You know what I'd risk for you."

I looked at him, looked at the creature pointedly, and then back at him.

"You saw what it did to Rowens' arm when he shot it," Walker muttered. "I want to keep both of mine attached to my body, thank you."

"He didn't have silver bullets. You do." I looked back at Rowens. The creature hadn't broken through the Kevlar yet, but Rowens wasn't conscious anymore. He was going to bleed to death. "We need to do something now while we still can."

Walker nodded slowly. "Ease back to the cave. When we're on the cave's ledge, I'll shoot."

"Shoot it now," I argued.

"No, we ease back first. If it comes at us, we can jump into the cave."

I raised my eyebrows. "I'm not sure I'd prefer falling to death over having my heart torn out."

"Bex won't let us fall." Walker jerked his head to the side, and against everything that felt right and humane, I eased back toward the cave.

The creature was getting frustrated with Rowens' Kevlar. It gave up with its claws and snapped at the frayed material with its teeth. The Kevlar still held, even against those long rows of sharp fangs, and the creature growled. It clamped its jaws around Rowens' torso and shook its head like a dog. I winced. If its fangs didn't puncture through the Kevlar, Rowens' ribs were surely crushed. If his ribs weren't crushed, his neck was likely snapped. And he was bleeding to death. I pressed my lips together in a firm line not to give voice to the ache in my throat.

We were only a few feet from the cave when the creature completely gave up on Rowens. Maybe it had sensed our escape or maybe it had grown impatient with the Kevlar and wanted easier prey. Either way, it dropped Rowens and turned its emotionless, black shark eyes on us.

Walker didn't hesitate this time. He squeezed off one shot.

One.

In the fraction of a second it took to blink, Walker was knocked back into the cave from one powerful swipe of the creature's arm. I fell back on my ass in the dirt and stone, and suddenly, inexplicably, the creature was inches from my face.

I heard Walker scream. I felt Walker's blood spray against my arm before he fell, and I saw Bex's shadow flit from the darker shadows behind the cave to catch him, like he'd known she would. But it wasn't what I heard, felt, or saw that would haunt my dreams years from now. Assuming I survived, it was the smell that would keep me awake at night.

The creature breathed on me in deep, ragged pants, and its breath was the choking, unbreathable stench of feces. My hair blew back and forth as it breathed in and out, flying into the creature's face and back into mine with each pant. It hadn't been winded by its attack on Montgomery or Rowens, but now, as it faced me, it inexplicably couldn't catch its breath.

I tightened my grip on the knife in my left hand, my finger trembling on the trigger of the silver spray in my right. The creature raised its claw, but it didn't strike me like I expected. It held my hair against its snout, closed its eyes, and breathed in another long gulp of air.

The creature was breathing in my scent. I swallowed, trying to stifle my disgust and trembling as I realized by its heightened pants that it liked what it smelled.

A low, rumbling growl erupted from the creature's chest. The growl was loud enough and I was close enough that I could actually feel its vibration against my skin. The creature let go of my hair and burrowed its face in the hollow of my neck. I winced back, bracing myself for its claws to pound through my sternum and rip out my heart like it had everyone else, but it didn't. It nuzzled its snout deeper into my neck and breathed in more of my scent.

I could feel the heat of my silver dangle earring burn its scaley skin. The sizzle of its flesh cooking against the metal was right against my ear, but the creature didn't react. Once again, it didn't even flinch.

Eventually, the creature pulled back to face me, nose to snout. I watched the blisters on its cheek heal where my earring had burned its scales. They popped, scabbed, and smoothed before my eyes more quickly than even Dominic could heal.

Its scales were tinged a sallow green color, but beyond its snout and black shark-eyes, the creature still retained some of its former, human-like features. It had short, black hair, longer and greasy on top but faded on the sides in a semblance of a faux-hawk. Its eyebrows were thick and dark, just like its hair. It was naked and obviously male, and despite its blood-coated snout, razor fanged-teeth, and thickened brow, its large, round eyes made it appear young, like it wasn't yet fully grown despite its size and strength and gruesome brutality.

I narrowed my eyes on its face as something registered about its appearance that I couldn't accept. Its nose was flattened and flared to points at the nostrils, just like all vampires' noses flared in their true, gargoyle-like form, but something on its nose glinted in the moonlight. My stomach bottomed out, and I wanted to scream. I wanted to lift my arm and stab the creature through its disgusting, unfeeling, heart-eating heart. I wanted to cry and rage and die, but I couldn't do anything but stare and deny the truth of what I'd just seen pierced through the pointed tip of the creature's nose.

The creature was wearing a nose ring.

NO! I instinctively screamed the denial inside my head, but I couldn't deny what was literally staring me in the face.

I swallowed and whispered in a shaky, hoarse voice, "Nathan?"

The creature let loose a sudden, ear piercing shriek, dipped his head into the curve of my neck, and clamped his massive jaws into my carotid.

The pain was instant and sharp and bone deep. I screamed and pressed the trigger on the silver nitrate, but the creature suctioned a pull of blood from my neck like a straw. I was instantly lightheaded and black starbursts danced over my vision. Another two gulps like that, and I'd be drained.

I tightened my hold on the knife, knowing that if I hesitated, I might not have the strength to stab him later. Still, I hesitated. The creature was no longer an "it." The creature was a "he," Nathan, my brother, and God help me, even if he tore my beating heart from my chest, I couldn't kill him.

That thought gave me pause. He should have torn out my heart like he had all his other victims, but he'd gone straight for my carotid instead. He might look and act like a mindless, blood-crazed monster, but on some level, did he know who I was, that I was his sister? There was only one way to determine the innerworkings of his thoughts, and he'd swallowed more than enough of my blood for me to do it.

"Nathan DiRocco," I commanded. "Stop feeding from me and step back three paces. Now," I whispered.

A whisper was all I could manage, but the strength of my voice didn't matter. I had an inner strength that belayed my diminutive stature, far stronger than this creature despite its muscles and claws and fangs. A mental twine tightened between the creature's mind and mine. Now I could pluck the strings. I'd never be equal to vampires in physical strength, but as Dominic so often reminded me, I didn't need physical strength to be strong, capable, and powerful. I didn't need physical strength to control their minds.

The creature swallowed another mouthful of my blood.

Another wave of starbursts darkened my vision. When I spoke again, I tried to force some strength behind the words.

"I command you to release my neck from your mouth and step away from me, Nathan DiRocco," I said, my voice a thready whisper.

The creature's grip on my neck tightened, and I realized that my commands weren't working. I focused on the threads connecting his mind to mine. I could normally easily manipulate those threads, but something was wrong. I could feel his deep, unquenchable hunger. His anger, so familiar to my own, was consuming and ravenous and unstoppable. He had been hunting for something specific, something familiar, and although he hadn't known what it was, he had found it.

He had been hunting me all along.

Besides instinct and sensory stimulation, the creature couldn't think or understand. I couldn't control his mind because he only understood the scent of my hair and the cramping burn of thirst. Words like "release" and "step back" and "sister" weren't part of his comprehension, so he couldn't respond to those commands.

If I couldn't control him mentally and I couldn't compete with him physically, I was next in line after Montgomery and Rowens.

I was dead.

The creature unexpectedly released his hold on my neck and stumbled back.

I crumpled to my hands and knees in the dirt. My hip ached. My neck ached. Everything ached, and I felt sick and shaky. I blew out a slow, unsteady breath and found enough strength to lift my head.

The creature had Bex pinned to the ground by her neck. She'd saved me. Bex had just *saved me*. I looked around frantically; if Bex was here protecting me, where the hell was Walker?

It took a moment, squinting through the darkness to discern the lump of his form from the surrounding boulders, but I spotted him. He was lying on his side next to the cave. My stomach hitched at the stillness of his body, and I crawled to him.

When I reached his side, I could see the steady rise and fall of his chest, but his shirt was drenched in blood. I whispered a rushed prayer that the damage wasn't irrevocable and peeked under the tatters of his shirt to face his wounds.

His skin was unbroken, smooth, healthy perfection.

"Now's not the time to get intimate, darlin'."

I snapped my gaze to his face. He was smiling at me.

"How?" I whispered. "I saw his claws gouge into you and all the blood..." I shook my head. "I saw—"

"Bex," Walker said, losing the smile. "You know better than me how well their saliva heals."

I turned back toward Bex, expecting the worst but hoping for the best, and as usual, my expectations were on target. Bex was losing her battle with the creature. She dodged and struggled against those massive claws as he stabbed for her heart, but with every near miss, he sliced through her forearms and shoulders and stomach. She was being shredded alive.

"Jesus!" Walker hissed. "Your neck!"

I turned back to Walker. "Do you still have your gun?"

He clamped his hand on my wound. The pressure of his palm hurt worse than the bite itself, and I experienced an eerie flash of deja vu. I jerked back, but he only squeezed harder.

"Hold still. Let me bind this with something," he said.

"I'm fine, but Bex—"

"No, you're not. Stop squirming," he snapped. "Bex has an entire coven of vampires to protect her. She'll be fine. It's you I'm worried about."

"That I can see, the only people here to help her are you and me." I looked around. "Where's Rene?"

Walker's jaw tightened. He pulled a packet of gauze from his cargo pocket and ripped it open with his teeth. He wouldn't meet my eyes.

I narrowed my gaze on him. "Was Rene there when she healed you? What did she say to him?"

"It doesn't matter. She told me to get you out of here, and that's exactly what I'm going to do."

"She told Rene not to leave the coven, didn't she?" I asked, and by the way Walker's jaw twitched, I knew I was right. "She's protecting us, but she can't fight that thing alone. She needs us."

"I don't care what Bex needs," he snapped. He pressed the gauze hard into my neck. "We're falling back."

I sucked in my breath against the pain. "She saved me, Walker. She saved both of us. We can't just leave her here to die."

Walker gave me a look. "Bex can't die." He ripped off a strip of his tattered, dirty shirt and tried to bind the gauze to my neck to keep pressure on the wound. "This isn't working," he grumbled. "It's too deep and there's too much fucking blood."

I grabbed his hands. "Listen to me. You can finish that later."

Walker tossed the strip of shirt and applied pressure to my neck with his hand again. He breathed a long, suffering sigh. "I'm listening."

"Wasn't it *you* who told me that vampires are only long-lived and hard to kill, not immortal?" I gestured to the injured, bloody mess that Bex was becoming as she continually dodged the creature's talons. "She won't last long."

Walker stared at me for a long moment before gritting his teeth in a frustrated groan. "Keep pressure on that," he demanded, pointing to my neck.

I slapped my hand on the wound.

He pulled out his gun.

"Shoot to wound if you can."

Walker looked down at me like I was crazy. "Why the hell would I do that?"

"Because I think that creature, whatever the hell he is, is my brother."

He stared at me and then back at the creature. "Fuck."

I sighed. "My thoughts exactly."

Walker lifted his gun and aimed. I braced myself for the shot and waited for the creature to turn on us.

And I continued waiting.

A full minute passed before I snapped. "You hesitated on Rowens and now you're hesitating on Bex. What are you waiting for this time?"

The creature jabbed at Bex, and she just barely rolled in time. His talons scraped her side, ripping open a flap of skin and exposing her ribcage. She screamed.

The creature lifted his arm back to strike again.

"I can't shoot. This may be the only chance I have," Walker murmured.

"Your only chance for what?" I said, beyond exasperated.

"My only chance to be rid of her."

The creature punched Bex's chest, and this time, she wasn't fast enough. His claw punctured under her sternum and buried his arm nearly elbow deep. Bex shrieked and struggled. Her movements turned frantic, slashing at the creature's arm with her own claws, but her efforts were only an annoyance, the buzz and tickle of a fly for the creature to swat away.

Tears streaked through the blood and dirt crusting her cheeks. She was losing and desperate, and we'd hesitated too long to prevent what was about to happen.

I tried to breathe, but the stink of blood and feces clogged my nose. I swallowed and tried not to throw up.

The creature twisted his arm inside Bex, and she shrieked even louder. Maybe it was the lingering thread of our mental connection or my own empathy—maybe it was my overactive imagination—but I could feel the pain of that shriek reverberate through my own heart.

The creature jerked his arm down in a rough, abrupt yank. Bex's screams cut short. Her arms were outstretched and her legs still kicked and fought, but the movements were awkward and flailing now. She went limp a moment later, and the creature tore his arm out of her chest cavity, heart in hand.

Chapter 11

I covered my mouth, horrified. That creature was Nathan. That creature was my caring, punk little brother, and he had just killed Bex. He had ripped her heart from her chest as she screamed and fought him, and by the motion of his tipped head, I had the disturbing realization that he was about to eat it.

I lost the battle with my stomach and puked Ronnie's homemade banana nut pancakes on the leaves and dirt in front of me.

Walker fired.

The creature jerked back and dropped the heart. He stared at us, looking stunned as the heart slipped from his claws and fell to the ground with a sick splat that did nothing to settle my already heaving stomach. The creature turned his head slowly to look at his shoulder. A tiny ribbon of blood trickled down his right arm.

Walker pulled the trigger a second time, and the creature jerked back again from the impact. A twin ribbon of blood streamed from his left shoulder. The creature glanced at both shoulders, stunned into inaction for one heartrending moment.

He disappeared in a blur of movement.

Walker was knocked off his feet. He fell back toward the cave's opening with the creature in midair. They landed in a rolling heap from the momentum, and before the creature could pin Walker to the ground, tear off his limbs, or rip out his heart, they skidded over the loose stone surrounding the coven's entrance and dropped into the cave.

I stared at the hole of the cave's mouth as they both disappeared from view. Everything had happened so fast, my mind was still trying to catch up and my body couldn't do much more than shake in shock. Bex was dead, and Walker had fallen into the cave with the creature. If the fall didn't kill him this time, the creature would.

Carefully, I crawled to the cave and peered over its edge, half expecting the creature to fly up and drag me down with him, too. I couldn't see any more than a few feet into the pitch black of its depths. I waited a moment, bracing myself for the jarring hit of their impact. The cave was unbelievably deep, but as I'd learned firsthand from my fall, thanks to Rene, it only took seconds to hit bottom.

Those seconds passed in silence.

I waited another moment before scuttling back from the cave's opening. They hadn't hit bottom. I felt relieved for Walker, but God only knew *why* they hadn't hit bottom. I wasn't loitering near the cave's opening to find out.

Turning away from the cave, I faced the nightmare behind me. Parts and pieces of Montgomery, Rowens, and Bex littered the ground. Bex's heart hadn't landed too far from her body. Its thick, muscled shape gleamed under the light of the moon. The slick, bloody arteries at its head had torn at varying lengths, and one artery in particular dragged along the ground a few inches longer than the rest. I couldn't pull my eyes from the sight even as I gagged.

As I stared at the carnage, I fingered the vial of Dominic's blood on the chain around my neck, and the thought that this wasn't the end, not for any of us, took root and wouldn't let go. After everything Bex had just sacrificed for me, saving her, no matter how unlikely, was certainly worth a try.

I crawled the twenty yards between Bex and me, but when I reached her side and stared alternately at the gaping hole under her sternum and the mound of bloody heart laying still and gleaming next to her, I needed a moment to come to terms with reality. I was about to physically pick up her severed heart into my own hands and stuff it back through the ragged hole in her chest.

Bex had been terrified at the end. Her face was bathed in blood. Her cheeks, neck, and shoulders were slashed to ribbons from dodging the creature's claws. The socket of her missing eye was somehow less gruesome now that she couldn't see at all, but the other eye, still and staring, haunted me.

This would have been me, torn apart and broken. Nathan would have swallowed another few mouthfuls. I would have been dead, and once I was dead, no one would be able to shove a heart back in my chest and hope for the best. Once I was dead, I stayed dead.

Vampires could heal catastrophic injuries. I'd seen Dominic heal after being impaled through his chest by another vampire's claws. I'd witnessed a vampire live through a throat slashing so deep I could see his spine, and I'd watched a vampire walk only minutes after having his aorta severed from his heart.

Bex was dead now, but she didn't have to stay that way.

I picked up Bex's heart from the ground and held it in my hand. *I held her heart literally in my hand.* The muscle was heavy and soft and slippery. Blood squished between my fingers as I adjusted my grip. The three arteries jutting from the aorta bobbed like springs at the top of the heart. I gagged, but the nausea was all bluster. I didn't have anything left in my stomach to throw up.

I unscrewed the lid from the vial of Dominic's blood and poured half of it on the severed arteries and the other half on the heart itself, hoping to increase the chance of its healing. The blood singed over the cuts on my knuckles, healing my wounds. Hopefully it would heal Bex's, too.

I stared at the heart in my hand, at Dominic's blood slick over its surface, and the burning scrape of thirst clawed down my throat. I had the immediate, insane urge to lick Dominic's blood from Bex's heart.

Oh Jesus, I thought, feeling my heart rate spike though my ears. *Not now.*

Drink! Jillian's whisper echoed insistently through my mind.

I wanted to. I'd tasted the heady spice of Bex's blood, and I knew with unparalleled certainty that Dominic's blood would taste even better—despite the fact that I'd tasted Dominic's blood on multiple occasions and hadn't liked one drop. But Jillian knew otherwise. All I'd need to do was lift Bex's heart and take one little lick. His blood was right there in my hand, dripping between my fingers in front of my eyes, and no one was here to know if I licked or if I resisted. No one, of course, except for me.

That was the fine line between temptation and addiction: how I lived my life when no one was looking. My throat was an inferno of thirst, but I'd survived this temptation before in another life, with Percs instead of blood, and I knew that even if the thirst burned my throat to ash, I'd prefer that pain than the consequences of giving into temptation.

Bex had protected me. She'd given me another chance at life, and I'd be damned if I let anything distract me from trying to do the same for her.

As gently as I could manage, I shoved the heart back into her chest through the gaping hole under her sternum. I could feel an unyielding cage of bone—ribs, I was assuming—and the soft, slippery, squish of other organs, maybe lungs. I knew the heart rested between the lungs and was angled toward the left, but I hadn't done particularly well in the anatomy portion of biology. The heart could be upside down, for all I knew. I hadn't had the stomach for dissection in high school, and biology wasn't a requirement for journalism majors.

I laughed to myself, up to my elbow in a corpse's chest and worrying about heart positioning, at the thought of having to slice into a toad now.

That I could tell, which wasn't saying much, the heart was roughly occupying the space in the chest it should. I held it there a moment, wondering if I should try to match the arteries together. The injuries I'd seen Dominic sustain seemed to heal automatically without the help of holding the pieces in place, so I decided against it. Besides, I couldn't decipher one artery from the other. If I held a vein to an artery, or vice versa, would I encourage the heart to heal incorrectly? I didn't know enough about anatomy or vampires to guess, so I eased my hand from her chest, hoping the heart would heal itself.

I waited, staring at the chest wound, her face, the empty hole of her left eye socket, and I held my breath for a sign of life. A flicker of movement. A rattling growl. Vampires didn't function like humans. She didn't need to breathe air into her lungs or have her heart beat to live—God knew why she even needed a heart if she didn't have a circulatory system— but I waited for some spark of animation to show that something was happening, that returning her heart to its position in her chest would allow her to heal and live.

Nothing happened. She didn't even twitch.

I was still kneeling over her—my hands outstretched from my body because they were disgusting, coated up to my elbows in grotesque, bloody gloves, waiting and hoping and trembling, my throat still burning with unquenched thirst—when I smelled it.

I knew he was behind me because I could feel the steady pant of his breath on my neck, but I hadn't heard him approach. I hadn't even known he'd exited the cave until I was suddenly gagging on the pungent, rotting smell of intestines.

I turned toward him slowly, inch by minute inch, until I faced him.

The creature didn't look any worse for having fallen into the cave. The bullet wounds on his shoulders from Walker's silver shot had already healed, and that I could tell, he hadn't sustained any new injuries from Walker or Rene or any of the vampires he might have encountered in the cave. I wondered how many hearts he'd eaten before coming back for me.

I plucked at the thread connecting our minds one more time, hoping to feel a glimmer of the man I loved and respected, the man I was proud to know I'd helped raise, but all I could feel was an inferno of his anger.

Decades of growing up together, years of mourning together, and a lifetime of arguing, scheming, and loving my little brother were gone. The anger had incinerated all thought, memory, and emotion from his mind except for one motivating drive to slake his thirst.

He recognized the brush of my mind against his and growled.

Nathan's eyes were a pale blue, identical to mine, but this creature's eyes were jet black. I couldn't distinguish pupil from iris from sclera. Staring at the diamond stud in his nose and knowing that Nathan was staring back at me didn't help. Whatever had composed Nathan's spirit or soul or mind or whatever made a person uniquely him, was gone. The creature stared back at me, not Nathan. The creature had followed me from New York, murdered Lydia, John and Priscilla Dunbar, the McDunnell brothers, and now Montgomery, Rowens, and Bex. Maybe even Walker and Rene.

I had an inferno of anger inside me, too, always boiling beneath the surface, stoked by my parents' deaths, Adam's lost love, and lately, the hopelessness of my career. Now, face to face with a mindless, murdering creature, formerly my caring, sassy little brother, what did I have to lose?

I tightened my grip on the Bowie knife Walker had given me, lunged forward in a desperate leap, and stabbed the creature in the side, attacking it before it could attack me.

I hit bone. The jarring vibration hyperextended my elbow, and pain *zinged* up my arm like lightning.

The creature let loose a high, growling shriek and swatted me away with a back-handed smack. Like four knives, its claws gouged into my ribs. I hit the ground hard on my back, my scream cut short as the wind knocked out of my lungs.

The creature was on me before I could breathe again, before I could even blink. Its massive, razor-tipped jaws clamped into my neck, and I felt the powerful vacuum of its extended snout sucking my blood. Black starbursts sprouted over my vision and merged together in a black blanket across the sky and trees and stars overhead. I felt my fists, which reached up in a futile effort to fight, fall limply to the ground. I felt the bone-sharp ache of its teeth gnarl into the meat of my neck and shoulder. I could both hear and feel the vibration of its rattling growl, and through the stink of its sewage breath, I inexplicably, unimaginably, smelled the distinct scent of Christmas pine.

Dominic, I thought, and a moment later I was ripped from the creature's jaws. By the freezing cyclone of wind and hair whipping around me, I imagined that I was flying. The clean scent of pine surrounded me. I breathed it deep into my senses, and the weak relief of knowing that I wasn't alone was almost like coming home.

The cyclone abruptly stopped with a rustle of leaves. Something probed into my neck, and I felt the familiar heat and unwelcome arousal of my flesh healing. I must have twitched, or maybe fought the emerging feelings—I couldn't tell which since everything was black and numb—because Dominic's hold around my body tightened.

His words moved against my ear in a noiseless whisper. "Keep still. It doesn't know where we are, and I'd prefer to keep it that way."

"Dying," I whispered back, but nothing uttered from my mouth except for the shape of the word on my lips.

Dominic must have read my lips or maybe the enhanced acuteness of his hearing could discern my voice better than even me.

"You?" He scoffed. "No more than usual."

"I haven't come close to dying in weeks," I argued.

I felt the silent rumble of his chuckle against my chest. "Seems like just yesterday. Can you open your eyes?"

I hadn't realized they were closed. I opened them, and as if through a narrow, dark funnel, I saw Dominic's face hovering over me. He looked worried despite the nonchalance in his voice. His thick brows were pinched into a frown, his expression severe in its seriousness. Except for the very tips of his fangs that poked from beneath his upper lip, his appearance was deceptively beautiful.

He'd already fed tonight.

The planes of his face were ripe with strength and stolen youth, and the solid line of his jawline was a chiseled block. Muscles chorded his neck, and biceps flexed against my back as he held me. Until tonight, he was the strongest living thing I'd ever known—using the term "living" loosely, of course. But now Dominic, formerly the biggest badass of the night, was hiding in a tree from my little brother, a mindless, heart-eating murderer.

Dominic's reflective, otherworldly eyes met mine, and he half smiled. The scar on the left side of his lower lip never stretched enough to accommodate a real smile, but I could tell from the worry clouding his eyes that despite the scar, his smile was half-hearted.

"Nice of you to stay with me," he murmured.

I raised one eyebrow. I couldn't move otherwise, but I could till convey my irritation. "It wasn't for your benefit."

I got the full smile then. His eyes crinkled at their outer corners, his scarred lower lip stretched and lifted lopsidedly, and his fangs flashed their full length in the moonlight. On any other night, I was terrified of those fangs, but after coming face to face with Nathan, Dominic's fangs simply couldn't compare.

"You're breaking my heart," Dominic said, the vibration of his words and breath like feathers against my ear. I shivered, not from the chill night air.

I opened my mouth to say something scathing, but Dominic placed a finger over my lips. His eyes locked on movement in the tree next to us. My heart leapt into my throat. He pointed down, and I looked at the scene beneath us. The creature was flipping out, smashing its claws into surrounding trees, stomping its hind legs on logs and shrubbery, and pounding its fists into the ground. It threw its head back and let loose a thrilling shriek that blew my eardrums and shot goose bumps through my spine.

I shook my head. "I think it's pissed at losing me. It followed me all the way from the city, after all."

Dominic narrowed his eyes. "Why was it tracking you?"

Admitting the truth made me nauseated, almost as nauseated as facing the creature itself. "It's Nathan. The creature is my brother."

Dominic sucked in a sharp breath. He looked down at the creature again and shook his head slowly. "No, it can't be."

I frowned. "He is. I stared at him face to face, and I'm telling you, that thing down there, whatever it is, was originally Nathan DiRocco."

Dominic stared at the creature a moment longer. It was still screaming and stomping in what was only comparable to a massive hissy fit.

"How long do you think he'll continue to freak before he tries tracking me again?"

Dominic shook his head. "We'll deal with him later. Where's Walker?"

"I, er, I don't know," I stuttered, thrown by the subject change and by the very realization that I wasn't sure if Walker had survived. "The last I saw, he'd fallen into the cave."

Dominic's strange, blue and ice eyes widened. "Fell? As in without any rappelling equipment?"

I nodded. "With nothing but the creature to break his fall. The creature came back out. Walker didn't." I narrowed my eyes on him. "How do you know about rappelling?"

Dominic waved away my question. "I've told you, I know everything."

The creature pounded its claws into the tree we were hiding in.

The tree swayed dangerously. We jerked forward and then suddenly swung backward, and Dominic lost his grip on me. I felt his hands slip from around my waist, and my stomach plummeted. Everything happened so fast, I didn't have time to do more than think—*NO!*—and then I was out of reach.

Dominic was faster than gravity. Before my thoughts could burst into a real scream, he dropped to a lower branch and caught me in his arms. I felt a warm rush of liquid gush from my side as he tightened his grip on my waist, and I remembered the creature's claws catching my ribs. I trembled from the pain and from enduring it in silence.

Dominic leaned in close. "You're injured worse than I first thought. It's more than just the bite on your neck."

I nodded.

"We need to find Bex's coven and seek shelter. Now."

I swallowed, trying to speak without screaming from the pain. "You don't know the location of her coven? I thought you knew everything."

"Cassidy—" Dominic growled, obviously not in the mood to deal with my attitude.

"It's the cave." The tree jerked again from the creature's beating, and Dominic's arm tightened around my ribs like a vise. I gasped. "The cave is the entrance to the coven."

"Ah," Dominic murmured, glancing at the cave. "Then I'm sure Walker fell into good hands."

I couldn't focus through the stabbing in my ribs. The pressure of Dominic's arm was relentless, and without any relief, I felt myself fade. The shadows of the woods and trees and leaves and Dominic all bled together into an inky landscape across my vision until nothing remained but the scraping wheeze of my breathing and the steady pound of my heart. And then even that faded to the demands of darkness.

* * * *

"Cassidy, don't make me command you to open your eyes."

The tree's swaying had stopped, and Dominic's grip was gentler than a moment before. I breathed a deep inhale of air, and although my side still twinged, the pain was bearable now.

I opened my eyes.

We were still in the damn tree, and the creature was still throwing a conniption below us.

I frowned. "How long was I—"

"Only a moment. I'll have to mind your injuries until I can heal them."

He sounded shaken. After existing for five hundred years, nothing could shake Dominic, but despite his extended existence, I'd heard the tremor in his voice.

I knew better than to stare into Dominic's strangely reflective eyes—
he could turn the parts of my mind that controlled my body to putty—but
I was breaking all the rules tonight. I stared deep into his eyes now, trying
to decipher how he'd done it. If it hadn't been for his uncanny timing,
if he hadn't arrived just when the creature was about to feast, I would
have died tonight.

"How did you know I needed you?" I whispered. "Why did you leave
the city? Tonight of all nights, why did you come for me?"

Dominic heaved a long-suffering sigh. "Would you believe me if I told
you that I heard your screams all the way from New York City?"

I grinned despite our situation. "I might have if you'd hid the sarcasm."

"I must remember that." Dominic stared at me a moment, but I couldn't
read his expression any better than I could the thoughts of a wild animal.
Both were beyond my comprehension, more instinct than logic, and
sometimes—less often now than when we'd first met—I swore Dominic
could turn on me as easily as he could save me.

"Well?" I prompted.

"Honestly?"

"Is there a better policy?"

"Several that I can think of," Dominic muttered.

I pursed my lips and waited.

"I didn't know you needed me."

I frowned. "Then how—"

"You didn't call me at sunset. I told you that I would damn the
truce with Bex and come here if you didn't call." Dominic gave me a
look. "So I did."

I blinked. "I forgot." I shook my head at our luck. "Thank God I forgot."

Dominic shrugged. "Or thank me."

I rolled my eyes. "I've mended things between you and Bex, so you
didn't break the truce. Not that that matters now."

"Why wouldn't the truce matter? What's happened?"

I bit my lip.

Dominic narrowed his eyes. "What did you do?"

"I didn't do anything! The creature tore out her heart. Walker had a
gun with silver shot, but he wouldn't—" I gasped, wincing as something
painful shot through my rib. "—and I couldn't—"

He placed a finger over my lips, cutting me off. "Don't distress
yourself. And lower your voice before Nathan hears us. Whatever you
did or didn't do is OK. I've seen her look worse."

I stared at him. "What's worse than dead?"

Dominic looked down and raised an eyebrow. "I could think of several things worse than death, but Bex is not dead."

I struggled to turn my head to see what Dominic was seeing.

"Just remain still. Is that too much to ask?" Dominic hissed. He adjusted his grip, so I could see more easily.

Bex was moving. She had dragged herself to the cave's mouth, inch by excruciating inch, while the creature was distracted over losing me. A trail of blood had soaked the moss in a bloody path behind her, but she was healing.

Bex wasn't dead.

I sagged with relief in Dominic's arms. "It worked," I murmured to myself. "It really worked."

"What worked?"

"Her injuries were so extensive—" I shuddered, thinking of her heart in my hand. "—I didn't think it was possible for her to heal, but I used your blood to save her, and it worked."

"Of course you did." Dominic narrowed his eyes. "Why didn't you try saving yourself?"

I frowned. "What do you mean?"

"I gave you that vial of my blood so you'd have it when you needed it, the subject of its healing being *you*, not me, not Walker, and certainly not Bex."

I snorted. "As if Walker would ever let me heal him with your blood. He'd rather die."

Dominic nodded. "Then let him, and *you* will use my blood to survive, as it was intended."

"I couldn't just leave her." My voice caught, and Dominic looked down to meet my eyes. "She sacrificed herself to save me."

Dominic raised both his eyebrows. "She probably feared the risk of another war."

Another? I thought, and then I realized that "truces" were often formed after wars. I sighed. "I doubt she had time to weigh the pros and cons of her actions. If you haven't noticed, that thing is fast, faster even than you."

Dominic shook his head. "I know Bex. She weighed her options."

"Fine, let me try in terms you might understand." I sighed, exasperated. "We wouldn't be very good allies if I let her die from injuries she sustained while protecting me when I had the means and the opportunity to help."

"Now *that's* an acceptable excuse for your actions," Dominic said, grinning. "But I know you, and you did not weigh your options before acting on them. That's what makes you such a risk and a reward." He brought his hand to his mouth and bit into his own wrist. I winced. "Next time, use my blood to heal no one but yourself. Promise me."

I rolled my eyes. "I promise."

Dominic shook his head. "You know what I want to hear. Swear by the certain passage of time."

Bex's warning about promises resonated within me, and I hesitated. I hadn't thought much of my promises to Dominic other than the fact that I always keep my word, so it didn't matter if I swore by the passage of time or certainty of the sun or whatever garbage Dominic invented because I'd keep my promise no matter the circumstances. But Bex's fearful refusal to swear by the sun made me wonder if Dominic's formalities were more than just words.

He leaned in close, forehead to forehead, until his bloody lips were inches away from mine. The blood had stained the divots and wrinkles of his scar, highlighting his natural sneer.

I cringed back, but he held my face immobile against him.

"You've been talking to people about us," Dominic narrowed his eyes. "Walker or Bex?"

Despite the fact that Dominic had just saved me, I felt cornered by danger from all sides: the creature below me and Dominic surrounding me. At least I knew the creature would drain me dry and rip out my heart. Three weeks ago, I'd have thought the same of Dominic, sans the heart, but now I believed his motives. He wanted more from me than just my blood, and sometimes, that was even more terrifying.

"I'm not asking you a second time," he growled.

"Bex," I confessed.

He smiled, but it didn't reach his eyes. His smile was all fangs. "I see."

"I doubt that," I muttered.

"Remain still." Dominic adjusted his hold so that his bleeding wrist pressed against the wound along my ribs. When his blood made contact with my wound, it sizzled, not necessarily burning but not pleasurable, either, like the overwhelming sensation of not stopping after climax. I clenched my teeth together to keep from crying out.

The creature stopped its tantrum.

I froze in Dominic's arms and opened my mouth to warn him, but Dominic covered my lips with his fingers.

The creature was still in the shadows below us. Without movement or sound, I couldn't pinpoint its exact location, but I could still smell the faint reek of its breath as it panted. Dominic and I waited in the stretching silence—the pound of my heart roaring in my ears—until my skin felt stretched thin.

If we couldn't see it than maybe it couldn't see us.

Faintly, nearly imperceptibly, I heard the underlying rattle of the creature's growl.

Dominic's answering growl rattled instinctively, deep from his chest. Pressed against him, I felt the vibration more than I heard it.

The creature heard it.

It turned its head, and I saw the glassy sheen of its eyes searching the trees and darkness. I froze, my heart a frantic, caged thing trying to beat out of my chest.

The creature didn't move. It waited, just as still and silent as us.

After a moment, it released another soft growl.

I closed my eyes, dread pouring through me. Dominic's answering growl would undo us.

Something growled in the tree next to us, and the creature launched itself at it.

Dominic braced his arms around me in an unbreakable hold, and we were suddenly a missile, launching from the tree and soaring. Through the whipping wind whistling over my ears, I heard the creature shriek and pound after us.

Dominic paused next to the cave entrance. We didn't have time to pause; the creature was in fast forward, gaining on us, but Dominic took the time to link arms with something cold and wet behind me. The sharp scent of cinnamon wafted from it, and the scent made my throat instantly, burningly parched.

Bex, I thought, recognizing the smell of her blood. *He's taking the time to save Bex.*

The creature swiped out with its claw, a hairsbreadth behind us. Dominic turned to give the creature his back, sheltering Bex and me with his body, before diving into the cave. Dominic stiffened in midair, and a wash of blood soaked between us.

We dropped headlong into the cave, more falling than flying. I looked up at the cave's entrance and the creature's outline, a darker shadow against the other night shadows. I expected it to dive in after us, like it had with Walker, but it didn't. It just watched from above, poised and waiting, as we fell out of reach.

* * * *

We crash-landed into the cave's bottom. Dominic tried to take the brunt of the landing, but Bex's injuries had crippled her strength and I was little better than dead weight. We hit hard. The impact jarred my hip. Pain seared through my leg. Dominic released Bex and tightened his grip on me as we bounced. Without Dominic to steady her, Bex hit the ground a second time, rolled a dozen feet, and slammed into a stalagmite.

Dominic skidded a few feet in the same direction as Bex with me riding on his stomach like a sled. The moment we slowed to a stop, I struggled away from him.

"Your back," I said, frantic. I tried to lift his shoulder to inspect his injuries, but my arms were as useful as limp noodles. He batted me away easily in my weakened condition, not that he couldn't bat me away easily otherwise.

"I'm fine."

"The creature flayed your back with its claws. I saw it. I felt you bleed." I said, glancing down at my stained shirt, although honestly, I couldn't distinguish his blood from Bex's and my own. My shirt was completely soaked through. "And now you've got dirt and gravel and cave grime embedded in the wounds," I continued. "You're not fine."

Dominic sat up with me in his lap and leaned forward to show me his back. I peered over his shoulder. Flickering light from the kerosene lamps illuminated the cavern just enough for me to see, but even knowing Dominic's penchant for healing, seeing wasn't believing. His button-up dress shirt was shredded—it was stained beyond repair by dirt and blood—but his skin was flawless.

"You're not hurt," I whispered. I grazed my fingers over his smooth flesh to reassure myself.

His growl was very soft, like velvet. I checked myself and pulled my hand away.

"I told you, I'm fine," he said gruffly. "I healed."

Bex groaned.

"Why hasn't Bex healed? She's more powerful than you. She should have—"

"How do you know who's more powerful?" Dominic interrupted, sounding offended. "My Leveling is approaching, if you remember. You've never actually witnessed my full strength."

"Yet even in your reduced state of strength, your wounds healed almost instantly. It's been at least fifteen minutes since I replaced her heart."

Dominic raised his eyebrows. "Replaced her heart?"

"Yes, Lysander, let's rip out your heart for twenty minutes or so and see how long it takes for you to recover after it's shoved back into your bleeding chest cavity," Bex moaned from her prone position next to the stalagmite. She hadn't moved since our fall. "It'll be a good test of strength for you, and the perfect comparison for me to see how you measure up, assuming you recover at all."

I craned my neck to the side, trying to get a better look at Bex in the light coming from the mineshaft. "I don't think that's necessar—"

"You said dinner with Bex went well. That you enforced our truce," Dominic interrupted me, his voice more a growl than words, as he caressed my collarbone.

I blinked. "It went better than expected," I hedged, unsure of his sudden mood swing.

"Who touched you?"

"I don't know what—"

"Your neck is black with bruises, Cassidy DiRocco," he purred, and I felt the caress of my name on his lips, like a pull on my tongue, urging me to speak the truth. "Someone's fingertips squeezed around your neck, here." He poked a thumb into a bruise on my throat, and I winced. "Here." He poked another bruise with his other hand so both his thumbs were at my windpipe where Bex had squeezed. "And here." He wrapped his fingers around the back of my neck.

I swallowed. "It's complicated."

"Unravel it for me, then."

"The other person looks much worse." I winced, the pain in my hip becoming unbearable from sitting sideways on his lap. "The truce was solidified, and that's what matters. Isn't that what you wanted?"

"Who?" Dominic growled. His grip around my neck tightened, but I could tell he was being careful with me. He was trying to rattle me, but he wasn't actually hurting me.

I kept my lips sealed.

"Me," Bex said from her shadow under the stalagmite. "It was me. I choked your precious Cassidy DiRocco, the perfect fucking little night blood. She deserved it. Or at least she did at the time."

Dominic released my neck and settled me on the cave floor. I sighed, relieved from the pressure on my hip for the moment. With a sudden flurry of wind and dirt, Dominic was gone.

He reappeared next to Bex and hauled her up in front of him by her upper arms.

"No!" I shouted, "Dominic, don't! I—"

Melody Johnson

"You want a truce, and you dare to touch my night bl—"

The light from the lamps crossed Bex's face. Dominic stopped mid-sentence, staring.

He glanced back at me before narrowing his gaze on Bex again. "The truce was solidified, despite Cassidy's neck and your…?" Dominic's voice faded, and that I could recall, it might have been the first time I'd ever seen him at a loss for the appropriate words.

Bex raised the eyebrow over her hollow eye socket. "And my what?"

She was going to make him say it.

"The loss of your eye."

Bex nodded. "Yes, although even if the truce hadn't been solidified then, after what Cassidy has done for me, it certainly would be solidified now."

I shook my head. "You saved me first. I couldn't do any less." I bit my lip. "I wish I could have done more."

"You did more than enough, unlike someone else we both know." Bex's voice ended on a warning growl.

The door to the mining shaft creaked open and flooded the cave with light. I winced away from the brightness, unable to lift my arms to shadow my face.

"DiRocco? Is that you?" Walker's deep bass vibrated through the cave.

"Shut the door, you idiot," Dominic hissed. Despite his threats, he instinctively turned his body, shielding Bex from the light. "Are you trying to spotlight us for Nathan?"

The door slammed shut. I opened my eyes, blinded by darkness after the loss of the light.

"I wouldn't be spotlighting anything if you weren't spread out like a buffet." I felt Walker's hand on my cheek. "I doubt the creature would risk diving back into the cavern, but better safe than sorry. Let's get you inside, darlin'"

I stared at him until my eyes adjusted to the darkness, and I could finally see the bold planes of his face, his bent nose, and curly-cue hair. I shook my head, feeling weak with denial and relief. "Walker, you're alive? You're OK?"

"It'd take a lot more than that creature to get rid of me," he said smugly.

"But how?" I said, stunned. "I saw you fall into the cave. I thought—"

"Rene caught me," he said, losing the smile.

I looked behind him, expecting Rene to make an appearance as well, to interject with an equally smug comment, but he wasn't there. "Where is he?"

"Didn't you hear his growl in the tree next to you?" Bex snapped.

I looked back at her, shocked. "I heard a growl, but I didn't realize that...." my voice trailed off, stunned. "That was Rene?"

"Who else would it be?" she said, her voice harsh and grating. And then she did something incomprehensible to me, something I'd never seen from a vampire. She dropped her face into her hands and wept.

Dominic adjusted his grip so he was holding her instead of man-handling her. Without his support, I think she would have collapsed.

"He'll return, Bex," he murmured. "And we can heal him if he doesn't."

Bex pursed her lips. "We can't heal him if it eats his heart," she murmured.

I looked up at the cave's entrance high above us, the size of a thumbprint from our view at the bottom. There might have been a shadow of the creature still peering over the cave's edge, watching us, but I couldn't say for certain.

"I should be out there," I said, more to myself than to anyone in particular. "It needs to be stopped."

The cavern's silence was a tangible, breathable heaviness in the air. I glanced back at Walker and realized that he and everyone else were staring at me like I'd lost my mind.

"What?" I asked.

"We only just narrowly escaped," Dominic said slowly, as if to the mentally deranged. "You're still bleeding."

I understood their hesitation but couldn't shake the frantic urgency clutching my heart. The creature was out there. That creature was Nathan, and he was eating people's hearts. He was likely eating Rene's heart as we spoke.

I wanted to scream. I wanted to stab something.

I contained myself to not falling over. It took more energy than I'd like to admit just to remain sitting upright.

"We can't hide down here and ignore what's happening outside this cavern. That thing is killing people right now!"

"And if we go out there, we will be the people that thing is killing," Walker said flatly. "We're going inside the coven. Now."

"I haven't extended you an invitation to my home," Bex growled.

"Unlike you, I don't need an invitation to cross a threshold," Walker snapped.

"On this, I must unfortunately agree with Ian Walker," Dominic interjected. "We should move this argument inside. Everyone. Now."

Bex ignored him to focus on Walker. "You're not welcome here anymore."

Walker snorted. "All these years I've refused you, but now that I'm here of my own free will, I'm not welcome. Typical."

"All these years I've held onto the *delusion* that you would see me and the life we could have together in the light you used to see me, before Julia-Marie died." Bex shook her head. "I was wrong to hold out for you."

Walker laughed. "And after all these damn years, what finally brought you to your senses?"

"You would have let me die. You had the opportunity to pull the trigger and help me, but you chose to let me die."

Walker shook his head in disgust. "Had I pulled the trigger, the creature would've attacked us."

"But you weren't torn by the decision. Staying your hand to protect yourself didn't cost you anything. You were *glad* to do it. I felt your relief and your hope that you would 'finally be rid of me.' Isn't that how you worded it?"

"My contempt for you is no secret, *darlin'*. Never has been."

The silence was thick and rotted the air between us.

"We can continue this conversation just as easily from the privacy of your coven, Bex. We are still open targets here," Dominic warned.

Bex didn't say a word. She nodded regally, and Dominic lowered her carefully to her feet. She didn't sway or flinch; by her movement and lithe grace as she walked forward, she had finally fully healed from her injuries. Or at least, she'd healed enough that she could mask the pain.

I, on the other hand, could barely crawl. My breath caught as I attempted to stand, and it was a small attempt.

Dominic was suddenly beside me on my left. Walker crouched to steady me on my right.

A low growl rattled from Dominic's chest.

"Play nice," I hissed. I glanced up at the cave's mouth, wondering if the creature was still there. "We don't want to encourage its attack."

"Nathan," Dominic said softly. "We don't want to encourage *Nathan's* attack."

I pursed my lips. "Just get me inside so we can figure out how to save him, and barring that—" I swallowed, not wanting to give voice to the inevitability of my brother's fate, but unable to deny the horror of everything I'd witnessed. "—how to stop him."

Chapter 12

The first time Nathan noticed I was high on Percocets, he didn't say anything. I'd known that he knew by his distant, disgusted expression. He'd never looked at me like that before, and that first time, it slayed me.

The second time I was high, he didn't keep it to himself. He asked me if my hip was still in pain. I'd told him the truth: I'd been prescribed Percs for the bullet wound to my hip, and although physical therapy was progressing, the pain was still there. I needed them to ease the edge off while I relearned to walk.

Slowly, painfully, I struggled through crutches and walkers until I was mobile with a cane, and with each progression at physical therapy, I earned back a measure of control in my life. Soon, I wouldn't even need the cane, and then life would finally return to normal.

Nathan waited several weeks before he brought up my addiction again. He waited until I could walk without a cane. He waited until I no longer limped, no longer needed physical therapy, and my only fear was the future threat of arthritis.

At the time, arthritis seemed a distant threat, one the doctors claimed would likely occur but may or may not be a serious concern. My recovery had been a success. Had I known how little time I'd have to enjoy life before arthritis did develop, maybe I would have lived a little differently. Maybe I would have set goals for marathon runs or rock climbing. Maybe I would have learned to rappel. But marathons and rock climbing weren't important to me back then. The only thing that was important was my career, which ironically enough, had sky-rocketed, not because of a breakout story like I'd hoped, but because I'd taken that bullet for my friend and fellow officer who'd been on the stakeout with me that night, Officer Harroway.

The police department was in love with me, and I planned on cashing in every last favor to climb and claw my way to the top of my career, just like I'd climbed and clawed my life back from the grave. I was determined and single-mindedly focused, but I was also undeniably addicted to Percocets.

When Nathan confronted me about my addiction, I denied it.

I didn't need Percs anymore for my hip, but I was terrified. I'd used Percs as a crutch to survive physical therapy, and I feared that if I stopped taking them the pain would return. I feared that I wouldn't be able to walk again, I wouldn't be able to work again, and I'd slide right back down the ladder where I'd started this mess, a lonely nobody, desperate for a breakout story.

I took Percs in the morning, throughout the day, and before bed. I was high at home, at the office, at crime scenes, and while I interviewed witnesses. I was high when I talked to Carter, Harroway, and Greta, but I wasn't the only one in denial. Everyone was happy I'd survived. Everyone was excited for my recovery and my return to work, and no one accused me of being anything less than a hero and a damn good investigative reporter.

No one, except Nathan.

He knew the truth and refused to look the other way. He flushed the Percs down the toilet, and when I bought more, he flushed those down the toilet, too. We screamed and fought and threatened each other, but nothing he said made an impact on my life because I knew he wouldn't rat me out to the police. He wouldn't flush my career down the toilet. No matter what he threatened, I knew he had a steel trap for a mouth, just like me, and he'd let me flush my own life down the toilet before breaking a secret when it mattered.

Eventually, he gave up. He stopped the interventions and the arguments. He stopped visiting altogether. His absence in my life was like a festering wound, worse than losing my parents and relearning to walk, because this time, the pain of losing him was entirely my own fault.

I visited his apartment to apologize, but one look through the peephole and he knew. I was high. He wouldn't let me in. He wouldn't even crack the door to talk to me. His voice was measured and calm and devoid of expression when he spoke through the door.

"You chose drugs over me. Over family. I don't want to see you. As far as I'm concerned, you died from that gunshot wound. Get the hell away from me and stay away. You're not welcome here anymore."

His words were harsh and cruel and tore my heart to pieces. And they were just what I needed. I requested a week vacation from work, flushed the rest of the pills down the toilet myself and never looked back.

After my parents died, family was everything to me, and Nathan was all I had left. I couldn't lose him, too, no matter the sacrifice, and although detox was the best thing for me anyway, it still felt like a sacrifice. It felt like dying all over again, but at the end of the week, I was reborn.

I waited until I'd returned to work and my life was back under control before visiting Nathan again. Walking up to his apartment door the second time was a nightmare. I feared that I'd failed, that he wouldn't forgive me, that I'd lost him forever just like my parents, and that fear made me sick.

I knocked. Seconds felt like hours.

He opened the door and stared at me.

I couldn't find the words. I'd practiced my apology the entire taxi ride to his apartment, but when the moment came, I couldn't speak. My throat was so clogged with fear and tears and regret, I couldn't have spoken even if I'd found the words, but I didn't have to. He took one look at me, and he knew.

He wrapped his arms around me, and I broke.

"I'm so sorry," I cried into his shirt.

"I know. Thanks for coming back," he said into my hair. His voice was suspiciously rough, too. He forgave me because we were family, and no matter my crimes against him, if I was genuinely sorry, he'd forgive me anything because that's what family does. Family stands by your side in the storm, fights for your life when you're drowning, and forgives you when the tide ebbs even if you don't deserve forgiveness.

I looked around at the variety of people—using that term loosely—gathered in Bex's dining room. We weren't a family by any means—not in love, selflessness, or devotion—but we'd been brought together as a united force against my brother, the only real family I had left. With the exception of Meredith, my partner at *The Sun Accord* whom I'd always considered more sister than friend, the people in this room were the only people who had my back.

I was sitting in one of Bex's plush dining room chairs, my hands on the table to keep my balance as the room spun and dipped and swirled in dizzying loops around me. I sipped on a glass of apple juice that Bex had graciously offered when it became evident that I was struggling to remain conscious. Dominic had stopped my bleeding, but I was still weak and lightheaded. Looking around at the silent, distrustful tension between everyone—Bex glaring at Walker, Dominic eyeing Bex, Walker keeping his distance from everyone, and everyone here because of me—I felt the last, frayed threads of my ambition to find and save my brother sever under the sharp, undeniable reality of our situation. We were in the eye of the storm, safe for the moment, but preparing for battle, but the battle was against Nathan. God help me, was there anything left of Nathan in that creature worth saving?

"My God, it's hopeless," I said under my breath, more to myself than anyone in the room. "I don't even know the creature he's become. How can we hope to save him?"

"I know exactly the creature Nathan has become," Dominic said. His voice was low, but it resonated in the silence of the hall.

I met his gaze squarely. "What?" I whispered, shocked. "How do you know?"

"It's not just me," Dominic said, raising his palms innocently. "I believe most of us, with one look at Nathan, would recognize the creature he's become."

Walker stepped forward. "I've seen some crazy shit, but I've never seen anything like that thing before tonight."

"It's because that thing is an abomination," Bex hissed. "It needs to be put down."

"That abomination is her brother," Walker snapped.

"And it needs to be put down," Bex repeated, a terrible finality in her voice.

"I know it doesn't seem possible, but some part of my brother is still alive inside him. It's not enough to communicate or see reason, but it was enough for him to bite from my neck instead of my heart like he did everyone else." I met Bex's eyes. "I think he recognized me—not as his sister, he doesn't think on a level able to comprehend family and friend from enemy—but his compulsion for human hearts wasn't enough for him to kill me. Something made him alter his pattern."

"Lucky you," Bex said waspishly, and she looked away.

I sighed. "What I'm saying is that a part of him might still be my Nathan, and if that's true, than he might still have a chance. We need to stop him no matter what, I get that, but maybe we can save him." I cleared my throat, trying to control my emotions. I turned to face Dominic. "And you," I pointed my finger at him. "All this time, you couldn't find my brother. You supposedly searched for him throughout the entire city—"

"I did search for him, and I found nothing," Dominic said, his voice carefully neutral. "Until tonight."

"This doesn't count as you finding my brother. I found him!"

"I believe your brother was the one who found you," Bex murmured.

I crossed my arms and turned on Bex. "And with one look, you recognized Nathan, too? Because he certainly doesn't look like the Nathan I knew, and he doesn't look like any creature I know." I looked back and forth between Bex and Dominic. "What the hell is he?"

"There is no official name for them," Bex said on a sigh. "Most of us refer to them as the Damned. A coven had a serious uprising of Damned vampires years ago, but they're typically rare." Bex's voice turned quiet. "I've never seen one in the flesh before tonight."

"He's a coven-turned night blood," Dominic clarified. "A rogue vampire drained him and attempted to complete the transformation instead of giving him to a Master. Their transformations produce single-mindedly bloodthirsty creatures, incapable of thought or emotion. They only feel the burning ache to slake their thirst, and they specifically crave the blood pumping directly from the aorta."

I narrowed my eyes. "Rogue vampire? Or did you mean to say *rebel* vampire?"

Dominic crossed his arms. "What are you implying?"

"Jillian once bragged that she could transform a night blood into a vampire." As the words left my mouth, I realized that the answer to the mystery of my brother's disappearance had been staring at me all along. "Jillian tried to turn Nathan into a vampire, didn't she? But instead, she got that... that..." I stammered, struggling for an appropriate word. "... abomination," I said, finally borrowing Bex's description.

Dominic rolled his eyes. "Considering Jillian was executed for her crimes against me and my coven, for her crimes against you, it's not as if I can interrogate her, now can I?"

"Swear to me on the sun that you executed her."

"Excuse me?" Dominic said, his body suddenly still as stone.

"You've told me time after time again that she was executed, but you've never sworn to it."

"That's like you swearing to become friends with Ian Walker. It's unnecessary to swear something that's already been done."

"I know that Jillian is alive, Dominic," I said, my voice barely audible.

Dominic crossed his arms. "And how would you know that?"

"She told me."

He was silent for a moment, and when he did speak, his voice was measured and soft. Much softer than mine. He could slice clean through silver with the softness in his voice.

"You've spoken to Jillian."

"Not exactly," I evaded, loathe to admit the truth. "It's more a one-way conversation."

"When?"

I sighed. "All the time. Lately, every day."

Dominic made a strange noise. "Forgive me, Cassidy, but I'm not following. You speak with Jillian every day? Even now, while you're here in Erin, New York?"

"I don't speak to her. She speaks to me."

"I don't know which is more impossible," Dominic murmured, and it sounded as if he were talking to himself. "You penetrating the depths of my coven, where I've imprisoned Jillian, or Jillian escaping from the silver I've buried her under."

"Kaden escaped from his imprisonment. I wouldn't be shocked to find that Jillian had escaped from hers," I said wanly.

"Jillian has *not* escaped from her imprisonment," he snapped, his anger a palpable weight in the air between us. "She is buried deep beneath the coven, under layers of silver and surrounded by rooms into which she is uninvited. Even if she managed to escape her confinement, she would never be able to navigate the labyrinth of that underground unscathed, nor without feeding. It's been three weeks since she's had a drop of blood. I doubt she's even conscious."

"I can hear her talking inside my head." I winced at how crazy that sounded. "So at the very least, she's conscious."

"That's how she speaks to you? Inside your head?" he asked. Even *he* sounded shocked.

I felt small, stupid and crazy, and all my self-doubt—the insanity of hearing Jillian's voice inside my head, of craving blood, my wasted efforts and dwindling hope of saving Nathan—erupted in a boiling, leveling geyser. When all my other emotions had been drowned by anger, Dominic remained standing, staring at me and waiting on my response. His innocent, inquisitive expression made me want to punch a dent into his beautiful face.

"This is your fault," I said.

He blinked. "Pardon?"

"You were supposed to have executed Jillian for her crimes against you and your coven. *For her crimes against me*," I said, throwing his words back in his face. I could feel my voice building up to a scream, and I didn't care if I sounded irrational. It felt good to scream. "Isn't that what you said?"

Dominic's eyes flicked to Bex and then back to me. "I don't think now is the time to—"

"You're right; three weeks ago would have been the time to excecute Jillian," I snapped. "You wouldn't allow me to witness her execution because of my 'weakened condition,' as you put it, but that was just a ruse. You lied to me."

"Cassidy, I—"

I slammed my fist on the table. "Did you lie to your coven, too? Did they trust you when you assured them that Jillian was dead?" I was on a rant now, and I couldn't stop. Dominic's ears had pointed and his fangs were lengthening, and Walker had positioned himself with his back against a wall, as far from the kill zone as possible, but like a derailed train whose tracks led off a plummeting cliff, I couldn't stop. "You need all the allies you can get to survive the coming Leveling; I wonder how your coven will feel, especially those most loyal to you, when they find out the truth, when they realize that you put them at risk. When they realize that you lied!"

Dominic gripped my shoulders and pulled me out of the chair to face him, eye to eye. "Jillian was like my sister!" Dominic shouted. His voice was grave and guttural and echoed through the great hall like thunder. "She was my second, the person I would have entrusted with my coven, the person who I entrusted with my life!"

"And she betrayed that trust!" I shouted back.

"Consider everything you'd be willing to overlook for your brother. Nathan has killed innocent people. He's dismembered their bodies, tortured them, and eaten their hearts. His crimes are worthy of excecution, but even after witnessing the horrendousness of his crimes, you ask Bex and I to have mercy."

"Don't try to twist this around," I said. "That creature isn't Nathan. He didn't choose this life."

"Nonetheless, he is the one responsible for his victim's deaths, but as his sister, no matter his crimes, you can't be his executioner, can you?" Dominic asked.

I pursed my lips.

"Can you?" he insisted.

"No, I can't, but—"

"Jillian is my family. I loved her as my sister for centuries. Literally, centuries. That kind of love, loyalty and devotion doesn't just disappear, no matter what she's done to betray it. That is the bite of unconditional love."

I shook my head. "But you lied about it. You told me she was executed. You *assured* me that I was safe from her, but you left me vulnerable to her in ways that neither of us could have imagined."

Dominic nodded. He set me back down on the chair gently and knelt in front of me. "And when you realized that she was still inside your mind, you should have told me." His hands were soft and caressing on my shoulders now instead of punishing. "It seems we are both at fault for things we should have told each other."

I narrowed my eyes on him "One more at fault than the other," I said stubbornly.

He shook his head, but when he smiled, his fangs had retracted to their normal length. "Perhaps."

I raised my eyebrow, but I let his noncommittal agreement settle between us.

"How long has Jillian been speaking to you?" he asked.

"Since I connected with her mind three weeks ago," I confessed. "It feels like a single thread still links us, and she won't let go."

"Jillian has been whispering in your mind for three weeks, and you never thought to tell me? You never thought that might be pertinent?" he asked, and there was a sudden sharpness that sliced through his tone.

"No," I said, suddenly feeling on the defensive. "It was pertinent to *me*, but I didn't think that you'd care. Frankly, I thought I was going crazy."

"Even if you were crazy, your mental health is my concern, is it not?"

"I suppose." I blinked, surprised at the intensity of his expression. He was livid. "I just didn't think of it. You never asked."

"Asking one if she is hearing voices in her head is not a commonly asked question," Dominic hissed. "That is something you would need to be forthright with me about."

"I didn't think that you—"

"That's precisely the point! You didn't think, but this is more than just about you. It's about Jillian. If she has latched onto your mind then she is not as contained as I had assumed. If you can hear her, can she hear you?"

I swallowed. "Yes, I believe so. I can also sense her suffering, so she might be able to feel my emotions, too." I frowned at that. "Although, come to think of it, beyond burning agony, she doesn't feel much of anything."

Dominic raised his eyebrows. "Perhaps because she is in complete darkness and silence. She has no sensory input where I imprisoned her."

He swiped his hand roughly over his face, his frustration plain. "Except for the sensory input she's feeding from you."

"Feeding from me?" I asked. His words resonated inside me, feeling suspiciously like hope. For the first time, I realized that maybe the thirst for blood I'd assumed was my own addiction was actually hers.

"You drank Bex's blood," Walker said, his eyes wide. "And you liked it."

"I've been craving blood lately," I admitted. "But I thought the craving was mine, that my repeated exposure to vampire blood was somehow addicting me to it."

Walker gave me a look. "I've been exposed to vampire blood my entire life, and it's never become more appealing over time, I can assure you of that."

"Bullshit," Bex growled. "There was a time when you pined for my blood."

"Only to spill it," Walker snapped.

"You once said that vampire blood *is* addictive," I hedged carefully.

"True, but you'd need to drink it regularly over a long period of time, several months I've been told." Walker glanced at Bex. "And even then, when your body craves it, the taste doesn't improve."

Bex hissed, baring her fangs.

"Quiet!" Dominic bellowed. "Stop bickering. This is serious."

Bex lowered her head. "My apologies."

Walker bit his tongue, but not happily.

Dominic focused on me. "You have craved blood and drank from Bex."

I nodded. "Jillian's not a picky eater. She encouraged me to drink everyone's blood, even dried blood at Ronnie's house and spilled blood at crime scenes."

"She is desperate for food, no matter the source," Dominic said thoughtfully. "Jillian may be literally drinking through you."

"But she wouldn't gain any nourishment, would she?"

"I don't know," Dominic admitted. "If she *is* gaining any nourishment, she may have retained some of her strength even while imprisoned."

I blew out my breath in a helpless sigh. "So what do we do? How can we cut her off?"

"If Jillian is your brother's maker, we may not want to," Dominic said.

A loud slam sounded from the doorway. I screamed instinctively.

Dominic appeared in front of me, his speed like magic.

Walker drew his gun.

"Whoa!" Rene said from the doorway, his arms raised in mid-air. "May not want to what?"

Bex cried out, somewhere between a wail and an unintelligible mash of words that sounded suspiciously prayer-like.

Rene was a torn, bloody mess. His hair was slicked and dripping streams of blood down his temples, forehead, and cheeks. His shirt hung from around his neck in tatters, like he'd been through a grinder, but the exposed skin of his chest and arms were whole and undamaged, despite the blood spatter. He stumbled toward us a few steps and then pitched forward.

In her weakened condition, Bex couldn't reach him before he fell, and Rene bit stone face first. The crystal on the dining room table shook from the hit. He didn't move, but he uttered a low, long moan. I winced.

Bex knelt on the stone next to him, turned him over, and held him. She cradled him to her chest, murmuring softly into his ear. Rene nodded and murmured back.

I watched them, frozen by the tenderness of their moment. I was fascinated by the depth of Bex's emotion, and a small, suspicious part of me wondered if it was an act, if a creature as instinctual and predatory as a vampire could harbor such tender feelings. I did honestly want to know if Rene was all right and thank him for saving Walker, but most of all, most selfishly of all, I wanted to know if all of that blood was his and only his.

Was Nathan still alive?

We waited in silence until Bex lifted her head. "He is no longer injured. He'll be fine after feeding."

Dominic nodded. "I'm glad for his safe return. I'm sure he needs nourishment and rest, as do we all. I propose that we retire for the day, recuperate our strength, and reconvene before sunset tomorrow to determine how best to move forward."

"Agreed."

Rene winced as Bex hoisted him from the floor. "Sounds good to me."

"No, not agreed," Walker looked around at the vampires like they were insane. "We need a plan now, not tomorrow."

"*We* need a plan?" Bex growled. "You are not a part of this coven. Is he your night blood, Lysander?"

Dominic glanced at Walker and laughed. "Certainly not."

Bex locked eyes with Walker. "You've found your way in and out of this coven on multiple occasions, with and without my consent. I have no doubt that you can see yourself out. If you're still here at sunset tomorrow, assuming you survive the day in my coven without my protection, I'll assume you mean me and mine harm, and I'll kill you myself."

Walker stared at her, the muscle ticking in his jaw.

Rene looked back and forth between them, and a wide, beautiful smile blossomed across his face. "Finally."

"How like you, unable to put aside petty problems for the greater good. We need to contain that creature!" Walker shouted.

"We need to *kill* that creature, but we don't need your help to do it. You're just a liability." Bex looked pointedly at the door and then back at Walker, her intentions like crystal.

Walker made a rude noise in the back of this throat. "I hope he eats your heart and you rot." He jerked his head toward the door. "Let's go, DiRocco."

I tensed to stand, but Dominic placed his hand on my shoulder.

"Cassidy isn't going anywhere," Dominic said, his voice amused.

I blinked. "I'm not?"

"No, you're staying the day with me. You're my night blood and as such, you're staying where you belong, by my side," Dominic said distinctly, obviously goading Walker, but also subtly reminding me of my role. Bex believed I was truly Dominic's night blood, so more than pretending at dinner, now that he was here, I needed to play the part.

Walker locked eyes with me. His hand adjusted its grip on his gun. "DiRocco?"

I swallowed. Even if I wasn't playing my part in this game, which I was, I wouldn't say otherwise. Walker with his gun against Dominic, Bex, and Rene with their preternatural abilities didn't stand a chance.

"I'm staying," I said softly.

Walker's hand loosened on his gun. He shook his head. "I was wrong about you."

"Walker, I—"

He lifted his hand. "I hope you figure things out with your brother. I hope you find a way to bring him back, and if you don't, I hope you can kill him quick and easy. I wish you the best, DiRocco, but between you and me, I was wrong." He turned to Bex. "I'll leave at sunrise."

Bex nodded. "Done."

Walker turned his back on us, walked out of the room, and slammed the door behind him without another word.

Dominic squeezed my shoulder gently, and I realized that I was trembling.

"I'm assuming that you have accommodations in which Cassidy and I may take our day rest safety?" Dominic asked.

I stared dumbly at the dining room door where Walker had just left, realizing with a type of slow-dawning horror that I would be staying the day with Dominic in Bex's coven.

Dominic squeezed my shoulder more forcefully.

"My vampires would never dare harm you. They know the punishment for such crimes," Bex replied, but she didn't sound offended. She sounded weary.

"I understand, but I do not take Cassidy's safety lightly. There may be one or two in your coven who haven't received word of our renewed alliance."

Bex nodded. "Of course. I'll show y'all to your rooms. I have an entire wing dedicated to guests. You'll be safe."

Dominic raised an eyebrow. "An entire wing? Do you host guests often? I can't imagine a rarer situation than the one we find ourselves in tonight."

"As you so acutely stated, I don't take the safety of *those in my coven* lightly. My vampires know the consequences of crossing me, but that doesn't mean I intend to provoke their disobedience."

"Tests have their uses but are better used when the coven itself is not being tested."

Bex nodded. "Precisely. One can only hope that prior tests have served their purpose, and with such preparedness, that we have a fighting chance."

I sighed, thinking of Nathan's sweet face compared to the impenetrable scales and lethal fangs of the creature. "Assuming we haven't already failed."

Chapter 13

Bex's guest bedchamber was very similar to Dominic's rooms in his own coven. The chamber was composed of several rooms—a bedroom, bathroom, and sitting room—complete with two sofas, a recliner, a coffee table, two lit scented candles, and a vase of Gerbera daisies. Fluffy area rugs spread over each room, softening the unyielding chill of the stone floors. The rooms were mostly gray and brown from the natural elements of stone and wood, but splashes of pink from the daisies, candles, and bedspread brightened the decor.

Dominic kept his coven relatively clean and inhabitable, and in some rooms, even personal, but a lingering dampness permeated his coven. Bex, on the other hand, had gone through some lengths to rid her coven of the dank, moldy humidity of the cave; the room smelled pleasant and fresh.

As I became more entrenched in Dominic's world, it became increasing difficult to accept the juxtaposition between the vampires' savage, instinctive, animal-like nature and their intellect, emotions, and personalities. I couldn't scrape the image of Bex gathering Rene in her embrace from my mind. She had worried over his well-being, and her joy at his return had been undeniable. It was unfathomable to me that beings who could rip each other's throats out, hunt indiscriminately, and kill without remorse could embrace a friend for returning safely, decorate a room with a pink bedspread, and light scented candles to counter the clammy air of the underground.

Seeing Bex's interaction with Rene and witnessing the care in which she kept her coven made me wonder if I'd been wrong about Bex and Dominic and vampires in general. They were lethal—there was no denying their strength and dietary preferences—but maybe there were more hues to their personalities than I'd ever considered. Maybe they were like humans in that the whole of their species couldn't be judged by the actions of individuals. Maybe some were monsters, like Kaden, some had conflicting agendas, like Jillian, and others, like Dominic and Bex, were leaders, forced to make swift, difficult decisions for the safety and security of their covens.

I could and often did deny Dominic's feelings toward me and my well-being, justifying them as shallow and selfish. I believed he only cared for me and not about me, like an owner cares for its guard dog. A guard dog isn't a loved member of the family. It might be fed and bathed and cared for physically, but when its purpose ends, whether from injury or age, the dog is replaced by a new guard dog that can better serve its purpose.

I was Dominic's daylight guard dog, his right arm in the sun, as he was recently fond of saying, but I worried that despite Dominic's intelligence and vast experience, the more animal, instinctive side of him was also utilitarian. Once my position as his night blood was no longer useful—after the Leveling—he would see me as more liability than asset, and I would be put down. Or turned into a vampire against my will.

I stood in the middle of the bedroom and stared at the single bed in front of me, the bed I would be sharing with Dominic unless one of us took the couch, and I couldn't decide what to believe. Was Dominic a leader, making difficult decisions to protect his coven, or a monster, using me and discarding me at will? Who could I trust? How would I survive? And if I aligned myself with the monsters to survive and hopefully save my brother, did that make me a monster, too?

I covered my face with my hands. The image of that creature, my brother, with its hand puncturing Bex's chest and tearing out her heart still haunted me, and I suspected would continue haunting me for the rest of my life. I shuddered.

"You are disturbed by the recent turn of events," Dominic said softly. "I knew that finding your brother, no matter the condition we found him in, would be difficult."

He had been standing near the bed to my left when we entered the room, but now his voice was directly behind me. I could feel his presence bearing over me.

I rubbed my eyes with the heel of my hands. "It's still out there, my own brother, killing something else because it couldn't kill us."

Dominic reached out from behind, wrapped his hands around my wrists, and pulled my hands down, away from my face. "That is very likely true, but there's nothing else to be done about it tonight."

I felt his presence, like a live wire, scorching my back. His thumbs massaged lazy circles on my inner wrists as he held me captive, and I felt suddenly trapped. He was my only protection here in Bex's coven, but who would protect me against him?

Dominic leaned into me. I felt his breath, hot and chilling, against my neck. Goose bumps puckered down my spine like a bolt of electricity. I froze.

"Dominic, let go of my arms and step back. Please," I added, trying to soften the request, "I need some space."

He nuzzled closer. His cheek was pressed to the back of my neck and his hands, so strong and unyielding, slid up my arms. "Your mouth says no, but I can smell you and the wet, heady scent of your desire. I can feel the vibration of your body, like a tuning fork, singing for me to touch you. I could taste the sweetness of your trust when we fell into the cavern. You were terrified, but you clung to me, trusting me to save us and protect you. Trust me now."

"One has nothing to do with the other. Let go." I turned my head, trying to face him and dislodge his grip, and my silver earring brushed his face as he nuzzled into my neck. I smelled the sizzling stink of burning skin before I realized what I'd done, but once I realized, I angled my head to press my earring flat against his face.

Dominic jerked back sharply, his expression fierce.

I froze at the sudden transition. "What?"

"Your earring burned my cheek."

I leaned in to inspect his injury, but his features were smooth and unblemished from my earring. He'd already healed. "Your cheek looks fine to me."

Dominic gave me a level look.

I sighed. "I asked you to let me go, and you didn't. What did you expect? For me to just take it?"

"After everything we've survived together, I expect your trust."

Most of what I survived, I considered having done so against him, not with him, but when my life was literally in his hands, he'd saved me without turning me into a vampire. He allowed me to keep my humanity, and for that, he'd earned a sliver of my trust.

"I trust you."

Dominic raised his eyebrows.

"I don't particularly trust your motives, but I trust you to protect me," I clarified.

Dominic nodded, still reserved. "Fair enough."

"But my brother is out there, just outside these walls and above this coven, and at the moment, there's nothing I can do to save him." I shook my head, sorrow squeezing my throat. "Nathan's a monster, and we're going to have to kill him to stop him." My voice squeaked on a sob at those last words.

Dominic walked passed me to the bed and climbed under the comforter.

I watched him cautiously, my eyes narrowed.

He patted the space next to him on the bed.

"Seriously?" I asked, looking down at the blood and dirt stains spread liberally over my clothing and then deliberately at Bex's clean sheets. "I don't think so."

He smiled, showing the full, lethal length of his fangs. "I promise not to bite."

I rolled my eyes. "I'm filthy. You could probably wring the blood from my shirt it's so soaked."

"Bex won't be surprised by a little blood on the sheets. I'm sure she keeps spares in the closet, as do I, for just such occations," Dominic said, dismissing my concerns with a flick of his wrist at the linen closet. "I have a story to tell you, and perhaps after you've heard my tale, you will gain a modicum of hope concerning your brother."

I inhaled sharply. Hope was Dominic's fangs against my neck, that poignant fear of my destruction should I concede, intermixed with the pain of the unknown should I resist. "You think we can save Nathan?"

"I think you owe it to him and yourself to try. He is already gone from you, so what do you have left to lose?" Dominic patted the bed again.

I sighed heavily and reluctantly conceded. I climbed under the comforter next to him and snuggled into its warmth with an even heavier sigh. I hadn't realized how cold I was until the warmth of the sheets, comforter, and mattress surrounded me.

"I healed you the best I could under the circumstances, but you need to rest and drink more fluids." Dominic looked around, and his gaze, so penetrating, seemed to look through walls. "I wonder if Bex keeps an IV in the coven."

"No IV," I said quickly. The last time Dominic had fitted me with an IV, he'd pumped me full of morphine. I was already resisting Jillian's cravings. I didn't need more of my own. "I'm healing just fine."

Dominic flashed me a look from the corner of his eyes. "I've never met someone so incredibly stubborn about her wellbeing. You would benefit from medical attention."

"I agree. It's too bad there aren't any trained medical personnel here to administer that attention," I said pointedly.

"My coven and I have survived for hundreds of years without doctors and nurses tending our wounds."

I leveled a flat look at him. "That's easy to say when your blood is rapidly self-healing and you don't age."

Dominic cracked a smile. "Some vampires in my coven heal rather slowly compared to me, and in those cases, I have administered my fair share of medical treatment."

I shook my head. "I thought you mentioned something about a story. Something that was supposed to give me a scrap of hope for my brother."

"Keep perspective in mind, but to be honest, I believe we have a little more than a scrap," Dominic said. He slouched into the covers until he was buried up to his chest in pink bedspread. "We have an inch or two of hope at best."

I shimmied onto my side to face him, my head in my hand and my elbow propped on the pillow. "Funny."

"I've been trying," Dominic said, and his expression as he turned his head to face me said it all. *I've been trying for you.*

"Well," I said on a swallow, "what can we do? What makes you think we have any chance at all?"

"When I found her, Jillian was one of the Damned."

I stared at Dominic in silence as that statement and its implications sunk into my brain. "What?" I asked, shocked.

Dominic smiled ruefully at my reaction. "Let me start from the beginning. This particular story took root when my younger brother and I were turned. After our transformation, we didn't understand what we had become. Unlike you, we'd never encountered vampires during our human existence, and we didn't readily accept our new life. We certainly didn't readily accept its limitations as described by our Master: avoid sunlight, drink blood, everlasting life. We questioned the existence of our immortal souls, and we resented our Master for damning us to an afterlife in hell."

I closed my mouth, realizing it was gaping. "I didn't know you had a brother."

"He wasn't around often. As first-born, I was to inherit my father's trade, so I worked with him in his shop. Desirius helped in the shop when he was younger, but once he was of age, he enlisted in the military. I rarely saw him through the years, maybe two or three times before we were transformed."

I frowned. The name Desirius nagged at a distant memory. I'd heard that name before, but I couldn't place it.

"Although I resented our Master, he was the only being who could teach me what I'd become, how to survive, and eventually, grow into the best version of that being possible. After years of his encouragement and praise as I surpassed his power, he became a second father to me."

I bit my lip, suspecting where the story was headed. "And your brother? Did Desirius stay and learn from your Master, too?"

Dominic shook his head. "No. As he had in his human life when faced with competition of our inheritance, Desirius left us to find his own way, to carve his own path. He learned from experience and the vampires he met along his journey, but he didn't believe all of the limitations that bound him. Avoiding sunlight and drinking blood are easy enough to prove, but more complicated matters, like Masters being the only of our kind able to transform night bloods into vampires, were more difficult for him to accept."

The name Desirius finally clicked in my memory, and I gasped softly. "Desirius was Jillian's Master."

Dominic nodded. "They fell in love while she was a night blood. He joined her intended coven to remain near her, but he wanted to be the vampire to complete her transformation. Eventually, so did she."

"Why would the current Master allow that? Why wasn't Desirius stopped?" I asked.

"He waited until the Leveling, when the current Master was powerless, and then he transformed other night bloods."

I frowned. "Not Jillian?"

"He thought it would work, but he wouldn't risk failing the first time with Jillian. So he experimented on other night bloods to perfect his technique. The creatures he transformed were Damned—horrific, mindless creatures who killed on sight—but as Desirius continued his experiments, the creatures became less mindless and slightly less horrific. He kept them caged beneath the coven, boxed in silver where no one would find them, not even Jillian. Similar, actually, to how I've contained Jillian now."

"Eventually his experiments were a success because he was able to turn Jillian, right?" I asked.

"Wrong. The creatures escaped their imprisonment and killed Jillian. They drained her nearly dry, and when every last drop of life had been stolen from her, they tried to eat her heart."

The image of Nathan eating Officer Montgomery's heart flashed over my vision. I swallowed the bile that rose in the back of my throat. "But?"

Dominic smiled. "But Desirius saved her before they could steal her heart and gave her his blood to transform her into a vampire."

"And it worked on her this time," I insisted. "She transformed into a vampire."

"No," Dominic said. "She transformed into one of the Damned."

I slid down into the comforter and laid on my back, my head on the pillow next to Dominic instead of facing him. "I don't understand. When I met Jillian, she was a normal vampire, her betrayal aside," I added at the skeptical look he shot me. "She wasn't one of the Damned."

"Exactly. She was one of the Damned when *I* met her, and we were able to transform her into a normal vampire, despite having risen as the Damned first."

"Oh," I said, barely daring to hope, but a kernel of nervous warmth spread through me. "You think Nathan could be transformed into a vampire, too?"

Dominic nodded. He propped himself up on his elbow to face me. "I think there's a chance. Make no mistake, the other night bloods who rose as the Damned died as the Damned. The damage done to them was irreparable. They killed on sight and massacred thousands of people—humans, night bloods, and vampires alike. Jillian was the only one capable of being saved."

I bit my lip, thinking of Nathan eating Officer Montgomery's heart and all the other people he had already massacred. "What was different about Jillian?"

"Love," Dominic said, and by his tone it sounded as if even after all this time, he didn't quite believe the words coming out of his own mouth. "And the fact that Desirius *had* improved upon the transformation with practice, but ultimately, love was what saved her. She didn't kill Desirius when he confronted her, like she had killed others. She hesitated, almost as if in recognition of him and her former feelings for him, and it gave us the chance we needed to kill her."

"Why were you there? Were you part of your brother's coven?"

"No, I was visiting. Word of the massacres and rumors of the existence of vampires were growing in the human population. I was there to find the source of the rumors and stop them. When I realized what my brother had done, it was only a matter of time before the Day Reapers came to rectify the situation. The Damned population was completely out of control."

"The Day Reapers are your government, right?"

"Yes, essentially. Masters ensure that their covens prosper in anonymity, and the Day Reapers ensure that Masters are keeping control of their covens. They are the most powerful of our kind and able to withstand sunlight."

I took a deep breath. "So what happened? How did you save Jillian if you killed her?"

"The Damned are unstoppable. As you've probably noticed, their scales are impenetrable, and their strength and speed can't be rivaled."

I nodded. "Yeah, I've noticed."

"But as her maker, Desirius had a modicum of control over her. His fangs could penetrate her skin. He drained her, and then I gave her my blood, the blood of a Master." Dominic sighed. "And then I killed Desirius."

I stared at him. "You killed your brother?"

Dominic nodded. "He'd created a horde of monsters that massacred thousands and exposed the existence of vampires. If Jillian hadn't been harmed, he would have happily continued his experiments. He didn't want vampires to remain a secret, to remain creatures of the night. Jillian agreed with Desirius, but after her experience, I'd thought her views had changed." Dominic was silent for a moment, staring down at the sheet between us. "I was obviously wrong about her."

I shook my head, stuck on one specific detail. "But he was your brother."

"The Day Reapers would have made an example of him to discourage other Masters from the path he chose. I spared him their torture," he whispered. "The memory of him and the rift between us still haunts me, but I take comfort in the fact that I protected him from the Day Reapers."

"Spare me your protection," I murmered.

"We heal instantly from devastating wounds, Cassidy. Torture for one of our kind in the hands of a Day Reaper can last several years without reprieve," Dominic said, his words clipped. "It was a fate he begged me to avert, and I willingly abliged."

"And Jillian?" I whispered.

"She transformed into a vampire, no worse for having first transformed into the Damned, and although she grieved Desirius' loss, as did I, she understood his fate otherwise. She forgave me. Supposedly," Dominic added. "When it comes to Jillian, I don't know what to believe anymore."

"So correct me if I'm wrong, but let me see if I understand the implications of this tale," I said carefully. "You want to drain Nathan and then give him your blood to transform him into a vampire?"

"I'll give him my blood to transform him, but I won't be the one to drain him."

I frowned. "If not you, who?"

"His maker transformed him into the creature he is, and she is the only one capable of taking it back."

I sighed warily. "She?"

Dominic didn't even hesitate. "Jillian, of course."

"Of course," I rolled my eyes. "How do you know Jillian's to blame for Nathan's transformation? It could be anyone."

Dominic shook his head. "No, it couldn't. Jillian believed that she, like Desirius, could transform a night blood, and she's the only vampire I know motivated enough to try."

"Fine. Let's assume Jillian is Nathan's maker. How do you suppose she drains him? Before or after he eats her heart for dinner?"

Dominic's smile was sheepish. I knew that look and his intension behind it before he even uttered a single word. "Now that we know Nathan is hunting you, we shouldn't have any trouble locating him.

"You want to use me as bait," I said flatly. "Again."

"Don't think of it as bait," Dominic said quickly. Too quickly. "I—"

"We've gone down this road before, and it didn't end well for me!"

"As I recall, it ended very well. We took back control of my coven, and we both survived. I consider that a win."

"I suffered! Kaden broke my leg, my ribs, and my arm. He snapped my finger and nearly drained me," I shouted. "I suffered terribly."

Dominic leaned forward. "And it was worth it. Think about it, Cassidy. This is your brother we're talking about this time, not my coven. Will you risk temporary suffering for the chance to save him?"

Fuck, I thought. When he put it in those terms, there was no question. "Of course," I ground out.

"So you lure him, Jillian drains him, I give him my blood, and to seal the transformation, I kill his maker."

I blinked. "You kill Jillian?"

"You'll finally get the execution you've been waiting for." Dominic's smile turned wary. "I will do what is necessary to protect us from the Day Reapers. If I don't instill order to their satisfaction, they will."

I pursed my lips, not entirely convinced. "What if his maker is Kaden? You don't know for sure that Jillian did this, and Kaden's already dead."

"Nathan recognized you tonight when he drank from your carotid instead of your aorta. He hesitated to kill you, just like Jillian hesitated when she faced Desirius. Kaden wasn't powerful enough to create a version of the Damned that could recognize love, but Jillian might."

I shook my head and blew the bangs out of my face. "There's too much at risk for 'might.' How do we find out for sure?"

Dominic grinned, and with that one look, I was suddenly very aware that I was lying in bed under the sheets with a powerful, dangerous, compulsive creature whose main source of food ran through my veins.

I eased away from him.

"Your heartbeat just escalated and the pitch of your breath deepened." Dominic leaned closer. "What are you thinking, Cassidy?"

"I'm thinking that you should keep your distance," I said in a careful, steady tone. Attempting to hide my fear when he could hear the change in my heartbeat was futile, but I attempted anyway.

"I could close the distance between us faster than you could think you wanted space."

"I'm already thinking it," I snapped.

Dominic raised an eyebrow. "Are you saying that you don't want me?"

That's exactly what I'm saying, I thought, but that wouldn't go over well. "I'm saying that I'm well aware of your strength and speed and physical superiority in every way. There's no need to show me how easily you could force me."

"I don't want to force you, Cassidy. I could if I wanted to, but despite my physical superiority—" His lips quirked at the phrase, and I got the distinct impression that he was laughing at me"—I want you to come to me of your own accord. I want your trust."

"Why is my trust so important to you?" I whispered.

He stared into my eyes, and I could feel the press of his mind against mine. I could feel the breathless ache inside him, like a kaleidoscope of desire, as it solidified and morphed shape with his thoughts. I didn't know his thoughts, but I knew by the crest and ebb of his emotions that he was conflicted and that the feeling was deeply rooted. Could I be the source of that conflict?

I shook my head and looked away.

"I can only trust you when I know you trust me," Dominic said. "Can you place your fears aside, just for a moment, and trust me now to determine Jillian's strength?"

I glanced up at him. "What do you need me to do?"

"I need you to trust me," he said patiently.

I rolled my eyes. "I've got that. What else do you need me to do?"

Dominic lifted his wrist to his mouth and bit into the vein. Blood welled in the deep puncture from his fangs and dripped down his forearm. He offered his wrist to me.

"I need you to drink."

* * * *

The heady scent of his blood wafted to me and scorched the back of my throat. Unlike the scent of cinnamon from Bex's blood, Dominic's blood had a fresh heat, like the effervescence of peppermint. I turned my head away but couldn't deny the unquenchable thirst. I burned with it.

Jillian stirred in my mind. His blood was familiar to her, and she stretched and shuddered with anticipation, luxuriating in the memories of his icy heat against her flesh.

Yes, she breathed on a long, trembling pant. *Drink.*

I raised my hand and blocked his wrist from coming any closer to my mouth. "No. This isn't going to prove anything."

DRINK! Jillian shrieked.

I winced from the volume of her voice resonating in my mind.

Dominic cocked his head. "How does my blood make you feel?"

I tried to breathe shallowly to avoid smelling its scent. "It makes me thirsty," I admitted. "My throat is on fire, as if I'll burn from the inside out without your blood to dampen the flames."

"Can you feel Jillian inside your mind?"

I nodded. "She wants me to drink. She's insisting, actually."

Dominic moved his wrist closer to me, undaunted by my efforts to stop him. "Comply with her, and let's see what happens."

Yes, Jillian purred. *Let's see what happens.*

I shook my head. "This isn't good. She's anticipating your blood."

"Of course she is. She's starving." Dominic stopped moving his arm closer, but he didn't pull back, either. "I won't let anything happen to you. You aren't drained, so drinking from me won't transform you nor harm you in any way. This is just an experiment."

"Nothing is 'just' an experiment."

"I need you to trust me."

I stared at Dominic's wrist, his blood thick like honey, and at that moment, there was nothing I wanted more than to lick his blood-slicked flesh. Desire and thirst incinerated my throat.

I shook my head.

Dominic sighed in frustration. "Why are you resisting? I know you trust me enough for this. You've risked much more for me than a simple lick. You've licked Bex's blood and nothing extraordinary occurred. Why not lick mine?"

"It's not about your blood. It's not about trusting you," I whispered, terrified.

"I know you want to help your brother. Your devotion to save him in undeniable."

I nodded.

"Determining Jillian's strength is our first step toward saving him."

"I can't."

"Why?" Dominic insisted.

I breathed in sharply from his tone. The icy heat of peppermint flooded my nose. A backdraft blazed down my throat to my stomach, and the truth burst through my lips before I even knew I was speaking. "I don't trust myself!"

Dominic stared for a moment, surprised by my outburst. "In what way don't you trust yourself?" he asked calmly, as if this were a normal conversation.

Tears streamed down my face, and it took every molecule of my control not to pounce on his arm and lap at the blood like an animal. Like him.

"I want it too much," I admitted. "I know better than to give into cravings when I want something this badly, when it feels like I'll literally die without it. It usually means I'll die having it."

Dominic narrowed his gaze on me. "These aren't *your* cravings, Cassidy. They're Jillian's. The few times you've tasted my blood, you were revolted. I had to force my blood into your mouth, and even then, instead of swallowing, you spat it back in my face, remember?"

I nodded slowly. "Yes, I remember, but these cravings feel like my cravings."

"I trust you," he said, his voice low and serious. "Drink."

I swallowed, and my saliva scraped like sand down my throat. His arm was suddenly closer. His blood smelled sweeter, and the scent stung my nose hairs in an icy burn. My mouth flooded with his blood before I even realized I'd moved. My hands on his arms, which were supposed to be resisting, had betrayed me and pulled his wrist to my mouth.

YES! Jillian shouted, her voice a breathy exhale of pleasure. *MORE!*

I swallowed and sucked in another mouthful of blood. The more I drank, the more I wanted, and the more I wanted, the more I drank. I was drowning in thirst and burning with need and without an anchor to steady me, I couldn't stop.

Dominic tried to pry my mouth from his arm gently, but I bit into his flesh and refused to budge.

"Cassidy DiRocco, you will stop drinking my blood, you will release your hold on my wrist, and look into my eyes."

Dominic's voice resonated in my head, turning my mind to putty and my will to his own. I stopped drinking his blood, released his wrist, and looked into his eyes instantly.

"No," I whispered. "You promised. You swore by the sun that you would never entrance me again."

"So did you, and when necessary, you broke that promise. As am I." Dominic looked deep into my eyes. "I can feel her in you." He didn't look away, but from the strain in his voice, it pained him not to. "I can feel your struggle. Why would you think you were addicted to blood?"

I tried not to think of that time, but not thinking about it was like someone telling you not to think about elephants. You were instantly and uncontrollably thinking about elephants.

I thought about my painful recovery from being shot, of my addition to Percocets and of my subsequent struggle to detox. I thought of my fight with Nathan and of my promise to never slip down that path ever again. I'd promised him that family would always come first.

"Ah," Dominic said, and that one noise said everything. He understood.

Dominic looked even deeper into my eyes, searching. "Jillian Allister, look into my eyes."

Impossible, Jillian thought.

Dominic released his hold on my mind, but the single thread that still linked my mind to Jillian's sparked to attention. I felt her look up through my eyes and stare into Dominic's gaze.

He was able to entrance Jillian through me.

"Oh, it's possible," Dominic said, his expression smug. "You made Cassidy drink my blood, which means you drank my blood, opening your mind to me. You know the consequences of drinking from another vampire, Jillian. And you know the consequences of hurting Cassidy."

I didn't make her do anything she didn't want to do, Jillian denied. *Release me.*

"I intend to, and when I do, you'll wish I had left you to rot in your imprisonment where you belong," Dominic hissed.

I felt Jillian's sudden, chilling fear.

"Did you attempt to turn the night blood, Nathan DiRocco, into a vampire?"

Who? Jillian asked, but a vision of Nathan flashed through my mind. His lifeless body was bent back over Jillian's embrace, his neck exposed, and the sweet cinnamon taste of his blood flooded her senses as she drank him dry.

"Did you give him your blood?" Dominic urged.

No, I did not, Jillian denied, but her memory of him sucking and swallowing her blood was all the answer we needed. Jillian had turned Nathan into the Damned.

Dominic looked away. His connection with Jillian severed, and almost instantly, Jillian severed the last remaining thread between us, so all that remained in her absence was a nauseating black void.

I could feel the sticky tack of Dominic's blood on my lips and chin, in my mouth and coating the back of my throat, and instead of the burning crave and unquenchable thirst I'd been struggling to stifle, I was revolted.

I gagged.

"She's gone?" Dominic asked.

I nodded. "Oh, God." I gagged again, fighting not to vomit. "I'm going to be sick."

Dominic's arms were around me in an instant, and with a rush of wind and a dizzying displacement in space, I was suddenly sitting on a shaggy rug on the tiled bathroom floor of our guest suite, draped over the toilet.

"Thanks," I muttered, and a moment later, my stomach convulsed. I closed my eyes, trying not to look at the contents of my stomach coming from my mouth, but I knew from the stench what it was and gagged even harder. I was throwing up blood.

"The blood you drank was nourishing her," Dominic said, sitting on the ledge of the shower beside me. "She might be strong enough to help with your brother after all."

"Great," I said. Although my words were true, sincerity was difficult to convey while hugging a toilet. I needed a shower. God knew I didn't have the strength to bathe on my own, but more than a shower, I wanted to hug the toilet without an audience. "Can I have some privacy?"

"You'll need help to clean yourself if you want a bath," Dominic said, his voice level and reasonable despite the words. "Let me help you."

My anger erupted in a hot blaze. "Get out of my head! You broke your promise! You swore by the sun that you would never entrance me, and you broke that trust."

"We swore that we would never entrance each other, but you broke that promise weeks ago."

"To save your life!"

"Which I accepted as an appropriate circumstance to break such a promise. I, in turn, was faced with a situation in which I felt it necessary to break that promise, and now, you're free from Jillian's hold on your mind. Also, we've confirmed that Jillian is your brother's maker. I apologize for the intrusion, for what it's worth, but it was necessary."

"Fine," I conceded between gags. Anything to make him leave. "Will you please go?"

Dominic stared at me in silence for a long moment. I attempted to ignore him and calm my stomach, but with the metallic stickiness of blood coating the back of my throat, I couldn't stop gagging.

The sink ran for a few seconds and then cut off.

"Here." Dominic leaned down and offered me a small paper cup filled with water.

I took a sip, gargled, and spat pink, diluted blood into the toilet. After a few more rinses my stomach settled, and I flushed.

"Thank you," I said, handing him the cup. "I suppose mind reading has its advantages."

"You know I can't read your mind unless you're entranced, and even then, I can only see your thoughts if I try very, very hard. Your defenses against me are better even than Jillian's," Dominic said, and if I didn't know any better, I'd say he sounded almost proud of me. "But that doesn't mean I can't anticipate your needs."

"And I appreciate that," I lied. "But at the moment, what I really need is some privacy." He still didn't look convinced, so I added, "Please."

"You will call for me if you need anything," Dominic said sternly. "I don't think you have the strength to bathe on your own, but I'll respect your wishes if you promise to ask for help if necessary."

"I promise," I said, thinking *not a chance in hell will I ask for your help bathing.*

Dominic's penetrating look pierced through my eyes and seemed to will my soul for more. I knew what he wanted, but I wasn't willing to give it to him.

"I'm not expanding on that promise, if that's what you're waiting for."

Dominic crossed his arms. He looked very comfortable leaning back against the side of the shower. Too comfortable. It didn't look like he was about to give me privacy any time soon. "Why are you refusing me now?" he asked. "You didn't before."

"Before, I didn't realize I was giving more than my word. I wouldn't have broken my word anyway, but now I'm wondering what else I'm giving you when I swear by the passage of time."

"Nothing more than what I'm giving you when I swear by the sun." Dominic grinned. "If you don't intend to break your word anyway, than what does it matter?"

"It matters," I said flatly. "When I asked Bex to swear by the sun, she refused. She told me that I didn't understand what I was asking of her, and she's right. What exactly was I asking of her, Dominic, that was more than a formal promise? What exactly have you been asking of me?"

"Nothing that I haven't given you. If you recall, I also swore promises to you."

I pursed my lips. "And what is it that we've given each other, Dominic? If I'm not aware of what I've sworn to you, does it even count as having been given?"

For the first time in our acquaintance, Dominic looked uncomfortable.

"After your experience with Jillian, I thought you wanted my loyalty of my own free will. It doesn't count as free will if you trick me along the way."

"You are very right." He stood. "Enjoy your privacy, Cassidy."

He shut the door behind him, leaving me to wash the blood and grime and memories of death from my body without him watching, without him near to confuse my thoughts and feelings. I'd won the battle for my privacy, but in terms of life as I once knew it, life as I preferred to live it, I was losing the war.

Chapter 14

Blood washed off my skin and out of my hair, some spots needing a little more scrubbing than others, until it all swirled down the drain. I let the water turn scalding. Steam filled the bathroom and my skin pruned as I boiled myself under the spray. Dominic's story about Jillian and how he had brought her back from the Damned and transformed her into a vampire was supposed to give me hope, but I couldn't quite accept his story as the beacon of hope he'd intended. Jillian had been saved from the Damned only to become a vampire.

Even if we saved Nathan, he wouldn't be himself again. He would be a vampire.

A week ago, I'd thought he was either dead or a vampire, and I hadn't known which would be worse. I'd never imagined that he would be the creature he is now, and I'd never thought that attempting to transform him into a vampire would be his salvation. Vampires were worse than death: they were undead, but dead or undead, anything was better than being Damned.

I dunked my head under the water, knowing that despite my healthy fear of vampires and placing my aversion to becoming one aside, being undead wasn't entirely the case.

After my continued experiences with Dominic, "undead" wasn't quite the term for his existence. "Mutated" was probably a better description. Night bloods transform into vampires by morphing their DNA with vampire blood. Dominic was once a night blood, too, just like Walker and me, with human worries and fears about disease, death, and his own mortality, but whether by force or by choice, he'd transformed into a vampire instead of dying.

I'd been so sure of right and wrong and good and evil. The distinction between vampire and human was black and white, but when I thought about Dominic and his stories—his attempts to comfort me, give me hope, and his plans to save my brother—everything was gray. Dominic wasn't pure evil, but did that mean I could trust him? Even if his motivations were selfish and self-serving, would he still pull through when I needed him most? When my brother needed him most? If everything was shades of gray, how could I find my way?

I turned my face into the scalding spray and let it all go. The suffocating uncertainties—whether Nathan was better off dead than a vampire, whether resisting Dominic was futile, whether facing my own mortality was really the preferable option—I let it wash over me and swirl down the drain along with the horrors of last night. I was alive. I was human. In this moment I was still me, and in that clarity, I could still breathe.

* * * *

Tendrils of steam followed me from the bathroom when I opened the door and walked into the bedroom. It hadn't occurred to me until after my shower that I didn't have anything to wear. The rags of my shirt and jeans that hadn't been torn were unmercifully stained with blood. My leather jacket, which had made me feel and look so badass, hadn't fared much better against Nathan's fangs and claws than the cloth of my fitted t-shirt. Even my phone was crusted with blood. At least the case had proven its worth and protected it from being damaged by Nathan's abuse.

Unfortunately, I couldn't say the same of my body. The shower had helped both my mood and my sore muscles, but I still ached in places deeper than a shower could reach.

I found a turquoise terrycloth robe hanging in the bathroom closet amidst the towels, so I wrapped that around myself, double knotted the cord around my waist, and held the lapels at my neck closed with my hands. For the first time in my entire adult life, my height came to my advantage. On a woman of average height, the robe likely cut off mid-thigh, but on me, it reached my knees.

I was still unsteady on my feet, battling the dizziness of blood loss and the usual grind of my hip. It took me eight excruciating steps, but with one foot in front of the other, I managed to cross the room without collapsing.

Dominic didn't move. He didn't turn to help me nor rebuke me for struggling on my own. He waited until I reached the bed, and then he walked into the bathroom, shutting the door with a soft click behind him.

It took me aback for a second, watching him enter the bathroom. I supposed he needed a shower, too—he'd been nearly as encrusted with blood and dirt as I was—but I never imagined him using a bathroom. The transformations between his many forms—his gaunt, emaciated body before feeding, the model perfection after, and the grotesque horror of his true, gargoyle-like form—were so unnervingly sudden that I'd somehow imagined that his hygiene and immaculately styled hair were simply products of that transformation rather than something he achieved by hand.

My preconceptions seemed silly now—I could hear the shower running and his belt hitting the tile floor—but that realization exposed an entire host of questions: did he cut his hair as well as style it? Did vampires' hair grow despite other bodily functions having stilled? Considering his liquid diet, did he need the bathroom for other, more basic necessities?

I took out my earings and placed them and my phone on the nightstand, but as I stared at the bed—more pointedly, as I stared at the soiled sheets on the bed—I banished those questions for tonight. I was exhausted. The more pertinent question, more imminent than my musings over Dominic's hygine, was where Bex kept clean sheets. Dominic was right, as usual—damn him—because I found a freshly laundered comforter in the linen closet.

Making the bed properly was beyond my current energy capacity, so I tore off the dirty, bloody sheets, left them in a twisted heap on the floor, and crawled into bed with the comforter burritoed around my body.

Despite the fact that sunrise was approaching and a new day was beginning, mine was finally ending. The guest bedchamber of Bex's coven wasn't the ideal place to sleep, but strangely enough, I felt safer here than I had in Walker's house. Walker had a safe room against the vampires, but here with the vampires, Dominic was the safe room.

Although, I had no real guarantee who would keep me safe from him.

I thought about the opulence of Bex's coven and the time it must have taken to establish her place here. I thought about Dominic's coven and the many vampires hidden under New York City, an entire city of vampires beneath our own, and I wondered at the other covens throughout the United States, hell, throughout the world, and how the Day Reapers thought to maintain and enforce such a widespread secret. If Dominic was having trouble convincing powerful and intelligent vampires like Jillian that secrecy was the best policy, I was willing to bet that in all the hundreds of covens in the world, Dominic wasn't the only Master struggling. It was only just a matter of time before someone powerful rose to Master with the opportunity and will to reveal their existence.

The bed dipped gently behind me. I opened my eyes, realizing I'd dozed off. Dominic's palm grazed my cheek.

"Don't let me disturb you," he whispered over me. "Go back to sleep. I need to rest as well."

I frowned, easing away from his hand. "You sleep?"

Dominic let his hand drop on a sigh. I could sense his disappointment, but I didn't bolt upright when he joined me beneath the covers. That was concession enough.

"In a sense," he replied, and it took me a moment to realize he was referring to sleep. "My brain doesn't have a REM cycle like yours; I don't dream, but I find a trancelike state in which I escape from reality. Like your sleep, my day rest is important for both physical and mental health."

"Oh," I said on a yawn.

"Sleep well, Cassidy."

"But what about—"

"Shhh," Dominic hushed against the back of my neck. The rush of his breath shot goose bumps down my spine. "Enough questions. We'll talk more at sunset."

"Fine," I grumbled. "Have a good night, er, day, I guess."

The rumble of his laughter vibrated between my shoulder blades. Considering we were sharing a king size bed, he seemed unnecessarily close behind me, but I refused to turn and give him the satisfaction of acknowledging that I'd noticed.

"A good day rest," he clarified. I could hear the smile in his voice.

I tried, I really did, but I couldn't contain myself. "Do you need a full eight hours, like us, to feel completely rested, or do you—"

"Sleep well, Cassidy," Dominic said, his tone cutting.

I sighed. "Have a good day rest, Dominic."

Moments later, when I had just slipped between waking and dreaming, I felt the weight of Dominic's arm drape over my hip and the press of his bare stomach against my back as he gathered me close, but I knew without a shred of uncertainty that I was dreaming when I heard his voice tremble as he whispered.

"Let the hours pass uncounted. I could rest for eternity if it meant resting with you."

* * * *

My entire backside and the line of my hip were ice cube cold.

Despite having snuggled under the layers of terrycloth robe and comforter, I woke with a disoriented suddenness, shivering and uncomfortable. The steam from the shower had long since dissipated, but without windows, deciphering the time was impossible. Even in a world of cell phones, computer screens, and watches, a world in which time was catalogued by mechanical hands and digital numbers, I never realized how telling the sun and shadows could be until I'd become obsessed with the exact moments of sunrise and sunset. Now my life's decisions hinged upon knowing the sun's rise each day and its fall each night, and being separated from that knowledge was like holding my breath underwater without access to breach the surface. I could grasp at guesses or check my phone, but I wouldn't breathe easy until I felt the warmth of the sun on my face and soaked the physical proof of its safety into my skin.

I wiggled my arm from beneath the covers and pressed the unlock button on my phone. The time glowed brightly through the room, and I blinked at it in denial.

8:17p.m.

The sun had already set.

I turned, about to blast my outrage at Dominic for allowing me to sleep the entire day away, but I stopped dead, realizing why it was so frigid under the covers.

Dominic wasn't himself. Or rather, he was a version of himself that I hadn't seen since we'd first met. He was staring at me, his eyes open and unblinking. His icy white irises were ringed by a dark midnight blue, and their pupils reflected a nocturnal green tint in the dim of the room. His face was gaunt, the shape of his features and skull nearly skeleton-skinny. The arm draped over my hip was nothing but skin and angled bones, and his entire body pressed against mine—from the top of his chest, down each protruding rib, and over his concave stomach—was naked and burning cold.

Although his eyes were staring in my direction, they looked through me rather than at me. I eased back, wondering if he was still "resting" with his eyes open. Maybe I could slip out of bed unnoticed. Even if I managed that, where would I go? All the vampires would be waking from their day rest, all hungry and in a similar state as Dominic.

I achieved an inch of distance between our bodies before he sprang from the bed. I bounced up from the absence of his weight and was just as quickly smashed back down into the mattress. He was on top of me, the length of his naked body only separated from mine by the fluff of terrycloth robe between us. I wriggled beneath him, desperate for some distance. My heart was a frightened, trapped thing, pounding for release.

His chest rattled, low and deep.

"Dominic?" I whispered. My entire body was shaking.

He buried his face in my neck, but this time I wasn't wearing any earrings to impede his progress. I'd removed them for bed. My weapons were still in the pockets of the ruined leather jacket I'd left in a heap on the bathroom floor, but my phone was on the bedside table and within reach.

I tried to squirm my hand loose between us. Dominic's chest rattled again. His lips peeled back, and I felt the press of his fangs against my skin. The heat of his breath chilled my neck, and I froze.

"Stop. Moving," Dominic growled. His body was shaking too. "God, your fear is so sweet. You smell delicious." He breathed in, and this time, the vibration of his growl shook the bed. "You smell like prey."

"Stop it. You're hurting me," I said, forcing the tremble out of my voice. "Don't make me entrance you."

His growl expanded. "You can try, but I thought we were past those petty tests. Haven't we already determined who would win?"

I cocked my head, trying to block his mouth from accessing my throat. "I thought we were past these petty threats," I threw back at him.

"You are not making it easy for me to resist," he said on a growl. He pushed my face aside, and despite my attempts to block him, he licked a long, slow path from my collarbone to my ear with his tongue. "I told you to stop moving!"

Goose bumps puckered my nipples. "I told you to stop hurting me!" I said, but my voice sounded less than convincing.

"I'm trying," he snapped back. His voice rasped like his throat was shredded by razors. "I've always had to hunt for my first feeding, but after rousing from my rest tonight by your smell—that delicious, spicy-sweet, cinnamon smell—I can't think beyond craving you." He was pressed so close to my skin that I felt his throat convulse as he swallowed. "Bex, Rene, and the others will expect me to feed from you. They will question my strength and your loyalty if I don't."

I bucked at him, anger finally incinerating the fear in a hot blast. "You knew that, and you shared your bed with me. You conveniently omitted that protecting me throughout the day meant killing me tonight!"

"You're being dramatic," Dominic growled. "Drinking from you won't kill you. You don't need the entire cow to make a hamburger, remember? And neither do I, concerning you."

"Number one, I don't like being compared to a cow. It's insulting. And number two, you may not need the entire cow for one hamburger, but the cow ends up dead anyway."

"We've argued over dietary preference in the past, and it's a conversation I grow weary of discussing," Dominic said. "Either you trust me, or you don't. Either you're my night blood, or you're not."

"I'm playing your night blood to uphold my end of our deal, but it's an act. I'm not really your night blood."

"Fine, but we're still within Bex's coven. You will continue the act until the deal is off, and as my night blood, it's your responsibility to sustain me until I can obtain a full meal," he said, and his tone brooked no argument.

"My blood will weaken you," I reminded him. "Losing more blood will weaken me, and we need to be our strongest to face Nathan tonight." I narrowed my eyes. "We are still facing Nathan tonight, aren't we?"

Dominic froze this time, his face still buried in my neck for a moment before he eased back. "Yes, of course. I haven't forgotten our goals for tonight." He pressed his thumb to the pulse at my throat and closed his eyes on another growl. "My own thirst, I'm afraid, prevented me from remembering your condition. You lost a lot of blood yesterday, too much for me to expect you to feed me now. Your health takes priority over appearances, and if questioned, even Bex would understand that. Forgive me."

I tried to ease back, but his hold was still impenetrable. "There's nothing to forgive," I lied. "Just get off."

He growled low in his throat, and I realized how my tone sounded.

More politely, I added, "Please."

The low, rattling growl in his chest persisted while he spoke. "There are ways to replenish your blood supply after I've fed, so your health won't be jeopardized."

"Dominic, let me up," I said reasonably. He moved his fingers down my neck, grazing my shoulder and over my bicep to the sensitive bend in my elbow. I shivered, no longer feeling cold while pressed against his iciness. "Please, don't do this."

"You smell differently now. The cinnamon's still there, but the spice is different. Chai, perhaps." He breathed in and groaned. "I don't know which is better."

Faced with my fear and desire, he didn't know which he preferred. Who was more sick, the monster or the woman who desired the monster?

Maybe if I changed the topic we could claw our way back from this madness. "You're naked," I accused, blurting the first thought that came to mind. Despite our situation, despite the real, physical danger vibrating from him, I blushed.

"Yes," he growled, and the rattling increased.

Not exactly the effect or topic change I'd hoped for, but I'd started it. May as well follow through. "There was another robe in the bathroom you could have worn."

"I'm not ashamed of my body. Why should I hide it from you?"

"I'm not ashamed—" I started, but I caught the smirk twisting his lips and cut myself off. I took a deep breath and tried again. "I would have appreciated you wearing the robe."

Dominic raised his eyebrows. "I would have appreciated you *not* wearing the robe, but you didn't hear me complaining."

I opened my mouth and closed it, not sure how the topic had so quickly flown off course. Again.

"Do you wear a robe for Ian Walker when you share a bed?"

He posed the question so abruptly and so devoid of inflection that I answered truthfully and without thinking. "Walker? I've never shared a bed with Walker." I frowned. "Not that it's any of your business."

Dominic smiled instantly and unabashedly, like a reflex and unlike any smile I'd ever seen from him before. He was normally so deliberate and calculating, but this smile erupted like a caterpillar from its chrysalis, finally free and unencumbered. Finally in its true form.

He threw his head back and laughed. His bellows shook the entire bed.

I narrowed my eyes. "I must have missed the punch line."

"That's all right, my dear, dear Cassidy. I thought it was funny enough for the both of us." He eased his body off mine and stood. "I've always known that Ian Walker was a fool where Bex was concerned, but I never thought him a fool in regards to his relationship with you. This once, it's very, very nice to be wrong." He held out a hand to me.

I hesitated.

"Come, now. It's just a hand."

"You promise not to bite?" I asked, my tone dripping in sarcasm.

"You'll need to touch more of me than just my hand to leave this coven, and I dare say you'd prefer to leave sooner rather than later to avoid contact with any of Bex's vampires before they've fed."

I shook my head. "We can't leave. We need to share our plan to transform Nathan with Bex and Rene."

"Before we share anything with them, I have business with Jillian to attend."

Dominic's tone on the word 'business' shot a thrill of goosebumps down my spine. I couldn't imagine what further punishment he could inflict that hadn't already been inflicted by her confinement—besides death—but I was more than happy, just this once, to remain in the dark.

"I'll return before midnight," Dominic continued, "but until then, you should stay out of sight. I don't care how your relationship with Ian Walker is or isn't progressing, I need you to lie low in the one place safe from all vampires." He sighed heavily. "Although if the Day Reapers come, no place is safe."

I raised an eyebrow. "Where exactly is the one safe place against all vampires? And what does my relationship with Walker have to do with it?"

"The safest place from vampires is within Ian Walker's basement."

Chapter 15

Dominic dropped me off at Walker's house with strict orders to stay inside and out of sight until he returned. Initially, I'd emphatically agreed. I didn't want Nathan to catch my scent and track me here—my very presence put the other night bloods in danger—but as the hours passed in seclusion and silence, not one night blood answered my calls, returned my voicemails, or arrived at the house.

For the first time since arriving in Erin, New York, absolutely no one, not even Ronnie, was home in the Walker-Carmichael household.

Three voicemails and five texts in two hours may have been overkill on a normal night, but nothing about tonight was normal. Despite our disagreement, considering everything at stake—lives were at stake—I'd expected Walker to pick up his damn phone. We assumed Nathan was hunting me, but after last night, he might be hunting all of us.

The hall clock chimed eleven when I finally heard footsteps on the front porch. The door's deadbolt snapped open. I leapt away from the breakfast bar and positioned myself next to the basement steps, tensed to dive into the safe room if need be, but my initial jolt of adrenaline quickly faded to relief before I even saw the person entering the house. Nathan wouldn't use a key, and vampires couldn't enter without permission. Whoever it was, the person coming through that door was human and a resident of this house.

I relaxed my guard and stepped toward the door. Maybe they'd have an update on the search for Colin. Maybe they'd know where Walker had disappeared—hell where everyone had disappeared. At the very least, they must know if anyone else had been murdered.

If Nathan had killed more people last night, did I really want to know?

The door swung open, and I froze mid-step.

Ronnie entered the house, but she didn't look like Ronnie. She had always been too skinny, but now she was gaunt. Her arms and legs were nothing but skin stretched over bones. Her clothes sagged on her emaciated body, several sizes too big on her skeleton-like frame. A low, weak rattle growled from her chest. She was scanning the house in jerky, bird-like twitches of her head, and when her luminous, reflective, nocturnal eyes spotted me, she hissed. Long, pointed fangs gleamed from her snarl.

Ronnie was a vampire.

"Holy shit," I whispered.

She charged me, moving with inhuman speed but not nearly as lightning-fast as Dominic or Bex or even Rene. I cut to the side, dodging her attack. She shrieked, baring her fangs at me as she whipped back around and charged again. I cut to the other side, but the kitchen counter blocked my momentum. She crashed into my back, knocked me into the counter, and we slammed to the ground in a tangled heap of limbs and boney joints.

She lunged for my throat.

I raised my hands instinctively, turning my face away from her snapping jaws. The moment my hands touched her shoulders, she jerked away and cowered on the kitchen floor.

I stared, first at her and then my hands. I was wearing silver rings on each finger. Dominic and Bex would laugh at the threat of my rings, but not Ronnie. Her shoulders were blistered and blackened from that one brief touch.

I shook my head at her, stunned. Ronnie never left the house. Ever. So how did a vampire enter and transform her? Why hadn't the safe room, supposedly the best protection against all vampires, protected her?

"What the hell happened, Ronnie?" I asked.

A low growl rattled from Ronnie's chest. Her wounds weren't blackened anymore, but they were still blistered and oozing. She was healing—slowly, but healing all the same.

I stood, trying to think of my next move, and Ronnie was suddenly on her feet, too. She knocked me back and cracked my head on one of the breakfast barstools. I hit the ground face first, and this time, I stayed down.

It took a moment for the room to stop spinning, but a moment was all Ronnie needed. Her fangs sank deep into my flesh, like two stabbing knives. I felt the hickey-like pull of her suction at my neck as she drank. Unlike Dominic, whose bite was pure pleasure, or Rene, whose bite was like a dream, Ronnie's bite was exactly that: fangs ripping into my skin and her greedy, urgent mouth sucking my blood.

I yanked out the silver nitrate from my pocket, aimed it behind me, and hit her with the spray.

She flew back, screaming.

I flipped onto my back, still aiming the spray and ready to hit her with another blast if she so much as twitched in my direction.

She eyed me warily. The skin over her right cheek, neck, and shoulder was pockmarked with boiling blisters. Despite being sprayed, she'd still managed to swallow a few gulps of blood, so her face had plumped, her arms and legs were defined with muscle, and her complexion had pinkened. She still didn't look like herself, but at least she looked less dead.

I stood carefully, using the barstool for balance as the floor shifted beneath my feet. My head was pounding. I touched my forehead tenderly and winced. I already had a goose egg growing under my hairline.

Ronnie lunged for me again, but I didn't hesitate this time; I didn't care if she was Ronnie. She was still a vampire. I hit her with another blast of spray, and she tripped backward blindly. One moment she was recoiling from me, and the next moment, she was falling through the open basement door and tumbling down the steps into the safe room.

I blinked, stunned into inaction by her sudden disappearance. Shaking off my shock, I ran to the top of the basement steps and peered down. Ronnie was at the bottom of the steps inside the safe room, curled on the floor, crying. Half of me, admittedly the stupid half, instinctually wanted to help her—this was Ronnie, for heaven's sake!—but the other half of me, the half that knew better, knew that she was a vampire. No matter how weak or injured or frail she seemed, her idea of a meal was to rip my throat out.

Ronnie opened her mouth, and between the whimpers and tears and that awful rattling growl, she whispered shakily, "Cassidy?"

The stupid half of me won. I walked down the basement steps to her despite my gut instinct to keep my distance.

I stopped near the bottom, far enough away that she wouldn't be able to lunge for my throat again. I hoped.

"What happened, Ronnie? Who attacked you?" I asked, trying to soften my voice and squeeze out some answers, but my head was still pounding and spinning.

Ronnie's sobs burst on a wail. "It hurts!"

I squinted at her as she squirmed on the floor. She couldn't be injured from falling down a flight of steps—she was a vampire now, after all—

but I noticed a thin ripple in the air above her skin, like the heat of a fire, and the noxious stink of burning flesh.

She wasn't injured from the fall. She was inside the silver walls of the basement safe room, and even without direct contact, the silver was burning her.

"I know it hurts," I soothed, "but I need you to focus. What happened to you? Who attacked you, Ronnie?"

"I was so thirsty," she gasped between sobs. "My throat was on fire, and I just wanted to go home."

Even as a vampire, she doesn't want to leave the house, I thought sadly. "Do you remember anything from last night?" I persisted. "Do you remember if you left the house or if a vampire broke in?"

"Everything was different when I woke up. I knew I wasn't dreaming, but it was like waking into a nightmare. The sounds and smells and flavors—" Ronnie pounded her head into the cement. "Nothing's right. Everything's different and nothing makes sense, and the life I remember having is a dream," Ronnie said, nearly hysterical. The expression on her face was haunting. "I just wanted to go home, but my home was part of the dream, too. And you can't go back to something in a dream."

I sighed. "You're home now, Ronnie."

"There's no going back, is there?" she asked, and the despair in her voice was pitiful.

"No," I whispered. "I don't think there's any going back."

"Hello?" someone bellowed from upstairs. "Anybody home?"

Walker, I thought. Ronnie must have thought so, too, because she was instantly on her feet, the fastest I'd ever seen her move.

I hit her with another blast of silver spray before she exposed herself. She cowered back against the floor, hissing.

"Stay down and shut up while I figure out what to do with you." I shook my head. "Jesus."

She listened to me and remained on the ground. I took a deep breath. She didn't look well, not that any vampire looked well before feeding, but Ronnie looked especially sickly. The word "deteriorating" came to mind. I wondered how long she could remain in the safe room, surrounded by silver, and not die.

"Hello?" I heard Walker bellow again, and this time, I also heard the accompanying snap of him loading the sawed-off shotgun.

Ronnie perked up, hearing his voice.

"Sit," I hissed, "and shut up."

Before Ronnie got any brave ideas, I shut the door and locked her in the basement. Who could have guessed that I'd use the safe room to protect a vampire against a night blood? The silver might burn her skin, but I had no illusions that whatever Walker would do when he saw Ronnie would be much worse and more permanent than silver exposure.

I turned on the steps to face Walker. Dread, like warm milk, soured in my mouth.

* * * *

I raised my hands and spoke before walking up the steps. I knew how trigger-happy Walker could be when provoked.

"It's just me. It's DiRocco. I'm coming up from the basement steps."

Sure enough, Walker turned the corner as I spoke, shotgun in hand and aimed at me.

I stopped cold, my hands already raised.

Walker dropped the gun. "Fuck, Cassidy. What the hell? What happened to your head? Are you all right?"

I touched my forehead, surprised. I'd forgotten about the goose egg. "I'm fine. Just leftover injuries from last night."

Walker leaned closer, his eyes narrowed. "That swelling looks pretty fresh."

"I'm fine," I insisted.

He crossed his arms. "Why was the door wide open?"

"When I got here the entire house was empty. Where is everyone?" I asked, avoiding his question.

Walker shrugged. "The last I saw, everyone was here this morning, taking shelter in the basement. No one seemed real inclined to leave the safe room after last night."

I raised my eyebrows. They'd obviously left the safe room. "Where were you? Why didn't you answer my calls?"

Walker leaned casually against the doorframe, but I noticed that he hadn't holstered the shotgun. "Some of us have lives to live, cases to solve, people to find. While you were playing night blood to Dominic, Officer Montgomery died and Agent Rowens isn't far behind."

"Rowens survived?" I whispered

Walker nodded. "He tied a belt around his shoulder in a tourniquet before passing out."

"Oh, thank God," I muttered. "Does he remember anything from last night? Has he said anything about—"

"He hasn't regained consciousness yet," Walker said, cutting me off. "He's just barely hanging on."

"Oh." I bobbed my head, half nodding and half thinking. Hopefully he wouldn't remember the details from his attack. Even if he did, no one would believe him, and the truth would only haunt him or drive him crazy for the rest of his life—if the vampires didn't silence him first.

"What are the police saying about the scene?" I asked. "Do they have any leads?"

"With Riley and Rowens hit, it's personal," Walker said. "No one knows we were at the scene yet, but they're questioning my absence from the search when they found Colin."

"They found Colin?" Relief made my voice tremble.

Walker nodded. "But we have another problem."

You have no idea, I thought. "Something worse than Nathan?"

He heaved a lengthy sigh. "Now we can't find Colin's father. Logan hasn't been answering his phone, he never stopped at the precinct this afternoon, and he still hasn't been reunited with Colin. I came back here for him, but—" Walker looked around, at a loss. "I'm guessing he's not here."

"No one's here but me. When was the last time you saw him?"

"He was here this morning along with everyone else."

"*Everyone* else?" I asked. "Ronnie was here this morning, too?"

"Yeah; Ronnie, Logan, Keagan, Theresa, and Jeremy. They were all here."

"And Ronnie was OK this morning?" I asked. If Ronnie had been here and human this morning, how had she been attacked, bitten, and transformed in less than twelve hours? According to Dominic, the transformation took no less than three nights. And where the hell was everyone else now if they had been here with her this morning?

Something thick and rotten settled in my gut.

"I don't know if Ronnie was technically, 'OK', but she was making pancakes this morning, like she always does," Walker narrowed his eyes. "What's with the twenty questions, DiRocco?"

I opened my mouth, closed it, and made a split second decision. I didn't know whether or not I'd be able to justify my decision later, but I knew how Walker felt about vampires. He wouldn't see Ronnie. He would only see a target. "When I came home, the house was empty."

Walker frowned. "Ronnie wasn't here?"

I shook my head. "No."

"That's not like her."

"No, it's not."

He pursed his lips. "You should've been here today."

I blinked, thrown by his flat, angry tone. "Excuse me?"

"I needed you here with Keagan and Ronnie. He's pretty good with my weapons, but he's still just a kid, and God love her, but Ronnie can't protect herself. She'd die of fright before the vampires even touched her."

"I don't see how that's my—"

"While I was protecting us from the FBI, I needed you here, protecting my home," Walker said, his voice hard.

"Why am I getting the impression that you're pissed at *me*?"

"There's that dead-on-target gut of yours again, DiRocco, never failing to point you in the right direction," Walker said, but his tone was ugly. He'd never spoken to me like that before.

"What the hell's your problem?" I asked, his anger sparking mine.

"You lied to me," He snapped. "I thought you came here for me, but you came here for Dominic."

I stilled, the validity in that statement far closer to the truth than I cared to admit. "That's not true. I came here for you."

Walker shook his head. "When it came down to choose between me or him last night, you chose him."

"We were two night bloods against three vampires. I chose to survive." *And I don't need to apologize for that,* I thought, Rene's advice ringing true in my heart. "And between the two of us, you're the liar."

Walker's face flushed a bright red. "I've never lied to you. Ever."

"We talked on the phone for weeks—three whole weeks—and not once did you mention that you were having seizures," I said, squeezing my hands into fists.

"I'm fine," he said tersely.

"Then I guess we differ on the definition of 'fine.'" I said, forcing a calm I didn't feel. "You were admitted into the hospital. Your skull was fractured, and you've been suffering for weeks. That's not 'fine,' Walker."

He just stared at me.

"I could have been here for you," I said, not knowing what more I could say to make him see reason.

Walker's jaw clenched. "I didn't want you here for that."

We were still an arms-length apart, but it may as well have been miles. "Then why did you even invite me here?" I asked, beyond exasperated.

He shook his head. "That doesn't matter now. I was wrong about us," he said. "I'll help you contain or kill Nathan—I'll help you in whatever you need to stop the murders—but I think we should keep things professional between us from now on. Once Nathan is stopped, you should return to the city."

A horrible, chilling wave of inevitability soaked over my anger. I laughed, partially in denial and partially fed up. "I thought you wanted me to live here in your house with all the other night bloods. I thought the city wasn't safe."

"It's not," he said. "But I don't want you living here anymore."

"So we're done." I snapped my fingers. "Just like that?"

He nodded.

I needed to swallow before I could talk, and I realized with startling horror that I might cry. "I thought something wonderful was growing between us. I thought—"

"I thought the same thing, but it's just not there."

I stared at him, incredulous. "It's just not there," I repeated numbly. "When we were kissing in Ronnie's old house, was it not there?"

"Cassidy, that's not—"

"Or when you felt me up on my desk at *The Sun Accord*, was it not there, either?"

Walker rolled his eyes. "You know that's not—"

"Because as I recall, it certainly *was* there," I interrupted. "That was never our problem. Our problem isn't about you and me. Your problem is with me and Dominic."

Walker snapped his mouth shut and glared at me.

"You're pissed because I spent the night in Bex's coven with Dominic," I said, plowing ahead over his telling silence. "You think I chose him over you, but it's not like that."

Walker crossed his arms. "Are you or aren't you his willing night blood?"

"I didn't choose this arrangement," I blurted. "Nathan was missing, and Dominic offered me a deal. If I mended ties between him and Bex as his night blood, he would help me find Nathan. I needed him, Walker, and I'd do anything for Nathan. My back was up against the wall."

Walker stared at me, and for once, I couldn't read the intent behind his stoney expression. I held my breath against the silence.

Finally, he whispered, "You said you came here to visit me, but really, you came here for Dominic, hoping he'd help you find Nathan."

I sighed. "I came here for you, too. You make it sound so cut and dry, but it's complicated. I needed Dominic's help to find Nathan, yes, but I wanted to see you, too."

"You should have asked for *my* help to find Nathan, but you only ever think to ask for Dominic's help. I can't abide anyone who sees the vampires as anything but creatures to put down."

"Life isn't black and white, good and evil, right and wrong. Everything in life, even the vampires, are shades of gray. Just because I ask Dominic for his help doesn't mean I don't want your help, too."

"You're either with me or against me, and if you're with Dominic, you sure as hell are not with me."

I shook my head. "Don't give me an ultimatum, Walker. I need all the help can get to save Nathan, and Dominic can—"

Walker raised his hand, refusing to listen. "It's how I feel in my bones, and I can't bend. Not on this. As far as I'm concerned, you made your choice quite clear last night."

I held his gaze, and an impenetrable wall of pride fused between us. "If you let me leave on these terms, I'm not coming back, not for the night bloods, not for a story, not for anything."

He didn't even hesitate before saying, "Good. That's exactly what I want, too."

Walker about-faced before I could respond and left the house, slamming the door firmly between us with a finality that staked my heart.

* * * *

Ronnie was trembling and moaning incoherently when I returned for her.

"I'm sorry," I said. "I didn't mean to leave you down here so long."

She looked up at my voice—her face burned, blistered, and pinched with pain—but she didn't focus on me. She looked behind me.

"Ronnie?" I asked, wondering if she was going into shock. Could vampires go into shock?

"Ian?" she whispered between cracked lips.

I shook my head. "He left. I wasn't sure how he'd react. Maybe you should drink and heal and look a little, um—" I struggled for the words. "Less grotesque" came to mind as I stared at her mottled red complexion, jerky bird-like twitches, and boney skeletal structure. "—more human before you break it to him."

Ronnie nodded and then started sobbing again.

I sighed, feeling horrible. Maybe Walker was right. Maybe if I'd been here, Ronnie wouldn't have been attacked and transformed. I didn't have much experience with newly transformed vampires, but she seemed especially pathetic compared to Dominic, Bex, and Rene.

I walked toward Ronnie slowly. "If I let you drink from me, will you promise not to attack? You can take a few swallows to heal yourself, but I'll spray you with the silver again if you go beserk."

Ronnie met my eyes, tears still flowing down her cheeks. She swallowed. "I'll try. Your blood, it's like—" Ronnie got a faraway look in her eyes, the way someone might try to describe heaven.

"Like cinnamon?" I asked dryly. "Like if you were to drink it too deeply and too quickly, it might burn?"

Ronnie's gaze widened. "Yes. It's exactly like that. And I'd want to burn."

I nodded. "I've heard that a time or two."

"But night blood weakens vampires, doesn't it?"

"Yes, but it's still food, and by the look of it, you're starving. Any blood, even night blood, is probably better than no blood at all." There was no helping it. Ronnie's transformation was partially my fault, and she was still Ronnie, for heaven's sake. I couldn't let her fry all night in the safe room. "Let's go into the kitchen. Maybe if we're over the sink, we'll make less of a mess."

Ronnie didn't have the strength to stand on her own, so I slung her arm over my shoulders and helped her up the steps. She was nothing but skin and bones, thank God, because with my hip clicking and scraping, I had trouble climbing the steps on my own, let alone supporting another person. Luckily, Ronnie wasn't dead weight, and once we were out of the basement and away from the silver, she regained some of her strength.

Under the kitchen's unforgiving overhead light, Ronnie looked exceptionally fried. The shine of blisters pocked her skin. Knowing this was a stupid idea and resigning myself to doing it anyway, I leaned against the sink and offered her my wrist.

A rattling growl vibrated from her chest as she stared at my upturned veins.

She shook her head. "I won't be able to stop once I start drinking," she said, her voice grave. "It's like my thoughts and actions are separate. I don't want to hurt you, but I can hear your heart beating. I can feel the pressure of your blood pulse through your veins like a vise around my own throat, and the inevitability of my need is like I've already hurt you. And that part of me doesn't care. I'll do anything for just one drop, but one drop won't be enough."

"You won't hurt me," I said. Her words about separated thoughts and actions sparked my inspiration. I didn't need to spray her with silver to stop her from drinking. Once she swallowed my blood, I could just order her to stop. I raised my wrist closer to her mouth. "Drink."

The growling rattle inside her chest heightened. I resisted the instinctive urge to run, but my heart didn't know that I was trying to help Ronnie. It sprinted, and I think Ronnie could hear its accelerated beat. She shook her head frantically, her eyes glowing, her fangs bared around her thin lips. I could see her will battling her instinct, and God help her, instinct was winning.

I bared my wrist under her nose. She breathed in the full scent of my pulse, and I saw the moment instinct took over. The fear and recognition in her eyes glazed, replaced by honed focus. She no longer saw me with her eyes but with her entire being, and her being saw me as food.

Ronnie took my arm in both hands and tore into my wrist with her fangs.

She wasn't gentle. Dominic could drink from the neat, double prick of his fang strike, but not Ronnie. Maybe from inexperience or maybe from the mindlessness of thirst, she ripped through veins and muscles like she was eating rather than drinking. She gnawed at my wrist, shaking her head like a dog with a bone. I couldn't take it. I screamed. She barely took three swallows, and I already felt dizzy.

"Veronica Carmichael," I commanded, and my mind instantly connected with hers.

I could taste the driving, aching burn in the back of her throat, only partially quenched by my sweetly spiced blood. I could hear the thousands of sounds that she could hear, my heartbeat and the expansion and release of my lungs through her ears. I could feel the prickle of silver still heating the exposed skin of her face, neck, and arms, even at this distance from the safe room. When I connected with Dominic's mind, I could only decipher a muddle of his senses and the vague imprint of his thoughts, but when I connected with Ronnie, I could hear and taste and feel through her as clearly as if I were experiencing the senses myself. Her thirst was my thirst. Her pain was my pain. And beneath it all, within the very foundation of her being, I felt her confusion and fear of becoming the very monster that had been her lifelong nightmare.

"Stop drinking my blood," I commanded.

Instantly, she stopped drinking, but her fangs were still imbedded in my wrist. She turned her head to look at me and inadvertently gouged deeper into my skin.

I gritted my teeth against the pain and barked more precisely, "Take your fangs out of my wrist gently!"

She did so, and gently.

I sighed. It was my fault. I should have been more specific. "Now, without cutting me with your fangs and without drinking any more of my blood," I said, giving my instructions precisely, no matter how obvious, "Use your tongue to slowly and *gently* lick into the wound and heal it from the inside out."

She slowly and gently licked into the wound and healed it from the inside out, exactly as I requested, but after a few minutes of licking, my blood was still pouring from the wound, pumping liberally into the sink. I grew increasingly light-headed. Her saliva wasn't clotting or healing my wound.

"Stop licking. Just stop," I commanded. She stopped licking, and I settled on a more traditional method. I grabbed the nearest towel and tied it in a knot at my wrist. Only a few moments later, however, and the towel was already a sopping mess.

I eyed Ronnie wearily. She was waiting, blank-eyed, for my next command, but I could still feel the thirst for more blood burning her throat. Her skin was now a healthy pink, so at least the blood had healed her silver burn. I wondered if the blood had been enough to sate her instinctual urge to hunt and kill, too.

"I'm going to release your mind, Ronnie, but I need you to give me an honest answer before I do. Now that you've fed, will you still try to attack me?"

"I don't know. I feel a little more like myself now that I've fed, but I'm still hungry. I don't want to hurt you, but when I smell your blood, what I want doesn't matter. I'll feed anyway."

I sighed. Well, I'd asked for honesty. If I didn't find help soon, I'd bleed out, and then it wouldn't matter whether or not she attacked; I'd already be dead.

I released her mind.

Instantly, the rattling growl vibrated from her chest.

"Oh, for the love of God, Ronnie, control yourself!" I snapped.

"I'm trying," Ronnie said, her voice desperate, but her growl swelled the air.

I shook my head. "I need you to leave and find Bex or Rene. Preferably Rene," I amended, thinking of the bad blood between Bex and Walker. "Dominic won't be back until midnight, but Rene will be able to heal me."

"Bex?" Ronnie squeaked, shaking her head. "No. You know I can't leave the house."

I stared at her, not believing what I was hearing. "Are you serious? Of course you can leave the house! You just came from outside the house."

Ronnie looked at me like I was the one who was insane. "It's after dark. Vampires are out there."

"*You're* a vampire!"

Her face crumpled. She was crying.

I closed my eyes, trying to focus now that the room was spinning. "Ronnie, please, pull it together. I need you to find a vampire, Rene specifically, and bring him to me. If you don't do this now, I'm going to bleed out and die."

Ronnie sniffled delicately, her face brightening at the thought. "Then I could turn you into a vampire, too. We could be vampires together."

"NO!" I swallowed the expletives that came to the forefront of my tongue. She couldn't even heal my wrist and now she wanted to complete a night blood transformation. I cringed inwardly and said patiently, "Only Masters can turn other vampires. I need you to leave and find Rene. I'm begging you, Ronnie."

Finally, blessedly, she nodded. "I'll try," she said. She took one last, long, lingering look at my wrist and the blood-spattered sink, and then she left the house, closing and locking the door behind her.

I pulled a stool from the breakfast bar and sat with my wrist over her kitchen sink. The floor was spinning and loop-de-looping around me. I laid my head in the crook of my elbow and took a deep breath, trying to fight through the light-headedness. After everything that I'd survived—my parents' death, discovering the existence of vampires, losing Nathan, finding him a monster—I refused to accept that my own compassion for Ronnie would be the mistake that killed me.

Chapter 16

The hall clock chimed midnight. I opened my eyes. My head was still on my arm, but my arm was numb. The towel around my wrist was soaked with blood and still dripping into the sink. I lifted my head slowly. The world somersaulted and dipped and spun in a whirling dance. I dropped my head limply back onto the counter before I fell off the stool.

If I ignored the gore spattered inside Walker's kitchen sink, his house smelled rather pleasant, like nutmeg and pecans. Ronnie had baked pancakes this morning like she did every morning, and they had probably been her famous banana nut pancakes. Thinking of Ronnie made me sick—not just nauseated, although that was there, too, but deeply sick to my soul—so I closed my eyes and stopped thinking. I just breathed.

The faint scent of pine drifted into the room, overtaking the lingering smell of nutmeg. My eyes snapped open, but I took care not to lift my head this time. Dominic was somewhere nearby, close enough that I could smell him.

"Dominic?" I whispered hoarsely. Walker would kill me for extending an invitation to a vampire into his home, but I was desperate. "Dominic, you may enter."

Something rammed into the kitchen door, hard enough to rattle its hinges. Normally, after being invited, Dominic simply swept into a room—sometimes I wondered if the invitation was simply perfunctory—but this time, the one time I truly needed him, he couldn't cross the threshold. He pounded into the door three more times, each more rattling than the last, but the frame didn't crack, the door didn't budge, and Dominic didn't enter.

"Why can't you come in?" I wheezed. I could barely hear myself speak, but with Dominic's fine-tuned senses, he should be able to hear my invitation. I tried to speak a little louder. "You have my permission to enter."

My words were answered with silence for a long moment. Dominic bellowed from the other side of the door. "It's not you whose permission I need!" he shouted. "Where are you in the house?"

"The kitchen," I said, dumbfounded. Why wouldn't my permission grant Dominic access?

"I can't sense you!" Dominic said. "I imagined that Bex had exaggerated Ian Walker's capabilities, but she was right. The house may well be impenetrable. I've never encountered anything like it."

I sighed. Here I was, dying, and Dominic was admiring Walker's handiwork. "I need you to penetrate it," I whispered. "I'm losing a lot of blood."

"I know. I can smell it," Dominic said, and this time, I heard the growl behind his words. "I can't enter to reach you, so you'll need to come to me."

"You really can't enter?" I asked numbly.

The door rattled on its hinges from what I could only imagine was Dominic body-slamming it. He let loose another string of curses that eventually succumbed to another bout of silence.

"No," Dominic said finally. His tone bit off the words, so they were clipped and pointed. "I can't enter."

A scab from a very nearly healed wound ripped open, and a flood of clarity and bone-cold anger gushed through it. Walker really did know how to prevent vampires from entering his home. Even though I already knew he was keeping that information from me, knowing it and actually witnessing it were two different kinds of betrayals. Dominic would always be a wedge between us, but Walker's own actions pounded the wedge deep enough to break us in half.

Walker was right about one thing: whatever was between us wasn't enough because something very important simply wasn't there to keep us together.

I focused my anger, like fuel, and stood. The world immediately spun off its axis, and I promptly fell to the floor. Hard. Pain blasted through my hip in an electric *zing*, and my forehead throbbed in time with my pulse.

The anger was still there, if not my strength, so I crawled. Hand over hand, inch by bloody inch, I struggled to the door. The wound at my wrist was still seeping, the soaked towel smearing blood across the floor. I'd been so worried about making a mess inside Walker's pristine house, but who was I kidding? Everything was already bloodstained.

By the time I reached the door, my vision was spotted in black starbursts. I stretched my arm up to grasp the doorknob, but my movements were clumsy, weak, and half blind. I could feel the knob at my fingertips. Its cold, smooth surface was slick in my hand. I strained to turn it, first one way and then the other, but it slipped from my grasp.

"Cassidy? What's happening? Are you coming out?" Dominic shouted from outside.

I slumped against the doorframe. "I'm trying," I whispered.

Dominic slammed against the door again, rattling its hinges, but otherwise, still not making much of a dent. It rattled my body against the door as well, and my hand slipped from the knob as I reach for it a second time.

I clenched my teeth. "You're not helping."

"Until you cross the threshold, I can't reach you," Dominic said. I could hear the desperation in his voice.

The floor and the ceiling whirled in kaleidoscopic somersaults. I blinked, trying to focus my vision, but when I reached up a third time to open the door, I couldn't feel the knob anymore. I couldn't feel anything.

"I can't do this," I whispered, more to myself than to Dominic. I would die because I was trapped in a house protected from vampires. I laughed at the irony.

"Yes, you damn well can," Dominic thundered. "You are the strongest, most determined person I've ever known in my very long life, and in this one moment when your strength matters most, it will not fail you. I want you to take a deep breath and think of why you're here. Why did you come to Erin, New York?"

For you, to mend your relationship with Bex. I thought. *For Carter, to finish my piece on crime fluctuation. For Walker, just for the pleasure of seeing him.*

There were so many reasons why I'd come here, but the real purpose of my visit made my heart quicken and my breath catch and my temper rise to a boiling swell. I took a deep breath, reached up, locked my hand on the doorknob, and tore the door open with all the anger and angst and uncertain love that made my heart beat.

Dominic was standing on the porch just outside the door. He'd fed since returning from the city. His face glowed with a youthful blush, and even from my view on the floor, his muscled frame defined his light blue dress shirt quite nicely.

"I came here to cement my end of our bargain, so you would help me find Nathan. I came here for my brother," I said, and then my hand slipped from the knob, my vision winked out, and I tumbled headfirst through the doorway onto the porch at Dominic's feet.

* * * *

Dominic caught my body before I hit the ground and cradled me in his arms.

"Cassidy? Can you hear me? How did you—" I felt him lift my wrist and unwrap the towel from the wound. "Who did this?" he asked, his voice a low, biting growl.

"It's not her fault," I murmured. "I told her to drink."

"Her?" he asked. I felt a flame light my wrist and a slippery probe slice into the wound. I knew without seeing that Dominic was licking into my wrist and healing me.

"Her saliva didn't heal me like yours always does. She tried, but it only hurt worse."

"Who?" Dominic asked.

"Honestly, it's not her fault. I encouraged her. She was so weak, and she was still *her* even though she wasn't, and I—" I sighed, knowing that I wasn't making any sense. "I thought she'd be able to heal me afterwards."

Dominic sighed heavily. "I will not kill whoever bit you. I'm simply trying to ascertain what happened."

"Ronnie," I whispered.

Dominic leaned forward. "Rene?" he asked, sounding shocked.

I shook my head, and I realized that I could see again. His face was inches from mine. His lips were stained a deep red from my blood.

"Ronnie, not Rene," I clarified. "She's Walker's childhood friend. She lives in his house with the other night bloods and—"

"Yes, I know who Ronnie is," Dominic snapped briskly. "I'm shocked Walker hasn't seriously attempted to kill Bex, considering Ronnie's transformation. I'd think that would be, what's the expression," Dominic said thoughtfully, "his last straw."

"Walker doesn't know. Ronnie was healthy and human this morning. She—"

Dominic cut his head to the side. "If Ronnie attacked you tonight, she was transformed three to five days ago."

"Walker saw her this morning. She was still human three to five *hours* ago," I insisted. "And she's a very weak vampire. The weakest vampire I've ever seen. She still moved nearly human slow, and she was able to enter the house uninvited." I laughed bitterly. "You couldn't enter with an invitation, but she used her own key to unlock the door."

Dominic raised his eyebrows. "She crossed the threshold into Walker's house?"

"Yes."

"You realize what this means, don't you?"

I hesitated. "That Ronnie is a sad excuse for a vampire?"

"Yes, but that's not the point. If—"

"That Walker is going to flip when he finds out?"

Dominic rolled his eyes. "Yes he will, but that's still not the point."

"It's going to be a huge point for whoever attacked Ronnie," I muttered.

"*That's* my point!" Dominic interjected. "If Ronnie was transformed three to five hours ago, before I left you earlier this evening...?"

I nodded.

"Then she was transformed during the day," Dominic finished, his voice grim. "And the only creature who can tolerate daylight and transform a night blood into a vampire is a Day Reaper."

"A Day Reaper?" I asked, trying to grasp the gravity of the situation. "I thought you said that we had some time before they came. *If* they came."

"We do! Or we should have. The police are still investigating the murders as human crimes. Day Reapers usually don't interfere unless our existence is at risk of exposure. Officer Riley Montgomery was a witness, but he's dead. And Agent Harold Rowens—" Dominic cursed. "Rowens hasn't even regained consciousness to determine what he remembers."

And if he remembers? I thought. Rowens didn't seem the type to easily or willfully forget. *Would you kill him for his silence?* I wondered.

"If a Day Reaper is here, does that affect our plan for Nathan?" I asked instead.

"It's something to discuss." Dominic bit into his own wrist and held the wound to my lips.

I eyed his bleeding wrist warily. "What are you doing?"

"You need it, and we really don't have time to argue at the moment. Bex is watching Jillian in my absence. Although I don't doubt Bex's abilities, Jillian is my responsibility. We need to return to Bex's coven, take ownership of Jillian, and discuss our plans to contain Nathan." He moved his wrist fractionally closer to my mouth. "Drink."

I turned my head away, but I was too weak to fight him if he forced me. "You've never needed me to drink your blood to heal me before," I said. "Licking my wounds usually does the trick."

"I've already healed you. You will live whether or not you drink my blood, but you won't have the strength to face your brother and wield Jillian against him unless you drink."

"I don't want to be a vampire. I don't choose that life."

Dominic rolled his eyes heavenward and muttered something foul under his breath. "You have enough blood of your own that you won't transform, I assure you."

I bit my lip. Dominic's intentions, and especially his intentions regarding my status as his night blood, were so complex that I couldn't see the big picture, but Dominic—five steps, two skips, and a bite ahead of everyone, as always—knew exactly how the pieces fit. Was this just another trick, like swearing on the passage of time, that I didn't understand or comprehend?

Dominic sighed heavily at my hesitation. I could feel the balance of all our lives in the weight of his sigh. "Do you or do you not trust me, Cassidy? It's that simple. When I tell you that drinking my blood will not transform you, do you believe me?"

"Yes, I believe you," I said, surprising myself. I really did believe him. He wanted to transform me, there was no denying that, but I believed without a doubt, more than his desire to transform me, that he desired my consent. "I trust you, but—"

"No. You either trust me or you don't, and if you don't, your brother's only chance at a normal, sane existence is lost."

I breathed in sharply. "Well, when you put it like that," I snapped.

"I'm not putting it any other way than how it truly is," Dominic said patiently. "In this, however, I won't force you. You must see reality for what it is and seize it with both hands. No one but you can do that for yourself."

Dominic pressed his wrist to my lips again, but this time, despite the instinctive urge to gag and bolt, I forced myself to stay the course. I sealed my lips around the wound, like I'd witnessed from him on multiple occasions, and sucked.

Any other time his blood made contact with my tongue—our experience with Jillian excluded—I'd spit it out instantly. This time, I allowed myself to taste it. I rolled its flavor over my tongue, feeling its texture, and to my surprise and deepening hate for everything concerning Dominic being right, the taste and texture was tolerable. His blood was cool and thick in my mouth, like chilled honey, but slippery against my tongue instead of sticky. It slid down the back of my throat before I could swallow, so I could either choke or accept it. Against my better judgment—against everything I thought I'd wanted for myself in this life—I swallowed.

Although his blood was chilled, heat spread down my throat, into my stomach, and through each limb. It swirled and crashed through my body like a riptide, unexpected and drowning, his blood in my blood, pumping through my veins in time with my heartbeat, healing and invigorating my body from the inside out. From chest to fingertip, head to toe, I was radiant.

Drinking Dominic's blood was a different experience now that Jillian wasn't leeching from my mind. In my wildest dreams, I'd never imaged feeling anything but disgust from drinking blood, yet I basked in it. But even the sun, providing light and life to the entire world, will incinerate whatever dares to venture too close. Dominic's blood was suddenly scalding. My skin stretched, like it might rip from my own body to keep from burning.

"Dominic? It burns."

"Your body must accept my blood as your own in order for it to strengthen you," Dominic's lips moved against my ear as he whispered, his voice rushed and urgent. "Otherwise, you'll just throw it up again."

"Something's wrong," I murmured. "I'm on fire, and my skin is tearing in half."

"No, it's not. My saliva burns, too, but it's just healing." Dominic moved his wrist away from my mouth and held my hand. He squeezed tightly. "Do you feel this?"

I nodded.

"Focus on my hand in your hand. Feel its cold soothing your heat, its strength protecting you. The coldness and strength that you feel in my hand is inside you now, anchoring you. Feel my blood course through you and embrace the gift it's about to give. You must accept it."

"Its gift?" I hissed through clenched teeth.

"Strength, Cassidy. Visualize my strength coursing through your veins. Let go of your fear and allow the blood access to your muscles and bones. Allow it access to your mind. Can you feel it in your veins?"

"Yes," I said. The blood was still burning and my skin was still tearing, but I could feel what he was describing, too. I focused on his hand and the anticipation of strength inside me.

"Visualize the blood soaking deep into your muscles, into the aches and soreness. Visualize it revitalizing you from the inside out. Can you feel your body healing, your vision sharpening, your muscles strengthening?"

"Yes," I whispered in wonder. "I can." I visualized what he described, seeing past the physical discomfort of my stretched skin to the miracle occurring beneath it. My heart shifted into third gear, and my biceps and triceps, my thighs and calves, my abdomen and all my muscles expanded, filling my stretched skin. My body fit inside itself again, but I was something more than I'd been before. I could feel it like tiny electrical snaps, the living electric pulse of his blood, now my blood.

"How do you feel now?" Dominic asked cautiously.

I glanced up into his face and stared. I could see the midnight energy of his being enveloping me. I could literally see his concern like a physical halo surrounding his body.

"Is this how you see?" I asked. I felt a strange, pointed whirl against my arm and cringed. A moment later, I felt the sensation again and again in concurrence with an owl hooting in the distance. I was feeling the vibrations of its hoot against my skin. I could literally feel his sound waves. "Is this how you feel all the time?"

Dominic stared at me like I was a stranger. "Every time I think I know you, every time I think I'm impressed by the woman you are and the night blood you're becoming, you do something extraordinarily unexpected, and I'm awed by you. Over and over again, you amaze me."

"I can feel sound waves and see emotions." I took a deep breath to calm my heart, and my mouth flooded with a muted, clean freshness, like peeled cucumber. "I can taste the air. Why wasn't it like this the last time I drank your blood?"

"Jillian was drinking from you, taking the nourishment that should have been yours, but she's not a part of you anymore. It's just me inside you. Knowing the night blood you are now, it humbles me to think of the vampire you'll become."

I narrowed my eyes, not so enthralled by my newfound senses to miss that last remark. "The vampire I won't become," I clarified.

"Don't," Dominic hushed, placing a finger over my lips. "Please, don't ruin this for me. You trusted me and took my blood into your body willfully and without the bloodlust of Jillian's cravings. Don't deny what you feel with pithy words. Don't cheapen this moment between us."

I wanted to deny it. I wanted to sneer and snort derisively *What moment? You can't cheapen what isn't there,* but after a lifetime of seeking and divulging the truth, I couldn't refute the undeniable, and the truth of the matter was that Dominic was, once again, right. Damn it.

I lifted my hand and touched Dominic's face. With his blood coursing through my hand, it somehow felt as if I was touching myself. Dominic shuddered, and by the bright, burnt orange burst through his aura, I knew he felt the same.

"How long will this last?" I asked.

I watched his throat work as he struggled to speak. "For most, mere hours. For you—" He shook his head. "Any guess would be speculation. Several hours to a day? I simply can't predict anything concerning you."

Dominic was inches away from my face, his lips breaths from mine, and inching closer.

"Long enough to save Nathan," I whispered.

He blinked, trying to focus. "Long enough for what?"

"Several hours to a day with these senses and added strength," I said. "It should be long enough to save my brother."

"Hmm," Dominic murmured noncommittally. I heard the snapping spark, like the spit of cracking logs in fire, of his hand sliding along the small of my back.

"Dominic," I warned. "Bex is keeping Jillian in your absence. You said yourself that we were short on time."

"They've waited this long," he growled. "They can wait a few moments longer."

His mouth sealed over mine in a blaze of exploding fireworks. My eyes widened, shocked by the explosion of light and heat between us, more shocked at first from the sensory collide than from the kiss itself, but as his mouth rocked over mine, my eyes shut of their own accord. His kiss was magnetic. His lips opened and fused against mine. I responded in kind, attuned to his movements like a choreographed dance. Where he led, I followed. I grasped at the collar of his shirt as the friction and pace escalated. His rhythm pounded though my blood, our blood, and its beat lit my lips and cheeks and neck. Everywhere his lips and tongue and teeth touched, I burned, and everywhere he hadn't yet touched burned even brighter.

Although his burnt orange aura and my own flaring burst of sparkling light collided, they resisted the merge. He pulled my hair back, exposing my neck. I angled my mouth on his and stroked my tongue over his lower lip. He growled and bit my lip. I bit him back, and I could feel him smile against my lips as we battled for control.

His hand against my lower back skimmed higher. I could smell the crack and smoke of the hearth from his movement. My breath caught, equally enthralled by his physical touch and the dynamic of my newfound senses. The callused pressure of his palm scraped from my lower back to my hip. His tongue slipped between my lips and curled against my tongue, and I forgot the movement of his hand in a blaze of light and rhythm until his calluses scraped against the tender underside of my left breast.

I tore my mouth away from his, panting, and stared into his eyes with wonder. Dominic, despite the fact that he wasn't panting—one of the perks, I suppose, of not having a circulatory system—met my gaze, and he looked just as devastated.

"Is this how it is for you every time?" I asked, gaining a newfound respect for his restraint.

"Everyone is unique—different auras colliding is always a unique experience—but yes, kissing you is like this every time."

"And everything else?" I asked. I broke our locked gazes to stare out into the vivid kaleidoscope that had become my world. "Is this how you see and hear and feel and smell and taste every day? Like magic?"

"My senses seem fantastic to you because they're new, but after hundreds of years, they become the norm. If I were to see, hear, feel, taste, and smell as a human again, I suspect I would feel bereft of my senses, essentially blind and deaf compared to the sensory input I've become accustomed to receiving."

I shook my head in wonderment at the prospect of living in such vivid Technicolor. "I can't imagine ever becoming accustomed to this."

"I never thought to live hundreds of years either, yet here we are," Dominic said, his gaze focused on me. "And thank God I have."

The look in Dominic's eyes as he stared into mine was unmistakable. I didn't need a vampire's senses to see the intent behind his gaze.

"They're expecting us," I whispered shakily, not sure I wanted to stop but knowing for certain that if we didn't stop now, we never would. "Nathan will attack someone tonight, and Bex is expecting us to help her stop him."

"So she is," Dominic said, his voice deliberately measured.

I extracted myself from his embrace and stood, tasting the heavy reluctance in my heart like syrupy medicine.

Dominic stood still, not pulling away but not stopping me either. I shook my head regretfully at his appearance. His clothes were ruined, stained by my blood.

"I don't know why you even bother dressing up," I commented. "That was one of your nicer shirts."

"All of my shirts are nice." He looked down at himself, as if just noticing his soiled clothing. He fingered a bloody patch on his shirt and then, locking his gaze on me, slipped that finger into his mouth.

I swallowed, partly disgusted because that's how I was supposed to feel, but the rest of me was intrigued. I could smell the sharp spice of my taste on his tongue. Later, I might blame his blood for tainting my judgment, but I wanted him in that moment like I'd never wanted anyone in my entire life.

"One day you'll look at me, not as a vampire or an ally or a problem to resolve, but as a man. And when that day comes, I'll be right here in front of you, the same man I've been since the first we met. It's you who will see me with new eyes."

I shook my head, at a loss. "Dominic, I—"

Before I could continue, Dominic took me in his arms, and we were soaring over the trees and through the darkness toward Bex's coven.

Chapter 17

Jillian was a walking, talking, living skeleton.

We were once again in Bex's main dining hall. Dominic, Bex, and Rene were arguing about the best means to capture and subdue Nathan, but I couldn't focus on their conversation without being distracted by Jillian, by the boney protrusions of her collar bones, the straggles of hair sprouting from her skull, and the revolting motion of her bare jaw as the tenuous strings of tendon and skin—the remains of her flesh—attempted to articulate words and expressions.

The last time I'd seen her, Jillian had been in the peak of health and challenging Dominic for the position of coven Master. She'd been uncommonly beautiful, petite, and voluptuous with rioting, curly blond hair that bounced down her back to the curve of her waist. She'd worn leather from head to toe and carried herself with a weight of power that belied her petite stature. I'd witnessed her rip a fellow vampire's throat out, exposing the gleaming bone of his spinal column, in punishment for speaking out of turn. I'd watched her impale Dominic with her claws—hell, she'd impaled me on her claws, too—and I'd felt the clever ruthlessness of her thoughts when our minds had entwined. But beneath the ruthlessness, beneath the raging thirst for blood, and deep beneath the power that she wielded like a shield as much as she did a weapon, was bone-deep betrayal and fear.

Now, Jillian struggled to hold herself upright. She was nothing but bones and blisters after enduring the last three weeks inside a silver prison. I wondered absently how long Ronnie would have survived in Walker's silver-lined basement before she looked like Jillian. Three days? Three hours?

Jillian's gaze met mine.

I breathed in sharply, caught staring.

"Miss me?" Jillian whispered.

A great, steaming wave of rage crashed over me, and for a choked, suspended moment as everything Jillian had inflicted on me and mine boiled through my veins in vivid, shining, red detail—impaling me on her claws, betraying Dominic, leading an uprising of murderous vampires, leeching onto my mind, nourishing herself on my life-force, and transforming my brother into a heart-eating monster—I couldn't do anything but stare open-mouthed at her, into those beautiful, icy blue eyes, nearly identical to Dominic's eyes, imbedded in that grotesque skull that was once her face.

"How dare you," I said, low and surprisingly calm-sounding despite the inferno inside me. "After everything you've done—"

"Everything *I've* done?" Jillian laughed, and the sound was like nails scraping across the back of my eyelids. "You've known Lysander for, what, maybe a month? I lived with the man for decades. This was not his path. His brother—"

"I know all about your sad, sob story. This is entirely *your* fault, so don't act the martyr. You have no right."

"I have every right. Vampires are confined to a mere shell of an existence, living in shadows and hiding underground. We deserve more. We deserve a leader who is willing to strive for more, for freedom from the night!"

"I've heard that speech before, too. I didn't buy it then, and I'm not buying it now," I snapped. "My brother was a night blood, a cherished future vampire, or so I'm told, yet look at the life you gave him! You transformed him into a monster!"

She smiled. Or at least I think she did. She didn't have lips, so her teeth and fangs were already exposed, but the muscles that remained over her cheekbones bunched and lifted.

"Sacrifice for the cause," she said.

I saw red. "He was my brother, you bitch, not some pawn in your fucking game for you to—"

"Cassidy!" Dominic's voice broke our conversation, and I realized that his hand was squeezing my upper arm, holding me back. "Now is not the time."

I met his gaze and looked around. Every eye in the room was on me.

"Sorry," I muttered. Having four vampires' eyes trained on me was not the attention I wanted.

Dominic released my arm. "Bex and I are both needed to restrain Jillian while we're above ground, leaving only Rene to guard you. I'd prefer to guard you myself, but—"

"—But Jillian is your responsibility. I know. I'll be fine with Rene."

Dominic shook his head. "It's not enough. Rene is powerful for someone so newly transformed, but he's still young."

I narrowed my eyes. "What do you suggest we do?"

"As much as it pains me to admit, Walker's skills could be useful. I would certainly feel more comfortable with you more heavily guarded."

"I don't know how much help we'll get from Walker," I admitted. "We had a sort of, er, falling out."

"I was only gone four hours," Dominic said, and I could hear a tinge of interest surface in his voice.

I sighed. "It's been an eventful four hours."

"Well, we won't have another four hours, eventful or otherwise, if we don't focus and finalize this plan. With the Day Reapers already here, there's no telling what kind of timeframe we should expect."

"The Day Reapers waited several years before intervening last time," Bex said, indicating Jillian with a tip of her head. "And the creature hasn't caused nearly as much destruction. I doubt they're here so soon."

"They're here already," Dominic said grimly.

"Y'all know that for sure?"

"They transformed someone mid-day, someone who never should have been turned."

Bex raised her eyebrows, her gaze darting between Dominic and me.

"Ronnie," I said finally, unable to stand the tension. "She was a human this morning, but sometime between then and sunset, she was attacked and transformed."

Bex frowned. "And you found her body?"

I shook my head. "No, she found me. Her transformation was already completed. She's a vampire."

Bex gaped at me. "She should still be transforming if she was just turned."

I nodded. "Yes, she should, but she's not. She attacked me."

"You saw her?" Bex asked sharply. "With your own eyes, you saw her?"

I frowned. "Yes, I saw her. She drank from me."

Bex's mouth opened and closed several times before she snapped it shut.

"More importantly than Ronnie's unfortunate transformation," Dominic interrupted, eyeing Bex intently, "is the fact that a Day Reaper transformed her. They're here."

Bex cleared her throat. "Right. Please continue, Lysander. If they're already here, then as you've already stated, we don't have much time."

Dominic's gaze lingered on Bex a moment longer before looking back at me. "If Walker won't help, than Rene will be your only guard."

"I'm better than Walker anyway," Rene said. He winked at me. "No worries there."

Dominic ignored him and continued. "Once we're outside the coven, Rene will bite you." He cut his eyes on Rene. "A small bite."

Rene smiled. "My pleasure."

"And you, Cassidy, will smear your blood on the ground and surrounding trees to draw Nathan to you. He's been searching for you and tracking your every move: to the first scene where you dropped your spray, to Ronnie's abandoned house where you cut your knees, and outside Bex's coven, where Walker smeared your blood on the ground. Considering he followed you all the way here from the city, I see no reason why he wouldn't continue to do so now."

I swallowed. "And when he shows up? Then what?"

"Then we subdue him," Bex said flatly.

I glanced askance at Bex. "And exactly how are we going to do that? He beat us to a pulp last night."

"You were taken by surprise last night. And now we have Jillian," Dominic said, gesturing to the skeleton.

Jillian looked at me, but what I saw in her didn't inspire much confidence.

I turned back to Dominic and raised my eyebrows.

Dominic pursed his lips. "Once Jillian drinks from Nathan, taking all of her blood back from him into herself, I will replenish him with my blood. The healthy blood of a full Master should revive him enough to complete a full transformation."

I took a deep breath. It was the plan Dominic had proposed when we spoke last night, but now that Jillian was here and staring at me with those icy blue-ringed eyes in that grotesque skull, it seemed impossible.

I leaned into Dominic and whispered, "Nathan's skin is different from yours. He has—" I swallowed, reluctant to admit, "He has scales, and from the firepower Walker blasted at him—silver firepower, mind you—those scales are pretty much impenetrable."

"Jillian is Nathan's maker. If there's anything that can wound him, the blow must come from her," Dominic assured.

I sighed. "What if she drinks too much? She's starved. What if she drains him?"

"You're lucky I'm not draining you for an appetizer," Jillian said coolly.

I straightened away from Dominic, chagrined. No sharing secrets with vampires around.

"Control yourself," Dominic growled, and the walls shuddered under the thunder in his voice.

"That is my very point," Jillian said, her voice still collected and measured. "I could drain her right now if I chose to, but I am controlling myself." She looked into my eyes, and this time I knew, even without lips or muscles to express herself, that she was smiling at me. "So if I do drain him, you'll know I did it on purpose."

I opened my mouth—God only knew what would have flown from my tongue—but Dominic lifted his hand in a halting motion. I swallowed the words and closed my mouth. I knew that look. I'd been on the receiving end of that look a time or two and it never boded well for me. I doubt it boded well for Jillian now.

Dominic cocked his head to the left, and Jillian stiffened, if a skeleton could become stiffer. Her bones, most of which I could see through the tatters of charred skin and muscle, seemed to vibrate.

"You couldn't drain Cassidy now because I won't allow it. You couldn't exist if it wasn't my wish for you to do so," Dominic said. Although his words were low and softly spoken, Jillian cringed away from them like they'd scalded what little remained of her flesh.

"I exist because you couldn't find it within yourself to kill me," Jillian whispered between gasps. "And I'm here now because Cassidy has you wrapped around her little finger. The man I knew and respected and trusted to lead our coven would have let her brother rot and transformed her, whether he had her permission or not. The man I knew wouldn't have wasted time on the whims of another."

Dominic shook his head sadly. "You didn't trust the man you knew to lead our coven. You tried to take it from me. Despite Cassidy's whims and my motives, you turned against me, your Master, and attempted to transform a night blood. And you failed. You created this mess, and I'll be damned if you don't clean it up."

Jillian laughed, and the sound was a shredding grate against my skull. "I'm here because you *need* me here. You can't retransform Nathan without me."

Dominic cocked his head again and Jillian's laughter cut short. Her limbs started vibrating again, but this time, he didn't let go. She shook so badly I feared that she might fall apart in a heap of bones and crumbled ash.

"Dominic," I said softly.

He let go. Jillian crumpled to her knees on the stone floor, gasping.

"You would do well to remember that you exist because I allow it. When this is over I may not be so generous," Dominic said, his voice shaking at the end.

"Yes, *Master*," she murmured, but even I could hear the sarcasm in her voice.

Bex sighed. "She can't be trusted. This plan is dangerous enough without relying on the very vampire who betrayed you."

"It doesn't matter if she can be trusted or not. She can be controlled," Dominic said. "Night is dwindling. We're running out of time."

"If you want to wait one more night, that's fine with me," Rene said jovially.

Dominic glanced at him, and his look could slice a lesser person in half. Rene just smiled. "Or not. That's fine with me, too."

Bex rolled her eye, but otherwise let Rene's sass go unchecked.

"Well," I said, gathering my nerves. "What are we waiting for? Let's go."

Something hard, pointy, and warm jabbed into my side. An arm yanked me back against a tall man wearing Kevlar.

"Don't. Fucking. Move. Any of you," Walker said, and I realized, somewhat belatedly and incredulously, that the object jabbing into my side was his sawed-off shotgun.

* * * *

It took a moment for his voice to register because I'd never heard it so cold and without its usual twang. My head instinctively swiveled up to see, but even seeing, I couldn't believe. Walker was splattered head to toe in a thick, sticky, dark crimson—nearly purple—liquid, and against everything I believed he was capable of doing, he was holding me hostage.

"Walker? Are you kidding me?" I asked.

He dug the gun deeper into my side when I moved. "I was talkin' to you, too, darlin'."

I winced, but with a weapon that could essentially blast me in half at this range, I did as I was told. I remembered all too well what happened to hostages when Walker aimed his sawed-off at them. I didn't dare move.

Rene raised his eyebrows. "I guess you really did have a falling out."

"Ian," Bex said, her voice soft and soothing and slow, very slow, like the way you shape your tone for someone balancing on the edge of a fifty-story building. "What have you done?"

Dominic's expression was unfathomable. He didn't so much as blink at Walker. It wasn't until I heard the low rattle and insect-like clicks of his growl that I knew how he felt. He was enraged.

"You can growl all you want," Walker snapped. "I'm pissed, too. Where are they, Bex?"

Bex blinked, her face transforming from worried to bland in an instant. "Where are who, Ian?"

"Don't fuck with me. You know exactly who I'm talking about," Walker backed up a step, dragging me with him. "I said, don't fucking move!"

"Calm down, Ian Walker," Dominic said, his voice low and on edge. He was minutely closer than he'd been standing a moment before. "You don't want to hurt Cassidy. You fancy yourself in love with her."

"You don't want me to hurt Cassidy," Walker snapped snidely. "You fancy yourself another vampire. But I'd rather see her dead than a member of your coven, and you know that's damn true."

Dominic sighed heavily. I knew that what he'd said was true, too, but hearing the words, "I'd rather see her dead," from Walker hardened a part of me I hadn't imagined could feel much of anything anymore.

"What do you want?" Dominic said, resigned.

"I want Bex to show me where she's keeping them."

"Where she's keeping who?" Rene said, exasperated.

"My night bloods. You have Ronnie, Logan, Keagan, Jeremy, and Theresa, and I want them back. Now."

Bex narrowed her eye. "*Your* night bloods?"

Rene glanced at Bex.

Dominic's gaze bore fiercely and fixatedly at Walker. "Bex?"

"Lysander?" she answered, nonplussed.

"Answer the man's question. We're losing moonlight as we speak. Nathan won't wait for us to get our shit straight. He'll attack someone tonight, and we want that person to be Cassidy."

"Thanks," I muttered.

"You said so yourself that a Day Reaper transformed Veronica," Bex said. "If I don't know where she is, how should I know where the rest of them are?"

"*I* know that," Dominic gritted, "So tell *him*."

"Where's Ronnie?" Walker insisted.

"Don't you listen?" Bex asked Walker, her voice turning ugly. "I. Don't. Know."

The gun jerked painfully into my side. I gasped.

Dominic's low growl reverberated through the cavern. "Careful, Walker."

"Where is she?!"

"At home!" I shouted. The dam inside of me burst at the sound of Walker's tears. I could hear their hollow keening as they squeezed from his tear ducts, thanks to my amplified senses, but that didn't make his pain any less real. I knew the tearing, helpless, hopeless pain of not knowing whether a loved one was dead or alive. I knew the ache of questioning when to let them go. Nathan's disappearance had consumed my mind every day since the moment I realized he was missing, but even had I tried to move on, the emptiness of his absence would have never left my heart.

I could only hope that Walker's love for Ronnie would never leave his, even after he knew the truth.

"What?" Walker asked, his voice soft, like a razorblade against the throat is soft, but still lethal.

I swallowed. "The last time I saw Ronnie, she was at home. But she was already a vampire."

The gun dug sharply into my rib. "You saw her? When?"

I breathed in sharply. "After our fight. After you left," I said quickly. I wasn't about to say otherwise while he jabbed me with the business end of his gun. "She came back to the house after she was transformed. She considers it her house, too, you know."

Walker shook his head. "Ronnie is not a vampire."

"I saw her, Walker. She drank my blood. She—"

"Shut up," Walker snapped. "I don't need to listen to your lies! Bex is pissed at me because of her eye, so she took Ronnie."

Bex laughed. Looking at him dead in the face, at his anguish and fanatic hope, she burst out laughing. "I'm not pissed at you about my eye. You were defending Cassidy, and you have impeccable aim. I wouldn't have you any other way."

The gun disappeared from my side. One moment there, its pressure bruising my ribs, and the next moment, simply gone.

I blinked, and amid rips of Velcro and snapping noises, a clatter rained over the stone floor around us. Walker's weapons—several knifes, multiple guns and their extra clips, various pens, pepper spray containers, a watch, and four aluminum tuna cans I'd assume no longer contained tuna—scattered across the stone floor around us.

Walker's arm bent back from the elbow, releasing me.

I felt the crack of his bone like ice on my wisdom teeth before I heard the high shriek of his scream. Something knocked me forward. Dominic caught me before I hit the floor. He tucked me behind him, and I couldn't see around his back. I squirmed to the side to peek over his shoulder and stared, shocked.

I don't know why I was surprised. Who else could have attacked us if Dominic, Rene, and Jillian were standing here, watching?

Walker had hit the floor, and by the looks of his twisted arm, busted knee, and a swelling bruise on his forehead, he'd hit hard. He was still struggling to move, fighting to sit up and defend himself, but Bex had a finger on the center of his chest. I could see the strain in the bulging veins at his neck and forearms, but all the effort Bex needed to put forth to keep him down was one little finger.

"What I *am* is furious," she growled, and her fangs seemed to grow longer as she spoke. Her nose flattened slightly, and the very tips of her ears poked through the sides of her bronze hair. "You would have let me die and been relieved to have me gone."

"You're a monster," Walker spat. "You deserve to die."

"I may be a monster of the flesh, but you, my dear, lovely Ian Walker, are a monster of the heart."

Bex sharpened her gaze on him, and her otherworldly, reflective, yellow-green eye bore into Walker in a blaze of inner light. He screamed.

"Finally," Rene muttered under his breath. "She's going to kill him."

"She is not," I snapped, but honestly, I wasn't sure. "Right, Dominic?"

"She's going to do what she should have done years ago, when he first tried to kill her," Rene muttered. The emphatic joy in his voice grated on my nerves. "She's going to kill him."

"Dominic?"

"Hush, both of you." Dominic hissed. "This is why I don't have newborn vampires."

"I thought it was because I refused you," I whispered.

Dominic looked down at me, his expression stern, but I could see the hint of amusement tip the corner of his lips.

"Do something," I said softly.

He shook his head slowly. "He just held you hostage and threatened to kill you, yet you want me to do something."

I opened my mouth to argue, but Dominic leaned in close, nose to nose. His fangs bared and his ears suddenly pointed. My argument choked in the back of my throat.

"He's lucky I'm letting Bex have him. If it was up to me, I'd tear out his throat," Dominic growled. "If he touches you again, he's dead."

I swallowed. There was no arguing with that.

I stared directly into Dominic's unnerving, otherworldly icy blue eyes, and I could feel the fuel of his rage. I could see it in the tightening of his muscles. I could feel it vibrating from his chest like the steady, constant heartbeat he didn't have. He didn't try to entrance my mind, to cloud my senses from seeing and feeling and knowing his mind like I'd never known before, and I wondered if he even knew it himself: more than my usefulness as a night blood and more than my potential as a vampire, Dominic Lysander cared about me, just for me.

Walker's scream cut short.

I tore my gaze from Dominic. Bex was standing over Walker, a strange, bitter, pain-filled resentment clouding her petite features. Walker was lying on the ground, struggling to move. I worried the pain was too much, that he'd seize, but slowly and shakily, he struggled to his knees. Eventually, he stood.

"Get out of my home," Bex growled. "And stay out."

"Damn," Rene said, obviously disappointed.

I blew out a shaky, uncertain breath.

"You can't keep me out, not until I find Ronnie." Walker panted, defiantly. "You have her somewhere, you have them all, and I won't stop searching until I get them back, even if that means killing every last one of you."

"You can try, and as always, I'm sure you will," Bex said, "And as always, you will fail. Goodbye, Ian. Let me show you the door."

The dining room hall door exploded outward in a mess of splinters, and they were gone.

I blinked a few times. "Where?" I stammered, unable to form complete sentences, "But how..."

"She'll be back," Rene said, his smile radiant. "Like she said, she's just showing him the door."

"I thought you said she liked that door," I muttered.

"She did, but she likes the flair for drama more. We needed a new door, anyway. That squeak was unforgivable."

I shook my head, in awe. "Bex *is* faster and stronger than you," I said to Dominic.

Dominic was still staring at the remains of the door when he said, "That's why she's our ally and not our enemy."

I shook my head. "She never displayed her power like this before."

"She's not one for bragging, but just because she doesn't show it off doesn't mean she doesn't have it."

I bit my lower lip. "Walker has considered her an enemy for years, but until now, Bex considered him her night blood."

Dominic lost his grin slightly. "Until now. I risked quite a lot to ensure that Bex remained my ally. Ian Walker risked everything to solidify Bex as his enemy. He has a long road ahead of him, one that I don't envy, but he paved the way himself."

I pursed my lips. He may have paved the way himself, but I still felt partially responsible. If I hadn't flaunted my relationship with Dominic, albeit a faked relationship, Bex wouldn't have realized what she was missing. She wouldn't have demanded that he lick her blood at dinner— he wouldn't have even been at dinner—and maybe his life wouldn't have spun so quickly out of control.

Dominic tipped my chin up, forcing me to meet his gaze. "I can feel your regret, and I'm sorry."

"You knew this would happen," I said softly. "Weeks ago when you first proposed that I come here to smooth your relationship Bex, you knew that Bex would be jealous of my loyalty to you, the loyalty she couldn't inspire in Walker. You knew that would drive a wedge between them."

"I knew that would forge a stronger alliance between Bex and me. What Ian Walker has done is between him and Bex is his own doing, not mine, and certainly not yours."

I rubbed my sore side where Walker's gun had bruised my rib. "Right," I said, unconvinced.

"Y'all coming?" Bex said, appearing in the doorway. "Nathan's feeding, and we don't have all night to clean up his mess."

Chapter 18

Nathan was feeding. That was one way to phrase what he was doing.

A body was crushed under the weight of his back leg, keeping his victim in place as he punctured the chest cavity, severed the heart with near surgical precision, and ate it. The person was already dead. Both its arms and one leg were torn off from what looked like a ragdoll beating, and the remaining leg was only attached by thin tendons. The bone was severed and poked through the wound like a gruesome flagpole, skin hanging loose and flapping from its tip.

We were outside Walker's house where Dominic had healed my wrist. My blood was now mixed with someone else's, but there was no denying that Nathan was still tracking me. He'd followed my blood here, so hopefully he'd follow my blood where we wanted him to go next.

I didn't have the chance to ask Bex if Walker was all right, and after he had threatened to kill me, I debated with myself whether or not I should even care. She didn't have bloodstains on her clothes or face when she'd returned, so I assumed that she'd left him unharmed, or at least not *further* harmed. Knowing her rage, however, that might be assuming a lot.

I squinted into the darkness from habit, not really needing to squint considering my temporarily enhanced vision. I didn't see Walker inside the house. None of the lights were on. I was perched thirty meters away, high in the treetops with Rene as my parachute, but from one glance through the trees, through the blackness of the night, and through Walker's dirty kitchen window, I could see that the basement door to the safe room was wide open, and his kitchen was still a bloody mess. My bloody mess.

If Bex hadn't harmed him, Walker would likely seek shelter to recover, but his home looked deserted.

I turned my attention back to the victim that Nathan, having finished with the heart, was now tearing to shreds.

Rene's lips touched my ear. "That's not Walker."

I jerked instinctively and then nodded. "That's nice of you to say, but you don't know that for certain."

"Sure I do. It's Buck McFerson."

It took a moment for the name to click, but I'd always been snappy with names. I closed my eyes as I realized what I was seeing. *Jeremy's uncle*, I thought. I was watching Jeremy's uncle being murdered.

I shook my head at the nightmare in front of me. It was either that or scream. Or throw up and then scream.

Rene nodded. "Yes, it is. I can smell him and the fry from his restaurant. If Jeremy's missing along with all the other night bloods who lived here, like Walker claims, it's no surprise his uncle came looking for him. He probably—"

I glanced at Rene. One look at my expression and Rene shut up.

Not far from there, only three and a half miles into the woods and down a steep decline, was a grove. The trees thinned and a shallow creek sliced the rolling hill in half. The water was shallow, mid-thigh at its deepest, and slow-running. If our plan worked, if Nathan followed my blood to the grove, Dominic, Bex, and Jillian would have higher ground advantage, better coverage, and space to maneuver.

Nathan finished what was left of his victim and stood at his full height. I held my breath. Knowing Nathan was this creature and experiencing it in the heat of an attack was somehow different at this impartial view. He was still horrifying, but he was like a lion, having ripped through a gazelle from instinct and hunger and the might to survive. He was as majestic as he was frightening. And he was my brother.

My throat burned with tears.

Nathan lifted his pointy-tipped nostrils and pulled long drafts of air into his lungs. His chest expanded, and after the first few breaths, a low growl rattled from his chest. I knew that insect-like rattle very well from my many attacks, encounters, and intimate interactions with vampires. He smelled something he liked and was going to hunt it.

With a grace that belied the weight and raw power of his frame, Nathan turned on his haunches and dashed into the woods toward the beginning of my blood trail and down the winding path that led to the grove.

I turned my lips into Rene's ear. "I think he's taking the bait."

Rene nodded, his eyes trained on the trembling leaves and rustling underbrush in Nathan's wake.

I fell silent, staring at the mess that was once a human being, a person with family and friends and a restaurant to run, who entrusted Walker with the safety of his nephew and had died worrying about him. Inexplicably, perhaps because he was my brother and none of this was entirely his doing—Jillian could rot for eternity for transforming him—I couldn't help but hope that despite the murders and wreckage and lives he'd destroyed, that he could still survive.

Staring at Buck McFerson's remains, however, I had my doubts that anyone—even my justice-seeking younger brother—could come back from this hell. And that made me want to curl in a ball and cry.

Instead, I turned back to Rene. "We should probably double back again to the grove. He's going to reach the stream soon, and we need to arrive at the clearing when he does."

Rene glanced at me and a small smirk pulled at his lips. "Nope. We're staying right here."

I frowned. "Why would we stay here? Bex needs you back there, and Dominic might need me."

"I've got my orders."

"Whose orders?" I snapped.

"Lysander," he said, and as I was becoming accustomed, Rene's grin widened when he delivered the news, like he'd been waiting in relish to divulge his little secret.

"What are you talking about?" I hissed. "Dominic made the plan with me, and the plan is to return to the grove and help them."

Rene shook his head. "That's the plan Lysander told you because he knew you'd never willingly agree to stay out of it, but if the creature took the bait, which he did, than the real plan was for you to stay here, out of harm's way."

"You're damn right I wouldn't have agreed to stay out of it. That creature, as you refer to him, is my *brother*, and I—"

Rene launched himself at me in a full body tackle, knocking me out of the tree, and we were suddenly airborne.

That was a bit of an overreaction, I thought, and then I saw Nathan, his jaws snapping at the tree branch I'd just been standing on a moment before.

Nathan hadn't followed my blood to the grove. He'd followed me here.

"Shit," I said, not realizing I'd even spoken until the word exploded from my lips.

Nathan spat the bark from his mouth and met my gaze. For one trembling throb of a moment, I thought I saw a glimmer of recognition, of thought behind the instinct. I thought I saw a choice to either pursue and kill or retreat, and the choice to retreat had merit.

Rene hit the ground running. I blinked, jostled from the impact, and Nathan let loose a shrieking roar that shriveled my bones. He jumped out of the tree, straight for us.

"He's coming after us," I warned.

Rene tightened his grip on me. He didn't turn to look, and he didn't stop running. Although a much younger vampire than Dominic, Bex, and Jillian, he could still move faster than my brain's synapses could fire, but with Dominic's added blood coursing through my body and enhancing my senses, even at this speed, my vision wasn't a complete blur. I could see the trees that Rene was dodging and the logs he was jumping over. I could feel his muscles straining, bunching, and pushing us as fast as possible through the debris and underbrush to beat Nathan to the grove.

But Nathan was faster.

"He's gaining on us," I hissed.

"I don't want to lose him," Rene said.

I watched Nathan over Rene's shoulder, pounding through trees instead of dodging around them. "You're not at risk of losing him."

"We don't have that far to go," Rene said. "We'll make it."

Nathan was close enough that I could see white foam gathering in the corners of his craggy lips. He was close enough that if I wasn't careful, he could eat my outstretched hand.

I kept my hands tucked safely around Rene's neck, but as if reading my mind, Nathan lunged forward, his jaws snapping. I jerked back instinctively and screamed.

Rene stumbled. My heart lurched as I fell backward in his arms. He rolled, trying to take the brunt of our fall, but we hit the ground hard on my hip. My vision blurred as a blaze of instant, radiating pain shot through my leg. I felt Rene bounce to his feet and lunge away from Nathan, evading the snaps of his teeth. I heard the clack of his jaws catching air and the rumbling rattle of his frustrated growl.

"Cassidy, snap out of it," Rene said. "Are you all right?"

My vision was starting to focus, but I didn't know which was worse: blind pain or the nightmare that was my brother, snapping at our heels. Literally.

"Cassidy?" Rene shook me as he ran, still whirling around Nathan's lunges, bouncing off tree trunks, and flipping over boulders and logs.

"My hip," I ground out. I took a deep breath against the rising nausea and the double fright of Rene's crazy acrobatics and Nathan's ferocity. "I'm fine."

"We're here. Take hold of my shoulders and hang on tight," Rene warned. I felt his arms squeeze more securely, nearly painfully, across my back.

I locked my arms around Rene's shoulders, and true to his word, the moment I held on tight, the woods dipped into a sharp decline toward the grove. Rene launched from the ground, from one step to the next into a flying leap, like Dominic could leap, soaring over the gorge and toward the meandering stream below. I tried not to look down, but my curiosity and bubble of burdening questions broke through my healthy fear, as usual. The wind from his flight whipped my hair in a wild cyclone around my head. I looked down through the whirling locks. If Nathan didn't catch us, tear us to shreds, and eat our organs, the fall from this height would kill us just as easily.

I tightened my grip on Rene's neck.

I looked up, daring to hope that Nathan couldn't fly. He was so heavy and muscled and monstrous that it seemed impossible that he could soar through the air like the rest of the vampires, but sure enough, just as Rene had launched from the crest of the grove, Nathan followed suit. He jumped after us, snapping and snarling.

"Rene, he—"

"He can't fly," Rene spat. "He can jump really far, but it wouldn't be fair if he could fly, too."

"Whether you call it flying or one really far jump, it doesn't matter. He's coming."

"It's not like I can soar through the air any faster."

Nathan was inches away. I gagged on the putrid smell of his rotting breath. "We need to do something! He—"

A glowing, black and blue blur collided into Nathan midair, knocking him off his trajectory and pummeling him down the thirty feet to the grove below.

Dominic.

I held my breath as they crashed. Their bodies dug a long crevice into the earth. Dirt and leaves uprooted and sprayed in an arch over them, and then, as unexpectedly as he'd appeared, Dominic's blur vanished into the surrounding trees and shadows.

Rene caught hold of a tree branch and pulled us into its vegetation. A few smaller branches snapped across my cheeks and snagged my hair as he yanked me inside. We collapsed against its trunk. His arms, still tight around my body and holding me sturdy against him, were shaking.

I pulled back to see his face. "Rene?"

"We must stay here, Lysander's orders," he said. His voice was steady and calm, not winded in the least, unlike my own ragged breathing, but then, Rene didn't need to breathe to live. Something wasn't quite right, however, no matter his calm countenance. His hands holding me were still trembling.

"What's wrong? Are you—"

The tree shook, like the violent sway of an earthquake inside a high rise. Rene and I tightened our grip on each other and the tree. As my hand curled into his back, fisting his shirt in my hand, I felt something wet and tacky coat my palm. Rene stiffened against me.

Nathan's soul-quaking roar echoed from below.

"He's certainly not taking any of this well," Rene commented dryly, but I could hear the strain in his voice.

"He got you," I said. I lifted my hand to see, and sure enough, my palm was gloved in Rene's blood.

"I'll heal. It just takes a moment longer than you're probably accustomed to with Lysander."

"How badly are you—"

The tree jarred again, this time with the force of being completely uprooted, and I was dislodged from Rene. The hot friction of Rene's grip tore at my skin as he attempted to keep me in the tree, but he was too late. I was wrenched from his embrace—my hands and forearms slick from his blood—and falling.

I screamed, as loud as I'd ever screamed in my entire life. "Dominic!"

Something pounded into my left side with the force of a Mack truck. Another something hit me from above with the same force, spinning me around in a 180. The three of us crash-landed, my body cushioned from the hit by their bodies.

The impact knocked the wind out of me despite their cushion. I gasped ineffectively, struggling to breathe. Rene was under me, lying flat on his back, unmoving. Dominic was in front of me, having already knocked Rene and me behind him with a swipe of his arm. I sat up and peeked over his shoulder.

Nathan stood in front of us, his sharp, crazed, black-eyed stare honed on me.

"What's the plan? Where's Bex with Jillian?" I whispered from behind Dominic, into his ear. "This might be a good time for her to start draining him."

"Timing is key. He was supposed to follow your blood trail further down the grove."

"He didn't, so Rene and I had to improvise," I hissed.

"Yes, and now you and I must improvise, as well," Dominic said. "Can you still feel Jillian inside of you?"

"No, you severed our connection, remember?" I blinked, wanting to stare daggers into Dominic, but I didn't dare take my eyes from Nathan. Maybe he wouldn't attack if we remained quiet and unmoving.

"Yes, I severed her connection to you," Dominic said patiently, "but not your connection to her. She has ingested blood that you swallowed. You should be able to find and control her."

I shook my head. "No, she's gone from me." And then what he really said suddenly clicked. "She ingested blood I swallowed."

"Yes," Dominic said. "I just said that."

"But I swallowed *your* blood. You should be able to feel her. You did last time."

"Yes, I did. Through you." Dominic's eyes narrowed on me. "Cassidy DiRocco, look into my eyes."

I felt his connection instantly, and my gaze tore away from Nathan's against my will to meet Dominic's gaze. *Damn it.* "Dominic, don't—"

Nathan roared. He swiped out with his talons, but with my mind entranced by Dominic, my body was pliant and defenseless—not that there was much defense against Nathan anyway—but I watched, helpless, as Dominic was knocked aside into an adjacent tree.

Rene was a sudden blur, out from under me and on Nathan. He tossed his head, swatting at Rene like a bee as Rene struck and zipped away in a brilliant attack and retreat maneuver. He wasn't inflicting much physical damage but was distraction enough that Nathan forgot Dominic.

"Merge a connection with Jillian Allister," Dominic commanded, purring his power through me from his prone position on the ground. "Now."

Dominic, as I was beginning to accept but still resent, was right: the severed threads of our connection were still there. Severed, but present. The power of his command sparked my awareness of them and the healing properties of his own blood flowing through my veins nourished them.

Suddenly, I was no longer myself. I was nothing but bone and skin and pain—horrible, burning, brittle, excruciating pain. The pain peeled over my entire body and scorched through my throat.

The new me cocked her head, recognizing my presence inside her.

"I was wondering how long it would take for you to realize that you needed me inside you again," Jillian said, the smirk obvious in her voice. "Longer than I'd thought."

"Jillian Allister," I commanded, ignoring the relish in her tone. I felt the threads of our tenuous connection weave between us, its twine strengthening a two-way street of my power over her and her leaching nourishment from me. I could feel the mirrors of her mind reflecting back at me, her mental barriers attempting to keep my commands at bay and her intentions secret.

The fact that she was planning to use our situation, her connection within me, and her temporary freedom to her advantage was unmistakable. We'd known she would betray us from the start, but that didn't change the fact that we needed her. At the moment, that would have to be enough.

"Command her to drink, Cassidy!" Dominic shouted through my mind. "She needs to drain him enough for the transformation!"

"Jillian Allister," I continued, struggling to focus. The triple personality of Dominic, Jillian, and myself inside my mind was like wading through molasses—my thoughts were slow and sticky and opaque. "I command you to drink from Nathan until he's drained enough to transform. But don't kill him," I added.

Dominic released my mind. I snapped back into myself, the twine between Jillian and myself still binding. I gaped at the scene in front of me.

Bex had joined the swarm, and all three of them—Dominic, Bex and Rene—were jabbing, twirling, slashing, and dodging around Nathan's head in Rene's rush and retreat technique. The scales along Nathan's face, neck, and chest were a mess of scratches, nothing deep or debilitating, not even bloody, but enough to have further enraged him. Enough to distract him.

Nathan slashed his arms through the air wildly, growling and hissing and roaring at them, but just when he reached out for Dominic, Rene scratched his chest. When he turned to backhand Rene, Bex ripped her claws up his back. When he whirled around to smack Bex, Dominic tore a line across his cheek. I watched their dance, fascinated and frightened by their movements, hoping against hope that they could hold him off, that this plan—if you could even call this failure of a plan a plan—would work.

A glowing black and blue blur rocketed into the air from one of the nearby trees next to me in a spray of leaves and raining twigs.

Jillian.

She cut through the blurred swarm of Dominic, Bex, and Rene surrounding Nathan and latched onto Nathan's back in full gargoyle form. Her fingers, still skeleton-like without the nourishment of skin or muscle, extended into thick, four-foot-long talons and pierced knuckle-deep into Nathan's shoulders.

Unlike anything else that couldn't penetrate his scales, Jillian's talons imbedded deep. Blood sprayed from both wounds and showered Jillian's face.

Dominic was right again, double damn him. As his creator, his Master, Jillian had the power to kill him.

Nathan roared and bucked at her, but Dominic, Bex, and Rene increased their onslaught, slashing and biting him, swarming his entire body, so he was blinded by pain and rage. His screams reverberated through the trees and choked my heart.

You can do this, I encouraged him, but really, the encouragement was equally for myself. I could survive witnessing my brother's death if it meant giving him back his life.

In one ferocious bite, Jillian clamped her jaws around Nathan's carotid and tore open his neck. She spat the meat of his flesh on the ground, and I gagged. The thick, bloody chunk of skin and muscle gleamed in the subtle glow of morning light

My stomach bottomed out as I realized that somehow in the time between finding Nathan and now, the sun was rising. In another few minutes we would still be outside, fighting Nathan and struggling to control Jillian, and it would be dawn.

Blood squirted in a vertical geyser from Nathan's neck. I stared, transfixed, too horrified to look away. Jillian let the spray settle to a steady pulse before extending her jaw, wrapping her lips over the wound, and sucking a long pull of blood into her mouth. There was so much blood, more blood than I could conceive of a body containing, and it gushed out faster than Jillian could swallow. It poured in a thick waterfall down Nathan's back. It coated Jillian's scalp, cheeks, and chin and dripped down the front of her body. It spattered on the ground as Nathan bucked and twirled, trying to dislodge Jillian and simultaneously fight Dominic, Bex, and Rene.

Jillian swallowed mouthful after mouthful of Nathan's blood, and I watched her transformation as she savored every sweet last drop. The straggles of Jillian's hair thickened and grew, pixie short but healthy. Muscle expanded and plumped over her bones, and the threads of skin that hung from her thin frame melded together, contoured over bone and new muscle, and revitalized into a glowing complexion.

Nathan fell to his knees. Dominic, Bex, and Rene were still swarming around him, still scratching and biting and stinging, but Nathan wasn't fighting them anymore. His hands remained limp at his sides, his face expressionless and yet somehow, maybe imagined from my own guilt, he seemed to look deep into my soul. I could see the devastating disappointment in his gaze.

Nathan collapsed onto the ground in front of me.

"She's had enough," I said, feeling my panic overwhelm my fear. I wanted Jillian to stop drinking. "She's going to kill him."

"You commanded her to drink until Nathan could be transformed, did you not? You commanded her not to kill him," Dominic said, suddenly solidly in front of me.

I opened my mouth to argue, but when I saw his appearance, I stared speechless. Dominic was a wreck. His cheek was split open, and a flap of skin hung loose from the bone. His clothes were in tatters. His shirt was blood soaked, and his chest and arms were a mess of jagged slashes and scratches. I swallowed, wanting to help in some way but too scared to touch him without causing further damage.

"Didn't you?" Dominic insisted.

I nodded numbly. "I, well, yes, I commanded her not to kill him."

"Then she can't kill him. She'll stop when he's ready to transform, not before and certainly not after," Dominic stated, and his confidence was like a balm soaking through the sting of my panic.

Jillian dislodged her talons from Nathan's shoulders but continued to swallow long pulls of his blood. Rene and Bex stopped their flurry of flight. Despite their injuries—they were just as slashed and scraped and bloody as Dominic—they stood shoulder to shoulder in a wall between me and Nathan, watching Jillian feed.

Nathan hadn't moved since collapsing. I bit my lip, waiting.

A minute passed. Jillian continued drinking, swallow after swallow, and with each second that passed, her eyes brightened shades brighter, her skin glowed more luminescent, and her power, like a pulsing, living swell in the air, expanded outward from her and snapped against my skin.

"I won't be able to give Nathan my blood," Dominic said.

I blinked, not sure I'd heard him correctly. He hadn't turned to speak to me. He was still watching Jillian, or rather, stalking Jillian with that unwavering, honed gaze.

"What are you saying?" I asked. "After Jillian drains him, you fill him back up. That's the plan, right?"

"That was the plan," Dominic said, his voice grave. "But when Jillian's finished, she'll have regained her full strength. She was my equal three weeks ago when we fought, and my powers have weakened since then. In order to contain her, I'll need as much of my strength as possible." Dominic sighed. "Which means I won't be able to give Nathan my blood."

"But you have to," I hissed. "You promised me. You swore by the sun. We had a deal!" I shouted, near hysterics. "I upheld my end of our bargain, and now it's time for you to uphold yours!"

"It's too risky. If I were unable to contain Jillian, she'd continue her mad cause, gain control of my coven, and life as we know it in New York would be irrevocably destroyed. I can't risk all of that. I can't risk my entire coven and your city for one man. I'm sorry, Cassidy. Not for your brother, not even for you, will I risk everything."

"I'll do it," Bex said. "I'll give Nathan my blood, so you can control Jillian and still uphold your promise to Cassidy."

Rene coughed. "If you don't remember, he tore out your heart and tried to eat it."

"You would do that?" Dominic asked, surprised.

Bex sighed. "Nathan may have torn out my heart, but Cassidy put it back in. We're allies, are we not?"

Dominic nodded. "Of course."

"Then one of yours is as welcome as one of mine."

"Thank you, Bex. That's exceedingly generous," Dominic said graciously.

"No, that wasn't the deal," I said.

Dominic turned to face me. "Bex is offering to save your brother. Take it and say thank you."

"I thank you, Bex, I really do, but I can't accept. This was *your* deal, Dominic. You promised that he would be a member of *your* coven."

Bex raised an eyebrow. "Dominic's coven is in tatters with the approaching Leveling. Nathan would be safer with me anyway."

"This isn't your deal to finish," I insisted. I knew I was being stubborn, but I didn't care. Nathan was my brother, and if he had to be a vampire, he would be Dominic's vampire in New York City, home with me. "It's Dominic's promise, and he's bound by it."

Sunlight crested on the horizon and glowed through the woods in streaks between trees. All three vampires in front of me jerked back. Bex and Rene actually ducked behind me to stand in my shadow. Only

Dominic remained in front of me, blocking Jillian from view. The air above his skin started to ripple, like the mirage of heat on asphalt.

"Honestly, DiRocco, if I were you, I'd take what I could get," Rene said. I shot him a glare.

"I'm serious! Compared to the creature he is now, anything is a step up, no matter the coven he joins."

"That's not the point. I—"

Rene's face stiffened and then contorted in pain. He pitched forward blindly toward a ray of sunlight. Bex was on him in an instant, knocking him to the side and dragging him back into the shadows away from the light, but she was too late. Although she'd saved him from the sun, I could see the silver broadhead of the wooden arrow protruding from the front of his chest. Black cracks, like poisoned veins, fissured from the wound and spread outward over his chest, neck, and shoulders, snaking down his arms and across his face.

An audible hiss passed over my shoulder. Before I could even register the flash of another silver broadhead or the streak of its wooden shaft, I heard Dominic's harsh exhale from the impact.

Dominic was shot through the heart with a wooden stake.

* * * *

Debilitating pain shot through my own chest, directly over my heart, and Dominic and I collapsed to our knees simultaneously. He gripped my upper arms before we both pitched headfirst to the ground, and we faced one another, nose to nose, the long wooden stake of one of Walker's arrows embedded deep into his chest.

I coughed, and blood poured from my mouth. The arrow had pierced his heart, not mine, but it was mine that was bursting.

"I'm sorry, Cassidy," Dominic whispered. "The bonds between us were supposed to strengthen you, too; it works both ways. My strength for your strength. But also, your life for my life."

"Bonds?" I whispered, but the gurgle of blood clogging my throat drowned the words.

"The promises. Sworn by the certainty of the sun and the passage of time, by the certainty of our deaths." Dominic shook his head. He lifted his hand to cup my cheek. His other hand fingered the arrow's shaft where it met his chest. "It's a death blow. I'm so sorry."

The sun rose fractionally higher in the pre-dawn sky, and a beam of pure, unhampered light pierced through the trees and poured over both of us.

Dominic instantly burst into flames.

The hands gripping my upper arms, now licking fire, scorched me. I screamed and instinctively wrenched away from him. Dominic threw himself back into the trees' shadows.

I looked around, desperate for something, anything, to help Dominic and smother the flames, but I didn't have anything on me except weapons to kill vampires. Nothing to save them. My own skin was starting to redden and blister, a slow, delayed version of Dominic's inferno, and I wondered if he was trying to take all the pain and injury and death into himself. It wasn't working. I couldn't feel the heat of the flames over his skin like I could the arrow through his heart, but my clothes were starting to blacken and split from the heat of his flames. I suspected that when he lost consciousness I would burst into flames, too.

I clutched my chest as my heart stuttered, and I wondered dismally which would kill us first: the arrow or the flames.

I turned my head toward Bex, trying to remain upright as my knees trembled. "Dominic. He's dying. I—"

Bex was openly sobbing. Her hands were outstretched, her trembling fingers clutching fistfuls of ash, and I remembered that Rene had been shot through the heart, too.

I stared, stunned. Rene was gone. The little that was left of him was in Bex's hands, flaking from between her fingers and floating like dust, away on the morning air.

My heart gave a last squish, trying and failing to pump, and I fell forward into the dirt.

Laughter, like nails across my eyelids, lit the air.

Trembling and wheezing, I looked up.

Jillian had dislodged her fangs from Nathan's neck. They were still in shadow, hidden from the sun under a large oak. She was watching Dominic burn, Rene float away on the breeze, Bex's grief, and my own struggle, and she was laughing.

I narrowed my eyes. She was laughing, but her throat—fully quenched from draining Nathan—still burned. Tears were streaming down her face, and I realized that she was hysterical.

"You think this is what I wanted? You think this was the path I'd envisioned for our coven?" she shrieked.

"You would have let Dominic burn in that alley when you betrayed him. This was the path you set for us," I reminded her. I didn't know if she could hear me or not. My words were nothing but the movement of my lips and a soft rasp.

She flew to him in a zig-zag, keeping to what little remained of the shadows. I twitched, trying to move toward him, to meet her there and protect him, but I couldn't move more than a few inches.

With a violent, powerful kick, Jillian knocked Dominic down the ravine, toward the bottom of the grove. The fireball of his body left a charred trail through the woods as he tumbled headlong over logs and boulders and finally plummeted into the meandering stream below.

I stared, stunned, as his body splashed into the water, dousing the flames.

Jillian was suddenly standing over me, her face a mask of blood. Tears exposed clean stripes of skin down her cheeks.

"He saved me once, a lifetime ago. When I was lost and my love had nearly given up hope of ever finding me, he brought me back to myself."

"I know," I whispered.

"I was never his night blood, but I was his all the same."

A hiss whizzed over my body. Jillian's hand whipped up and caught the arrow mid-flight, centimeters before it pierced her chest. She scanned the surrounding woods, and a growl rattled from her chest as her gazed honed on target.

I turned my head to see what she'd seen.

Walker was standing less than a hundred feet away in the thick of the woods beneath a patch of brilliant sunlight. His blond, curly hair glowed like a halo around his head, but his expression was anything but angelic. I'd witnessed his single-minded vendetta against vampires before, just like I'd witnessed him aim his sawed-off shotgun at hostages, but I'd never been the hostage until last night. Until now, I'd never been his target. I felt my heart twitch in my chest, and I struggled to breathe past the pain as the blind hatred in his expression spread from Jillian to me.

Walker aimed the crossbow at Jillian. Protected as he was by sunlight, he was untouchable, and he knew it. Jillian couldn't give chase. She'd have to retreat toward the river, into the deep woods and shadows, to survive.

"I will be the Master Vampire of New York City," she said, her voice like ice. She snapped the arrow in half with her fingertips. "But not like this."

I blinked, and she was gone. I turned my head and scanned the surrounding forest for a blaze of her catching fire or the rustle of her retreat through the shadows, but nothing remained of her presence except for the serene exhale of her absence.

I turned back to Walker. He'd re-aimed the crossbow. Without Jillian for a target, he was aiming at something over my shoulder, but he was staring directly at me. He watched me struggle to breathe, to keep my eyes open and locked on his. He glanced at Bex behind me—still in shadows but surrounded by sunlight, still incoherent with grief—and then he locked eyes with me again. I could see the struggle in his face as his feelings warred with his instinct to kill.

He was aiming at Bex.

Could he aim his crossbow at a grieving, sobbing woman, a woman who had saved his ungrateful ass several times throughout his life, and pull the trigger when she wasn't looking? He knew that wasn't self-defense, no matter how he spun the details. Whether he considered Bex a woman or a vampire, whether he considered her living or existing—even I wrestled to distinguish those details—I didn't have any trouble distinguishing self-defense from murder. And if Walker shot and killed Bex in this moment, that was murder.

Before I could shout in warning to Bex or block Walker's line of sight, he dropped his aim. I sighed in relief and then coughed from the pain in my chest. I didn't have a physical wound, only the metaphysical one Dominic had created with his bonds, but physical blood spewed from my mouth. Walker watched me cough and struggle, and the telltale clench and unclench of his jaw tightened his expression. He wanted to help me. He hated seeing me struggle, and he wanted to be the man by my side to help me survive.

He didn't kill Bex—he'd let the sun do that for him—but he didn't help me, either. He watched me struggle to breathe and he watched me bleed and tremble on the ground for a long moment, and then he turned his back on me and walked away.

The woods was thick with foliage, so one moment to the next, Walker was there and then he was gone, but I could hear the leaves rustle and branches snap at his retreat. I stared out into the woods long after the sounds of his steps faded, listening to the rhythm of waking birds and their calls and the constant, steady, trickling flow of the nearby stream. The gaping emptiness of what we'd accomplished on full display in the dawn light shamed me to tears. Nothing had gone according to plan. Nothing had ended like it was supposed to have ended.

Bex was still grieving. I could hear her moans and coughing sobs behind me.

Nathan was still protected by the shadow of a large oak, but the shadows were shrinking, lifting under the morning dawn. He would be exposed to the sun in another minute and burst into flames, just like Dominic.

This was never supposed to be the end, not for any of us.

I dug my elbows into the dirt and struggled over the stones, twigs, and blood-soaked earth to crawl next to my brother. He needed someone's blood to transform. Dominic wasn't here anymore to uphold his end of our deal, and Bex was as good as gone without any shadows to hide beneath. I was all Nathan had—vampire or not, healing blood or not—but whether this worked or not, we would both die anyway. The chance of holding on to breathe another breath, no matter how infinitesimal, was still a chance and worth the fight.

Nathan was unmoving and unresponsive when I reached him. In repose, he was just as monstrous and unreachable as he had been while tearing through limbs and ripping out hearts. His black hair was a matted mess of knots, grease, blood, and fouler things. His face, tipped to the side and slack with unconsciousness, didn't resemble anything I knew as my brother. This creature's face was a scaly gleam of scratches and hunger and ferocity. His brow was jutted in a thick frown, and his teeth, too large and too many for his mouth, protruded from his lips, each tooth a razor, shark-bladed point, except for his fangs, longer than the rest, that curled down like sabers.

His nose, flat and pointed and pinched at the corners, glittered from the diamond pierced though the left nostril. I stared at his nose stud for a long moment, reminding myself of who he was, who we were, and that if this worked, everything we'd sacrificed for this moment wouldn't have been an empty accomplishment. It would be the very accomplishment I was willing to die to achieve.

In a gesture that was becoming all too familiar, I bared my wrist and lifted it, trembling, to Nathan's lips. His mouth was slack, so I braced the tender inner flesh of my wrist against the sharp point of his fang and sliced in deep.

Blood poured from my wrist into Nathan's mouth.

Almost immediately, a low, vibrating rattle growled from Nathan's chest. I sighed, wondering if I was transforming him or feeding him, and honestly, at this point, wondering if it really mattered. With Jillian on the loose, she would reign over Dominic's coven, and God only knew the monstrosities she would create while in power. I closed my eyes. Nothing could be worse than the monster she'd created in Nathan.

Exhausted and helpless and nearly hopeless, I collapsed next to him, resting my wrist over his mouth so my blood could drain down his throat. *I'd* be Damned if I didn't see this through to the end.

The tremors were minute at first—a twitch against my wrist, a tremble that could have been the vibrations of his growl—but they deepened violently into convulsions within a matter of seconds. He was seizing. Or having a stroke. Or maybe his blood was clotting, like Walker had once described, and he was suffocating.

Or maybe—even if the chance was infinitesimal, it was still a chance—maybe he was transforming.

Minutes passed. Nathan's convulsions didn't ease, and the blood loss was too much for my body. I drifted into a swirling numbness and felt myself being gently lifted from the ground. Nathan was somehow rising with me; I could still feel his seizing shivers and convulsions next to me, closer to me somehow and yet further away. The sun was a brightening brightness over my vision as I squinted into the full morning rays of sunlight, and I wondered if this was more than sunlight, if we were rising to the final light.

Arms tightened around me as my vision darkened in pulsing, black bursts. The voice was a soft, southern twang, her words like feathers as she spoke.

"Hang on just a little longer, Cassidy. Your strength for his strength. His life for your life, remember? If not for yourself, hang on just a little longer for him."

Bex's soft waves of bronze hair glittered like a halo of fire around her head as she looked down on me, her expression serene and encouraging and hopeful. She stood with us in the rays of morning light, gathered us tightly in the strength of her arms and carried us as she took flight through the clear, crisp morning air, not a shadow of protection between her porcelain skin and the sunlight.

Chapter 19

The scratchy scent of antiseptic, the ache of an IV in the bend of my elbow, and the steady beep from the machine monitoring my heart were becoming unfortunate familiarities.

Someone was in the room with me, two someones actually: a patient and a visitor. I knew not because of a colored aura surrounding the room or the pump of their heartbeats or the smell of their perspiration or the heat of their focused gazes. I knew because I could hear them with my very human hearing. The steady beep of the patient's heart monitor was competing with mine, and the visitor was speaking softly.

I was alive. The grateful relief of simply surviving was becoming overly familiar as well, but each time was like the previous. It didn't matter if this was the first time opening my eyes after facing death, and it didn't matter if it was my last, although I'm sure it wouldn't be considering my proclivity for doom and gloom. I took a deep breath despite the sting of antiseptic and enjoyed the simple pleasure of feeling my lungs expand, knowing I would open my eyes to see another day.

I opened my eyes, but the person looking back at me wasn't anyone I could have anticipated; my newfound feelings of grateful relief plummeted.

"Special Agent Rowens?" My voice cracked, not entirely from disuse.

"Please, it's Harold." He walked to me at a brisk clip, picked up a plastic cup from the bedside table, and tipped the straw toward my lips. "Here, take a sip. I'm sure you're parched," he said. "I know I was."

I licked my lips, but my tongue was dry. I could feel the flakes of cracked skin on my lips from dehydration, so I strained forward, took the straw in my mouth, and drank.

The water was cool, if not entirely fresh, and moistened the sand and hair from the back of my throat enough that I could use my voice and not feel like coughing.

I eased back and cleared my throat. "Thanks."

Rowens nodded. He set the cup back on the bedside table and sat on the chair nearest my bed.

I eyed him warily, too many emotions constricting my throat to really speak, despite the water. He was still wearing his hospital gown along with a pair of green gym shorts, so he was decent if not technically dressed. The room was cool, even for me with my own gown and wrapped in blankets, but after the exertion of walking and standing, sweat slicked over Rowens' brow. He wiped his forehead with the sleeve of his left shoulder, shrugging.

He was missing his right arm at the shoulder, and in its place were wads of gauze and padding held by a sling around his neck and upper chest.

He noticed where my gaze had wandered and the corner of his lips tipped in a self-deprecating grin.

"My supervisor wants me to take leave for physical therapy. He knows better than to broach the topic of leaving the field, but I could hear the order loud and clear even if he didn't voice it. A fucking desk job." Rowens shuddered. "Rip off both my arms, why don't they?"

I didn't know what to say. My empathy for him and guilt for my part in his injury were overwhelming and poignant, but my uncertainty over what he remembered, what Bex had allowed him to remember, choked my response.

He held up a hand, letting me off the hook. "Sorry, I'm not here to grouse. I just wanted to thank you."

I raised my eyebrows. "Me? The last time we spoke, you were the furthest thing from thanking me."

"Your tip on Colin was instrumental in his rescue. He might not have survived much longer, and the search party found him relatively quickly, thanks to you."

I nodded, waiting on the catch. "You're welcome."

Rowens' hand curled into a fist. "And I thought you'd like to know, for everyone's peace of mind, that Walker was able to track and put down that bear."

I blinked, hating that I was playing catch-up with the one person capable of exposing everything and endangering all of us. "Bear?" I asked.

"Rabid bear. Not particularly common, apparently, but not unheard of, either."

"Right. Good," I said, trying to drum up some necessary enthusiasm. "That's great to hear. I knew Walker would come through for us."

"There were other reports that I'd read concerning the deaths of Lydia Bowser, John and Priscilla Dunbar, and William and Douglas McDunnell, that did not support a bear attack," Rowens leaned forward, his gaze more intense than any other man I'd known, except for maybe Dominic. The focus and intent in his eyes made me hold my breath. "But no one remembers writing those reports."

I opened my mouth, not wanting to gape at the familiarity of his frustration and at the implication of what that meant for him, but I gaped anyway.

"And the few people who were stupid enough to open their mouths about it decided to take a sudden vacation or leave of absence. I haven't seen them since, and their phones are either disconnected or they haven't returned my voicemails."

I closed my mouth and swallowed. "You'll have to remember that while you're taking leave. No work for you while you're off duty," I said lightly, trying to feign ignorance of what he was implying.

Rowens shook his head. "My reports reflect that Officer Riley Montgomery and I were attacked by a rabid bear, so I won't be going anywhere, off duty or otherwise."

He knows, I thought, and I could hear my heart racing a double crescendo from the increased beeping on the monitor and the pounding, like punches, pumping inside my chest. I didn't know if he knew everything—who would come to the true conclusion, *vampires*, after facing the creature that Nathan had been, assuming he remembered—but he knew something. He knew enough.

"Rowens," I whispered, "There's some things about this case that you don't know—"

"No, there isn't," he said. "I'm telling you this because you sat across from me in that interrogation room without any real answers to my questions when I knew you had them, and now I know why. So I don't care what it is I don't know, I'll figure it out on my own terms, like I've done my whole life, but I'm telling you that whatever it is that you think I don't know, you don't know either. You didn't know anything about this case when you were in my interrogation room, and you *still* don't know. Got it?"

"Yeah, I got it." Rowens was a survivor. He wasn't going to be one of the people to disappear, and he didn't want me disappearing on him, either. "I haven't taken a vacation in years, and I wasn't planning on taking one anytime soon."

"So if I call you in the next few weeks, you'd better answer your damn phone."

I nodded. "I will."

"Good." He stood. "Just one last question, DiRocco. How common are rabid bear attacks in the city? All this time off and leave of absence nonsense, it might be nice to get away, to see a friendly face."

I raised my eyebrows. "I'm a friendly face?"

"You're not bad on the eyes. Not bad at all."

I laughed, and then I met his eyes squarely. "Rabid bear attacks are more common in the city than you'd think, but when I write my article next week on city versus country crime rates, that's not what you're going to read."

Rowens inclined his head. "That's what I thought. Take care, DiRocco."

"You too," I said softly.

"And take care of that brother of yours. It's not every day that a family visit goes so awry. Nothing like a bear hunt for brotherly bonding."

"What do you know about my brother?" My voice cracked, nothing to do with disuse this time.

Rowens nodded, indicating the bed next to mine.

I turned my head, not daring to breath, barely daring to look, but like synapses that had already fired, turning my head was an inevitability that I couldn't fight even if I'd wanted to.

Nathan was the patient next to me.

"Oh my God," I breathed on a harsh exhale. "Nathan."

"I'll leave you two alone," Rowens murmured. I heard the door click shut behind him, but I didn't turn to look or bid him goodbye. I couldn't look away from my brother's beautiful face.

His skin was soft and tan and glowing. The scratches that had reflected like metallic scrapes against his scales were now thin, scabbed paper cuts, crisscrossing his cheeks and nose and chin. His lips were pink and plump. His hair, though still matted and greasy, was now framed by rounded ears and thick raven eyebrows. No protruding brow. No shark-pointed teeth crowding his mouth. The sun was streaming through the cracked window panes, casting rows of horizontal light over his bed, arms, and face, that beautiful face that I could recognize as Nathan.

Tears streamed down my cheeks. I felt my throat constrict even as I tried to breathe calmly and slow my heart, but the telling beep from the monitor betrayed my efforts. Remaining calm was impossible.

Nathan was my brother again.

I struggled upright and out of bed, careful not to jar the IV or machines or other various clamps and stickies they had monitoring my body. I didn't want anyone rushing into the room because they thought I was coding.

The few steps to the side of his bed were dizzying, but seeing wasn't believing. I sat on the edge of Nathan's bed and cupped his face in my hands. I couldn't look away. He was here, and he was himself, and more than any relief I could have felt at having found myself alive, I felt the relief of guilt and grief and heartache that I'd carried for three long weeks suddenly shower over my body, like a burst dam, and I broke along with it.

I doubled over, rested my forehead against his chest, and sobbed.

"Cassidy?"

My cries choked in the back of my throat, and I froze. I sniffed, wiped my face on the blankets, and slowly, disbelievingly, I peeked up at his face.

Nathan's aqua-colored eyes, the very reflection of my own, stared back at me. We held each other's gaze, lost in the wonder that he was here, that we were finally together, and that the feelings of joy and grateful relief that everything was right in the world was our reality. After living a nightmare for so long, I didn't dare move or breath or speak, fearing that the moment would shatter.

"Nathan," I finally whispered. "I don't know what you remember. Or the last thing you might—"

"Everything. I can still smell their fear, and I still remember my hunger, like unslakable flames, fueling my hunt. I can still taste their—" He stopped, unable to continue, and he turned his head from me. "I can still taste you."

And there it was, our reality in shards and splinters around us. Just when we thought to find our footing, reality embeds swift and deep in tender places where we never would have thought to take care with our step.

"It's all right. It's over. You're back now, and it's all over," I murmured.

I wrapped my arms around him, needing to feel the give and warmth of his skin to comfort myself, but the arms he wrapped around me trembled. They clutched me to him, digging his hands into my back and crushing the breath from my lungs as he struggled to find an anchor in the nightmare he was just waking into. It wasn't over. But for the moment, with Nathan in my arms and his arms, not talons, holding me back, I could accept that most everything—everything I could want and stand to live without— was indeed all right.

* * * *

With the possible exception of doing your own taxes, recovering from injury is the most physically and mentally draining achievement. I've done it—both the taxes and the recovery—and no matter how many times I swear it's the last, the second, third, and forth time prove me wrong over and over again.

According to my chart, I had good reason to feel fatigued. Nathan and I were discovered collapsed and unconscious at the emergency room entrance. Apparently, I'd driven us there. Walker's truck was found in the parking garage, and our human-shaped bloodstains were soaked into the fabric. Nathan suffered minor lacerations and blood loss, but otherwise, the bear hadn't mauled him as much as it had me.

I'd suffered from severe blood loss, internal bleeding, irregular heart palpitations, and severe sunburn. My nurses said I'd been invited to observe and report on the bear hunt as thanks for my tip to the police about Colin. The hunt had gone well but not without a few injuries to Rowens, my brother, and myself. No one commented on the fact that Rowens had been admitted to the hospital the day before, nor that with the exception of my torn wrist, none of my injuries were consistent with a bear attack. I suppose anyone who might have questioned those inconsistencies were already on permanent vacation like Rowens had warned.

Although I was recovering remarkably well for someone who had flirted with death, my doctor decided to keep me overnight. I'd developed a slight fever after receiving a blood transfusion, and until that fever settled, he didn't recommend discharging me. Since the next bus to New York City didn't leave until tomorrow evening anyway, I decided to comply with doctor's orders for once.

Sunset came and went, blanketing my room and the entire hospital in a silent, beep-filled hush. Despite my exhaustion, I rested with one eye open all night, waiting. I was on the fifth floor. My window was closed and locked, but Dominic had proven himself adept at entering locked fifth-story windows.

I waited and continued waiting until the first rays of dawn broke the horizon and flooded through my window, bathing the room with light. Nathan didn't comment on our undisturbed night—he had his own demons to fight—and I certainly didn't mention it, but Dominic's absence left an unexpected hollow inside me. I'd expected him to visit. I'd anticipated and braced myself for him—every gust of wind against the windowpane, every floorboard creak, every long stride down the hall—and until last night, he'd never been one to disappoint.

I ate a toasted bagel with cream cheese and rubbery eggs for breakfast, dragged my IV into the bathroom with me before the nurse returned to take my temperature, and laid on my back in bed, waiting for lunch. Otherwise, Nathan and I sat in uncomfortable, tension-filled silence for the majority of the day. Our bus departed at nine o'clock, but until then, there was too much to say and feel and do between us to express it all at once, and too many people to overhear what we might say. At least, that's what I told myself as my thoughts strayed all day to Dominic.

The last I'd seen him, he'd been a ball of flames. I'd assumed that if I'd survived, he'd obviously survived, but what if he hadn't? He'd created bonds between us with our shared promises, but what if when the moment came, he couldn't bring himself to use them to keep himself alive if it meant killing me?

Nathan was being discharged just in time to make our evening bus into the city, and God help anyone who said otherwise, so was I. Despite a persistent, mild fever, I felt fine, and I was not staying out of the city for one moment longer than necessary. I'd had my fill of trees and cows and cavern covens, and if one more nurse referred to me as *ma'am*, I was going to physically maim someone.

By eight o'clock, I was sink-showered, dressed, and if not presentable, at least decent for public display. The few things I had here at the hospital—my phone, recorder, and inexplicably, Walker's truck keys—had been enough to corroborate my story as a bear-attack victim; I cringed at the mounting lies, but I suppose I should have felt grateful that Bex had chosen bear attack over serial murderer. Before I left for good, however, I'd need to swing by Walker's house to pick up my luggage. My stomach cramped, thinking about that potential confrontation.

Nathan left the room to bring the truck around front for me. I'd insisted that bringing the truck to the entrance was unnecessary, that despite a mild fever and the usual grind of my hip, I was perfectly capable of walking an extra seventy feet to the parking garage. Nathan had been adamant, and if there was one person as stubbornly single-minded as I was, it was my brother. I didn't like having him out of my sight. Even in the short interims of using the bathroom, washing, and dressing, I felt on edge having walls between us, but I was getting the impression that the very opposite was true for Nathan.

The scent of Christmas filled the room, seemingly more prominent than in the city, where pine is scarcer, but nonetheless unmistakable even here. I didn't need to turn around to know who was behind me.

"I was wondering if you would visit. You did last time," I said, continuing to make and smooth the covers on the bed. The nurses would likely strip and change the sheets anyway, but I needed to do something to hide how my heart tripped and stuttered at the mere smell of his presence. Not that I could physically hide anything from him, anyway. If he hadn't already heard it, he undoubtedly smelled it on me. I was relieved and grateful to see him.

"I was wondering if I'd ever catch you alone," Dominic said, his voice deep and somehow cautious. "Congratulations on transforming Nathan. I couldn't have done better myself."

"Thank you," I laughed, but the sound was harsh and grating. "It's strange now that he's himself again. When he's out of my sight, I'm worried he'll turn back." I knew how unreasonable that sounded, but I couldn't help how I felt. "After having just found him, I'm terrified of losing him again."

"I know the feeling," Dominic murmured.

The bed was smooth and crisp and completely wrinkle-free. If I smoothed it out any further, I'd create wrinkles. I sighed deeply, gathered my fortitude, and turned to face him.

Dominic stood against the far wall next to the now open window, his shoulder leaning against the windowpane, his legs crossed at the ankles. He'd recently fed. His skin glowed in a warm, healthy complexion over his sculpted face, his scar a slightly less prominent shade of pink against the radiance of his skin. He wore navy dress pants, brown wingtip shoes, and a brown and navy checked button down tucked into a brown belt. I'd never seen him in a patterned shirt. He still looked posh and very New York City. If he thought the checkered shirt would help him blend with the country folk, he was seriously mistaken.

I frowned at him, a sudden realization wrinkling my thoughts. I hadn't invited him in.

Dominic looked down at himself, mistaking my frown for disapproval. "Solids are typically my mainstay, but I thought you might appreciate some variety. Compared to our last encounter, I think there's little risk of you ruining this shirt like you did the last."

I laughed. "Me? *I* ruined your shirt?"

"That's how I remember it, yes," Dominic said, but his lips smirked in that crooked, self-deprecating half-smile.

I crossed my arms. "I don't suppose being impaled through the heart or engulfed by flames contributed to the destruction of said shirt."

"Nonsense," he said, truly smiling now. "You'd ruined that shirt long before I caught fire."

I nodded, wanting to remain apprehensive in his presence, but after everything we survived, my caution seemed false. He was still dangerous. He was still a creature I couldn't implicitly trust, a creature who schemed and bent me to his will on command, but unfortunately for my sanity, he wasn't the monster I'd labeled him. He was just as complexly good and evil, selfless and selfish, and open and guarded as everyone else. I couldn't categorize him on a high shelf and ignore his actions because of who or what he was; besides being a vampire, he was a man who had helped me save my brother at the risk and expense of his own safety and the safety of his coven, the very coven he feared losing. I wouldn't forget that sacrifice.

"The shooter was Walker," I said, and even after I'd hardened my heart against him, or at least I thought I had, the wounds, still so fresh and raw, bled inside. I had to swallow before I could continue. "He saw me there, dying right in front of his eyes, and he walked away." I shook my head. "He left me to die."

"I'm truly sorry, Cassidy. I know how much Ian Walker meant to you, as a man and as a fellow night blood," Dominic said, and God help me, he sounded sincere. "I wish I could ease your suffering. I'd kill him if I thought that would make you happy, but even now, I know that would only worsen the situation. Unlike Ian, I know when to hold my fire."

I looked up sharply at the words "kill him." Dominic's smirk was contagious. "Not funny," I murmured.

"On the contrary. I find myself hilarious."

I sighed deeply. "And I'm glad you're all right," I whispered, finally voicing the fear that had burdened me all day.

Dominic inclined his head. "I know."

"I know you know already—you can probably smell it on me—but I needed to say it," I said in a rush. "The last time I saw you, I didn't know if you were going to live, if either of us would live." I narrowed my eyes on him. "You could have warned me about the bonds between us. Don't think you're off the hook for that."

"Had I warned you about them, you wouldn't have agreed to them."

I raised my eyebrows. "That's your defense?"

He shrugged. "Sometimes it's more prudent to act in the moment and to ask for forgiveness later."

I crossed my arms and waited.

He sighed extravagantly. "Must I apologize for something that benefits both of us? That helped us survive?"

"That helped *you* survive," I reminded him. "And yes, you must, because you put my life at risk without warning me."

He nodded. "You are correct about that. I do apologize for not informing you that you were at risk."

"Thank you," I said, mildly shocked that I'd actually extracted some form of an apology from him. "It's a kind of betrayal, you know, to bond our lives like that without my permission. It's not something I would've wanted."

Dominic leaned forward. "But?"

I sighed. "*But—*" I continued, "I'm glad that the bonds were in place when they were, so I was able to keep you alive. Rene disintegrated into ash in Bex's arms. If you—" I shook my head; the thought of him floating away on the air like that made my gut squirm in ways I'd never thought applicable to him. "I don't like you, Dominic, but I don't want you to burst into flames and ash."

Dominic's smile was instant and rapturous. "Oh, you more than like me."

I pointed my finger at him. "Don't push—"

He held up a hand. "I'm glad for the bonds as well, and if the time comes—God help us if they do—I hope they serve you as well as they've served me."

"Without the bonds, would you have died as quickly as Rene from the arrow through your heart?"

"Yes. A wooden stake through the heart is a lethal blow, and I should have burst into ash within moments. The same goes for sun exposure for most vampires, but I can burst into flames and still survive, as you well know."

I bit my lip, thinking of the last moments before I'd given into unconsciousness and who had saved me. "But you always burst into flames?"

"Always."

I rubbed the back of my neck, uncertainty warring with the proof of everything I'd witnessed. "I don't think the Day Reapers were ever in town, Dominic. I think Walker was right about Bex attacking Ronnie and the other night bloods."

"Careful of who you accuse of what, especially Bex. She's our ally, and we've worked hard to keep her that way." Dominic narrowed his gaze on me. "Veronica Carmichael was attacked and transformed during the day. You said so yourself. And Rene never saw her last night. After you sent her in search of him, no one has seen her since, so we can't confirm either way who her maker is."

"I know what I said, and she *was* transformed during the day, but I don't think Day Reapers transformed her. I don't think Day Reapers came here to resolve our situation with Nathan, either. Have you actually encountered any Day Reapers? Wouldn't they have made their presence known to you, to deal out punishment or fines or whatever they do?"

Dominic straightened from the wall. "What's your point, Cassidy?"

"Bex didn't burn in the sunlight," I whispered. "She stayed with me, sobbing over Rene's ashes, and then after I let Nathan drain me, she picked us up and brought us to the hospital. We were in full sunlight, and she didn't burst into flames or turn to ash. I've seen her skin boil and steam in the sunlight before, but this time, she didn't even wince."

Dominic was on me in an instant, his nose centimeters from mine, his eyes blazing with that inhuman internal glow, and his fangs bared mere inches from my lips. My heart plummeted in a hard fall into my gut.

"Don't speak of it again. I don't know how Bex was able to withstand sunlight, if she was able to withstand it." He eyed me quizzically. "You were dying and near unconsciousness. You don't know what you saw."

"I know exactly what I saw," I insisted, despite the threat of his fangs and lethal strength. I reminded myself that he couldn't kill me without inadvertently killing himself because of the bonds, and that gave me courage.

"No, you don't. She could have formed bonds of her own with a night blood."

"With Walker?" I scoffed. "I don't think so."

"Bex doesn't claim allegiance with the Day Reapers, and her allegiance is all I care about until the Leveling. What you saw is our secret. Swear it."

"On the certain passage of time?" I asked dryly.

He stared at me, nonplussed.

I sighed. "I swear, I won't mention Bex or what I saw again. Until the Leveling," I added.

"Thank you," Dominic said, and the blazing light glowing from his eyes dulled to a less intense shade.

He stared at me a moment, still inches away—close enough that I could feel the radiant chill of his body—when something minute changed in his expression. His face slackened slightly, his eyes widened, and he stared at me like a stranger stares at someone they think they know but can't quite remember.

"What?" I asked, feeling more uncomfortable than usual under his gaze. "Is something wro—"

Dominic dipped his head to nuzzle within the curve of my neck. He took a long, deep breath, and the rush of air against my skin tingled down my spine.

He jerked back as if *I'd* been the one to scald *him.* "What did they do to you?"

I blinked. "What are you talking about? What's your problem?"

"You smell different. Wrong, somehow," Dominic said.

I frowned, resisting the urge to lift my arm and sniff. "I haven't taken a full shower yet, but I don't think I'm really that—"

"It's more than that," Dominic dismissed. He leaned in again, slower this time. Carefully and quietly, he sniffed the air around me. His eyes searched mine, as if he could peel away the layers of my mind with a single glance, which was a closer truth to his capabilities than I liked to ponder.

I held his gaze from pure stubbornness, envisioning a mirror in my mind to reflect his commands if he got any brave ideas about entrancing me.

"Describe what transpired from when you left the grove to now," Dominic demanded. His voice was sharp, formal, and wavering. I'd seen Dominic in many stressful, life-threatening situations in which he remained aloof and stoic, but if I didn't know any better, I'd say that as he stared at me, his eyes scanning over my face, up and down my body and everywhere in between, he looked near panic.

I shook my head. "I don't know, exactly. I was unconscious. Why is this so important?"

"It's more than important. It's crucial," Dominic said. "Endeavor to explain in detail despite your unconsciousness."

I lifted my hands and let them fall back to my sides, at a loss. "I woke up in the hospital. I'm assuming Bex brought me and Nathan here, but whether she flew or took a more conventional method of transportation, I don't know. Walker's truck is parked in the garage, so I guess she could have driven us."

Dominic nodded and lifted his hand in a circle, encouraging me to continue.

I sighed. "When I woke, Rowens visited me and thanked me for my help on the case," I said, glossing over our conversation. "I reunited with Nathan, stayed the night here as per doctor's orders, and now, I'm being discharged from the hospital. And here I am now, conversing with you," I concluded. "That's it."

"Doctor's orders?" Dominic asked. "Why were they concerned that you spend the night in the hospital?"

I shrugged. "I had a mild fever. I suppose it's standard procedure after a blood transfusion, but I don't—"

"Blood transfusion?" Dominic growled.

"Yes, I'd lost a lot of blood." I took an instinctive step back from the ferocity in his expression. "What's wrong with you?"

"You don't smell like you anymore. That cinnamon spice that drives me mad, it's not there." Dominic said, and I could tell he was truly upset. For a man who prided himself on his control, he was losing it. The tips of his ears pointed through his hair. "You don't smell like a night blood."

I narrowed my eyes, not liking what he was implying. "You're insane. I might have come this close to dying—" I squeezed my fingers together, barely a centimeter of air between them. "—and needed a blood transfusion, but that doesn't change anything. I'm still me. People receive blood transfusions all the time. It's a part of modern medicine."

Dominic eyed me speculatively, and I met his gaze squarely, daring him to argue.

"There's only one way to find out."

"I don't think there's any way to really prove—"

"Cassidy DiRocco," he commanded, and I felt the mental twine pull taught between us before I could re-envision the mirror to reflect his command.

"—Oh, for heaven's sake, Dominic, not again. Your word doesn't mean shit if you don't keep your promises."

"You will forget my name," he said, and his command reverberated over my mind like all his commands, firing my synapses and forcing my actions, but as usual, my thoughts remained my own. "You will look upon my face and remember me, know me, and trust or distrust me as you always have, but when your tongue shapes to address me, nothing will remain of your memory concerning my name beyond hollow, unforgiving doubt."

He released my mind, and I rolled my eyes at his ridiculousness. "Are you done? My bus leaves for the city in thirty minutes, and I don't care if I smell like manure. I'm not missing that bus."

He cocked his head. "By all means," he said, stepping aside in a gallant gesture. "I hope you have safe and smooth travels back to the city, Cassidy."

"Thank you, D—" My voice choked and my mind blanked on whatever I was about to say.

He raised his eyebrows and leaned closer. "What was that?"

I cleared my throat. "I said, thank you. I'll see you back in the city."

"Say my name, Cassidy."

I rolled my eyes, but a cold lump of doubt coiled in the back of my throat. I forced a laugh. "You're being ridiculous."

"Say it," he insisted.

I opened my mouth to say something scathing.

He leaned in close, his mouth centimeters from my mouth, his icy eyes blazing into mine.

My breath caught in my throat, and I hesitated.

"Say. My. Name," he roared, and the low vibration of his growl rattled from his chest.

I screwed my lips shut tight, aching inside from the unforgiving emptiness inside me where I *knew* I knew his name.

But I couldn't remember.

He leaned away from me, his expression blank and incomprehensible. "That's what I thought."

I reached out—not sure what I was about to grab or touch or take hold of, maybe anything of him—but as usual with his frustrating speed and grace and otherworldly, unfathomable illusions, I blinked, and he was already gone, leaving me alone with my thoughts. Leaving me alone with the knowledge that even though I knew without a doubt that I knew his name, I didn't know if I was still me.

Keep reading for a sneak peek at the next book in the Night Blood Series

ETERNAL REIGN

Available Winter 2017

I emerged from the rooftop access staircase of my new, vampire-proofed apartment, and Dominic was lounging in my hammock.

I glared down at his reclined form and crossed my arms. "Don't get comfortable. This is one of the few nights I have with Meredith, and I don't want to waste it."

He lifted an eyebrow. "You see Meredith every day. Sometimes you see her every night."

"I *work* with Meredith every day. We're hanging out tonight. There's a difference."

"So there is," Dominic patted the miniscule space in the hammock next to him.

I shook my head. "I believe that would constitute getting comfortable."

Dominic leveled his eyes on me, those otherworldly, icy blue eyes. They often looked through me, seeing my innermost fears and desires, more than they looked at me, but they looked at me now. He knew how I felt about him. He didn't need proof of it by reading my mind when he could taste it on my skin, feel it like a wood-burning stove wafting from my thoughts, smell it in the cadence of my breath. He knew, but I'm sure the confirmation of it on Technicolor display was gratifying, too.

He grinned, confirming my suspicions. "Would getting comfortable really be so bad?"

I nodded. Dominic was my friend but that didn't change who and what he was. "Getting comfortable could be deadly," I said.

"Being comfortable and becoming complacent are two very different things, and I would never accuse you of complacency," He cocked his head, smiling. "Is this a hard, fast rule of yours, remaining uncomfortable?"

I sighed, knowing from experience what was coming next. "No, it's not a hard, fast rule. It's more of a personal preference."

He cocked an eyebrow. "You prefer to remain uncomfortable?"

I rolled my eyes. "Fine. A cautionary measure."

He growled. The low rattle was deep and predatory, but it didn't have anything to do with anger.

Involuntarily, I took a step back.

"Cassidy DiRocco," Dominic rumbled through the growl. I could feel my mind perk at the call of my name, like how a dog cocks its ears forward to receive the next command. I envisioned a silver framed mirror protecting my mind, like he'd taught me, but I knew that it wouldn't work against him. Not anymore.

"Come here, and lay next to me in this hammock," he commanded.

Instantly and uncontrollably, I stepped forward. I went to him as he commanded, my actions not my own, and laid next to him in the hammock. To my credit, I laid opposite him, but that was only because he hadn't specified the exact position I should lay.

Dominic shook his head at me from across the hammock, his lips tugging into a reluctant smirk. "Even now, you're impossibly obstinate."

I smiled. "Thank you."

"Did you envision something to reflect my command? Did you try to protect your mind?"

"Of course. I didn't just lamely await your command," I scoffed.

His lips twitched. "Well, besides your stubbornness in refusing to lay 'next to me,' I didn't sense any resistance from you. Not like I used to," he added softly.

I sighed. "You didn't see my mirror?"

He shook his head.

"When I spoke to Dr. Chunn, she mentioned that the female body typically takes sixteen weeks to replenish blood cells after donation. It's possible that—"

"We don't have sixteen weeks," Dominic interrupted. "It's been over a week since your blood transfusion. My Leveling is in five days, and if you haven't regained the advantages of your night blood by now, it won't matter if you regain them sixteen days or sixteen years from now. We need them for the Leveling."

"I'm sorry my recovery isn't on your schedule," I snapped.

"Me too," Dominic said gravely. "If you don't have them for the Leveling, I need to consider an alternate plan to protect my position as Master."

I crossed my arms. "It's not my fault that this happened. I didn't ask for a blood transfusion. I didn't want to lose what little protection I had against you and the other vampires. I was unconscious, I was dying, and the doctors were just trying to save my life. They succeeded, if you haven't noticed, but you've been less than grateful."

"You're damn right I'm less than grateful. If I was there, I could have—"

"But you weren't," I interrupted. "You weren't there, and the doctors did the best they knew how."

Dominic looked away. "I'm just telling you what must be done."

"And what exactly must be done?" I demanded. "What are you saying?"

He stared off into the distance, across the expanse of city lights. We couldn't see the stars here, not like I could upstate when I visited Walker last week, but I'd missed the city. I'd missed the bustle and life and conveniences I'd taken for granted, like streetlights and taxis and the absence of wild animals. I'd especially taken for granted the protection of Dominic's presence.

Before my visit upstate, I'd felt constricted by his visits and considered his limitless reach an unwanted invasion of my personal, physical, and mental boundaries.

Until he'd been out of reach.

I would have died upstate without Dominic, killed by my own brother when he didn't know anything but how to kill. When I'd needed Dominic most, despite the risk and distance and my own reluctance, he came.

I stared at the scarred side of Dominic's face as he continued studying the expanse of city below us, and I had the sudden, insane, urgent impulse to kiss those luscious, imperfect lips. In this form, his lips were the only feature that was imperfect, and I cherished that reminder of his former life, a life in which despite our age, gender, and moral differences, was very similar to my own in the fact that we were at one time both night bloods and bore the physical reminders of our mistakes.

He met my gaze, and I looked away, embarrassed by my thoughts and urges. We wanted two very different futures for ourselves and this city, but the one want we agreed upon—very recently and only sometimes, although with increasing and alarming regularity—was his lips against mine. He hadn't kissed me since that crazy moment upstate in Erin, New York, when I'd been high on his blood, but I thought about that moment every day since. I'd relived the smell of his longing and the heat of his breath and the demand of his lips in the quiet solitude of my hammock on this very roof every night.

But I wasn't alone tonight.

I forced myself to meet his gaze. By the intensity in his eyes, I didn't need my night blood back to know that he thought about that moment as often and with as much longing as I did.

"I've never faced a situation quite like this before," he said. When he finally spoke, his voice was coarse, like he needed to clear his throat. "A human knows of our existence, knows about me and the inner workings and location of my coven intimately, and I have allowed her memory to remain intact. If my coven knew, if the Day Reapers found out, it would ruin me."

I frowned. "Who are you talking about?"

Dominic blinked at me. "My dear Cassidy DiRocco, I'm talking about you."

"Oh," I said. I remained quiet, waiting for his next words. My gut churned; I didn't like the direction this conversation was headed. "You're asking me my preference?"

He nodded.

He knew my preference, and if he didn't, he didn't know me as well as I thought he did. "I'd prefer to keep my memory." I gave him a look. "Obviously."

"Think on it, Cassidy. Without your night blood, you have no protection against other vampires, and if I don't survive the Leveling, Jillian will come for you. She knows where your loyalties lie. She will not tolerate you or any of my supporters, but if you no longer remember me or her or any of us, if you don't know that vampires even exist, she may allow you to live. You might be able to carry on with your life as you did before we met. Isn't that what you truly want?"

I shook my head. "What I truly want is for vampires to not exist at all, but they do. To pretend anything else would be a lie, and didn't you once say that I'm in the business of exposing the truth?"

Dominic nodded.

"I have no interest in living a lie, no matter how pretty that lie is. You know me better than that, or at least I thought you did."

"I suspected you would say as much, but knowing what may become of me and also knowing what Jillian may do to you, I couldn't live with myself if I didn't at least offer that option."

"Wiping my memory doesn't ensure my safety anyway," I argued. "If Jillian comes for me, I want to know exactly why she's here and why I'm being killed. I wouldn't change anything I've done for you or Nathan, so if Jillian wants to kill me for it, that's her prerogative. I don't want to forget it happened."

Dominic reached across his body and touched my ankle. "You say that now, but you may sing a different tune when she breaks you. I couldn't bear to witness your suffering."

"You won't be witness to anything. If Jillian comes for me, you'll already be dead."

He leveled a look on me. "I couldn't bear the thought—"

I pulled my foot from his hand. "Save it. You watched Kaden break me. Literally limb by limb, you sat back and watched him break every bone in my body as he tortured me to get to you."

"I intervened before he went too far," Dominic growled.

I laughed. "Your threshold for 'too far' is way higher than mine."

"We did what was necessary for the bigger picture."

"That's exactly what I'm asking you to do now. If you fail, Jillian won't just come after me. New York City as we know it will be devastated. Vampires will be exposed. People will need someone who knows what the hell's going on. I can be that person."

Dominic was quiet for a long moment, so long that maybe he was reconsidering his stance on allowing me to keep my memory. I bit my lip.

"Letting me keep my memory is the bigger picture," I said softly. "For humanity." I winced inwardly. Even I could tell that was pushing it a little too far.

"Allowing you to keep your memory puts you at risk, but it also puts me and my coven at risk," Dominic finally said.

"That's typical!" I snapped, exasperated. "As usual, your coven comes first, even before common sense. This was never my choice at all, was it?"

"Cassidy, please—"

"No! If you think I'm going to agree to let you wipe my memory for the benefit of the coven, you've lost *your* mind. I'm not letting you off the hook so you can feel better about mind-raping me. I'm not agreeing to this. I'm not your martyr!"

Dominic's face tightened. "If you would shut up and listen—"

"Screw you," I snapped.

Dominic was suddenly on top of me, his hands grasping my shoulders, his body pressing across my body, his face in my face. "I'm not going to wipe your memory!"

I blinked up at him. Squished into the hammock from his weight on top of mine, I could barely breathe, let alone think. "Oh," I said. "But you said—"

"I said for you to shut up and listen." His voice was a growl, and I could feel the hard proof of his anger and excitement dig into my hip. He was a vampire and he was dangerous—there was no denying the facts of his existence—but in many ways, he was still very much a man. Lately, he seemed determined to remind me of that fact, too.

I shut my mouth.

"Are you listening now?"

I nodded.

"Allowing you to *keep* your memory compromises the security of me and my coven, so I need you to promise me that you will keep our secret. Promise me that you will not expose our existence before Jillian does, that you will only acknowledge our existence after I'm gone, after she makes vampires a known threat to humanity."

I glared at him. It was impossible to impress an advantage from my prone position beneath him, but I glared anyway. "I don't want to expose your existence," I denied, "but if your existence is going to be exposed anyway, I—"

He put up a hand. "You don't want to be out-scooped. I understand, but this isn't your career on the line. It's your life."

"My career is my life," I grumbled.

"Not anymore. To survive, you need Jillian to take the fall for exposing us."

"Why? What's the harm in writing my article if she's going to expose you anyway?"

"It matters because when the Day Reapers come, and believe me, they will come, they will come for her and not you."

I closed my mouth. I hadn't considered the Day Reapers. Dominic spoke of them like boogiemen in the shadows, reigning justice and order over our heads, but I'd never experienced their wrath. From the horror of Dominic's own personal experiences with them, I wanted to keep it that way.

"Promise me," he insisted.

I sighed. "I promise."

He opened his mouth.

"I promise by the certainty of time that I will not expose the existence of vampires before Jillian," I clarified. "I promise to keep your secret until it's already exposed."

Dominic smiled.

"What's another bond here and there when you're already linked for life, right?"

"Right." He eased his grip on my shoulders and laid next to me the way he'd intended for me to lay next to him. "Kiss me before I leave."

I raised my eyebrows. "Is that a request or a command?"

"If I'd commanded you, your lips would already be pressed against mine instead of arguing with me, would they not?"

I pursed my lips.

"Almost, but not quite. You need more of a pucker."

I smacked his shoulder. "And why in the world would I do that?"

"I want to say goodbye. I need to make other arrangements to secure my standing in the coven since my original plan has failed me, and I need a token of courage to give me strength."

I placed a fist over my heart. "Ouch."

He crooked his finger, beckoning me.

"That's a reason why you should kiss me, not why I should kiss you."

Dominic raised an eyebrow. "I should kiss you because I ache for you." He pressed against me again, as if I wasn't already perfectly clear on the part of his anatomy that was aching.

I nudged him away with my shoulder. "If it's just physical satisfaction you're looking for, I'll pass."

Dominic groaned and flopped back on the hammock to gaze at the sky. "You're insufferable. What about allowing you to keep your memory is just physical satisfaction?"

I rolled my eyes. "If you're looking for a thank you for allowing me to keep something I already have the right to keep, then fine. *Thank you,*" I said snottily.

"Wiping your memory was never truly an option. I just needed to ensure that you'd considered all of your options. That we were, as you say, on the same damn page."

I couldn't help but smile. He really did listen to me when I spoke. "And why is wiping my memory not an option? Not that I want to encourage you, but it's the option I'd thought *you'd* prefer."

"If I wiped your memory of vampires, I'd be wiping your memory of my existence. Of everything I can and can't bear, everything I'd do for the bigger picture and for my coven, I could never do that."

I stared at him, trying to determine the truth in his words.

He gave me a long look. "I can't bear that you forget my name on command. I can't imagine you forgetting me entirely." He made a strange noise in the back of his throat that clogged my own. "It's unthinkable."

I touched the scar on his chin and urged his face toward mine. He looked at me, wary now that I'd pissed him off, but still willing.

"I'm sorry that I can't help you on the Leveling. I really am. And I'm grateful that you're allowing me to keep my memory, that you're choosing me over your coven. I understand how big that is."

He nodded.

"But you and I, whatever this is between us, is wrong. I'm human, and you're—"

"And I'm a monster," he interrupted bitterly.

"And you're a vampire," I said firmly.

"It's just a kiss."

I laughed. "With you, it's never just anything."

His focus honed on my lips, and my laugh died from the seriousness of his expression. I wanted him. God help me—vampire or not, monster or not—I wanted to kiss him.

"Tell me you don't want to kiss me," he demanded.

"Stop reading my thoughts," I snapped.

"I'm not. I'm reading your expression. Say it," he urged.

I shook my head. "I want to kiss you, damn it. But that's not the point—"

"That's exactly the point," he growled. Dominic took my acknowledgement as permission, and he kissed me.

And damn me, I kissed him back.

Don't Miss

THE CITY BENEATH

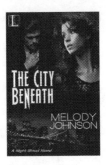

The first book in the Night Blood Series

Available now

As a journalist, Cassidy DiRocco thought she had seen every depraved thing New York City's underbelly had to offer. But while covering what appears to be a vicious animal attack, she finds herself drawn into a world she never knew existed. Her exposé makes her the target of the handsome yet brutal Dominic Lysander, the Master Vampire of New York City, who has no problem silencing her to keep his coven's secrets safe...

But Dominic offers Cassidy another option: ally. He reveals she is a night blood, a being with powers of her own, including the ability to become a vampire. As the body count escalates, Cassidy is caught in the middle of a vampire rebellion. Dominic insists she can help him stop the coming war, but wary of his intentions, Cassidy enlists the help of the charming Ian Walker, a fellow night blood. As the battle between vampires takes over the city, Cassidy will have to tap into her newfound powers and decide where to place her trust...

About the Author

Melody Johnson is the author of the gritty, paranormal romance Night Blood series set in New York City. The first installment, *The City Beneath*, was a finalist in several Romance Writers of America contests, including the "Cleveland Rocks" and "Fool For Love" contests.

Melody graduated magna cum laude from Lycoming College with her B.A. in creative writing and psychology. While still earning her degree, she worked as an editing intern for Wahida Clark Presents Publishing. She was a copyeditor for several urban fiction novels, including *Cheetah* by Missy Jackson; *Trust No Man II* by Cash; and *Karma with a Vengeance* by Tash Hawthorne.

When she isn't working or writing, Melody can be found swimming at the beach, honing her recently discovered volleyball skills, and exploring her new home in southeast Georgia. You can learn more about Melody and her work at http://www.authormelodyjohnson.com, https://www.facebook.com/pages/Melody-Johnson and https://twitter.com/MelodyMJohnson. Keep up to date on new releases and author events by signing up for her newsletter.

Printed in the United States
by Baker & Taylor Publisher Services